A Very
Pukka Murder

Books by Arjun Raj Gaind

The Maharaja Mysteries
A Very Pukka Murder

A Very Pukka Murder

A Maharaja Mystery

Arjun Raj Gaind

Poisoned Pen Press

Copyright © 2016 by Arjun Raj Gaind

First U.S. Edition 2016

10 9 8 7 6 5 4 3 2 1

Library of Congress Catalog Card Number: 2015957979

ISBN: 9781464206436   Hardcover
       9781464206450   Trade Paperback

Poisoned Pen Press
6962 E. First Ave., Ste. 103
Scottsdale, AZ 85251
www.poisonedpenpress.com
info@poisonedpenpress.com

Printed in the United States of America

Dedicated to my mother

*If I had half your intelligence and a quarter of
your integrity, then I would be a truly
extraordinary human being.*

Acknowledgments

Writing a book is a journey in many ways, and I have been fortunate to have many wonderful people help me complete this arduous voyage.

First and foremost, I must thank my agent, Kanishka Gupta, for his unflinching support. If not for his valiant efforts, this book would still probably be moldering in a slush pile somewhere. I must have done something right to have him in mine, and Sikander's, corner.

I am truly grateful to Manasi Subramaniam, who was kind enough to take a leap of faith on this book. If not for her, and Karthika VK, from Harper Collins India, Sikander would most likely remain a figment of my rather over-stimulated imagination.

I also owe a great debt to Barbara Peters and Robert Rosenwald from Poisoned Pen Press in the United States for bringing this, Maharaja Sikander Singh's very first adventure, to American readers. In particular, I cannot praise Barbara enough. As a writer, it is easy to think of editors as your foes. However, if you are lucky, as I have been, you get to meet that rarest of species, an editor who possesses both patience and skill, and who genuinely wishes to elevate your work, not hack it to pieces. Barbara, this is as much your book as it is mine, and I can only hope I have the delight of working with you again.

I must also offer my sincerest gratitude to Shobhaa De for her enduring support. It is rare to find someone who will help another person selflessly, but if not for her kindness, this book would never have seen the light of day.

I am very thankful to Sreeram Ramakrishnan for his invaluable assistance with an early draft, and to Ambar Sahil Chatterjee for his insightful and helpful commentary. I feel extraordinarily blessed to have met and worked with such considerate and gifted editors.

Also, an appreciative salute to Beth Deveny, the hardest working copy editor in the world, who spent countless hours making sure every paragraph was perfect, and to Diane DiBiase for all her help.

Last but not least, thank you, Amitabh Nanda, for enduring my endless diatribes, and the rambling phone calls I insisted on making to you each time I uncovered any abstruse fragments of research that caught my fancy.

And of course, I must thank my mother, for being there unconditionally, and for helping me fulfill this seemingly impossible dream.

Chapter One

From the northernmost borders of icy Kashmir to the shark-infested shores of the Malabar Coast, Major William Russell, the Resident of the princely state of Rajpore, was renowned for being a man of unshakeable habit.

Each morning, as regularly as clockwork, he rose at the stroke of six. After taking a tepid cup of Earl Grey to settle his humors, as the first smoky slivers of dawn began to color the distant horizon, he would change into his jodhpurs and set out to exercise his favorite horse, a dun gelding of fine pedigree named Cicero. On most days, it was his custom to ride toward the deep ravine that separated the British Lines from the native town, cantering onward until the sweltering heat became unbearable and sent him galloping back to the shelter of the Residency.

Upon returning to his quarters, he would invariably spend the better part of an hour perusing the latest dispatches from Calcutta as his valet, Ghanshyam, shaved him and trimmed his sandy whiskers. At nine-thirty precisely, Major Russell dressed for the day in a lightweight linen safari suit and his customary wide-brimmed pith helmet before hurrying through a small breakfast of one-half boiled egg accompanied by a healthy helping of kedgeree. After this abstemious repast, he would be driven to his offices at the City Palace. Once there, he heard petitions through the day, pausing only for a brief spot of tiffin around noon before pushing on till three, when he returned home to enjoy a siesta under the watchful gaze of the punkah-wallah whose onerous duty it was to fan him as he rested.

At fifteen minutes past four, not a moment later, he would rise refreshed from this brief slumber and dress for dinner, an austere meal that was almost always the same: cold mutton and suet pudding accompanied by fresh salad and perhaps a jug of apple cider, after which on most evenings he liked to ride across to the Rajpore Gymkhana and indulge in a game of billiards and perhaps a rubber or two of bridge before returning home to retire for the night.

This was the routine from which the Major rarely ever varied. Perhaps once or twice every month he accepted an invitation to dinner or chose to make a social call, or was compelled by duty to leave the comfort of the city and take a tour of the more rural districts of Rajpore.

That is what made it so unusual when on this, the inaugural morning of the year 1909, Major Russell failed to rise at his prescribed hour. When his valet, Ghanshyam, knocked on the bedroom door, he found it securely bolted from within.

"Sahib," he said, "I have brought your *chota hazri*," but received no reply. Bewildered, Ghanshyam waited patiently outside the door for almost half an hour, knocking sporadically but to no avail, after which he retreated to the kitchen and gulped down the tea and biscuits himself, thinking that perhaps the Resident Sahib had tired himself out a little too much at the New Year's Ball the night before.

But then, as the morning withered and the sun climbed to its fiery zenith above the City Palace, Major Russell's dewan, Munshi Ram Dev, began to worry.

The Sahib would never miss an occasion as auspicious as the first darbar of the year, he thought anxiously, scratching at his bald skull. *It is not in his nature to be so tardy.* Suddenly stricken by the certainty that something dreadful had happened to his master, Munshi Ram arrived at a decision. Briskly, he marched out of the Resident's office and commanded the grumbling, restless throng of petitioners gathered in the waiting room to disband, informing them brusquely that the Burra Sahib would not be accommodating any visitors that day.

At first, the mob of supplicants refused to leave peaceably. Many of them had arrived well before dawn and waited patiently for hours, having traveled to Rajpore from great distances to seek an audience with the Resident Sahib. As a result, when they found themselves treated to such a summary dismissal, they surrounded the Munshi, arguing and complaining at the top of their collective voices.

Nonplussed, the Munshi summoned a native watchman with a shout and ordered him to make sure that the crowd was dispersed immediately. The watchman set about this task with great gusto, waving his rattan cane as if herding a throng of unruly cattle, and in a matter of minutes, after cracking a few recalcitrant hands and shins, managed to drive the angry multitude away.

His unease growing with each passing moment, Munshi Ram waited impatiently till the last of the grumbling petitioners had departed, after which he thanked the watchman with a half-anna tip and hurriedly bolted and locked the Resident's office. Then, grasping his spotless white dhoti in one wrinkled hand so that its immaculately embroidered hem would not drag in the dust, he set off with the utmost haste.

It was a distance of several kilometers from the City Palace to the Resident's bungalow, but the Munshi made the journey in record time. His apprehension continued to swell as he bustled along until, by the time he finally reached his destination, he was breathless with foreboding, shaking like a leaf in a hurricane.

Upon arriving, he found that the Resident's bedroom door was still firmly shuttered, and that the Major himself had not yet emerged from within, even though it was well past midday.

"Sahib, it is I, your faithful servant," the Munshi croaked, rapping his knuckles upon the door's obdurate face politely. "Are you feeling quite well?"

Leaning forward, he pressed his ear to the smooth surface of the wood, hoping for some reply, however feeble. To his dismay, he detected no discernible answer, naught but a silence so absolute that it seemed to magnify the dull thump of his own heartbeat, resounding deeply through his wizened frame like the beating of an ominous jungle drum.

Decidedly unnerved, Munshi Ram scurried off to question the Resident's valet, Ghanshyam. He found the boy in the stables, eating peanuts and spitting out the shells indolently as he watched Gurung the syce curry the horses and polish the Resident's number one saddle.

"Ghanshyam," the Munshi asked urgently, "did Russell Sahib take his exercise this morning…?"

"No, he did not." With a sly smile, the valet lowered his voice to a conspiratorial whisper, so that his words would not carry to the syce's ears. "I think, Munshiji, that perhaps the Burra Sahib is drunk."

"Nonsense," Munshi Ram snorted. "You know as well as I that Russell Sahib does not take hard liquor."

But even as he said those words, a tremor of doubt clawed at his ancient chest. What if the Sahib was indeed intoxicated? Although he had never known the Resident to imbibe to excess before, perhaps he had chosen to partake of a burra peg or two the night before amidst the revelry of the Rajpore Club's annual celebration. *What am I to do…?* He wrung his hands in despair. How was he expected to make sure that Russell Sahib was well? It would be unseemly, even indecent for him to barge into the Sahib's room, for though the Resident was a confirmed bachelor, the old clerk was understandably reluctant to intrude upon his privacy.

It took Munshi Ram several minutes to make up his mind, but then, with a sigh, he turned to Ghanshyam, beckoning the boy to follow his lead

"Come," he said, "we must go see the Captain Sahib. He will know what is to be done."

With that brusque command, off the Munshi went at a vigorous trot, his leather slippers crunching like bone on the gravel of the curving driveway. The valet trailed in his wake, hobbling after the old man as he made his way towards the adjoining bungalow, where the Commandant of Cavalry, Captain Fletcher, was billeted.

Marching up to the verandah, Munshi Ram called out for the Captain's manservant, who was taking a catnap nearby beneath the shade of a freshly washed bed-sheet.

Yawning, the boy sat up with a groggy curse.

"*Kya hai?*" He snapped, "What do you want, heh, disturbing my sleep like a barking pie-dog?"

"Fetch the Captain immediately," the Munshi commanded brusquely in Hindi.

"I cannot, Munshiji," the servant replied ruefully. Being the Resident's personal clerk, the Munshi was a man of some distinction amongst the native community of Rajpore, and accordingly, the Captain's servant, a gangly pock-faced teen named Govinda, moderated his tone with measured respect.

"The Sahib is painting, and he has left strict instructions that he is not to be disturbed."

"Nevertheless," Munshi Ram insisted, "you must disturb him. It is a matter of the utmost urgency."

"I cannot," Govinda whined. "He will whip me if I do."

Ignoring these protestations, the Munshi frowned and clapped his hands impatiently.

"*Jaldi karo,*" he declared imperiously. "Go quickly, and call him. I will take the responsibility."

Grumbling beneath his breath, the Captain's boy obeyed without offering any further argument. He hurried away to return a few minutes later, followed by his master, a short, gray-whiskered cavalryman with the perpetually bowed legs of a horse soldier.

"What is the meaning of this?" The Captain's face had flushed a deep scarlet to match the red velvet smoking jacket in which he was clad, glowering at this unannounced intrusion. "What on earth do you want?"

"Huzoor," Munshi Ram apologized with an obsequious half-bow, "I am sorry to disturb you, but I fear something terrible has happened to Russell Sahib. He has locked himself into his bedroom and will not emerge."

Captain Fletcher, a career soldier who had known the Resident long enough to be well aware of the regularity of his habits, responded immediately. Without stopping to change into more suitable attire, he snatched up a battered terai hat and commanded the two men to follow closely as he strode towards the Resident's bungalow.

The Munshi struggled to keep up as the Captain dashed through the front door and hurried up the stairs two at a time. Raising one calloused fist, he started to pound at the bedroom door as hard as he could, a staccato of impatient hammer-blows.

"Russell, dear boy, are you quite well in there?" Fletcher shouted hoarsely.

There was no response from within. The Captain, an earnest man who far preferred action to deep thought, wrapped one hand around the doorknob and rattled it as mightily as he could, but the door was solid Burma teak and refused to budge, not even when he threw his shoulder against it with a grunt.

It took two more feeble and altogether fruitless attempts that almost managed to dislocate his clavicle before he realized that he was not going to be able to break the door down by himself. Scowling, he turned to Ghanshyam and snapped out a terse string of orders, dispatching him to the bungalow's gatehouse to fetch a burly sergeant and two sepoys with the greatest possible haste.

Upon the arrival of these reinforcements, under Captain Fletcher's supervision, the soldiers fashioned a crude ram from a sturdy kitchen-bench, and set about at battering down the intractable door. Once, twice, thrice, they swung the heavy bench back and forth until at last the thick teak splintered with a resounding crack.

Hastily, Captain Fletcher barged in through the resultant gap as if it were a breach in Seringapatam's walls, followed closely by Munshi Ram's slight figure.

A moment later, a shrill scream rang out, alarming the crows dozing in the skeletal trees and sending them fluttering up into the sky, a murder of ominous black that seemed to block out the sun itself. The District Magistrate, The Somewhat Honorable Mr. Lowry, as he was known in local circles, was out walking his basset hound, Bluebell, on the town maidan when he heard this terrifying shriek. Without a moment's delay, he slipped the dog from its leash. Bluebell raced away, dashing uphill towards the Resident's bungalow in great, leaping bounds. Somewhat more sedately, the Magistrate hobbled after her, holding desperately to his feathered Tyrolean hat, huffing and puffing as he struggled to keep up, for he was a plump man rather too fond of sugared drinks and chocolate éclairs from Flury's.

As they crested the narrow rise atop the hill and turned to enter the wrought-iron gate that guarded the Residency, Bluebell gave a yelp of surprise, colliding headlong with Munshi Ram, who was staggering down the driveway drunkenly, his turban unwinding behind him like a bride's train.

When the old clerk saw the Magistrate he collapsed to his knees and began to weep. Mr. Lowry came stumbling to a halt. Frowning, he glared down at the old man, his fleshy face purpling in disbelief at this utter breach of good manners.

"What is it, Moonshee?" He pulled the old man to his feet roughly, his voice stiff with disapproval. "What has happened?"

"He is dead, Lowry-ji," Munshi Ram declared breathlessly, gazing up at the Magistrate with tear-stained eyes.

"The Resident Sahib…he has been murdered."

Chapter Two

For His Highness Farzand-i-Khas-i-Daulat-i-Inglishia Mansur-i-Zaman Maharaja Sikander Singh, Light of Heaven, Sword of Justice, Shield of the Faithful, sole ruler of the princely state of Rajpore, the year 1909 began with a headache.

Groaning, he threw back his ornate duvet, a quilted brocade coverlet made especially for him by Yves Delorme of Paris and embroidered with his personal crest, a pair of leaping stags with antlers of spun gold, and beneath it, an ornate hamsa, an open palm with an unblinking eye at its center.

As slowly as an invalid, the Maharaja sat up. It took a few heartbeats for his senses to steady. He shuddered, recalling with some measure of repentance his antics from the night before. Regrettably, he had allowed his enthusiasm for the New Year celebrations to get away from him, leaving him nursing a hangover that could only be described as monumental.

His eyes felt gummy; his purple satin pajamas were drenched with sweat. The inside of his mouth was as dry as a desert, and for some inexplicable reason, he could hear a dull hissing echoing through his ears, an insistent tinnitus, like the buzzing of a particularly excited beetle.

Turning, he saw that he was not imagining things after all. His manservant, Charan Singh, was standing by the door, clearing his throat discreetly as he waited patiently for his master to acknowledge his presence.

"What time is it?" Sikander croaked. His voice felt strange in his mouth, rasping at his throat like sandpaper.

"Just after noon, Sahib." The manservant replied, pulling open the thick brocade drapes that cloaked the bedroom in claustrophobic darkness. Sikander blinked, temporarily blinded by this sudden onslaught of bright sunlight. A spasm of dizziness wracked through him, a sharp ache jagging downwards from his forehead, making him gasp with pain.

"I thought, Your Majesty, that perhaps you might wish to be awakened while it is still daylight."

As his eyes met the Maharaja's, the manservant stepped forward with a bow and offered Sikander a tray bearing a sparkling goblet of champagne. Sikander winced, trying not to retch. Ordinarily, he liked to begin his day by enjoying a Veuve Clicquot cocktail before breakfast, served to him in a decanter made of beaten gold, frosted lightly with fresh Kashmiri ice, but on this particular morning, much to his disgust, he found that he could hardly bear the thought of a drink, much less the taste of it in his mouth.

"Get that swill away from me." Unsteadily, he rose to his feet, teetering as the sway of gravity began to exert itself upon his limbs, like a tree being buffeted by a squall of wind. "Fetch me a cup of coffee instead, you immense oaf," he hissed crossly.

Without a word, the servant obeyed this command, impassive except for the slightest hint of a smile. Charan Singh was massive, almost seven feet tall, a bull-necked giant of a Sikh whose barrel-shaped body was surmounted by an enormous pugree and a leonine mane of a beard that swirled halfway down his chest. Like all Sikhs, he treasured his warrior heritage and did not trim his hair and whiskers, and was never to be seen without an ominous-looking dagger tucked into his belt, the iron kirpan that marked him as one of Guru Gobind's stalwart chosen.

With a grace that belied his size, he retreated to a baroque side table upon which a covered breakfast service waited. Deftly, he measured out a draught of viscous Yemeni kahva from a steaming samovar into a delicate Sevres cup, stirring in two heaping spoons of sugar before returning to offer it to the Maharaja.

Sikander accepted the cup shakily, cursing as his trembling hands managed to slop half its contents onto the front of his satin dressing gown, causing Charan Singh to grin.

"What do you think you're smirking at, you fool?"

"You are getting old, Huzoor," Charan Singh replied. "It saddens me to see you in such a sorry state."

"Oh, do shut up, won't you?" Sikander snarled, and settled into a silver-backed Gouthier chair, taking a tentative sip of the cloying yet bittersweet coffee, which was so strong that it made him shudder with disgust.

While he waited wearily for its revitalizing warmth to spread through his aching body, he watched his manservant go about his duties. Over the years, Charan Singh had managed to turn even a task as mundane as laying out the Maharaja's day-clothes into something of an art form, wasting not a single motion as he fetched each item of clothing from the Boulle cabinets in the dressing room next door and arranged them efficiently upon a black velvet Chippendale settee.

"Well," Sikander asked, "what have I planned for today?"

"Oh, you have quite a hectic day ahead of you, Sahib. The shipment of books you ordered from Hatchard's has arrived at last, and also the hamper of edibles from Fortnum and Mason. The Gamekeeper has a boar cull scheduled for this afternoon, and I have taken the liberty of cleaning and preparing the number two Purdey, if you should wish to attend. Also, the Chief Minister has asked for an audience, when you are feeling suitably recovered from your late night."

In spite of the gentle tenor of recrimination in his manservant's tone, the Maharaja could not help but smile. To most observers, Charan Singh might have seemed little more than a faithful retainer, but in his own manner, the Maharaja loved the old Sikh like a member of his own family, thus permitting him liberties in private that propriety prohibited in public. *In many ways*, Sikander mulled, *he has been more of a parent to me than my own father ever was.* It was Charan Singh who had been the Captain of Sikander's honor guard during his childhood, and who had taught him to ride and shoot and duel with a sword. It was Charan Singh who had protected him stalwartly through the many dangerous escapades Sikander had managed to mire himself in over the years, and it was Charan Singh who, over time, had grown to become his closest confidante, the one person he trusted implicitly, without reserve.

"Sahib," the manservant declared, unable to resist the temptation to needle his master, "perhaps I should hurry and fetch the English doctor, yes? You do not look at all well."

"Silence!" Sikander exclaimed, feigning disapproval. "If you must fetch something, old man, go and get my newspaper. Run along, make yourself useful, or I will have to send you back to your farm and you can spend your dotage chatting with your cows."

Giving his master an exaggerated bow, the large Sikh turned and vanished through the door. As for Sikander, he spared a moment to gulp down the remainder of his coffee before rising to stagger toward the bathroom.

His personal bath-chamber was vast, as large as a concert hall. Beneath a vaulted ceiling covered entirely with a sparkling carapace of glazed mirror-work, the floors and walls were lined with a mosaic of alternating black and white Carrara marble tiles, imported from distant Venice. At the center of the far wall, an arched picture window framed a vista of the snowcapped peaks of the Himalayas. Opposite this dramatic panorama, an immense sunken caldarium in the Roman style awaited the Maharaja, filled to the brim with searingly hot water that had been heated in the boiler room two floors below and cunningly piped upwards to pour forth in a torrent from six solid gold taps shaped like the mouths of roaring lions.

Biting back a groan, Sikander shucked off his dank nightclothes. Once naked, he paused briefly in front of an ornately embellished Louis Quatorze mirror, purchased in Paris and said to have belonged to the Sun-King himself. Grimacing, he studied his reflection critically. What he beheld was a slender, elegant man with a well trimmed beard, not tall, just a little over five and a half feet in height, but gifted with a regal bearing made him seem somehow more imposing. His eyes were peculiar and pale in contrast to his walnut-brown skin, as gray as a thunderstorm, and unlike most Sikhs, his hair was cut short, cropped almost to his skull, beneath which a hard angular face frowned back, hollow-cheeked with a strong jaw and a cruel, rapine hook of a nose, that saturnine beak which was the particular birthmark of the ancestral rulers of the kingdom of Rajpore.

It was the nose that made him an ugly man, for though his features were attractively formed, its angularity spoiled the symmetry of his face, making him seem ruthless, almost predatory. As a boy, Sikander had despised the immensity of his nose. At Eton, when he had been packed off by his father to learn how to be a gentleman, his classmates had never stopped making fun of its size, nicknaming him Corvo, the raven of ill luck. They had tormented him with such unforgiving relentlessness that he had sometimes wished that he could amputate the offensive appendage with a knife and make himself blandly handsome, with a plain, unremarkable face, the unexceptional visage of a commoner. *But that was not my destiny,* Sikander thought with a wry smile. *I was born to be a King, and if an unfortunate nose is the price I must pay for it, then so be it. The Romanovs are hemophiliacs, the House of Hanover porphyritic, the Norwegian Oldenburgs have their heterochromic eyes, the Hapsburgs their prognasthic lips, and I have the monumental Rajpore nose. That is my birthright, the surest sign of my regal lineage.*

Unlike many of his princely peers, who were ample-bodied, almost Rubenesque, Sikander was lamentably thin, as skeletal as a laborer. But his wiry build did not mean he was weak. On the contrary, this slimness disguised a strength which had on more than one occasion surprised those who had tried to take advantage of the Maharaja during his youth, thinking him ineffectual because of his fastidious nature and fussy habits.

Arching his back, Sikander stretched like a cat. It never ceased to please him that despite his sybaritic lifestyle, he was just as strong as he had been at twenty. He made a great effort to take care of himself, not just out of vanity, but because if there was one fate which terrified him above all others, it was the thought of growing old and going senile and becoming so weak and helpless that he would have to come to depend on others for even the simplest of actions.

I would rather die tomorrow while I am still young and vital, than live a long life and become debilitated, he thought, gritting his teeth, remembering his own grandfather who had stumbled on till the ripe age of eighty-seven and gone utterly mad in the end, conversing with flowerpots and dancing with a hat-stand, thinking it his long dead English mistress.

No, although he had little interest in athletics—thinking perspiration to be entirely unsuitable for a man of his stature and much preferring pursuits that occupied his mind and his libido—Sikander had managed, thanks to a rigorous session of yoga daily and martial art instruction thrice a week with Yin, his Japanese cook, to ensure that his posture was still ramrod straight and his stomach admirably flat.

Satisfied with what he saw in the mirror, he hummed an old ghazal beneath his breath and dabbed some of his favorite Farina Eau de Cologne on his cheeks, before helping himself to a generous handful of pomade which he proceeded to daub liberally onto the drooping tips of his mustaches, twirling them with his fingertips until they stood erect with piratical abandon.

When he was finally satisfied with the state of his whiskers, Sikander retreated to the tub. Stepping slowly into the water, he eased himself into its scorching depths until he was immersed up to his neck. Sighing with satisfaction, he leaned back, savoring the heat as it seeped into his bones, refreshed by the aroma of rose oil and fresh lavender.

Closing his eyes, he began to hyperventilate, like a deep-sea diver, inhaling and exhaling deliberately, an old yogic trick which served to slow his heartbeat. Gradually, the worst effects of his hangover began to fade away, and a deep calm enveloped him, a rare sense of peace.

Sadly, it was not to last. Just as Sikander had begun to doze off, a tactful knock on the door shook him from his slumber.

Struggling to contain his annoyance, the Maharaja sat up with a splash.

To his fury, he found that that Charan Singh had returned, but without the requested newspaper.

"What is it now, you tiresome toad?"

The Sikh stood framed in the bathroom doorway, his eyes glowing with excitement. "Sahib, you had better get yourself dressed double quick."

"Why?" Sikander said, intrigued by the flutter of urgency in his manservant's ordinarily imperturbable voice. "Whatever is the blasted hurry…?"

"Murder, Your Highness," Charan Singh replied with a grim smile. "It seems that there has been a murder in Rajpore."

Chapter Three

Grinning like a madman, Sikander swerved recklessly through the immaculately maintained palace grounds. In his wake, he left a broad swath of destruction—a row of trampled hedgerows, one very perplexed peacock who squawked in outrage as he trundled by, a herd of terrified silver antelope who skipped away as rapidly as they could, and worst of all, a maze of deep tire tracks in the grass that was certain to make his long-suffering gardener wail with despair.

It was an ungainly, noisy behemoth, a Rolls-Royce Silver Ghost touring car painted in the royal colors of yellow and scarlet with the Rajpore coat of arms emblazoned on each door, a rising sun flanked by two rampant golden lions. Sikander had imported three of these magnificent vehicles at great expense the year before. Unfortunately, he was still not entirely accustomed to their raw power and heavy handling, as was evident when he rounded a corner sharply, and the car nearly got away from him, sideswiping a large flowerpot with a resounding crash and sending a scarlet shower of stricken geraniums tumbling into the path of the Ford lorry which was trailing behind at a discreet distance, bearing his personal bodyguard.

Beside him, Charan Singh gripped his seat desperately, jostling from side to side each time Sikander twisted the steering wheel. The Maharaja cast a sidelong glance at his manservant. The massive Sikh's face was frozen into a rictus of terror so absolute that it made Sikander laugh.

"One of these days, old man," he said, raising his voice to be heard above the drone of the engine, "you will have to let me teach you how to drive a car."

"Never, Sahib," the big Sikh groaned, shaking his head fervently in vehement refusal. "If God intended us to drive, then he would have had the foresight to provide us with wheels instead of legs."

Sikander snorted. It never ceased to amuse him that while the old Sikh was willing to face down charging elephants and wrestle man-eating tigers, he was scared to death of cars. It was an attitude he had seen often, particularly amongst the poorer classes who had never had occasion to travel abroad beyond the borders of Rajpore. To a man, they were terrified by machinery, by progress of any kind, a fear so stubborn that Sikander, who prided himself on being a man of science, simply could not comprehend. Why would anyone be afraid of change? Change was a wonderful thing, something to be welcomed with open arms, not despised. The Maharaja relished the new, the modern, the innovative, and he was appalled by the way most of his subjects clung blindly to tradition, that unyielding rigidity with which the citizens of Rajpore, Charan Singh included, preferred to blunder along with both feet firmly planted in the Dark Ages.

As if to illustrate that very thought, his manservant chose that moment to speak up. "It is not too late to turn back, Huzoor. I cannot comprehend why you are so eager to get involved in this matter personally. Why not leave it to the Superintendent to sort everything out?"

"I think not," Sikander snorted. "For one thing, I doubt that Superintendent Jardine could find his own feet, much less solve a crime of this magnitude. Besides, my friend, don't you understand how long it has been since I have had any fun?"

The old Sikh clucked his tongue.

"You know, Your Majesty, you have a very strange sense of what is fun."

Sikander laughed merrily. "Oh come on, old man, don't be such a spoilsport. Would you deny me this small distraction?"

In reply, Charan Singh shook his head, his face taut with disapproval. "It is most undignified, Sahib. You are the King, not some bazaar thief-taker. It is very bad form for you to traipse around like a common Havildar, poking about for clues."

But even the patent displeasure in the old man's voice could not dull Sikander's enthusiasm. A nervous tension quivered through him like a jolt of electricity, making him feel as if his very skin were ablaze with anticipation.

What a strange breed we princes of India are, he thought. *What peculiar passions we have, eccentric fascinations that boggle the very mind.* For Baroda, it was jewels, and for Junagadh's boy heir, curiously enough, dogs. Jayaji Rao Scindia had been utterly mad about electric trains, and the mighty Nizam of Hyderabad, the *éminence grise* amongst India's royals, was passionate about fashion to the point that he had dedicated an entire wing of his palace just to house his wardrobe. And then there was his old friend, Jagatjit, the prince of Kapurthala, who had a well recognized penchant for French tarts of the most vulgar kind.

But for Sikander Singh of Rajpore, well, it was mysteries he loved above all else. Try as he might, he simply could not resist an enigma. If asked to explain this unhealthy preoccupation with the baffling, Sikander would have been hard pressed to find the words to articulate precisely how he felt. How could he justify the depths of his obsession without seeming foolish or trivial? How could he describe the headiness of anticipation he felt when he encountered a riddle yet to be deduced, an inscrutable sense of mystification that was as utterly intoxicating as a drug? And how could he explain the thrill that seized him when he finally managed to unravel a conundrum which no other man had been able to solve, a sense of accomplishment so potent that it far exceeded any pleasures of the material realm?

It was a small vanity of his, but he preferred not to think of himself as a common detective. On the contrary, he imagined he was what the continental philosophers called a Ratiocanist, a solver of puzzles not on the basis of assumption and guesswork, but rather through careful and deliberate logic.

That was what Sikander had always believed himself to be—a creature of reason questing for meaning in an age mired in absurdity, a seeker after truth as the great Guru Nanak had intended every Sikh to be, searching for the faintest glimmer of illumination in a world shrouded by impenetrable darkness.

But the truth was rather more mundane. Sikander adored mysteries, not just because he had been blessed with a curiosity so perfidious it brinked on the crass, but also because he was cursed with an innately profane nature that only felt excited by the unknown. It never ceased to amaze him, but nothing else—not women or wealth, nor fame or power—gave him the same thrill he felt when confronted by a case of cold-hearted, bloody murder.

"Sahib," Charan Singh's urgent voice jolted him back to reality, "Watch out!"

Sikander had been so lost in the cadence of his daydreams that he didn't realize he was on a collision course with a large and rather ugly Venetian marble statue depicting a very voluptuous Leda being ravaged by a reluctant-looking swan. Desperately, he twisted the steering wheel with all his strength. The car veered with a deafening screech, and almost managed to avoid the unfortunate monument, clipping it only slightly with one front fender to leave the unfortunate swan with a truncated wing.

"Huzoor, please," Charan Singh groaned, an abject look of terror distorting his bearded features. "I beg of you, keep your attention on the road! I would like very much to live long enough to see my grandchildren become grown men."

Sikander stifled a chuckle and slowed down marginally to reassure the old man. Up ahead, he spotted the grand edifice of the wide gateway that led out of the Fort, an immense arched doorway called the Elephant Darwaza, because it was flanked on each side by a pair of monumental sandstone pachyderms, each thirty feet high, their trunks raised in perpetual salutation to trumpet a stern greeting to all who passed beneath.

As the Rolls-Royce rattled through this colossal portal and surged across the drawbridge spanning the deep moat that surrounded the inner citadel, a platoon of the Rajpore Lancers, resplendent in pink breeches and lemon yellow tunics piped with scarlet braid, crashed to attention in a royal salute even as the brass band on duty struck up the state anthem, a stirringly martial thunder of drums and flutes which never failed to rouse Sikander's passions.

Rajpore was not a large kingdom, one worthy of just a twelve-gun salute, but its strategic position on the map of India made it an important ally of the British.

To the north it was bordered by the Hill States and the vale of Kashmir. To the east lay Chamba and the Kangra Valley, and to the west, Sialkot and Rawalpindi. To the south was Lahore and the vastness of Punjab with its five noble rivers, bisected by the ancient Sadak-e-Azam, Sher Shah Suri's great highway, undulating like a plump snake towards the bustling entrepôts of Delhi and Agra and Benares, and on towards distant Calcutta, the capital of British India. The capital city of Rajpore, from which the kingdom drew its name, was located at the center of this ancient trade route, at the very cusp where the grasslands of central India ended and the great crags of the Himalayas began to rear like a giant's broken teeth.

Rajpore was actually two cities spread across a pair of neighboring hills: the English settlement covering the lower of the two hillocks and the valley below, and the native town that sprawled across the escarpment of the larger crag, overlooked by the imposing edifice of the Golden Fort, the famed Sona Killa, which could be seen from miles away.

Built atop the implacable heights of a sheer cliff-face, poised almost a thousand feet above sea level, the Sona Killa's impenetrable ramparts could proudly boast that they had never fallen to an invading army, not even to the Highlanders with their mournful pipes and tartan kilts. Hidden behind four concentric walls built of yellow Palitana sandstone which gave the fortress its name, the Sona Killa was a miniature city in itself. At the center of the fort stood the Raj Vilas, an imposing sixty-eight-room palace built in the old Saracenic style. Beside it was the smaller Sheesha Mahal, the Mirrored Palace, whose walls were covered with glass mosaics in the Rajput style And finally, at the very edge of the cliff, looking down at the distant plains beneath, was the Hawa Mahal, the Pavilion of the Winds, its façade decorated with a hundred arched windows from which it was said Sikander's ancestors had flung their enemies to be dashed to pieces upon the jagged rocks far below.

Surrounding these palaces spread a neat array of well tended gardens, and bordering them, an impregnable barrier of tall ramparts which could only be entered by two gates, the Elephant Darwaza to the south, and to the north, the Lahori Gate. Beyond these two doorways, encircling the killa, shored up against the walls like the flotsam of a great shipwreck, the old city sprawled, a hodgepodge of gaily painted bright yellow houses separated by a network of teeming lanes and gullies that seemed as complex as a maze. It was an oddity unique to Rajpore, the startling shade of yellow that all citizens were expected to paint their walls to complement the Sona Killa's tawny façade, but it was one of his grandfather's few whims that Sikander still enforced. As a result, yellow had become the trademark of old Rajpore, not just mere ornament, but also a useful device because it reflected away much of the sun's unforgiving heat and kept the havelis cool during the hottest months of summer.

Much to Sikander's consternation, as he entered the crowded lanes of the old town, he was forced to slow the Rolls almost to a crawl. Since it was the first day of a new month, it was market day in Rajpore and the vegetable bazaar, the sabzi mandi, was swarming with people. Every street, every single lane was as thick as flies with farmers and workmen and ruffians and thieves, jugglers and peddlers and hawkers galore.

Irritated by this unexpected obstruction, Sikander honked the car's horn raucously, but it did little to disperse the crowd. As the trailing lorry caught up with him, with a nonchalant flick of his wrist, he commanded his guards to dismount and clear the way. Immediately, a troop of burly Sikh sepoys poured forth, resplendent with their matching yellow pugrees and puttees, fanning out to force a passage through the unruly mob.

At first, in typical Indian fashion the crowd resisted, jostling and hooting and screeching vehement abuses at the Sikhs, but then, when they noticed the royal pennant fluttering on the bonnet of the Rolls, that resplendent red sun that was the stanchion of the House of Rajpore, they moved aside hurriedly. As soon as a wide enough path had been cleared, Sikander sped up once more, sending a tardy camel-drover scattering out of his way, followed by his strident beast. Once past the old city's massive outer gateway, he ground down eagerly on the throttle lever until it could yield no further. Hurtling down towards the base of the hill, throwing up a thick cloud of dust behind him, the Maharaja pushed the six-cylinder engine to its very limit. It buzzed as loudly as an infuriated mosquito and the speedometer slowly crept up towards its maximum speed of forty miles an hour.

"Sahib," Charan Singh cried, "slow down! We are leaving the escort behind."

Sikander ignored the old Sikh's entreaties. Instead, almost as if to spite him, he flung the car around each hairpin bend at breakneck speed. Six times the highway undulated sharply, six jagged switchbacks before the new city came into sight, gleaming beneath the haze of the sun like a mirage. At the base of the hill languished a teardrop shaped lagoon called the Khamosh Jheel, the Silent Lake, because it was rumored that another of the Maharaja's ancestors had drowned all who had dared to question his rule in its murky depths, thus guaranteeing their eternal obedience. Skirting the Silent Lake, the verdant expanse of the polo ground flanked the gated enclosure of the Army Cantonment, where the British Garrison was housed. Bordering the Cantonment was the railway station with its Gothic watchtower, and next to that the deep gorge of the river Oona, now straddled by a modern suspension bridge built at Sikander's behest, gleaming dully like a rusty metal cobweb.

On the other side of the bridge lay the neat expanse of the English town. At its center stood the whitewashed edifice of the Town Hall, flanked on one side by the High Court with its Doric colonnades, and on the other by the imposing spire of the Afghan Church, rising above the city like a broadsword. A few meters away from the Town Hall, the City Palace was visible, a sprawling monument built in the Saracenic style which Sikander's father had chosen to formally hand over to the English upon his ascension to use as their permanent Residency. Beyond the Residency sat the Royal Hospital, and the smaller, less ostentatious façade of St. Mary's Catholic Church, and beside it, the walled expanse of the English cemetery, with its tidy rows of graves, like an orchard of macabre marble crosses, baking bone white beneath the noonday sun. Then came the Lower Mall with its row of Indian shops and, and past that, the Upper Mall where all the English boxwallah shops were located. And finally, the Civil Lines, an orderly rank of neat bungalows that housed the British population of Rajpore, dotted across the heights of the English Hill, at the very crest of which was the walled compound where the Resident had lived, and towards which Sikander was now headed with such great haste.

Even as the Rolls-Royce's wheels clattered loudly across the suspension bridge, raising a thunderous din, Sikander found himself thinking, rather unexpectedly, of his mother. It was from her that he had inherited his intelligence and wit, his icy eyes and impeccable manners, and most of all, his love of mysteries. That had been Maharani Ayesha Devi's one abiding passion—mystery stories, like those written by Paul Feval and Emile Gaboriau and Arthur Conan Doyle and her personal favorite, Pierre du Terrail and his clever rogue Rocambole. While her husband had preoccupied himself with hunting and polo and pig-sticking, Maharani Amrita Devi had found refuge for her razor sharp intellect not in card-play or zenana gossip, but in her books. How well Sikander remembered her delight each time a fresh parcel arrived from Paris, or a new copy of *La Presse*, with its tidbits of true crime and its serialized *feuillitons*…!

His mother had made it a habit to read these macabre tales out to him over breakfast each morning, peculiar, convoluted adventures of deception and discovery that had quickly become his passion as well. Although he knew that his rank and birth made it quite impossible, as a boy it had been his most cherished dream to become a professional detective, an unraveler of conundrums like Auguste Dupin. In fact, it was this very dream that had driven Sikander to travel to Europe so that he could learn about the nascent science of criminology, studying phrenology and sociology under Lacassagne in Lyon and forensic psychology and criminal anthropology with Cesare Lombroso in Turin.

Sadly, upon his elevation to the throne, he had been forced to abandon this boyish dream. Quite naturally, the role of investigator was an entirely unsuitable profession for a prince from one of the most exalted royal houses in India. Nevertheless, that did not mean Sikander had not found ample opportunity to put his analytical skills to the test since becoming the Maharaja of Rajpore. On the contrary, in spite of Charan Singh's constant and unwavering disapproval, he had managed to make quite a name for himself as an amateur sleuth. There had been the case of the Maharani of Jodhpur's missing diamonds, and the supposedly unsolvable Ferguson triple murder in Bombay which Sikander had unraveled in less than a day. There had been the murder at the Savoy, and the Cotswold affair, and of course, the incident of the Nawab of Palanpur's racehorse last year which had been the talk of princely India.

Much to Sikander's chagrin, very little of interest had occurred either to test his ingenuity or tease his imagination for almost six months. Instead, he had found himself restricted to the tedious rigmarole of statecraft, day after endless day of placid inaction which had grated at his nerves and very nearly driven him to the brink of despair. While Sikander was a prudent man, not a profligate and a philanderer like his cousin Bhupinder of Patiala, or a pervert like Jey Singh, the Kachhawa king of Alwar, who was said to be a sadist and a pederast with a preference for ball boys from his local tennis club, he knew all too well he lacked the temperament to be a good bureaucrat. Try as he might, he simply could not bear the mountain of work that went with being a Maharaja, the endless, tiresome red-tape that accompanied the day-to-day running of a kingdom, albeit one as small as Rajpore. No, he had always much preferred to leave those annoying details to his Chief Minister, Ismail Bhakht, who had served his family with great loyalty for more than five decades, choosing instead to expend his energies indulging his three great passions: mysteries, books, and women, in that order precisely.

At least, he had until Major Russell had arrived in Rajpore. Sikander stifled a grimace as he thought of the recently deceased Resident. He had disliked the man immensely, thinking him a martinet, a bounder of the worst kind. He let out a sigh as he remembered the man who had preceded the Major. Sir James Foote had been a gentleman in the truest, most meaningful sense of the word, a man of gargantuan size and Dionysian appetite, quick to laugh, always more than a little drunk and a great connoisseur of port and sack and female flesh alike. In many ways, he had been as much of a local institution as the Sona Killa. An inveterate Orientalist from the John Nicholson school, he had spent the better part of his life in Rajpore, from his arrival in Sikander's grandfather's time as a humble under-secretary, through four long and tumultuous decades during which he had managed to weather the terrors of the Mutiny and the turmoil of Lal Singh's ascension and Sikander's father's all-too-brief reign and, finally, played a pivotal part in seeing Sikander's own elevation to the throne.

Sikander had been a great admirer of the late Sir James. Scandalous though the man may have been, the Maharaja had thought him a thoroughly charming fellow, a scholar who spoke Urdu and Punjabi with the fluency of a native and was rumored to have sired sixteen illegitimate children with five different Indian bibis. He smiled fondly as he recalled the many evenings he had spent in heated debate with Sir James, arguing about Voltaire and Rousseau. How he missed the old scoundrel, not just because he had been a staunch ally and an entertaining raconteur, but also because as long as Sikander had kept him well supplied with generous amounts of alcohol and tender young girls well versed in the arts of love, the man had left him entirely to his own devices, preferring to indulge his insatiable appetites rather than nag the Maharaja about the duties inherent to his position.

Sadly, it had been those very appetites that had led to Sir James' untimely demise. Late in 1904, during a banquet in Lucknow, he had choked to death on a chicken leg while trying to sing a verse from *Pirates of Penzance*.

A few months later, early in 1905, the new Resident had arrived to take his place. Unfortunately, Major William Russell had turned out to be a man quite the opposite of the insouciant sir James, one of those lamentable Utilitarians cut from starched Victorian cloth. Sikander had held great hopes for the man before his transfer, praying that they would forge a fine partnership based on mutual trust and respect, but to his infinite regret, his high expectations had quickly been dashed. Within weeks of his arrival, Major Russell had managed to make himself a righteous pain in Sikander's regal behind with his tiresome attention to custom and formality, a canker that had continued to fester even further, due to his insistence that the Maharaja leave all major decisions concerning the governance of Rajpore to the Crown.

As if such blatant self-righteousness hadn't been enough to invite Sikander's scorn, the Resident had proven himself to be one of those insufferable Englishmen who took great pride in harboring the post-Mutiny attitude that Indians could not be trusted to manage their own affairs. Rather than seeing the Maharaja's many merits, he had chosen to treat Sikander as if he were little more than a spoiled, unruly child, thinking him a playboy and a wastrel like most of the other rulers of princely India. Why, on more than one occasion, he had even dared to lecture him with tiresomely Christian zeal about the extravagance of his lifestyle and the unsuitability of his penchant for mysteries, haranguing him like a common nag until Sikander had been reduced to inventing exceedingly imaginative excuses to avoid him entirely.

And now he is dead, he mused, *and part of me cannot help but celebrate.* That consideration inspired an uncharacteristic tremor of guilt, a chill that had little to do with the misty morning. Was he somehow responsible for the man's death? He had certainly cursed the Major often enough, imagined how good it would be to be rid of him, not unlike Henry the Second praying to be free of Thomas Becket. Could some higher power, or for that matter, a lower one, finally have decided to answer his prayers, and struck the Resident down?

"Bite your tongue, Sikander Singh," he muttered to himself, knowing that he was being unnecessarily macabre. He did not even know for a fact yet that the Major had indeed been murdered. All that was certain was that the man had been found dead. How and why, that could only be determined after a thorough and exacting investigation.

Still, he thought mordantly, *the Major could not have chosen a more opportune time to kick the bucket.* Frankly, Sikander had been bored halfway to death himself, all but ready to quit the city and set off on a jaunt to London in time for the start of the season, or to Paris for a brief dalliance at the Ritz and a spot of shopping at the Rue du Faubourg Saint-Honoré—anywhere where he could experience a change of scenery and rid himself of his doldrums.

But then, on this, the very first day of a new year, here was a most unexpected puzzle, and that, too, at his very doorstep.

And not just any old mystery, Sikander thought, letting out a ghoulish chuckle of anticipation, *but for once, what I suspect could in all likelihood turn out to be a very pukka one!*

Chapter Four

The Resident's bungalow was located at the very peak of the English Hill. To get there, the Maharaja had to first maneuver his way through those serried rows of whitewashed colonial bungalows where the majority of the British denizens of Rajpore resided.

As the Rolls lurched through these serene streets, Sikander took the time to cast a jaundiced eye around him. He rarely strayed this far into British territory. It was an unspoken part of the detente he had with the Colonials: he kept to his side of Rajpore and left the Sahibs to their own devices. On the rare occasions he did venture over to the British settlement, it was only to go as far as the Rajpore Club. But now, as his vehicle lurched through this utopian enclave, it struck him quite forcibly how different a world this was from that which he ruled. The Indian side was as chaotic and colorful as Hieronymus Bosch's proverbial Garden, a maddening maze of ancient, mismatched kothis and narrow, cobbled alleys that seemed to twist towards nowhere in particular. In utter contrast, the English Lines were tidy and well-planned, a fine testament to the orderliness of Empire. Here, there were no stinking middens, no wandering cows foraging in the middle of the road, no overflowing drains, no rickshaws and bullock carts jostling against each other for space. Most of all, he was surprised by the complete absence of noise, unlike the old city, where the din was always deafening, a thousand voices speaking in unison, Hindi and Urdu and

Punjabi, bargaining and arguing and gossiping, all mingling into one boisterous cacophony.

In many ways, the Civil Lines epitomized all that was commendable about the British—organization, orderliness, and of course, cleanliness. But at the same time, it exposed their greatest flaw as well. In spite of its crowds and its filth, old Rajpore had a hectic charm, an undeniable vibrancy. But here, there was a sterility, a barrenness that was hard to avoid, not to mention a raggedness around the edges which was apparent when he took the time to look around more closely. His observant eyes could not help but notice that in more than one place, the walls of the cottages were scarred by web-works of musty cracks that no amount of fresh chuna could disguise, as if to suggest that the English were fighting a losing battle against the inevitable entropy of India's heat and dust.

Cresting the final rise that preceded the ornate wrought-iron main gate of the Residency, Sikander found that the native police had erected a hasty cordon of bamboo across the road to keep out unwanted interlopers. Not far from this flimsy barrier, rather a sizable crowd had gathered, a buzzing cluster of memsahibs congregated beneath the shady canopy of an immense Indian banyan. And at the heart of this gaily bedecked brood, slinking about like a shiny lizard, Sikander saw the rotund figure of the local newspaperman, Miller from the *Rajpore Gazette*, dressed in his usual rumpled white tropical suit and tattered straw boater, trying his level best to bribe his way past the trio of native policemen guarding the barricade.

As the Rolls approached, one of the policeman, a red-turbaned Havildar with a large pot-belly, stepped out and raised one hand to obstruct the car's passage. When he saw it was the Maharaja behind the wheel, he bowed hurriedly and waved him past the flimsy obstacle, snapping out an obsequious salaam.

"*Chalo, chalo,*" he squawked to his compatriots. "Hurry up, you donkeys! Can you not see who it is?"

Sikander eased past the gate when the guards pushed it open with a rusty screech, and brought the Rolls-Royce to a lurching stop at the berm of the gravel driveway, making sure to engage the parking brake. Even before he had turned off the engine, Charan Singh leaped from the passenger side, relief patent on his shaggy face to have solid ground beneath his feet once more. Stumbling slightly, he scurried around to hold open the door for his master. It was a cool morning. The air was tart with Himalayan frost. Sikander shivered slightly as he dismounted from the vehicle, rubbing his hands together to keep them warm. Grimacing as the circulation flooded back into his legs, he shucked off his driving gloves and tossed them onto the back seat. Next he removed the woolen army greatcoat he had belted around his waist, pausing with a moue of distaste as he noticed that several strands of lint had managed to adhere themselves to the thick silk of his tunic.

Impatiently, he snapped his fingers, and Charan Singh retreated to the rear of the vehicle, where a capacious Goyard trunk had been strapped to the chassis, filled with the necessities required for any royal outing. Sikander was a great believer in being prepared for any eventuality. Inside the trunk could be found several bottles of mineral water, a haunch of baked venison, a brace of pickled partridges, two freshly baked loaves of rye bread, four bottles of Laurent Perrier Cuvée Blanc packed in a copper bucket of fresh ice, a large tin of his favored goose liver and truffle pâté, a jar of Wilkin and Sons marmalade, as well as two large oilskins, a canvas expedition tent, a full complement of mountaineering equipment, several lengths of rope and a comically large grappling hook which he had never found occasion to use, a pair of matched Holland & Holland .375 caliber hunting rifles, an expedition telescope and its accompanying tripod, and of course a large Gladstone bag containing a folding camera and his detective apparatus, complete with a magnifying glass and a fingerprinting kit.

As Sikander waited, Charan Singh extracted a clothes-brush from inside the trunk and hurried forward to brush away every scrap of annoying lint from the Maharaja's shoulders.

"There you are, you little peacock!" he declared.

Sikander was tempted to stick out his tongue at the old man, just like he had as a boy. Instead, he gave Charan Singh a withering glare. Turning, he marched toward the Resident's bungalow, an obviously regal figure, even though he had done away with much of the pomp and circumstance with which most Maharajas chose to surround themselves. Sikander snorted as he recalled the spectacular tamasha that had ensued each time his grandfather had left the confines of the killa. The old man had been terribly old-fashioned, and insisted on playing the role of an Oriental despot to the hilt. He had refused to move an inch unless mounted high atop a gilded and brocaded elephant, seated beneath a chatri of pure gold, looking down at his subjects like an avatar of some imperious god, his progress heralded by a dozen trumpets and a retinue of some two hundred hangers-on, led by a cavalcade of twenty-four chobdars and bhaldars to announce his coming, accompanied by forty bannermen bearing the golden morchal standards of Rajpore. A bevy of thirty-six scantily clad serving girls had preceded his every step, tasked with strewing fragrant rose petals in his path so that the noxious odors of reality would not permeate his hallowed nostrils, followed by a troop of sixteen chamardars waving whisks made from yak tails, tasked with driving away any flies before they could disturb his Highness with their buzzing.

Contrary to the Burra Maharaja, Sikander had little stomach for making a public spectacle of himself. Rather than cloaking himself in gilded robes and bedecking his body with gold and jewels until he looked like some pantomime caricature of a Turkish sultan, he preferred to dress simply and practically in a black high-necked doublet and a pair of spotless white riding trousers stitched to his precise specifications by the famed Parisian *chemisier* Charvet and tucked into supple black John Lobb calf-leather riding boots that came almost to his knees. Atop his head, he wore a royal blue pugree tied in the Sikh fashion, and around his neck, a matching cobalt ascot, also by Charvet, bound tightly into a Ruche knot and fastened with a peacock-shaped gold stickpin. Other than that, he wore little jewelry, his sole concession to ornament a pair of square emeralds in his ears and a single ring on his left hand, designed by Asprey and Garrard, a massive fifty-four-carat blue-white diamond cut in a distinctive Asscher octagon mounted upon a simple setting of silver, with the regal seal of Rajpore, a rampant lion, etched into its glittering face.

Ordinarily, it was his habit to wear a ceremonial sword, but on this occasion, to allay the natural suspicion of English minds, since he was making an uninvited foray into the white township, he had chosen to leave it behind. Instead, he carried a handsome ebony cane topped by an ornate golden lion's head with twin glittering rubies for eyes. Absently, he found himself tap-tapping it upon the gravel as he walked, like a blind man feeling out his passage. The cane seemed innocuous enough; only Sikander knew that disguised within its slender length was a short-bladed rapier, handcrafted for him by Kliegenthal of France. It wasn't much of a weapon, and while Sikander knew that Charan Singh would gladly lay down his life before he let his master come to any harm, his innate paranoia wouldn't allow him to visit the Angrezi settlement without the reassuring weight of a blade close at hand.

Imperiously, he strode up the eucalyptus-lined pathway that led towards the bungalow, ignoring the inquisitive glances his advance drew from the crowd assembled outside the gate. It didn't escape his notice that his unexpected arrival had managed to create quite an uproar, not only because of the mode of transport he had chosen, but also because Sikander was a native Indian striding deep into the heart of the English establishment and thus a creature to be viewed with suspicion. Many of the memsahibs took a breather from their gossip-mongering and turned to watch his progress. Those who had not heard of his reputation for sleuthing, peered in his direction with a mixture of bewilderment, curiosity, and distrust, wondering why an Indian monarch had decided to put in such an impromptu and unheralded appearance at the scene of a crime. A few stared with open disapproval, particularly two of the senior memsahibs whose crepey chicken necks bobbed up and down in choreographed condemnation, quite offended by the thought of a native Indian invading the sanctity of what they considered their exclusively English domain. And yet others—like a young girl with flaming russet curls and a lovely complexion quite untainted by the harsh Indian sun—gazed at him with more than a little admiration in their eyes, for he cut a compelling figure, noble of bearing and dashing of demeanor.

A few steps behind him, Charan Singh followed as faithfully as a hound, carrying the patent leather valise bearing Sikander's sleuthing equipment in one hand, careful to keep at a respectable distance because he knew better than to intrude upon the Maharaja's line of sight when he was in an investigatory frame of mind.

As Sikander strolled slowly up the gentle incline of the driveway, almost like he were taking a leisurely constitutional, his sharp eyes swept from side to side, studying the scene, seeking out even the slightest hint of anything irregular. The bungalow was at the center of a self-contained estate, perhaps two acres in size. It was a long, low structure with chuna-whitewashed walls and a sloping, eaved roof covered with bright terra cotta tiles that seemed to glint beneath the sun, as though aflame. There were two floors, the upper storey bedecked by a thick mat of verdant ivy framing a row of Jalousie windows painted an appealing shade of bright blue, and a lower floor surmounted by a wide verandah bordered by a row of six polished teak pillars, between which a wooden railing stretched like a farmyard turnstile.

Rather than directly approaching the front of the bungalow, the Maharaja decided to take a tour around the grounds first. Behind the main building he came across a smaller structure, ostensibly the guesthouse, and at a right angle to it, a small tin-roofed shed that he took to be the servant's quarters. Behind that rose a large barn-like enclosure which was obviously the stable, since he sighted the Resident's barouche half hidden away within its shadowy confines, an old-fashioned four-wheeled buggy with a collapsible roof.

Between the main house and the guest quarters, in the shade of a stand of silver-barked eucalypti, he encountered a small garden, so well kept it made the Maharaja hum with approval. He noted that the Resident had been a fan of roses, mainly of the Chinese variety. The winter blossoms he had planted in careful rows were still in late bloom, blazing pink and yellow in a riot of unruly color. Briefly, the Maharaja paused to sniff at one of the flowers. Its sickly sweet odor filled his nostrils, making him feel a little dizzy and reminding him that in his hurry to get to the scene of the crime, he had neglected to take a proper breakfast.

Sikander frowned, trying to ignore the insistent rumbling in his belly. Just then, the shrill clamor of loud voices from within the bungalow assailed his ears, causing him to quicken his steps. To his surprise, the front door was unguarded. Once inside, Sikander found himself in a large vestibule, bare except for a skeletal coat-rack. Beyond was a large parlor that took up the heart of the bungalow, an oblong room with polished hardwood floors and a high vaulted roof crisscrossed by bare rafters. The walls were papered in a hideously brown Lincrusta that was peeling from the humidity. A musty smell hung in the air, the faint odor of moldy wood and decay. Added to that, the room was much too dark, every ray of natural light blocked out by thick velvet curtains drawn tightly across the windows, thus making its interior oppressive, trapped in a perennial twilight.

Sikander glanced around him curiously, pursing his lips in a faint moue of distaste. Like so many English residences, he thought the bungalow excessively furnished, every corner crammed with heavy Georgian furniture which he guessed the Resident must have imported specially from England. He winced as his eyes fell on a particularly egregious cupboard, a mahogany and rosewood monstrosity carved with enough gorgons and cherubs to give a man with even the slightest semblance of good taste nightmares for a week. Personally, the Maharaja preferred the modern when it came to decoration, simple furnishings and a lot of light, not this cave that made him feel claustrophobic, eager for a breath of fresh air.

To his immediate right, a small Victorian *chinoiserie* table was topped by an alabaster vase filled with fresh white roses, their bright presence somehow out of place in this mausoleum of a house. Next to the table, a stairway led upwards toward the bedroom where the Resident's unfortunate corpse waited, undoubtedly already moldering in the midday heat. Adjoining these stairs was a door which Sikander guessed was the way to the kitchen. Next to it, a long row of shelves stood, piled high with rows of musty books, little more than a tall stack of cloth-bound volumes of the *Imperial Gazetteer* that were almost half a century old and which Sikander guessed must have predated the Resident's occupation of the bungalow.

His circumnavigation ended before a pair of ornately embel-lished double doors. Judging by the clamor of loud voices emanating from behind them, Sikander deduced that this was where the argument that had assailed his ears with such strident volume was playing out. Rather than surrendering to his innate inquisitiveness and barging in, the Maharaja hesitated, easing open one of the doors a few inches so that he could eavesdrop on the confrontation unfolding within. Peering through this narrow gap, he saw a formal dining room. Inside, standing splay-footed in front of a mahogany sideboard, Superinten-dent Jardine's barrel shape loomed as squat as a brick wall, his back turned to the Maharaja as he volubly chastised Magistrate Lowry's more rotund figure which was hunched over in a chair, his head slumped forward in his hands.

For a large man, Jardine's voice was surprisingly shrill, so high-pitched that it made Sikander cringe. As he lurked by the door, witnessing the man's thorough browbeating of Lowry, he found himself wishing that the Superintendent would be stricken by a sudden and miraculous attack of laryngitis, thus affording them all a moment of peace.

Huddled on a bench behind the arguing Englishmen sat Munshi Ram. The Resident's secretary looked even older than usual, the very portrait of a broken man, still sniffling and dab-bing at his eyes with a corner of his dhoti, while at his feet the basset hound Bluebell, leashed firmly to a chair, was engaged in licking his private regions which such utter thoroughness that Sikander had to stifle a smirk.

It was the Munshi who noticed the Maharaja's presence first.

With impressive haste, he tottered to his feet as quickly as he could, bowing creakily to pay his respects, but Sikander waved him back with a gentle gesture, indicating that he could dispense with the formalities.

"Mr. Lowry," he said, abandoning his sophomoric attempts at stealth and pushing through the doors now that he had been noticed. "I take it, my dear fellow, that you are the senior man present."

The Magistrate acknowledged him with a grateful nod, immeasurably relieved at being rescued from Superintendent Jardine's invective. "Yes," he said, bewildered, as if the thought had not occurred to him before, "I guess I am."

"Excellent! In that case, I would like your permission to view the body."

Before Lowry could grant his assent, Jardine hustled forward to bar the Maharaja's passage. The Superintendent was a tall man, with the flaming complexion of a perennial sampler of arrack. While his shoulders were still wide, his belly was rapidly going to fat with the onset of middle age, straining the buttons of his uniform almost to splitting. Coupled with his bulging brow and hairy arms, it made his appearance seem almost simian. Sikander scowled, struggling to conceal his distaste. Even though it was not yet noon, already the underarms of the policeman's chambray uniform were ringed with damp circlets of sweat, and from the strong vinegary stench emanating from him, Sikander guessed that Jardine was one of that noxious breed of old-fashioned Englishmen who believed that baths were injurious to one's humors.

"I am sorry to say," the Superintendent snorted dismissively, "that you are not needed here."

With one sausage-like finger, he made as if to jab at the Maharaja's chest, to emphasize his point, but before he could touch Sikander, Charan Singh, who had shadowed his master into the room and had been trying his best to stay inconspicuous, growled menacingly and stepped forward, holding up the Maharaja's valise threateningly, as if it were a weapon. Dwarfed by the big Sikh, the Superintendent recoiled, eyeing the Maharaja's manservant warily, unaccustomed to any displays of defiance from a native.

"I must insist he leave immediately," he barked at Lowry. "This is a gross obstruction of my duties. There has been a death here, sir, of a high-ranking British official, and that is a matter best left to trained officers of the law, not dilettantes who fancy themselves detectives."

"I think, Superintendent, that you will find that in Rajpore, I am the law," Sikander said, refusing to rise to the bait and permit Jardine's obvious impudence to goad him. "As for the matter of training, tell me, have you ever had the pleasure of studying Gabriel Tarde, or Quetelet, or Andre Michel-Guerry?"

"They sound French to me," Jardine said, with a massive frown.

"Oh, that they are, Superintendent, although I do believe Quetelet might be Belgian. Nonetheless, that isn't the point. These gentlemen happen to be pioneers in the field of a new science called criminology, a discipline I am more than familiar with."

Jardine grunted, a pig-like growl of disdain. "I don't need any damned frogs to teach me about criminals. The only good thing the damned French ever did was run away every time they got into a scrap with us English."

"Come now, Mr. Jardine," Lowry spoke up at last, "Let us not be rude. I think in this case, given the seriousness of the situation, we should defer to the Maharaja's expertise."

He rose to his feet, stooping slightly in welcome, his fleshy mouth twisting in silent apology for Jardine's belligerence. "We would be grateful for your help, Your Majesty. You will let the Maharaja through," he commanded Jardine wearily, "and do everything in your power to render whatever assistance he may require."

"But he is a civilian," Jardine glowered at the Magistrate, "and this is a police matter. Need I remind you that the English town is under my jurisdiction, not the Maharaja's?"

"I think, Mr. Jardine, you will find that the Maharaja has quite a reputation for being an expert decipherer of puzzles. And I have every confidence that if any man can deduce the cause of the Resident's unfortunate death with due haste, it is he."

"But," Jardine began to object, "You can't…"

"For God's sake, man, just do as you're told." The uncharacteristic forcefulness of this exclamation from someone as docile as Lowry took Jardine entirely by surprise, striking him temporarily dumb. His face darkened, turning almost purple with fury. His mouth flopped open and shut like a beached fish, so overcome with emotion that he could barely string together a coherent string of words.

For a split second, Sikander was convinced that he was going to disobey the Magistrate and stand his ground. But then, to his relief, the Superintendent seemed to subside.

"Very well, Mr. Lowry," he mumbled, shuffling aside, "but be certain that I intend to carry on a parallel investigation of my own."

"And I look forward to hearing your conclusions," Sikander said, trying not to laugh at Jardine's peevishness.

His amusement deepened even further as Jardine shot him one final glare before spinning on his heels as neatly as a clockwork soldier to stomp away with a thunderous clatter of boot-heels.

"You must forgive the Superintendent," Lowry said wearily, scratching absently at an angry red mosquito bite on his cheek. "He gets a touch excitable in the pursuit of what he perceives to be his duty."

"There's no need to apologize, Mr. Lowry," Sikander said magnanimously. "There will always be men who do not know their place, yes?"

"Absolutely, sir," Lowry agreed, bobbing his head like a bird. "If you don't mind my inquiring, how do you intend to proceed?"

"Well, first, I want to take a look around upstairs, and then, I have a few questions to ask you. And you, too, Munshi." Sikander directed a smile at the hapless old man who had remained cowering in the background, as quiet as a dormouse. "Is that entirely agreeable with you?"

"Of course. I shall do everything I can to help your efforts."

"Capital!" Sikander smiled widely and started toward the staircase that led to the upper floor and the Resident's bedroom, followed closely by Charan Singh.

Lowry, however, hung back, wincing as if he were afraid to leave the safety of the dining room. "If it pleases Your Majesty, I will stay here. I don't think I can bear to go up there."

"I understand," Sikander said sympathetically. "We shall be fine without you."

"It's the damnedest thing," Lowry whispered, his voice trembling with emotion. "The door of his bedroom…it was locked from inside, you know, and they had to break it down. And the windows were firmly fastened. I just can't understand it." He shuddered. "Jardine is convinced that William took his own life."

"And you, sir, I take it you disagree with that theory?"

"Absolutely," Lowry insisted with uncharacteristic vehemence, "Will would never have done that. He was Catholic, you see, just as I am, and suicide for us is a mortal sin."

"He was your friend, wasn't he?"

"Yes," Lowry said softly, "he was. We were very close once. Like brothers, we were."

In spite of his aversion to the man, Sikander found himself feeling more than a little sorry for the Magistrate. It must be immeasurably difficult for him, to first suffer the shock of having a dear friend die abruptly, and then have the mantle of responsibility thrust upon him without any warning. Judging by the pallor of his face, he was close to breaking point, and no wonder. From what Sikander knew of him, at least by reputation, Lowry was a weak, altogether venial, fellow, interested only in good food and gossip, and he doubted if the man possessed nearly enough backbone to shoulder the Resident's job, even temporarily.

"Don't you worry, Mr. Lowry. I shall do everything in my power to find out what happened to the Resident."

"I cannot thank you enough, sir," the Magistrate said gratefully. "And I, for my part, will endeavor to keep Jardine well out of your way."

Chapter Five

Charan Singh vaulted up the stairs, displaying an impressive agility for a man his age. At the top, he took up a position directly opposite the mangled remnants of the Resident's bedroom door, a sentinel to prevent intruders from disturbing the Maharaja as he carried out his investigation.

Sikander's advance was altogether more leisurely. Rather than approaching the bedroom directly, he took several detours, first to examine an unexpectedly elegant chair that caught his interest and then to peer into the guest bedroom. This apparent indolence was of course a ruse. To someone who didn't know him, it may have seemed that he was browsing through a shop trying to choose something expensive to purchase, not conducting a murder investigation. But his razor-sharp mind was racing, filing away every detail, however insignificant.

Finally, he came to a halt opposite his manservant. Rather than charging right into the bedroom like Cardigan at Balaclava, Sikander spared a moment to compose himself. In the blink of an eye, his entire demeanor seemed to alter. The absent-minded half-smile that had decorated his face till that moment melted away, to be replaced by a hawk-eyed frown. From one of the pockets of his tunic, he extracted a pair of slim white gloves, not unlike those which gentlemen wore to the opera, which he proceeded to slip onto his hands with fastidious exactitude. Then, watching his steps carefully, he tiptoed past the splintered remnants of the door.

Charan Singh began to follow, but before he could enter the bedroom, the Maharaja fixed him with a baleful stare.

"Wait there, will you?" he said stiffly. "I need a few minutes alone."

Once inside the room, for one long heartbeat, Sikander stood perfectly still. He had a system he liked to follow. Ignoring the body at first, he took his time to scan his surroundings, trying to discern if anything, the most minute detail, seemed out of the ordinary. The bedroom was smaller than he had expected, perhaps twenty feet by fifteen with a wooden floor and artichoke-papered walls, furnished in the same cluttered style as the rest of the house. Sikander winced when he set eyes upon the large four-poster bed that dominated the center of the room and the lank mosquito net that hung from its wooden arms, as hazy as a shroud. At the base of the bed, a brass-buckled canvas campaign trunk sat with its heavy lid ajar, revealing three pairs of immaculately polished boots and a small mountain of balled-up woolen stockings. An ornately carved Victorian red walnut wardrobe stood opposite the trunk, tucked into one corner of the room, its front surmounted by a tall beveled mirror in which Sikander spotted a fleeting glimpse of his own reflection, his eyes as shiny as newly minted coins.

Crossing to the cupboard, he tried its door. To his surprise, it was unlocked. Inside, there seemed to be nothing remarkable, little more than a row of badly cut safari jackets of the variety the Resident had favored hanging in a tidy row above a pile of folded shirts and neatly pressed trousers.

Stifling his disappointment, Sikander turned his attention to the row of three drawers at the base of the cupboard, pulling them open one by one. The first was filled with the Resident's personal possessions, a gold Elgin hunter and watch chain, a pipe and two tins of Wills Capstan tobacco, a neatly folded arrangement of neckties and handkerchiefs. The second drawer revealed an assorted array of bric-a-brac, a small wooden music box and a chipped bowl full of coins, an unopened jar of Calvert's carbolic toothpaste, and a jar of what turned out to be very pungent pomade.

Finally, he pulled open the third drawer. Inside, to Sikander's unmitigated delight, he uncovered a heavy cast iron strongbox tucked away under a heap of assorted unmentionables. The Maharaja's eyes widened with anticipation. Squatting over, he eased one long pin from his turban, a sliver of metal some three inches long with a razor-sharp tip, which he carefully inserted into the strongbox's lock and began to jimmy back and forth. Amongst his many dubious achievements, Sikander had at one point spent three weeks with a screwsman in Paris, mastering the art of lock-picking, and it took only a matter of seconds before the box's lid snapped open with a barely audible click, bringing a satisfied smile to his face.

Sikander eased the box open. Inside, to his disappointment, all he found was an Enfield Mk1 revolver, a box of cartridges, and a meager wad of banknotes, which he guessed was the Resident's petty cash. Carefully, the Maharaja picked up the gun, snapping open its breech to check if it was loaded, but it was not. Lifting its barrel to his nose, he sniffed at it tentatively, to see if it had been fired recently, but could find no trace of the telltale stink of cordite. Muffling a curse, he replaced the gun and slotted the strongbox shut, before putting it back in the drawer.

"Have you found something, Sahib?" Charan Singh craned his neck forward to peek over the threshold, but was careful not to disobey Sikander's orders by actually setting foot inside the room.

"Nothing at all, old man. Just the Resident's long johns which, while intriguing from a purely scientific point of view, really don't help our cause."

In the other corner of the room, a rather handsome escritoire stood bordered by a Bombay chest, both in matching rosewood. The table's surface was cluttered, piled high with letters and envelopes and a stack of manila folders through which Sikander leafed briefly, making a note to return and examine their contents more carefully at a later time.

Next to this mess of papers lay a covered dinner plate, flanked by an empty glass and a half-consumed bottle of wine around which a few desultory flies buzzed. Curiously, Sikander lifted the napkin that covered the plate to reveal the half-eaten remnants of a mince pie daubed with congealed gravy, and a piece of moldy cake from which rather a large bite had been taken. Next, he turned to the bottle, picking it up with a squint to inspect its label. Much to his surprise, it turned out to be sherry, not wine, a very dark Manzanilla Oloroso of a decent vintage, the kind of bottle that he would have been happy to store in his own cellars, but which was rather an unexpected discovery in the house of an alleged teetotaler.

Well, he thought, *perhaps the Major had not been a complete barbarian after all, not if he had chosen a sherry as fine as this.* And of course, the irony of it did not escape him. *As a final drink before dying went*, Sikander thought, *few bottles could be more worthy.* Shaking his head, he put down the sherry, before turning towards the window. From one of the pockets of his impeccably tailored tunic, he withdrew a small monocular reading glass, a contrivance of his own design able to magnify anything to six times its original size, manufactured for him especially by the renowned German lens-maker Carl Zeiss. Scrutinizing the windowsills, he saw that the Magistrate had indeed been correct, and that they had been shuttered from the inside. The locks remained fastened, and from the thick sprinkling of dust that speckled the murky glass, it was easy for him to infer that they had not been opened for some time.

He unlatched one of the windows now, struggling with the clasp briefly before the louvered shutter slammed open with a loud crash. Bending forward, Sikander studied the sill *outside* carefully, looking for any trace of a fingerprint or for any telltale scratches or marks marring the wooden frame that would suggest that it had been pried open. As he had expected, he found nothing. Straightening up, he leaned out of the window precariously and saw that there was a steep drop to a flowerbed some fifteen feet below, noting there were no trees nearby from which an intruder could have gained access to the Resident's bedroom, not unless he were part langur.

Sikander carefully latched the window shut. *So Lowry was correct*, he thought. It had indeed been firmly locked from the inside, and had not been tampered with in any discernible way. Wrinkling his brow, he crossed to the door once more. Taking a knee, he examined the crumpled wood of the jamb, noting that the latch had been snapped cleanly in two when the door had been battered down. A closer scrutiny revealed that the lock still had part of a brittle iron key jammed deep inside it, and Sikander found the other half on the floor after a minute or two of scrabbling amidst the assorted shards of debris on the floor. It too had been sheared cleanly in twain, which reconfirmed Lowry's statement that the door had indeed been locked and bolted from within.

Puzzled, the Maharaja rose to his feet and, at last, turned his attention to the body that lay on the bed.

The Resident's corpse had been covered hastily with a parrot-green chintz bedspread which some kind soul had draped across his face so that he would be spared the ignominy of having to suffer the stares of gawking strangers.

Solemnly, Sikander lifted one corner of the thin cotton sheet, folding it back neatly to expose the gory sight hidden beneath. Major Russell had not died well. He lay on his back. His eyes, which were as green as the shroud that had cloaked him, Sikander noted absently, were wide open, bulging from their sockets, staring up at the roof with an expression of shock so palpable that for a moment, the Maharaja couldn't help but feel sorry for the man.

As if that was not macabre enough, his handsome face was distended into a horrifying rictus, not a grimace of agony but a ghoulish grin, almost as if he had been laughing as death took him. Sikander knew that most corpses tended to look like they were peacefully asleep because, at the time of death, the muscles of the face relaxed, subsiding toward an almost serene appearance. But here, curiously enough, the Major's jaw was locked rigid, leaving him with an expression as unnatural as a gargoyle's leer, suggesting that his muscles had contracted, convulsing at the moment of his demise.

He pulled the sheet back farther to reveal that the Major's body was twisted into a most unnatural posture as well. His back was arched quite distinctly, lifted clear off the bed to leave his weight resting on his heels and his occipitalis. Even more curiously, he was already petrified as stiff as *stone*, his arms held out in front of him, his hands curled into claws. *It doesn't make sense*, Sikander thought, *How could it be rigor mortis quite so soon?* The Major had not been dead long enough to justify such rigidity. His body was obviously still only in the second stage of death, although bewilderingly his face had turned an icy shade of blue. Still, putrefaction had not yet begun to cause the corpse to bloat, which would have been the case if he had died more than a few hours ago. The Maharaja hunched over to take a closer look. He knew from his studies of Lacassagne that it took roughly between six and twelve hours for gravity to cause a body's fluids to congeal in the extremities, leaving the upper hemisphere of the victim's body with a distinct chalk-like pallor. That was certainly not the case here. Although the Major's lips and cheeks were definitely bluish, his neck and torso were still quite pink, which confirmed his assertion that the man could not have been dead for longer than six hours.

It was obvious that he had choked to death, he inferred, most probably on his own effusions, since the front of his blue-striped cotton nightshirt was crusted thick with dried blood and vomit. Sikander guessed that he must have begun to retch violently before losing consciousness for one last time and drowning in his own bile.

Grimacing, he pulled a perfumed handkerchief from his pocket, clasping it to his face as he turned towards the bedside table. Upon its polished surface, an assortment of objects lay, amongst which were a small glass bottle, a pair of reading spectacles, a tawdry potboiler with the florid title of *The Seething Pot*, and last but not least, a small ivory snuff box.

First, Sikander examined the glass bottle. He uncorked it to find that it was almost empty. Bringing it to his nostrils, he sniffed at its contents cautiously. The fumes made his eyes water, the raw odor of tincture of opium so strong that immediately he was overcome by momentary dizziness. *So the Major was a habitual user of laudanum*, he thought with a frown. He would never have guessed, for the man had completely lacked the emaciated pallor associated with an opium addiction.

Just as he was about to replace the bottle where he had found it, an unexpected sparkle from beneath the table distracted him. Leaning forward, he found that the glint had come from the glass fragments of another bottle, a cracked blue decanter of what seemed to be Philip's Milk of Magnesia, which he guessed had been knocked over and shattered by the Resident just as the ravages of death had seized him.

Biting his lip, the Maharaja knelt down to study these scattered shards. With a curt snap of his fingers, he called for Charan Singh to bring him his bag. The Sikh entered the room with immense reluctance, placing the valise on the floor and quickly scurrying backwards, letting out a low moan when he glanced at the body on the bed. Wide-eyed, he made a hasty sign against the evil eye, no doubt trying to ward off the Major's restless spirit, in case it still happened to be lurking in the room.

Snapping open the valise, Sikander rummaged through its contents until he found what he needed: a set of bright red silken envelopes of the sort used by Hindus during religious festivals to give each other gifts. He had ordered a thousand of them made up to utilize as evidence bags. Very carefully, Sikander bent forward to retrieve a glass fragment from the broken bottle of Milk of Magnesia. Next, he collected the bottle of laudanum and the empty snuffbox and finally, as an afterthought, from the writing desk, the remnants of the Resident's dinner and a few drops of sherry, which he poured carefully into a glass test tube, stoppering it with a cork. Then, turning once more to the Resident's corpse, Sikander pulled out a small clasp knife and cut off a lock of the dead gentleman's hair. Next, he carved a narrow scrap from one of his fingernails, and finally helped himself to a scraping of the bloody efflux that caked his face and chest, all of which he bundled carefully into individual silk purses, before tucking them away in the Gladstone bag.

"Well, Huzoor," Charan Singh said, trying to keep his voice light to obscure his obvious distaste as he watched his master curiously, "what do you think happened to him…?"

"I have the beginnings of a theory," the Maharaja replied, "but I need some more time. A theory is like a good curry, old man. You have to let it simmer, stay on the boil for a while. Besides," he beamed genially, "it's not like the Resident is in a hurry, is he?"

Charan Singh groaned at this awful attempt at humor and shot his master a look of pained disgust. "The fat Superintendent seems to be quite certain that this is a suicide."

"The Superintendent is a fool," Sikander retorted, "and I doubt he would know the difference between a suicide and a murder, even if he were the victim of either one."

"Forgive my impertinence, Your Majesty, but what makes you so sure he is wrong?"

Rolling his eyes, the Maharaja stifled a sigh. Charan Singh was admirably faithful, but he simply could not help but play the role of devil's advocate. It came to him all too naturally, for it was his innate tendency to accept things at face value. He was a soldier after all, and it did not suit a soldier to ask too many questions. Sikander on the other hand refused to accept anything at its word. It was his natural condition to question everything, and it would be anathema to his very character if he conceded so easily, not without making a thorough investigation first.

"I mentioned a man named Michel-Guerry to the Superintendent earlier," he said indulgently. "Tell me, old man, have you ever heard of him?"

Charan Singh snorted, recognizing this question for what it was, the prelude to one of Sikander's habitual dissertations about some abstruse subject or the other.

"Of course not, Sahib, I am an illiterate soldier. What do I know of these things?"

"Oh, he was a terribly interesting fellow, a Frenchman, the son of a poor building contractor who educated himself and became a lawyer, and then wrote a truly monumental book called *An Essay on the Moral Statistics of France.*"

Charan Singh mimed a shudder. "It sounds utterly dreadful, Huzoor."

Sikander nodded, cracking a wry smile. "In many ways it is, a piece of writing so unbearably pedantic that it would put all but the most dedicated scholars to sleep. But at the same time, amidst reams and reams of mind-numbing numbers, Michel-Guerry managed to discover something truly amazing.

"He was an amateur cartographer, you see, a map-maker, and he devised a series of six maps based on fifty years of crime statistics, which was interesting enough in itself, but what really caught my eye was that one of the maps actually charted out the suicides in France according to different regions."

Sikander paused, staring at Charan Singh, his eyes gleaming with boyish enthusiasm.

"Think of it for a moment, old man. An atlas of suicide. Why, it absolutely boggles the mind!"

"Very good, Sahib, but what in God's name does your Frenchman's map have to do with our Major's death?"

Sikander rolled his eyes. "It has everything to do with this case. You see, while compiling this map, Michel-Guerry collected together all the suicide notes left behind for over a half a decade to try and analyze not just why, but *how* people decided to kill themselves. And do you know what he realized? That when they took their own lives, young men generally favored pistols, while older men chose to hang themselves."

The Maharaja held up one hand, miming a noose.

"You see, my friend, the fact is that when it comes to suicide, males resort to poison very, very rarely. It's a woman's way out, not a man's."

"Poison!" Charan Singh gawked. "Do you mean to say that the Major was poisoned?"

"Yes," Sikander shrugged, "I am almost certain he was."

Chapter Six

"What makes you so sure of that, eh?" A belligerent voice announced. "Are you a blooming magician now?"

Sikander turned to see Jardine looming at the door, flanked closely by the Magistrate, Lowry, whose eyes widened with horror as they settled on his friend's ghastly corpse. The Maharaja tried not to scowl, infuriated by the thinly veiled disrespect in the Superintendent's manner. Part of him, the Sikander who was sick of being insulted so flagrantly, wanted nothing more than to respond by berating the man, hurling curses at him. But another, more circumspect instinct warned him to hold his tongue, that getting him to lose his equilibrium was exactly what Jardine was trying to achieve, so that he could have him removed from the case.

Instead of surrendering to the onrush of bile burning in his throat like acid, Sikander concentrated his attention on his trousers, whose sharply creased knees had become somewhat wrinkled when he had knelt to examine the Resident's body. Clucking with agitation, he rubbed against the expensive broadcloth, trying to restore some semblance of its pristine neatness.

"If you bother to actually examine the corpse, Mr. Jardine," he said, "it is quite obvious that the Major did not kill himself. For one thing, you will see that he died a very violent and painful death. In my experience, I have found that victims of suicide prefer to take the path of least resistance, and ordinarily choose a way out that is as painless as possible. In fact, if you take a look in the cupboard, you will find a revolver in there. If the Resident really wanted to take his own life, why didn't he shoot himself? It's quicker and less painful, and certainly less complicated, don't you think?"

"That's all well and good, but how do you explain the door being locked from inside?"

Sikander waved a hand dismissively. "That's simple enough. I am almost certain that is one of our friend William Cobbett's infamous red herrings." He cleared his throat. "Of course, there are elaborate answers we could grab at, if you wanted to waste your time and my own. We could theorize that the murderer had a duplicate key, or that this is a conspiracy of some sort, a grand plot to rob of us of Major Russell's tedious company, but I suspect the explanation is somewhat more mundane."

Sikander arched an eyebrow at the Superintendent. "Tell me, Mr. Jardine, have you ever read an author named Gaston Leroux...?"

In reply, the Englishman shook his head with almost clown-ish vehemence. "I told you, I don't have time to read Frenchy rubbish. I am a hard-working man, I am."

"Of course you are," the Maharaja retorted. "The very epitome of John Bull reborn. Rule Britannia, death to the Frogs, and all that. Still, if you do happen to have an evening to spare, I recommend Leroux highly, particularly his most recent book, The *Mystery of the Yellow Room*. It really is an excellent bit of writing, perhaps one of the finest mystery stories I have had the pleasure to read."

"I fail to see what that has to do with the Resident's death."

"Oh, I think it has everything to do with Major Russell's unfortunate demise. You see, the story begins with a young woman being discovered beaten to death inside a locked room. Leroux's detective, a very intelligent journalist named Rouleta-bille, is perplexed by how she was killed, and after a dazzling example of logical analysis, he manages to deduce that the murderer, who incidentally also happens to be the chief detec-tive investigating the case, never entered the room at all. As it turns out, the young lady was beaten rather severely some time before she died when she and the policeman in question had a lover's tiff, and then she succumbed to her injuries after locking herself into the room for the night."

"What are you trying to suggest?" Jardine bristled. "Are you insinuating that I had something to do with this?"

"Of course not. I wouldn't expect you to have the imagination." Sikander sighed. "The reason I mention Leroux, and the fact that makes the book so interesting, is that he based it on an actual case. Some eight years ago—or was it ten, never mind, I really am getting old—but in either case, Elisabeth, the Empress of Austria-Hungary, was assaulted by an anarchist who stabbed her in her heart with a needle. However, the wound was so narrow that it didn't kill her immediately, and she walked away, apparently in perfect health, only to collapse some hours later and hemorrhage to death after she had locked herself in her room."

"And you think someone stuck a needle in the Resident...?"

"Of course not, Mr. Jardine. Don't be purposely obtuse. What I am trying to say is that whatever killed Major Russell occurred before he retired for the night and locked the door behind him as was his habit. That is what I believe happened here. The substance that killed the Resident was administered to him sometime late last evening, but its fatal effects only seized him much later, when he was overcome by a paroxysm which claimed his life while he lay in bed. That explains the locked door perfectly. It's really quite obvious."

"Hah!" Jardine snorted. "That's a pretty piece of supposition, Mr. Singh. Perhaps you should have been a writer of penny dreadfuls like your Frenchman, heh?"

Sikander stiffened. Abruptly, he found himself overcome by the keen desire to hit the man, a single swift jab to the soft spot below his Adam's apple, before taking a step back and watching Jardine choke to death on his own vomit, just like the Resident had.

It took all of his rapidly fraying gravitas to keep his face impassive. "Tell me, Superintendent, what do you believe the cause of death was?"

"Why, poison of course," Jardine grunted. "I have to agree with you there. It is really quite obvious that the Resident was poisoned."

"Very good," Sikander said. "And pray tell, who do you think would want to poison Major Russell? Who are your suspects?"

"It doesn't really matter," Jardine said pointedly. "That is precisely what I have been trying to explain. You see, while you have been up here, crawling about on your knees, I have already solved the crime."

Jardine's florid face broke into a grin, distended by a smile so vast that it would have put the Cheshire Cat to shame. "What do you think of that, eh?"

"Can this be true, sir?" Lowry asked Sikander, his bewilderment suggesting he could not fathom a universe in which Jardine could possibly achieve such a feat of deduction.

Though inwardly he was equally baffled by this unexpected revelation, the Maharaja made a tremendous effort to keep his expression neutral. "The Superintendent certainly seems to believe so," he replied softly, "though personally, I think it would be best to reserve judgment until we have had a chance to determine whether he is correct for ourselves."

"Oh, I can assure you, I have Major Russell's killer in custody," Jardine crowed. "Would you care to meet him, *Your Majesty?*"

"I would dearly love that, yes," Sikander said demurely, refusing to show his vexation even though the fatuous look of self satisfaction on the Englishman's face was causing his hackles to rise.

"Come along then," Jardine declared with an asinine chuckle before turning and plodding away. After a heartbeat, Sikander followed with a most unprincely alacrity, with Lowry hard at his heels. The Superintendent led them back downstairs. Coming to a stop outside the kitchen, he pulled open the door, beckoning impatiently with one brawny hand that they should pass through. Inside, most of the space in the small, smoke-stained room was taken up by a large wood-burning iron stove and chimney. Opposite it stood a row of stained cabinets and a cast-iron ice box, arranged at a right angle to a wooden counter and a tall metal barrel filled with stagnant water. At the base of this drum, squatting on his haunches, an elderly man cowered, so portly and well fleshed that he could only be the khansameh.

When the Maharaja entered, he scrabbled desperately towards him, whimpering and pressing one hand to his eye, which was swollen half shut.

"Help me," he gasped in Punjabi, "I beg of you."

"Silence," Jardine growled, shaking one callused hand at him. "You shut your bloody darkie mouth."

A frisson of absolute disgust shuddered through Sikander. It was bad enough that the man had the gall to insult him, but it was nothing short of appalling that Jardine had the chutzpah to treat one of his subjects with such brutality, and that, too, right in front of the Maharaja.

"What exactly is going on here?" he snarled, his voice taut with barely repressed outrage.

"Well," Jardine announced, "while you were wasting your time poking around upstairs, I was able to deduce that this is the villain who murdered the Major so brutally."

"Him?" Sikander exclaimed, barely able to contain his surprise. "This fellow? Really?"

"Indeed! I am sure of it."

"And how, might I ask, did you arrive at this most unshakeable of conclusions?"

Sadly, sarcasm was quite wasted on Jardine's thick hide. "It was simple enough!" He gloated. "All it took was a bit of good old-fashioned police work. The Resident, it seems, was inordinately fond of mushrooms, and this rogue here," he pointed at the cook, who shrank away from the accusation, "he was the one who was responsible for gathering them."

As pompous as a peacock, Jardine strutted to the counter and gathered up a small wicker basket filled to the brim with mud daubed morels, proffering them at Sikander, inviting him to examine them.

"This knave has admitted that he picked a fresh lot of mushrooms just yesterday, from which he prepared an omelet for the

Major's supper last evening." Jardine smiled and puffed out his chest self-importantly. "From that singular snippet of information, Mr. Singh, it took me only a moment to deduce that he obviously slipped a poisonous specimen into the dish intended for the Resident's table. That, I believe, was the cause of Russell Sahib's unfortunate demise."

Sikander smiled, bemused by Jardine's posturing. He raised his hands and gently applauded, in mock approbation of the Superintendent's performance.

"I must confess, that is a most interesting theory, my dear Jardine." He picked up one speckled mushroom and sniffed at it tentatively before replacing it with exaggerated carefulness. "But what makes you so certain that this hapless fellow is the culprit? I have found that people rarely kill without a reason. Tell me, what possible motive could this poor fool possibly have to murder the Resident of Rajpore, and thus render himself without employment?"

"Come now," Jardine hissed hotly, his face reddening. "You know how these bloody natives are! All that they want is to kill the Gora Sahibs. My father saw a hundred of these bloodthirsty little bastards during the Mutiny, I tell you. Bloody insolent wogs! Don't know their blooming place, do they?"

Sikander flinched at this flood of invective. "You do realize, Superintendent," he said frostily, "that I am a bloody wog as well."

Jardine blanched as the immensity of his gaffe dawned upon him.

"Oh, I didn't mean that way." Reluctantly, he bowed his head, a half-hearted apology if ever there was one. "Of course I wasn't talking about you. You're a pukka sort of native, a man of good birth and upbringing. I meant these low caste heathen scum. They have no breeding, no education. Why, they're little more than animals. They'd kill a man in the blink of an eye, they would."

Sikander ignored his blustering and turned to the khansameh. "Do you know who I am?" he asked imperiously, in perfect Punjabi.

The man gazed up at him, cringing visibly. "Of course, Sahib," his voice wavered as he stammered a hesitant reply. "You are the sun and the moon to me. You are my father, and I am your loyal servant."

Sikander fixed the man with a stern stare. "Then you know that it will do you no good to lie to me? I am your Maharaja, your Lord and Master, and if you dare to lie, I shall have your skin flayed from your body. Do you understand?"

"Lie, Sahib?" The man said, recoiling before the intensity of Sikander's pale eyes. "Why would I lie to you? I am but a worm, unworthy of even being in your presence."

"Enough of that! This fat white baboon, he thinks that you killed the Resident Sahib. Tell me now, is this true?"

The man's eyes widened in shock, and he shook his head vehemently. "By golly, Sahib, do not even think such a thing! Why would I kill the Burra Sahib? Without him, I have no livelihood. I will starve on the streets." Letting out a vast groan, he threw himself at Sikander's feet. "Please, you must believe me. I swear by the spirits of my ancestors, I have done nothing."

It was as convincing a denial as Sikander had ever witnessed.

"Very well, I believe you."

"You are a star fallen to Earth, Sahib, a god reborn in human guise, unlike this nasty Angrez, who smells like a pile of manure, this English donkey, this son of a pox-ridden whore who seeks to blame me for another man's crime."

"What is your name?" Sikander asked, unsure of whether to be amused or mortified by the colorfulness of the cook's vocabulary.

"I am Khayyam, your Eminence," the man replied, performing an elaborate kornish. "Like the poet, only I create my poetry with a spoon and saucepan, not a quill."

Sikander grinned, delighted by the man's theatricality. "For now, you may go, Khayyam, but stay close by. I have many questions for you."

"I am yours to command, Huzoor."

Springing up, he dashed for the door, but not before taking a moment to make an exceedingly rude gesture at Jardine with his thumb and forefinger.

"What on Earth do you think you're doing?" Jardine

exclaimed, reaching out to grab at Khayyam as he shuffled by. "He's my prisoner, he is. I intend to question him further, once I can get an interpreter who speaks his bloody foreign tongue."

"Let me save you some time, Mr. Jardine," Sikander said. "The man denies everything, and I believe him."

"He's lying! They're all liars, these native bastards." He turned to look at Lowry, trying to garner the Magistrate's support. "Look, just give me twenty minutes in a cell with the little bugger, and I promise you, I will get a confession out of him. Oh, he poisoned the Resident; I know it in my bones. Probably got caught stealing, and didn't want a beating. How's that for a motive, huh?"

"Bravo, Superintendent," Sikander said dryly. "That's absolutely brilliant, as shaky a piece of sophistry as I have ever encountered, with one regrettable exception, I am afraid. You see, the Resident was not poisoned by a mushroom."

"What makes you so sure of that…?"

"Well, for one thing, if you take a careful look at the mushrooms we have here, you will realize that not a single one is of a poisonous variety."

Jardine frowned, too bellicose to take the Maharaja at his word. Obstinately, he picked up a particularly dangerous-looking mushroom from the basket and held it up, a large specimen with a bright orange cap and stem. "What about this one, eh?"

"Ah, that is the Caesar mushroom. *Amanita Caesarea*. It is really quite delicious. You grill it with some butter, and some thyme…"

"And this one?" Jardine held up another even more ominous-looking piece of fungus, with a dirty brown cap covered with strange dark scales that resembled a bird's plumage.

"That is a Dryad's saddle, I believe. It goes very well with a nice, dry white wine."

"This one has to be poisonous," Jardine said tenaciously, holding up one last morel, this one bright yellow, with a wrinkled cap shaped somewhat like a funnel.

"Oh my!" Sikander clapped his hands together in delight. "*Craterellus lateritius*. You have no idea how rare these can be." Beaming, he grabbed the mushroom from Jardine, and then, to a collective gasp, took a large bite. "Absolutely marvelous! A delicious specimen, if somewhat immature." Smacking his lips, he offered the remainder back to Jardine. "Here, why don't you try it? It tastes rather like an apricot."

The Superintendent snorted brusquely, giving Sikander a look that was far more poisonous than any mushroom could ever be. "That doesn't prove anything," he groused. "Murderers don't just leave evidence lying about, do they…? For all we know, Major Russell could have eaten the poisonous one."

Sikander tried not to laugh. "Very good, Mr. Jardine," he said patiently, as if he were speaking to a child. "That is certainly a possibility, just as it is equally possible that the Major was killed by a magic spell, or perhaps by a malevolent djinn bent upon unearthly revenge. However, being a keen amateur botanist, the one thing I can testify to quite conclusively is that there are few species of fungi in Rajpore that can kill a man, particularly at this time of year. It's because of the cold weather, I believe, which can really be quite harsh on plant growth. Of course, if you doubt my word, I would be happy to lend you my copy of *Hooker's Flora* so that you may verify my conclusions for yourself. I also have an excellent edition of Ainsworth and Bisby I could let you have if you wish to explore the science of mycology in greater scientific detail."

Lowry struggled to stifle a smile as Jardine's expression darkened, galled by the Maharaja's blatant needling. "There'll be no need for that," he hissed through clenched teeth.

"Marvelous!" Sikander said expansively. "Now, as I was saying, we are both entirely correct in our assumption that the Resident was poisoned. However, what remains to be established is precisely which poison was used. Luckily, at this juncture, I believe I can provide an answer to that riddle." He paused, as theatrically as an actor about to deliver a grand denouement, reveling at being the center of attention. "Without a shred of doubt, I am convinced that it was a substance called strychnine that killed the Major."

"Good God!" Lowry gasped. As for Jardine, he glowered at the Maharaja, his face tight with mistrust.

"I don't understand. Is this another of your theories, Mister Singh?"

"Not at all," Sikander said. "I have more than enough proof to back up my assertion." He looked squarely at the Superintendent. "When you examined the Major's corpse, you must surely have noticed his unearthly expression. That is what is called Risus Sardonicus, Satan's smile, a condition that occurs to anyone who has suffered an overdose of strychnine. Also, the way his spine is arched so prominently, it suggests opisthotonus, the severe paroxysms that victims of such cases undergo just before they suffocate."

"Are you confident of this, Your Highness?" Lowry said, trying not to let his skepticism show. "It seems rather unbelievable. I mean, where does one even find this strychnine? You can't just buy it in a shop, can you?"

"Oh, to the contrary, it is dreadfully easy to come by. Nux vomica, for one, is a derivative of strychnine and is quite commonly used as a tonic. Besides, the tree is native to India and grows wild. All one has to do is get their hands on some of the fruit, and presto, you have all the poison you need. Of course, I cannot be absolutely definite until I have carried out a few laboratory tests, but I can say that I have more than a little faith in my analysis. The evidence never lies, Mr. Lowry, and from what I have observed upstairs, it was strychnine that killed Major Russell. I am willing to stake my reputation on it."

His face hardened. "Someone wanted the Resident to die slowly and painfully. Someone who was clever enough to know his habits and patient enough to wait for the perfect opportunity to strike. And most of all, someone who hated him a great deal and wanted him to suffer terribly."

"But why…?" Lowry asked. "Why would anyone want to kill poor Will?"

"That, my dear man," Sikander replied, "is precisely what I intend to find out."

Chapter Seven

In spite of this persuasive explanation, Superintendent Jardine remained as intractable as a mule.

"This is all utter conjecture." He let out rather a forceful sniff. "As far as I can see, the case is open and shut. The native cook is to blame. If only you will allow me to question him further…"

"Mr. Jardine," the Magistrate interjected, "would you be so kind as to step outside and check that the crowd is not getting out of hand?"

"Here," He offered Jardine his dog's leash. "Please take Bluebell with you. She gets terribly impatient when she is cooped up inside for too long."

"You must be joking," Jardine objected, aghast at the thought of being reduced to little more than a glorified dog-walker. "This is intolerable! I have yet to conclude my inquiry!"

"Do as I say, please," Lowry commanded, an edge of steel hardening his ordinarily placid voice. "I would like to speak to his Majesty in private."

Clenching his fists, the Superintendent gave first Lowry and then Sikander an irate scowl, before taking one half-step forward. For a moment, the Maharaja thought the man meant to assault him. His hand dropped to the Kliegenthal cane, bracing himself. Behind him, he sensed Charan Singh stiffen, preparing to intervene. Sikander stilled him with the barest nod of his neck. His lips twisted into a sardonic smile as he held Jardine's gaze levelly, challenging him, almost hoping that he would resort to belligerence so that Sikander could put him firmly in his place for once and for all.

This tense impasse held for two long heartbeats until at last something in Jardine seemed to deflate. His shoulders slumped in visible defeat, and he snatched the leash from Lowry's hand. Muttering angrily under his breath, he shuffled away, tugging at poor Bluebell so viciously that she let out a rather affronted yelp.

"I fear you have made yourself an enemy, your Highness," Lowry said.

"I couldn't care less, not as long as he stays well out of my way. Can you see to that?"

"I shall try, but the Superintendent is a very headstrong man." Lowry shuddered. "Good lord, what is the world coming to when a man is poisoned in his own home?"

Shaking his head, he offered Sikander a sorrowful nod. "Do let me know if there is anything else I can do for you."

This was precisely the opening the Maharaja had been waiting for. "Actually, now that you mention it, I was hoping we could have a bit of a chat. I have a few questions about Major Russell, concerning his history and his habits, and your opinions, of course, about what sort of man he was, so that I can build a mental picture of his personality. I find that in getting to know a victim, you also manage to learn a lot about his murderer."

At the mention of the Resident's name, Lowry's eyes widened with palpable distrust. "I don't see how I could help you," he said woodenly. "We were no longer close, the Major and I."

Sikander forced himself to smile, trying to allay the man's obvious misgivings, baring such an expanse of perfectly polished teeth that he could feel the seldom used muscles in his jaw stretching and creaking with complaint.

"Come now, Nicholas," he said, purposely using the man's first name to try and disarm him. "It is well known that you are one of the most erudite gentlemen in Rajpore. And your time on the bench, it has given you a fine understanding of human nature. If anyone can help me, surely it is you."

As he had hoped, flattery was indeed the key to thawing Lowry's reservations. His chest swelled with pride, and his plump features broke into a pontifical grin.

"Well, I guess I can spare a few minutes, if it helps." Turning, he waddled goutily into the parlor. Sikander followed after him, gritting his teeth impatiently as the man made a great show of pulling out a chair and offering it to the Maharaja. With a brusque nod, he sat down, eager to begin asking the many questions frothing at his lips.

To his chagrin, he was forced to wait, because rather than taking a seat himself, Lowry decided to shuffle over to a large cabinet abutting the bookshelves. Opening it with a rasping creak, he spent what felt like an eternity rummaging through its shelves, before proudly brandishing a dusty, corked bottle.

"Ah, so that's where he hid it, the clever bugger," he exclaimed, bringing the bottle and two dented silver stirrup cups back to the table and easing his rotund frame into a chair directly opposite the Maharaja. Sikander pursed his lips, watching impatiently as he struggled to pry loose the bottle's cork, which seemed to be jammed as firmly in place as the proverbial sword in the stone. When it did finally pop free, it came away in a cloud of musty dust that made Lowry sneeze violently. Sniffling, the Englishman proceeded to pour out a generous measure of muddy liquid, which appeared to be medicinal brandy, into each cup, one of which he pushed towards Sikander with a wink.

"It isn't quite the finest malmsey, but I find myself sorely in need of a drink after this morning's trials."

Sikander declined politely with a curt shake of his head. While he was as parched as a wanderer lost in the Sahara, he had no desire to try a glass of something as obviously turpentinish as the Magistrate's brandy. "I am afraid that I am still recovering from yesterday's festivities, but why don't you go ahead?"

Shrugging, Lowry put the cup to his lips and quaffed it in a single, eager swig. He then picked up the second cup as well and greedily gulped down its contents before settling back with a voluble groan, his cheeks gleaming bright red from the fiery spirit.

"God, he's really gone, isn't he…?" He sighed loudly, his corpulent frame shivering. Glancing up at the ceiling, he crossed himself, a devoutly superstitious gesture, as if he were afraid the corpse in the bedroom above their heads could somehow overhear them. "I just saw him last night, you know. He seemed in perfect health."

The Magistrate shook his head sadly, almost as though he still couldn't believe that the Major was well and truly dead. "You know, I always thought old Will was indestructible. He fought in Burma and Baluchistan, and then the Afghan war, and never once took a wound, not even during the rout at Maiwand. He made it through it all, and not a scratch on him, and now he's gone, like this…Gosh, how dreadful!"

He let out a most unmanly sob. Sikander averted his face hastily so that the man would not see how embarrassed he was to have to bear witness to such a public display of grief. The Maharaja was a man who believed in keeping his feelings closely guarded. From childhood, he had been trained to keep a perpetually detached expression on his face, to remain as emotionless as the Buddha himself, because in the game of kings, even the slightest flicker of sentiment at the wrong time could give his opponents a precarious advantage over him. But now, confronted with open emotion, he found himself thoroughly nauseated. Nonetheless, Sikander kept his face composed, letting the Magistrate regain control of himself before continuing with his questions.

"From the way you speak of him, it seems you had known Major Russell a long time?"

"Yes!" Lowry nodded, his jowls wobbling in garrulous agreement. "Will and I were at Cambridge together. He was a year ahead of me at Magdalene, and took me under his wing and protected me from the attentions of the senior lads, if you know what I mean."

"I have always wondered what the Resident was like as a boy. Was he just as stiff and aloof?"

"Absolutely! Will was always a stuffed shirt. We are the same age, you know. I shall be forty-three this summer, and he was just a few months older, but he always acted like he was so much more mature, even when we were boys." His voice grew pensive. "Of course, he was unbearably brilliant. An exceptional scholar, mind you. The Masters were quite dazzled by his skills in languages, but he did not make friends easily. Neither did I, for that matter. I was a slack Bob, you see, didn't play cricket or row, and to make things worse, I was a poor colleger, attending school on a scholarship, which made me quite the object of scorn for the wealthier fellows. But Will, he was always there to watch out for me. He got me through the worst of it, he did."

"Do you happen to know anything about his antecedents, his family history?"

"He told me he grew up in a small village in Kent, I believe. He said that his father was a soldier, a Captain in the Hussars. He died at Sebastopol, when Will was very young, and his mother remarried."

"Were they a wealthy family?"

"Oh no, not at all. His father died deeply in debt, and his stepfather did not get along with Will, and turned him out when he was just sixteen. Luckily, his father had made an arrangement so that he could attend Charterhouse, and then he won a Catholic bursary to Cambridge." He sighed, his rotund face shiny with remembrance. "I think that was what drew us to each other. We were both as poor as church mice. But unlike me, Will was the ambitious one, bloody well ambitious enough for the both of us. He always wanted to be someone, you know. He wanted to be important, powerful, a proper nob, not a humble drone, like me."

Shaking his head, Lowry leaned forward and fumbled with the bottle, pouring himself another generous dram of brandy, which he guzzled with even greater alacrity than before.

"He left Cambridge early, and came out to India long before I did, to take up a writer's position in Calcutta. I took up practice in Gray's Inn for a bit, but it didn't suit my temperament. I was lucky, though. I had an uncle who was a bit of a Nabob with connections in the India Office and he got me a position out here."

Lowry frowned, pausing to collect his breath. "By the time I arrived, it turned out that Will had managed to make quite a name for himself. He was Deputy Commissioner for Khairpur by then, if I recall, but he had to abdicate hurriedly, I believe, under a bit of a cloud."

"And why was that?" Sikander said, leaning forward interestedly as he sensed a hint of scandal.

"I am not sure, and I wouldn't want to put down on him. There was some salacious gossip, something about a garbarh of some kind. Who knows if it was even true?" He looked at the Maharaja cautiously, a shadow of unease flickering across his face, a sudden wariness. "Will wasn't an easy man to like, Your Highness." Lowry spoke slowly, as if he were choosing his words with great care. "He was often priggish, and much too full of himself. Worst of all, the poor fellow had great expectations, sir, aspirations that were staggeringly vaulting."

Sikander frowned, sensing a deep bitterness behind the Magistrate's words. Mentally, he took note of it. There was something else here, something Lowry was not being completely honest about, a rivalry perhaps, or a resentment, which he would have to investigate further.

At that moment however, he chose not to interrupt the Magistrate. "After Khairpur, Will was at Makran, and then at Sirmur for a bit, I believe, and finally, here at Rajpore, sir, just after your mother's unfortunate passing."

"And you stayed in touch with him throughout?"

Lowry shrugged, indicating the negative. "Oh no! The truth is I lost track of him after he left Cambridge. I regret to say we had a bit of a falling out."

With that declaration, the Magistrate fell silent, peering into the empty glass in his hand with a brooding expression on his face, as if he were searching its depths for some measure of reassurance.

"How did you happen to find yourself here, in Rajpore?" Sikander asked politely after a momentary pause.

"Oh, that was Will's doing, strangely enough," Lowry said sadly. "I hadn't heard from him in years, until last Christmas, when he wrote and asked me to take up the Magistrate's post here."

"It was an offer which I accepted, with some eagerness, I might add." He smiled weakly. "I am...I was not like Will, sir. I never did have his ability, his drive."

"Come now, Mr. Lowry, there is no need to be so self-effacing. You seem like a fine enough fellow."

"It is kind of you to say so, but I know the truth about myself. I am a venial man. I drink and eat too much, and on most mornings it takes all my strength to drag myself to the cutcherry and maintain a solemn face as I listen to the cases brought before me." He groaned. "God, if only I could go back in time and change the choices I have made..." Lowry seemed to realize that he was babbling, and he paused, collecting himself with an embarrassed grimace. "The truth, Your Majesty, is that I just do not possess the drive to be much more than a humble district Magistrate. But Will, he would have made it all the way to the governorship of Punjab, I tell you, if it wasn't for this unfortunate incident."

His voice tapered off, lapsing into despairing silence. He hunched over the table, cradling his head in his hands, as if speaking of the past had worn him out completely.

"You mentioned several times the Major left Cambridge prematurely? Would you happen to know why?"

Lowry stiffened. "I am afraid that I don't remember. It was a long time ago."

It was an obvious lie, and Sikander was not at all convinced by this fumbling denial. "He is dead, Mr. Lowry. The truth cannot hurt him now, but it may very well help me apprehend his killer."

The Englishman bit his lip, struggling visibly. "It was one of Will's most closely guarded secrets. You see, he was sent down just before he could take the finals. That is why he had to leave."

This explanation managed to arouse Sikander's curiosity. What could have happened to have Major Russell expelled from Cambridge? It took a lot for a college, even a Cambridge one, to send a man down. Sikander knew that for a fact, from personal experience. He had nearly been sent down himself while at Caius for supposedly ungentlemanly behavior, but had been exceedingly fortunate that the authorities were very careful before taking this most drastic of steps. After all, a sending down could smear a gentleman's reputation and ruin his prospects almost entirely. Russell would have had to have done something truly dreadful to have been turned out from Cambridge, guilty of a sin so unmitigated that it would have left the senior collegians no other choice.

"Would you happen to know why he was sent down?"

"No." The Magistrate shook his head with great finality. "I have no idea, and this time, I am not lying, I assure you."

He gave Sikander a pained, almost offended look. "That really is all I can say, Your Highness. The truth is that I lost touch with Will a long time ago. You know how it is with old friends? When you meet after a long interlude, sometimes there is a discomfort too difficult to surmount. Some people change, and find it easy to forget their own sins, whilst others are cursed to remember." With that cryptic remark, Lowry fell silent.

Sikander waited for him to say something else, but he remained adamantly close-mouthed, staring down at the floor, his expression grim with regret.

"If it isn't too much of an imposition, might I ask, why exactly you and the Major had a falling-out, all those years ago?"

The Magistrate winced, darting a furtive glance at the Maharaja. "It is a private matter, and frankly, I would much rather leave it in the past," he mumbled. His voice tapered away, the words catching in his throat. "Will that be all, your Highness?" Extracting a silver hunter from the pocket of his waistcoat, he peered down at its dial with a squint. "I really should be getting back to the City Palace."

"I am grateful for your patience, Mr. Lowry. I have just a few more questions. You say you last saw Major Russell last night. Was that at the Ball?"

"Ah yes! The Ball." This subject seemed to cheer Lowry up immeasurably. "As it so happens, I was elected as the Chairman of the organizing committee this year, and we pulled off a bit of a triumph, if I may say so myself!"

Lowry sat up, and offered Sikander an avuncular grin. "In fact, I think I looked particularly elegant last night," he smiled, as vain as a peacock. "I had a brand new suit made just for the occasion, you see, crushed red velvet with a high collar and ruffled sleeves."

Lowry looked to the Maharaja, eager for his approval. "Personally, I find that red can be quite slimming, don't you think, Your Majesty?"

Even an entire vat of crimson dye couldn't make you look anything but corpulent, Sikander wanted to reply, but instead, he cleared his throat rather pointedly, cutting the Magistrate off just as he was about to launch into an extended description of the hors d'oeuvres.

"What time did the Resident arrive?"

"Oh, he came in at about eight-thirty, I think. Yes, I am sure of it. I remember distinctly, I was chatting with Lady Fitzgerald, and she had just asked me the time."

"Was he alone, or did he have an escort?"

"No, he was quite alone." Lowry's mouth twisted into a grimace. "In fact, I am almost certain he had come there straight from his duftar."

"What makes you so sure of that?"

"Well, he hadn't even bothered to change, for one thing. Even though the invitation clearly called for tie and tails, he was wearing his day-suit. And then, when I came out to welcome him, he was downright rude to me."

Lowry sounded quite hurt at this recollection. His face purpled with an echo of outrage.

"Rude? In what way?"

"Why, he told me that…that I looked like a giant tomato!"

Sikander stifled a grin, trying to maintain a professional demeanor. "Is that all? Did he say anything else?"

"Yes, as a matter of fact, he took me aside and said he wanted to speak to me privately. He told me that I should come find him before he left, and that it was a matter of the utmost importance."

"And did you have a chance to speak to him?"

"No, I came looking for him when there was a lull in the festivities, but sadly, he had already departed.

"And what time was that?"

"Oh, an hour or so before midnight, I think. Let's see." The Magistrate wrinkled his brow. "Hmm, he was chatting with Captain Fletcher, and then he enjoyed a dance with a very pretty young lady. And then, of course, there was the altercation he had with that foolish young officer."

"An altercation, you say? What sort of altercation, and who was this officer exactly?"

"Oh, he's the pretty young woman's husband, in fact. A harmless enough lad, just a little too big for his boots, that's all. His name is Bates, Peter or Paul, one or the other. He is the son of Lieutenant Colonel Ernest Bates, of Chitral fame. Perhaps you have heard of him?"

"I cannot say I have."

"Never mind, it isn't important anyway." He shrugged. "Young Bates, he's our new Quartermaster over at the Cantonment. I must say, fresh from Sandhurst and thinks he is Caesar reborn. He kept pestering the Major to have him sent onward to a better posting, but Will refused to get involved. I think that was what the argument was all about."

Lowry snorted disdainfully, wrinkling his nose in patent disgust. "It was just hot air, of course. Lieutenant Bates is the sort of jumped-up bounder who likes to show off, he is."

"What do you mean?"

"Oh, it's just a lot of little things. He wears his hair unfashionably long, you see, and primps and curls it like a woman, for one, and the silly bugger likes to carry a sword, of all things, like he's some sort of modern-day Cavalier. And if that isn't bad enough, he is always telling everyone that he has high and mighty connections at the Foreign Office who are watching out for him. As if there is a grain of truth in that, hah? If the poor fool had such great and powerful friends, I wonder, how did he end up stuck in Rajpore in the first place?

"Not that Rajpore is such a bad place, mind you," the Magistrate added hurriedly. "It's a fine posting, really, Your Majesty. It's just that for a young officer looking for quick advancement, it can be a dead end, especially since you have done such a fine job of keeping the peace."

"Yes, of course," Sikander said absently, barely noticing this ham-handed attempt at sycophancy. He was more interested in what the Magistrate had indirectly divulged about Lieutenant Bates. So the man was a popinjay who had been angling for a transfer but had been frustrated repeatedly by the Resident, to the point where it had resulted in a public quarrel between the two men. It was this confrontation that intrigued Sikander more than anything else. It took a lot to push an English gentleman to a point where he was willing to put aside propriety and make a public spectacle of himself, particularly at the Rajpore season's most celebrated social event, not to mention risking damaging his career irrevocably by arguing with a senior officer in front of half of the city's most influential residents.

"You say the Resident left before midnight…?"

"Yes, he was feeling rather poorly by then, I think. He had a bit of a dizzy spell, and Captain Fletcher offered to escort him back to his cottage."

"And the Lieutenant? What time did he depart the Ball?"

"Oh, I had him packed off well before the Major, and that wife of his with him, the little minx. I can confirm they were long gone by the time Will and the Captain departed."

"Hmmm." Sikander wrinkled his nose, as if he smelt something odd. "So Fletcher was very possibly the last person to speak with the Resident before he died, and the first to find his body this morning? How very convenient!"

Lowry sat bolt upright.

"Good heavens," he exclaimed, struggling to contain his astonishment. "I didn't realize that before."

He leaned forward, coming so close that Sikander winced, put off by the reek of cheap brandy on the Englishman's breath.

"Do you think he did it? That he's the one who, you know…" He ran one finger across his own plump neck with a loud clack of his tongue, macabrely enacting a gruesome decapitation.

"Why?" Sikander retorted. "Can you think of any reason that Fletcher would want to see the Resident harmed?"

"Oh, no, of course not." Lowry shook his head. "Captain Fletcher is a very respectable man, a pukka fellow, if there ever was one."

As an afterthought however, he made a great show of wrinkling his brow quizzically.

"Although…now that I do stop and think of it, I happened to hear about a rather angry exchange between Will and the good Captain a few weeks ago. I wonder, what was that all about…?"

Sikander arched one sardonic brow. The man was so transparent it was almost insulting. It was obvious he bore a personal resentment against the Captain, which explained why he was so eager to steer Sikander towards him as a suspect.

"I thought they were the dearest of friends?"

"Oh, they were, indeed, but if the scuttlebutt is to be believed, I think they had some sort of kerfuffle recently."

Sucking in his breath, he cast a wary eye first left then right, as if he were afraid of being overheard. "I really think you should talk to the Captain, Your Highness."

There was something in his tone, a whiff of insistence bordering on anxiety, that made Sikander's nostrils flare with suspicion. The man was far too quick to be helpful. Even though the Maharaja hated to look a gift horse in the mouth, Sikander had more than enough experience with interrogations to sense that Lowry's willingness to volunteer information had to arise from motives that were not entirely charitable. No, the Magistrate was hiding something, most likely some fact that might serve to incriminate himself, given how eager he was to name others as suspects.

Sadly, before he could delve deeper into Lowry's motivations, the Magistrate's dog began to howl, a throaty lament that made him sit up impatiently. "I should really be getting poor old

Bluebell home," he said. "It is long past time for her breakfast, and you know how bitches get when they aren't fed, eh?"

Lowry smiled tentatively, exposing an expanse of cracked and yellowing teeth, but the Maharaja noticed that his eyes remained sullen, watching Sikander with an almost reptilian intensity.

Even though he was quite irritated at being left with so many half-answered questions, Sikander suppressed his exasperation. "Thank you very much for your time," he said, "You have been very helpful."

"Of course, Your Majesty," Lowry responded. "Always glad to be of assistance! Do remember that when Simla asks you to recommend someone to take Will's place, won't you?"

Lowry rose to his feet, teetering slightly from the after-effects of his trio of brandies. It took him a moment to compose himself before he felt stable enough to lurch toward the door, but before he could leave, Sikander was struck by a sudden afterthought.

"A moment, Mr. Lowry," he exclaimed, raising one hand to delay the Magistrate's unsteady departure. "You have been more than kind, but there are two more favors I am afraid I must ask of you."

Lowry halted, and turned to face Sikander with bleary eyes. "What more can I do for you?"

"First, I would be grateful if you would allow my doctor, Roy, to examine the Resident's body and perform an inquest."

At this request, Lowry's face tightened. "I am afraid I cannot consent to that."

"Why not?" Sikander asked, taken aback by such an adamant dismissal. "Is it not customary for the detectives at Scotland Yard to hold a public inquest to ascertain the causes of a man's death, particularly when it is a violent murder? All that I am asking is that we hold a similar autopsy and permit Dr. Roy to confirm my suspicions that the Resident was indeed poisoned? Is that such an unreasonable expectation?"

"Not at all," Lowry replied with a civility so overbearing that it was almost condescending, "and much as I would like to help you, I regret to say that it would be highly improper for me to allow a native doctor to examine Major Russell, especially one with as colorful a reputation as your Dr. Roy."

He gave Sikander an apologetic shrug. "Might I suggest an alternative instead?" he offered. "Why don't I have Dr. Mason examine the body, and share his findings with you?"

Sikander raised one eyebrow. "And this would be the same Dr. Mason who still believes that bleeding and trepanation are both legitimate medical procedures...?"

"I am afraid that there is no other English doctor in Rajpore, Your Highness. If you truly wish an inquest, then I am sorry to say that Dr. Mason is the only person who can perform it. If he permits it, your man Roy may attend and assist him."

"Very well," the Maharaja declared acidly at last when he realized the Magistrate was bent upon being intractable, "I don't see what other choice I have."

"And your second request?"

"I would like very much to interview the Munshi, as well as the Major's other servants."

"I...I am not sure that Superintendent Jardine would approve, Your Majesty."

"Oh, come along now, Mr. Lowry, surely you can accommodate this one whim of mine. I have come all this way in the heat."

Predictably, Lowry quailed before Sikander's intransigence, wilting like a piece of soggy lettuce.

"Very well," he said resignedly. "I will see what I can arrange."

Chapter Eight

With a clap of his hands, Lowry summoned a native Havildar from outside.

"Go and fetch the Major Sahib's servants at once," he commanded the man who answered the call, a pock-skinned, squint-eyed Bihari who looked more a villain than a policeman. "Tell them that the Maharaja of Rajpore wishes to interrogate them, and that they are to co-operate fully, or else."

As the Havildar scurried away, Sikander stifled a yawn.

"Good man!" Waving one indolent hand, he dismissed the Magistrate. "You may leave now. And have someone bring me a glass of lemon water, will you? I find that all this talking has left me quite parched."

Lowry stiffened, his pride sorely wounded at being spoken to like a mere attendant.

"Is that all? Would you like me to have someone fetch you a snack as well? Some fresh fruit perhaps?" He directed a wintry look at the Maharaja, his eyes so scathing that they could have curdled milk, but Sikander did not notice. He had already lost interest in the Magistrate, his formidable intellect now focused squarely on the riddle at hand.

Aggrieved at being treated with such contempt, Lowry waddled away in a huff, leaving Sikander to consider what he had discovered in the Major's bedroom. As far as the Maharaja knew, there were five conceivable reasons why any man was driven to commit murder—greed, rage, jealousy, revenge, and pride. Which one of them had been the cause for the Resident's death? Had he any enemies who would profit from murdering him? Or was this a case of retribution? Had the Resident managed to offend someone to such a degree that they had decided to get rid of him, a scorned woman perhaps, or a wounded husband? Or was the killer someone he knew, someone who had ready access to his quarters, which certainly explained how the poison had come to be administered? Was it someone who had once been his friend but had come to hate the Resident so much and envy his success that he had been driven to poison him? Someone like Lowry, perhaps, however mild-mannered the man may have seemed at first glance?

What was taking that damn Havildar so long? Abruptly, Sikander found himself haunted by an inexplicable unease, an intuitive inkling that there was something that he was missing, nagging at him, like a piece of corn stuck in his hind teeth. Impatiently, he sprang to his feet, and crossed over to the bookshelves lining the wall nearest the kitchen, leaning forward to take a closer look at their dusty inhabitants. The first three shelves held nothing of interest, but as he scrutinized the fourth, the very top shelf, his eyes settled upon one book in particular, a thick volume bound in expensive red calfskin with gilt-edged pages that immediately gripped his interest. Sikander pulled the book out, leafing open a page at random. He had hoped it would be something interesting, but it turned out to be a rather long-winded biography of Gordon of Khartoum. Wincing, he slapped it shut and was about to replace it when he noticed that there was something half-hidden behind its nearest neighbor, secreted away in one corner, a volume so slim that he would have missed it entirely had it not been partially uncovered by his inquisitive rearrangement of the Resident's meager library.

Rising up on his tiptoes, he reached out curiously, only to find the errant book was wedged much too tightly to extract without going through the effort of removing the others first. Nonetheless, Sikander, who was an exceedingly stubborn man, refused to surrender quite so easily. Wiggling his fingertips back and forth, he managed to pry it loose, and the flimsy book fell to the floor at his feet, its pages flapping loosely like an angry bird's wings.

Eagerly, the Maharaja leaned forward and scooped it up. Much to his surprise, it was not a book at all, but rather a thick cloth-bound envelope, folded over double and bound with a band of rubber. *Another secret!* Sikander thought, his ennui fading, replaced by a surge of enthusiasm. Impatiently, he pried open the envelope's flap with one thumbnail. Inside, to his amazement, he discovered a slim collection of photographs. It was a set of six, an array of sepia-stained calotypes featuring a young Caucasian girl, barely out of her teens, dressed as an Oriental courtesan. She was entirely naked, as pale as a ghost except for a large gem-crusted necklace around her neck and a belt of coins around her pelvis, clasping her pubescent breasts in a sad parody of sexuality as she gazed out at the camera-lens with dull lifeless eyes.

Sikander grimaced, overcome by a pang of embarrassment. Once more, the Major had managed to surprise him, and he was not an easy man to surprise. Other than his love of good sherry, it seemed, the Resident had possessed another hidden passion, a penchant for the lowest variety of Victorian erotica. The Maharaja had seen this type of thing before, cheap pornography which could be purchased discreetly in Holywell Street to satisfy gentlemen of certain tastes. In fact, he knew of one or two Maharajas who were avid connoisseurs of such rubbish, one in particular who would remain unnamed who had an entire room in his palace stuffed chock-full of French postcards. Of course, Sikander had never needed to resort to such trite measures himself to satisfy his carnal needs. Personally, he much preferred the real item—what had always attracted him to women was not the concupiscence of their flesh, but rather their quintessence, what the Romans had called the animus, that germinal of taste and smell and touch and soul that could never be substituted with stiff paper and silver nitrate.

A frisson of disgust shook him as he imagined how many times the Major must have stood there and stared down at those very photographs. *God only knew what the man had gotten up to,* he thought, glad that he was wearing gloves.

Unfortunately, the Havildar chose that very moment to return with the first of the servants, who was none other than the khansameh, Khayyam.

Sikander hastily stuffed the photographs back into the envelope and shoved the whole scandalous bundle right back where he had found it. Then, turning, he ran a critical eye over the cook as the Havildar pushed him into the room, like a drover herding a particularly recalcitrant sheep. The man was about sixty-five, with lank white hair and a well-trimmed beard. His shoulders were stooped, and his protuberant belly suggested he enjoyed partaking of his own cooking a little too much. He was dressed like a dandy, in a red silk kurta that came to his knees and a silver embroidered waistcoat, as if he were off for an evening in a kotha. Sadly, his encounter with Jardine had left him somewhat worse for wear. The kurta was filthy, streaked with sweat and dirt, and the waistcoat had a rather prominent rip across the back. As for his bruised eye, it had darkened to a rich shade of purple, as livid as a ripe plum. It made Khayyam seem untrustworthy somehow, duplicitous, an impression that only deepened when he immediately began to complain vociferously.

"Oh, Sahib, I am innocent," he wailed piteously, pulling at his hair and dissolving into a cataclysm of theatrical sobs. "Let me go, I beg of you. I have seven children and one of them is lame. If you harm me, who will care for him?" He fell to his knees, groveling. "Why do you punish me when I have done nothing? Are you not afraid of Allah's wrath?"

Sikander watched this overly dramatic performance with detached disinterest. Melodrama came naturally to most Indians. It was like a sixth sense they had, the ability to cry and wail and curse their ancestors and make a general spectacle of themselves at will, and he was much too experienced to be duped so easily.

"I have no intention of harming a hair on your oily little head, Khayyam the bawarchi," he said patiently. "All I wish to do is have a conversation."

As if by magic, a gold coin appeared in his hand, a heavy sardari he pulled from his cummerbund faster than the eye could see. As expected, the gleam of gold bought an immediate end to the cook's caterwauling, curtailing his complaints immediately. The Maharaja hid a smile. Yet again, his instincts had been spot-on. The cook's eyes never once left the scintillating coin. He licked his lips hungrily, his face flushed with piggish greed, and no wonder. To the Maharaja a gold sardari was a pittance, but to the cook it was a veritable fortune, probably worth at least a month's wages, if not more, and from the naked desire on his face, Sikander guessed, the man looked like he would sell his own mother for a quick profit.

"What would you like to converse about, Huzoor?" The man asked. "I am your faithful servant."

"Oh, I don't know," Sikander replied. Nonchalantly, he sent the coin dancing across his knuckles, flipping it from finger to finger as easily as a professional prestidigitator. "Why don't you surprise me?"

"I know many things, Sahib," Khayyam said, his face twisting into an expression of pure avarice. "The Major had many secrets."

"Is that so?" Sikander bared his teeth like a starving raptor which had just scented its prey. "Well then, regale me. I'm all ears."

He threw the coin at Khayyam, who snatched it out of the air greedily. Grinning, the cook bit it once and then made it disappear into his clothing with blinding alacrity.

"Did you know," he whispered, lowering his voice so that only Sikander would hear him, "that the Major Sahib was very fond of low women?"

The Maharaja raised one eyebrow.

"Low women?" He echoed quizzically.

"Oh, yes." Khayyam's lips broke into a leer, exposing an expanse of cracked, paan-stained teeth. "Every nine weeks or so, he would tell us he was going on an overnight inspection tour of the border outposts, but in reality, he would pay a visit to the English havakhana. You can ask his driver, Sahib, if you do not believe me."

This tidbit made Sikander gasp. In Lahori cant, a havakhana was a brothel, a house of ill repute of the lowest kind, even cheaper than a tawaifkhana or a khopcha, the sort of place patronized only by the poorest of patrons who could not afford to take their pleasure on their backs in a bed beneath a roof, and were thus forced to carry out their business propped against a wall or squatting under the open sky, hence the slang, to "eat air," or *hava khana*, in Hindustani. Could the cook possibly be trying to insinuate that the Major had been a patron of such a low-class establishment? It made no sense, unless…Could he possibly mean Mrs. Ponsonby's? No, Sikander scoffed, it couldn't be. The man had to be lying, spewing out whatever salacious rubbish popped into his skull to try and extort a few coins out of the Maharaja.

"Have you any proof?" he asked, unable to disguise his dubiety.

"Proof, Sahib?" the man echoed, as if he couldn't quite understand what Sikander was talking about.

"Why should I believe you? Without proof, how can I be sure that you are not lying to me?"

"I am telling the truth, I swear it," Khayyam exclaimed, bristling with indignity, visibly affronted that the Maharaja would question his veracity. "You can ask anyone. It is well known that Khayyam the bawarchi never lies."

The forcefulness of his insistence caused Sikander's brow to knit into a perplexed frown. Of all the things he had expected to uncover while interrogating the servants, this was by far the most unimaginable. On the face of it, it was hard to think of the Major as the sort of immoral degenerate who patronized prostitutes. In fact, Major Russell had always struck Sikander as an unmitigated prude. Why, less than a week previously, he had accosted the Maharaja at the Imperial and insisted upon giving him a stern telling to about what he had called Sikander's dissipated lifestyle, calling it a grave affront to both good taste and decency.

Still, what if the bawarchi was telling the truth? An unexpected stab of doubt clawed at the Maharaja as he sat back, weighing this new snippet of information against what he already knew about the Major. Curiously, it did not surprise him as much as it should have. In fact, the more he contemplated it, the more it seemed to make sense. Was it really that hard to accept that Russell had sought the company of low women? If there was one truth Sikander knew all too well, it was that no man, however strong-willed he might be, could muzzle the beast inside him completely. And the Major, it seemed, had been no exception. Behind his stiff exterior, he had concealed a prurient side, as was clearly evidenced by the photographs Sikander had uncovered, and now, if the bawarchi was to be believed, by this revelation about his salacious proclivities.

True, the Resident had managed to be admirably discreet about indulging his vices, but that was a carefulness born out of pragmatism, Sikander suspected, not shame. Most likely, he had tried his best to keep his base desires hidden, because if even the slightest hint of impropriety, particularly of the sexual kind, had leaked back to Simla, it would have prevented his advancement. But unfortunately, that was the damning thing about a man's carnal desires. They were instinctual, a visceral need, like hunger or rage, and no man could live without losing control of them from time to time.

Could that somehow have contributed to his death? Inexplicably, Sikander was struck by the conviction that it was somehow at the very heart of why he had been killed. Lust, desire—those were the oldest and fleshiest justifications for murder of all, having caused more fatalities than all the other sins put together. And when thrust together with power, it made for what was a truly intoxicating cocktail of motives.

Sikander bit his lip, trying not to let his excitement show. Once more, his eyes swiveled upward, in the direction of Major Russell's moldering corpse.

"Oh my, you were a naughty boy, weren't you?" He let out a vicious little cackle. "And that, I suspect, is exactly what got you killed."

Chapter Nine

The next servant to be ushered in was the dhoby.

Sikander attempted to question him, but the man was obviously simple-minded and knew nothing other than the frequency with which the Major's underwear was laundered and how much starch he liked in his shirts. Annoyed, Sikander sent him packing. He had equally little luck with the pair that followed, first the bhishti who was a deaf-mute and then the ayah, an angry old crone who spent ten minutes chastising him for the spiraling prices of vegetables in the market as if it was all his fault personally.

"Who is next?" he asked the Havildar once he finally managed to shoo this vociferous grandmother out of the room. Before the man could answer, a tiny man marched stiffly into the room. He was even shorter than Sikander, just a shade over five feet tall, but very fit, as wiry as a bantamweight prizefighter, dressed in rough breeches cut off at the knee and a tattered vest that stank of sweat and horse-dung. The Maharaja surmised from the Oriental cast of his features that he was a Gurkha, an ex-soldier, he thought, a man who had seen battle and not blinked in the face of death. He could infer at least that much from the imperturbability of his gaze and his ramrod straight posture, not to mention the distinctive curved knife he wore at his hip. The oversized kukri was as much the trademark of the Garwhali tribesmen as the kirpan was to the Sikhs.

Rather than bowing to the Maharaja, he snapped to attention instead and gave him a prim salute, so crisp that it would have put any parade ground soldier to shame. Sikander smiled, and mirrored this gesture. He had nothing but respect for Gurkhas. The mountain men were doughty fighters, as valiant as lions. It was said that a Gurkha would rather die a thousand deaths before surrendering to an enemy, and their sense of honor was so rigid and unyielding that it could have been cast from stone, a stalwartness which made them excellent friends and formidable enemies.

"I am Gurung Bahadur, Sahib," the man said, inclining his head slightly. From his weather-beaten visage, Sikander guessed he was in his early thirties, although he could have been younger. It was always hard to tell the age of mountain men, given their wizened features and leathery skin, but in Gurung Bahadur's case, it was made doubly difficult because his face was horribly scarred, marred by a serpentine bolt of dead-white flesh that jagged wickedly across one cheek and the bridge of his nose to twist his left eye into a perpetual wink. Sikander recognized it as a bayonet wound. *The man was damned lucky to be alive*, he thought with a shiver, *an inch higher and he would have lost an eye.*

"It was at Gyantse Dzong, Sahib," Gurung Bahadur said when he noticed Sikander staring at his face. "That was where I got this little memento. The Tibetans mounted a surprise attack on our camp and very nearly routed us, but we managed to push them back after some spirited hand-to-hand fighting." He smiled sardonically, baring his teeth. "Whenever I look in the mirror, I tell myself it could have been worse. At least I still have my head on my shoulders, by the grace of the goddess."

Sikander shuddered, an involuntary tremble of his shoulders. He had heard terrible stories about Younghusband's campaign, especially what the Tibetans did to British troops unfortunate enough to be captured, particularly the Gurkhas, whom they hated with an unholy vengeance. The lucky ones died, but if they were taken alive, the Tibetans had strung them up and cut them apart piece by piece with their own kukris and left them to die slowly, pecked at by crows and vultures until all that was left was carrion.

"What regiment?" he asked.

"Eight Gorkha, Sahib," the man snapped back, staccato-voiced.

"Rank?"

"Havildar Major, Your Highness."

This gave Sikander a moment's pause. It was the highest rank a native officer could achieve, the equivalent of a Sergeant Major, which meant the man must have been a halfway decent soldier. Sikander felt his opinion of the Gurkha changing. Though he was poorly dressed, and at first glance, looked as slovenly and unkempt as a beggar, beneath the surface Sikander could still discern the drab vestiges of the soldier he had once been, the seasoned veteran who had survived the Tibetan debacle and rallied other men in battle.

"You seem to be a brave man, Havildar. What are you doing as a mere syce? Surely you could do better for yourself...?"

"Times are difficult," the Gurkha mumbled stoically, "and a man does what he must to survive."

There was something very evasive about the way he gave this vague reply, a close-mouthed reticence that made Sikander suspicious, certain that there was far more to the truth than what the man was willing to reveal.

"How long have you worked for the Major?"

"Not long," the Gurkha replied, "only a few months, since September."

"How did you happen to end up in Rajpore? It is very far away from your homeland."

The man winced. Momentarily, his carefully maintained mask wavered. A tremor of barely hidden sorrow flickered across his face like a shadow. This slip lasted less than a heartbeat, before the Gurkha managed to get his emotions under control and resume his stony faced demeanor.

"I was discharged in Lahore, Sahib, but my sister was here in Rajpore. She was..." The man hesitated, as if he were struggling to find the right words. "She was taken ill, and I came to care for her during her convalescence. By the grace of god, the mess club of my old regiment put me in touch with one of the stewards at the Rajpore Club. He was kind enough to help me in my time of need, and found me this position."

Sikander nodded. The brotherhood of old soldiers was a sacred thing. He found himself wishing he could help the man, an impulse he promised he would see through if the Gurkha answered his questions honestly, without guile.

"Tell me, was the Major a good master...?"

The man did not reply. Instead, he held the Maharaja's gaze. Somehow, the epicanthic folds of his eyes made his expression inscrutable, difficult to read.

"I cannot answer this question, Sahib," he said softly. "It would not be fitting."

His tone was respectful, almost deferential, as if to convey he had no desire to offend the Maharaja but at the same time, there was iron in his voice, to suggest that he would not be swayed. From any other man, such a blunt refusal would have made Sikander angry. But this once, the Maharaja understood why the Gurkha had refused to speak, even as he knew instinctively that no threat of violence would loosen his tongue. It was their way. No Gurkha would ever willingly betray his master. Once they had sworn to serve a man, they would never betray his confidence. Loyalty was like a religion to them. They would give up their lives, but never surrender their honor.

"Very well," he said with a sigh, "let us talk about last night instead. Are you comfortable with that much at least?"

The man nodded, a curt bob of his head.

"Good. I believe it was you who escorted the Major back after the disturbance at the gymkhana."

The man's face tightened. "Yes," he said warily, "we did."

"By we, I presume you mean yourself and Captain Fletcher, yes?"

Another brisk nod of agreement, followed by the briefest flicker of hesitation across his face, so tenuous that most men would have missed it, but Sikander's skilled eye recognized it immediately. The syce was hiding something, and it involved Captain Fletcher.

"Is there something you wish to tell me?" He asked softly. "There is no dishonor in telling the truth, I assure you."

The man's jaw clenched. He seemed to struggle to make a decision, before finally replying in a stifled monotone. "There was an argument, Sahib."

Sikander wrinkled his brow, assuming that he was speaking of the altercation between the Major and the Lieutenant at the Ball.

"Yes, yes," he said impatiently, "I know all about that."

"No, Sahib, not the fight at the club. The Captain and the Burra Sahib, they exchanged angry words on the way back to the bungalow." He paused, and looked at Sikander sheepishly. "They did not realize I understand English, Your Majesty."

"What was this argument about?" Sikander said, intrigued.

"The Captain was very angry. He called the Major some rather harsh names."

"What kind of names?"

"I would prefer not to repeat them, sir," The Gurkha said, his mouth tightening with distaste. "Let me just say this much, if any man were to call me such names, he would not have long to continue in this world."

Sikander hid a smile. He was starting to like the doughty little man. The Gurkha had gumption, which was so rare a quality that it managed to take Sikander by surprise. Most people were terrified of him, and wilted in his presence, but for once, he found it refreshing to face a man who was not afraid to speak his mind.

"Did the Captain threaten the Major?"

"Yes," the man grimaced. "He said that he would get even with the Major, if that was the last thing he did. I was about to halt the carriage and step in to stop their argument before it could become more heated, but luckily, we arrived back at the bungalow before I had to get involved."

"And after helping you escort the Major into the house, what did the Captain do then?"

"He left, Sahib, without another word."

Even as he said those words, he betrayed a momentary nervousness, absently lifting one finger to rub at his scar, an unconscious gesture that he ceased as soon as he noticed it, dropping his hand back to let it rest uncomfortably at his side.

"You're lying," Sikander said flatly.

"I am not, Sahib, I swear it."

"Do you take me for a fool?" Sikander snapped. "I know when a man is lying to me. That was not the last time you saw the Captain, was it?"

The Gurkha paused, clenching his jaw and gathering a deep breath, as if he was trying to find the strength to step across an invisible barrier, a Rubicon he was reluctant to cross.

"No, Sahib, it was not." His voice was sepulchral, barely more than a murmur. "It is my habit to oil the traces and the reins before I retire for the night. It normally takes me a little over an hour. As a result, by the time I was done currying the horses and polishing the Major's tack last night, it was very late. I was about to return to my quarters when I heard noises coming from the direction of the Sahib's bungalow, so I decided to check if everything was fine." He hesitated, disinclined to say anything more. "I went up to the main house, and that was when I encountered the Captain Sahib, dashing down the driveway toward the gate, in a great hurry."

"Did you ask what he was doing here at such a late hour?"

The Gurkha looked down at his feet shamefacedly. "No, I did not. It is not my place, Your Majesty, to question the Sahibs." Gurung grimaced. "That is all that I know about last night, Your Majesty, I swear it on my honor."

Sikander fixed him with his most penetrating stare. The Gurkha held his gaze stolidly, not shifting an inch, even as the intensity of this scrutiny grew awkward to bear.

"I find myself confused by you, Gurung Bahadur," Sikander said, "You seem like a good man, but at the same time, I am nagged by doubts about your trustworthiness. Why should I believe you now, when you have already lied once?"

The man frowned. "I did not mean to be deceptive, Sahib. It is just that it is best for someone like me not to get involved too much with the Burra Sahibs. That is something I learned in the army. When two elephants are raging, it is best for the ant to burrow deep into the ground and try not to be noticed."

Sikander furrowed his brow. He couldn't help but agree with the Gurkha. Discretion was often the better part of valor, especially when it came to the English.

"Very well," the Maharaja said with a perfunctory wave of one hand. "You may go, but stay in the vicinity. I might have need of you later."

The Gurkha clattered to attention, as neatly as a clockwork soldier.

"As you command, Sahib," He offered Sikander another perfect salute before backing away with that rigid gait of man more accustomed to marching than walking.

Sikander wrinkled his nose. Sadly, just like the cook, the Gurkha's testimony had managed to leave him with more questions than answers. What had it been that Fletcher and the Major had quarreled over? Could it had been something so vicious that Fletcher would actually contemplate murder?

"Who's next?" Sikander turned to the Havildar, who had been watching the Gurkha's little performance unfold with a look of disapproval writ on his ugly face.

"You should be wary of that man," he volunteered. "Never trust a Gurkha, Sahib. They are too clever for their own good."

Sikander frowned, annoyed by this unsolicited piece of advice. How dare the man speak out of turn, and with such overt familiarity? An ember of irritation flared inside him, and he gave the constable a stern glare, a look so vituperative that the man involuntarily took two quick steps backwards.

"What is your name?"

"I am Jha, Sahib. Uttam Kumar Jha of…"

"It would please me, Jha," Sikander said, cutting the man off before he could launch into a detailed description of his genealogy, "if you kept your opinions to yourself, and brought in the next servant immediately."

Havildar Jha's face tightened. He bristled at this rebuke, squaring his shoulders before stalking away with an air of wounded dignity.

The next witness turned out to be the Major's valet, Ghanshyam. Sikander recognized the boy as soon as he entered the room. He had been a servant at the palace until a few years earlier, a cheeky cretin with sticky fingers who had been caught trying to pocket a pair of silver spoons and thus dismissed from his post. Since then, he had taken service with the Resident, although Sikander suspected he had been placed there deliberately by Ismail Bhakht to serve as a spy.

Ordinarily, the boy was as brash and cocksure as a bantam rooster, strutting about as if his closeness to the Resident made him invulnerable, but now, he seemed surprisingly timid. As soon as Jha relaxed his grip on his shoulder, he immediately collapsed to the ground in an untidy heap, to grovel at Sikander's feet.

"You have to protect me. Please, you are my only hope."

"Protect you from whom?" Sikander exclaimed, alarmed by the child's desperation.

"I know, Huzoor. I know who killed the Major."

Sikander's eyes widened in disbelief. "Who was it? Tell me immediately."

Ghanshyam let out an immense groan, his pockmarked face slack with fear except for his thin lips, which had contorted into a rictus of pure horror.

"It was the churail, Sahib," he moaned. "She cursed him, and now he is dead."

"What churail?" Sikander said with a frown, unable to make sense of this incoherent rambling.

"Day before yesterday, Sahib, on the night that there was no moon, I saw a ghost, a woman in black. She was wandering in the mist, as if she were searching for someone."

Sikander looked down at the boy, trying not to let his skepticism show. As a rationalist, he had no patience for the supernatural, and found it difficult to accept such a far-fetched story at face value.

"Where? Where did you see this churail?"

"Just behind the guest bangla, Sahib. It was very late, well after midnight. I had woken to go into the bushes to do my business. That was when I saw her. She came up the hill and stood beneath the large peepul, watching the house like a hawk. That was how I knew she was a churail, you see. It is well known they haunt peepul trees, that they lie in wait beneath their shadowy branches to pounce on unwary travelers and suck out their eyes."

"She just stood there…?"

"Yes, Sahib, she walked back and forth for some time, talking to herself in a low whisper. I was hiding of course, cowering behind a bush. I decided I would wait until she had left before I tried to make a run for the shelter of the stables, because I did not want her to see me and eat my eyes as well. But I think she must have heard me, because all of a sudden, she looked in my direction, and then floated away with great haste."

Sikander rolled his eyes. What a ludicrous tale! Most likely it had been a trick of the light, or a hallucination where the boy's overactive imagination had turned the shadows cast by the trees into something infinitely more fanciful.

"Are you sure that she wasn't one of the Major's lady friends? Perhaps a late night visitor?"

"Oh no, Sahib. She was a churail. I am sure of it."

The Maharaja pursed his lips, his doubts wavering in the face of such staunch insistence.

"I want you to describe this apparition to me," he urged.

"She was very beautiful, Sahib, as slender and lissome as a young girl. Her skin was pale like a corpse and she was clad from head to toe in blackest black, darker even than the night."

"Her face, did you see her face?"

Ghanshyam hastily made a gesture to ward off the evil eye. "She had no face, Sahib. Nothing but two shiny eyes which burned like coals. Everything else, it was black, like a shadow."

He uttered a shrill whimper which made Havildar Jha gulp and take an involuntary step backwards. Sikander shot him an annoyed look. What a pair of superstitious ninnies! More likely that she had been wearing a veil, a scarf wrapped around her face perhaps, to obscure her features and hide her face from sight? That made more sense than this description of a faceless wraith.

"Stop being such ignorant fools, both of you! There are no such things as churails, or curses for that matter!"

"But...but I saw her," Ghanshyam objected piteously. "I swear it, I did!"

"Oh, just take him away!" Sikander snapped.

Reluctantly, Havildar Jha complied, shuffling forward to pull the boy up bodily to his feet, but not before his saturnine face twisted into a grimace, as if to illustrate how unwilling he was to even touch Ghanshyam, terrified that his talk of churails would somehow contaminate him.

As the boy was marched away, Sikander mulled over what he had revealed. Churail indeed! What a load of nonsense! It was patent, even to a child, that what Ghanshyam had seen was certainly not an apparition. No, there was a straightforward explanation to be had, and a logical one at that. Quite obviously, the so-called churail had to be a woman, and most likely, an Englishwoman, judging by the boy's description.

Who could she be? he wondered. *And what in God's name was a memsahib doing skulking about in the middle of the night like a thief?*

Frankly, it made no sense.

Not unless she was the one who had poisoned Major Russell.

Chapter Ten

Choking back a weary groan, Sikander pinched the bridge of his nose, trying to gather his strength for one last interrogation.

When the Munshi limped into the room, he could not help but feel a pang of sympathy for the old man. He looked haggard, on the very brink of collapse. His once spotless dhoti was now bedraggled and stained by dirt, his lined face wearing an expression of stricken exhaustion, as if he had seen too much for any one man to endure.

"Hello, Munshiji," Sikander offered him a compassionate smile. "Come, sit down for a moment."

He pointed toward a nearby chair. Wide-eyed, the Munshi hesitated, terrified perhaps of taking such a liberty in the Maharaja's presence. A long moment passed before he realized that this overture was not a request, but a command, and hastened to obey, shuffling over to take a precarious perch on the chair's very edge, as if he were afraid that it would collapse under his scant weight.

"Lowry Sahib said you wished to speak with me, Your Highness," he said, his voice wavering with barely repressed emotion.

"Indeed, I do, Panditji." Sikander decided to use this honorific to put the man at ease. "I understand that you have had a terrible shock today, but I have a few questions and I would appreciate it greatly if you would answer them."

"As you wish, Huzoor. I am your loyal servant."

"I am glad to know that. I have heard much about you,

Munshiji. You are said to be an honest man. Is this true? Are you indeed as trustworthy as they say?"

This comment seemed to rouse the man's spirits, and he sat up straighter, as proud as punch.

"My reputation is well founded, Sahib. From East to West, it is known that Munshi Ram Dev is as pukka as a Swiss clock."

"Bravo! Then I can trust you?"

"Of course!"

"Excellent! Tell me then, if you will, about your master."

At this mention of Major Russell, the old man's enthusiasm waned visibly.

"What would you care to know, Huzoor?" He said, unable to hide his reticence.

"Let us begin with how long you have been his clerk, shall we…?"

"Some four years. Before that, I was a chuprassy in the employ of your father, but when Russell Sahib arrived, I was seconded into his service, and he trusted me enough to make me his Munshi."

"And what was your opinion of him as a man?"

Another hesitation, before he answered, selecting his words very carefully.

"He was a good man, Huzoor. Strict, but fair, and not the sort of Sahib who was given to foolish or impulsive behavior. I had great hopes for him." The Munshi paused, biting his lip. "I am not comfortable saying more. I have eaten his salt, and it would be most rude of me to indulge in bazaar gossip."

"I understand. You are a loyal man, Munshi Ram, to keep your master's faith with such conviction, even though he has left us."

"Thank you, Sahib," the Munshi said, preening. "From your exalted lips, that is a great compliment indeed. Who knows, perhaps someday I can serve you again, as I served your father before you? That would be an honor indeed."

Sikander smiled, brushing aside this lame attempt at sycophancy.

"Tell me, Panditji, did the Resident have any enemies that you know of?"

"Enemies, Your Highness, I cannot imagine anyone would think poorly of the Resident Sahib," the Munshi said, feigning bewilderment, but Sikander could see that his bafflement was just a sham, as thin and unsubstantial as Lahori muslin. It could be a natural close-mouthedness, or perhaps the man was afraid, but whatever the case may have been, Sikander could tell he knew something, but had decided to keep it hidden.

"Let me rephrase myself. Can you think of anyone who may have held a grudge against the Resident?"

Instead of replying, the Munshi's eyes flickered toward the door, as skittish as a lizard. Sikander realized the man was petrified, scared half to death of something. Or was it someone? The English, he understood with a start, the Munshi knew something important but was afraid to reveal it because of the English.

"Go on, Munshiji," he said, leaning forward. "Do not be afraid. You are under my protection, and nobody will cause you a whit of harm. As God is my witness, I promise it."

This pledge went a long way toward reassuring the Munshi. "The Captain, Your Majesty," he said in a low whisper. "Fletcher Sahib had a terrible argument with the Resident some weeks ago. They almost came to blows."

Sikander sat up. "Can you tell me what they were arguing about?"

Circumspectly, the old man nodded. "As a matter of fact, I happened to overhear their exchange."

The Maharaja hid a smile. The Munshi made it sound like a fortunate accident, but most likely he had been listening at the door.

"The Captain was expecting to be raised to Major, you see, but his promotion was refused." Munshi Ram clucked his tongue. "He blamed the Resident for it. The Major tried to explain that the rejection had come from Simla, but the Captain was beside himself with fury. He threatened Russell Sahib, and promised he would get even with him someday, and now this…?"

Puckering his brow, Sikander pondered this snippet of information. It could be a motive for murder, but where was the proof…? He knew the Captain socially, and while he did not like the man, thinking him rather too pompous and abrasive, he could not imagine him resorting to poisoning a man. No, Fletcher had an old-fashioned sense of honor, and if he wanted to kill someone, it would have been the route of grass before breakfast, not strychnine in a bottle of tonic. That seemed quite anathema to the man's nature, not to mention too clever by half for someone of such limited intelligence.

Unconvinced, Sikander turned back to the Munshi, who had begun to wring his wrists and rub at his arms tenderly. For the first time, Sikander noticed that the man's wrists and forearms were covered with angry bruises. Most of them were old enough to be fading to yellow, but at least two looked freshly inflicted, still bright red.

"Who did this to you?" he asked sternly. "Was it the Havildar?"

The Munshi shook his head. He tugged at his sleeves, trying to hide his injuries, his wrinkled face coloring with guilt, as if he had been caught doing something wrong.

Suddenly, a flash of insight struck Sikander.

"It was the Resident, wasn't it?"

The Munshi did not reply. He bit his lip, staring pointedly at the floor, as if to hide his obvious discomfort.

"Did he whip you?" Sikander said, his outrage mounting. If there was one thing he could not abide, not in the least, it was the mistreatment of an underling by his master. As far as he was concerned, there were few things more barbaric than a man grossly misusing his power to abuse someone powerless to resist, and though he had an inkling that such behavior was quite common, particularly amongst the British, who tended to treat their Indian servants like beasts of burden, being confronted with such blatant evidence of the Major's viciousness made his blood boil.

"It didn't happen very often," Munshi Ram said in a dead monotone, too ashamed to meet the Maharaja's gaze. "Only when I did something wrong."

He finally managed to look up at Sikander, his mouth twisting into a piteous smile.

"You have to understand, Huzoor, the Major Sahib was a demanding person. He was very set in his ways and could be short-tempered at times, but that does not mean he was not a good master most of the time. It was only over these last few weeks that he had been behaving erratically."

"Why?" Sikander inquired with great interest. "What brought about this sudden change in behavior? Was he having an affair, perhaps?"

"I cannot say," the man replied stiffly, as if he were deeply offended by the intimacy of this query. "My duties were confined to the City Palace, and I was not privy to the Major Sahib's personal habits. For that, I think, you will have to speak with Jane memsahib."

"Jane memsahib? Who in God's name is Jane memsahib?"

Abruptly, a spasm of horror flashed across the Munshi's wizened face.

"Oh no! I had forgotten all about her," he exclaimed. "She is the Resident's housekeeper, Your Majesty."

"What?" Sikander hissed, sitting up with a start. "Where can I find her?"

"I do not know, Sahib," the old man whined. "I have not seen her since I got here." Even as he uttered those words, his eyes widened with dismay. "*Hai Ram*, you don't think she has been murdered as well?"

Sikander cursed, springing to his feet. That was it, the source of the unease that had been nagging at him since he had first entered the bungalow. The Residency was far too neat to be a bachelor's home. A woman's touch was evident everywhere, from the roses in the parlor to the faded scent of jasmine hanging in the still air.

I really should have seen it sooner, Sikander chastised himself.

"You fool," he growled at the Munshi. "You unmitigated idiot! How could you not have mentioned this before…?'"

"Forgive me, Huzoor. I forgot, I swear it. I barely know the woman. She only took up service with Major Russell a few months ago." The Munshi slumped forward, his shoulders shuddering as he cradled his head in his hands. "Oh, no! It is all my fault. She is dead, just like the Major Sahib, I just know it."

"Compose yourself, you fool," Sikander barked. "We must find the memsahib immediately. She could be a vital material witness to what happened here."

With a visible effort, the old man manage to pull himself together. Raising one skeletal finger, he pointed out towards the small cottage which Sikander had passed while exploring the grounds.

"The guest quarters, Sahib," he groaned wretchedly. "There, just behind the main house. That is where she lives."

Immediately, as if his very life depended on it, Sikander vaulted to his feet and dashed towards the front door, only to barrel straight into Jardine.

"Hie there," the Inspector squealed, "what in blazes is going on here?"

"There is a woman who lives here with the Resident," Sikander paused momentarily to explain. "His housekeeper, a Miss Jane. She hasn't been seen since last night."

Jardine may not have been very bright, but it did not take long for the full implication of the Maharaja's words to dawn upon him.

"Of course," he gasped. "I should have remembered about her. We must search the grounds immediately."

"What a good idea!" Searching the grounds would keep the Superintendent busy and thus ensure he remained well out of the Maharaja's way, which was exactly how Sikander preferred it. "Do that immediately."

Even as the Superintendent lumbered away, barking out a string of urgent orders at his Havildars, Sikander broke into a run once more. Rounding the corner of the house, he put his fingers to his lips and let out a shrill, most ungentlemanly whistle. A moment later, as if by magic, Charan Singh materialized, dashing up from the direction of the stables, brandishing his kirpan menacingly in one immense hand.

"Oh, do put that away, will you, before you poke out someone's eye?"

Reluctantly, Charan Singh sheathed the dagger at his waist and glowered at his master questioningly, as if to inquire why he had been summoned with such exigency.

"There is another victim," Sikander growled. "A woman, the Resident's housekeeper."

The giant Sikh's face hardened. Wordlessly, he fell into step behind Sikander as they hastened through the back garden and up the narrow curving path that led to the guest cottage. It was much smaller than the bungalow, a single-floored structure with a thatched roof and a front porch enfiladed by twin Palladian columns.

Without bothering to knock or announce himself, as propriety demanded, Sikander marched up to the front door and tried to wrest it open, only to find that it was securely bolted.

"Well," he turned to Charan Singh, "don't just gawk at me. Break the damned thing down."

"If you insist!" the Sikh said. Grinning wickedly, he raised one massive boot and brought it crashing down just above the lock. The door didn't just splinter. Like cheap glass, it shattered apart, one half remaining locked, and the other flying open with a resounding crash.

Rather than waiting for his manservant to enter and make sure that the guesthouse was secure, Sikander pushed past the old Sikh and barged into the room beyond, nearly tripping over a table in his haste. A few heartbeats passed before his eyesight adjusted to the shadowy gloom within, and he was able to discern that they were in a small, sparsely furnished parlor. At the far end of the room, two closed doors led towards what he guessed were the bedrooms.

"You take the one on the left. I'll take the right."

Charan Singh nodded, tiptoeing across the room with laughable daintiness. Once he was in place, Sikander surged forward and shouldered open his chosen door at the same time that his manservant slammed open the other. Gritting his teeth, he barged into what seemed to be a storeroom piled high with old boxes. A moldy smell permeated the air, as if to suggest that it had obviously had not been occupied for some time, and Sikander let out a loud exhalation of relief, glad to discover that the place was quite empty.

Sadly, this reprieve was destined to be short-lived. A heartbeat later, Charan Singh called out, "Sahib, over here. I have found her."

Outside the other room, the giant Sikh hulked, hunching his broad shoulders solemnly. When Sikander approached, he bowed his head, as somber as an undertaker. The Maharaja's heart sank as he elbowed past and was greeted by the sight of a supine form lying sprawled on the floor in the distant corner. It was a woman, clad in a thin nightgown of cotton that left little to the imagination, barely able to conceal a figure so slender that Sikander thought that she could be little more than a child. Undoubtedly, this was the missing Miss Jane, and just as Sikander had feared, she had been murdered as well.

Since she was lying facedown, he couldn't see her features, but he had no doubt they were distended by a rictus of anguish quite as horrible as the Major's. Biting back a sigh, he approached her corpse, reaching out to turn her over gently, almost reverently. When he saw her face, the Maharaja let out a gasp. He had expected an Anglo-Indian ayah, but the housekeeper was an Englishwoman and a striking one at that. He realized he had been quite mistaken about her age. This was no callow child, no. On the contrary, she was very nearly his own age, well past thirty with cuprous hair cropped unfashionably short and a strong face so pale it seemed almost eldritch. And her body, while slender, was that of a woman in her prime, broad of hip and shoulder, with firm breasts that strained at the thin fabric of her nightdress and briefly caused Sikander to shudder as a frisson of desire ran through him.

The Maharaja pushed aside these entirely inappropriate thoughts, and reached out to take her wrist so that he could check for a pulse. That was when she surprised him. With an almost imperceptible shiver, she let out a soft whimper and for an instant, her eyelids flickered open, revealing irises as green as cabochons, before fluttering shut once more.

"She's still alive!" Sikander exclaimed.

"Are you sure?" Charan Singh leaned forward to stare down over his shoulder.

"Of course I am, you bullock. I have seen enough corpses to tell the difference between dead and alive. "

"*Wahe Guru*, it is the will of God!" The big Sikh made a gesture thanking the heavens, and then turned and shouted at the top of his voice. "Call for the horse ambulance. The memsahib is still alive."

"There isn't time," Sikander said roughly. Sweeping the duvet off the bed, he wrapped the woman in the thick bed-cover to keep her warm. Then, as if she weighed nothing at all, he gathered her into his arms effortlessly.

Charan Singh tried to intercede. "Give her to me, Your Majesty," he said, stretching out his massive hands. "I will carry the memsahib."

"Leave it be," Sikander snapped. Cradling the insensate woman close to his chest, hefting her as easily as a pile of laundry, he pushed past his manservant. Charan Singh began to follow after him, but a curt snarl stopped him dead in his tracks.

"You stay here! Secure the crime scene. Make sure nobody tampers with the Resident's body, and ensure that my samples get to the palace."

With that final command, Sikander turned and dashed through the door, grimacing beneath the weight of his unconscious burden.

A few meters away from the front gate, very near where the Rolls was parked, Lowry was lurking beneath the leafy shelter of a jamun tree, enjoying the attentions of the ladies of the Rajpore Garden Society. Abruptly, one of the women let out a scream, a strident shriek of pure horror. Immediately, the buzzing hum of conversation died out, withering to a stunned silence. En masse, Lowry and the rest of the Garden Society turned to be greeted by the shocking sight of the Maharaja of Rajpore tramping towards them, his face red with exertion from the effort of carrying an insensible Englishwoman in his arms.

"Your Majesty," the Magistrate squeaked, aghast, gazing down at the girl with barely repressed dismay, "what on Earth is going on...? Is she...is she dead?"

"Not yet," Sikander grunted, "but she soon will be, if I don't get her to a doctor."

Brusquely, he brushed past Lowry and made for his car, struggling to shoulder a path through the assembled mass of curious onlookers surrounding the Rolls-Royce. Unaccustomed to anything but servility from native Indians, they drew apart, slowly at first, but then beating a hasty retreat to give him a wide berth, as if he were the carrier of some deeply infectious plague. A scandalized murmur ran through the crowd as the Maharaja lowered the unconscious memsahib into the passenger seat of his car, handling her as gently as if she were made of glass. Then, vaulting into the driver's seat himself, Sikander pushed the gear lever into reverse, but before he could move an inch, Superintendent Jardine marched up and planted himself directly behind the car, standing squarely in his intended path of egress, as squat and immobile as a block of granite.

"Stop right there!"

"Out of the way, you baboon!" Clenching his jaw, Sikander reversed the Rolls directly towards the Superintendent with a shrill screech. Jardine's eyes widened as he realized that the Maharaja had no intention of slowing down. Even though he was a large man, he managed to move with surprising speed. As nimbly as a dancer, he backed away from the path of the car, but sadly, he wasn't quite quick enough. One of the flapping royal pennants caught his arm with a glancing blow and, like a falling redwood, Jardine reeled, collapsing backwards with a surprised yelp that quickly turned into a howl of agony as his large rump settled squarely onto a patch of thorny nettles.

Sikander did not spare him a second glance. Once he was clear of the gate, he performed a reckless turn and crunched down on the throttle so hard that the lever almost broke in two. The Rolls sped away, quickly racing to its maximum speed as it hurtled down through the English town towards the Cantonment.

Next to him, the girl had slowly started to recover her wits. Her eyelids flickered slightly, and each time the car juddered over a pothole, she let out the faintest of groans.

The Maharaja shot her a sidelong glance, his face stiff with concern.

"Hold on, girl," he growled. "Don't you dare die! That's an order!"

Chapter Eleven

There were two hospitals in Rajpore.

The first was the British-run Royal Hospital adjoining the Cantonment which tended largely to the soldiers and the English populace. The other was the newly constructed Rajpore Sanatorium, built on the outskirts of the native town. It was a free hospital, set up by Sikander in memory of his mother, and managed by a fine doctor from Calcutta, Dr. Roy, who had been barred from practicing in Bengal because of his involvement with the National Congress.

At first, it had been Sikander's plan to drive the girl straight to the latter, but then, as he drew closer to the center of the English town, it occurred to him that it wasn't really safe to take her to a hospital at all. Rajpore, particularly English Rajpore, was a small place, and the news that a memsahib and, as such, the only witness to the Resident's murder, had survived being poisoned would spread like wildfire through the Cantonment and the club. It was much too salacious a piece of gossip to go unnoticed, and in his heart of hearts, Sikander knew that he had to keep Jane's survival a closely guarded secret because the murderer, who had already proven to be very clever, would certainly come after her again when he found out that she was still alive.

Added to that, he was certain that Jardine would be on the warpath as well, and that if he left Jane alone for even one moment, the Superintendent would move immediately to place her in British custody.

And once that damned fool gets his sweaty hands on her, he thought crossly, *I can kiss goodbye any chance of questioning her.*

No, he frowned, *I shall have to take her somewhere where I can protect her, somewhere secure where no one will think to look for her.*

The only logical choice that remained was the Imperial Hotel.

Located at the distant end of the Silent Lake, some four kilometers from the outskirts of the English town, The Imperial was the most discerning of the handful of establishments that catered to visitors who happened to pass through Rajpore. Unlike the Grand which prohibited Indians entry, and the Ross Common, which was patronized largely by boxwallahs and tradesmen, the Imperial was an exceedingly civilized establishment, catering only to travelers hailing from the upper classes. Many of them were visiting rulers of other Princely States, who made it a point to visit Rajpore each summer in time for the hunting season, since it was widely acclaimed that there were few finer places to shoot wild fowl than in the marshy fens surrounding Ranibagh, seventy miles north of the capital.

The Imperial had begun its life as the Star of Punjab, the grandiose dream of a Scotsman, George Campbell, who had made a fortune in prize money while campaigning against the Rohillas and come to Rajpore with the intention of founding an establishment that was a homage to the Savoy. His timing had been impeccable. For a brief while in the 1840s, Rajpore had enjoyed an economic Renaissance, and had become the center of the cotton trade in North India, particularly as the Civil War in America had reduced their own cotton exports to a trickle. Sadly, this boom had not been destined to last long. With the cessation of hostilities between North and South in the United States, the cotton bubble had burst and soon the deluge of visitors to Rajpore had reduced to a trickle. This left the unfortunate Mr. Campbell to watch his dream crumble, along with his grand hotel, until in the end, overcome by grief and failure and a mountain of mounting debts, he had chosen to take his own life the same year that Sikander's father had inherited the throne.

After its owner's death, the hotel had remained deserted, dwindling slowly to a ruin until the Maharani, Sikander's mother, had purchased the property on a whim, and done a remarkable job of renovating it and turning it into one of the better establishments east of Suez. The Imperial was the tallest building in the city, an astonishing triangular-shaped structure built entirely of iron beams that had been molded in the same foundries that had cast the frame for the Crystal Palace. The results were quite striking, a complete contrast from the rest of Rajpore's traditional architecture—a modern building constructed in the neo-classical style, five floors each fronted by arched plate-glass windows elaborately embellished with ornately wrought art nouveau details. Of the forty rooms, ten were suites with private balconies overlooking the placid waters of the lake. At the center of the hotel was a glass-roofed atrium that housed a fine ballroom and a theater and what the Maharaja considered unarguably to be the best restaurant in Punjab where diners could enjoy both French and Indian cuisine.

Sikander had inherited the hotel when he had taken the throne, but had held onto it very briefly, choosing instead to give it away for the princely sum of a single rupee to its current owner, Madame Helene Beauchamp, who unbeknownst to most people also happened to be his long-suffering mistress. A narrow smile played across the Maharaja's lips as he thought of Helene. It seemed like a lifetime had passed since they had first met. Sikander had been just a callow boy then, trying to live incognito in Paris and pass himself off as a penniless student. That was when he had first met Helene's sister, Camille, who had been a dancer at Le Chat Noir. He had fallen head over heels in love, only to lose her when she had been murdered under mysterious circumstances. That had been his very first case, and though he had ultimately managed to apprehend Camille's killer, he had nearly ended up half in the grave doing it, had it not been for Helene's tender ministrations.

She was the one who had nursed him back to health, and slowly, his respect for her had grown into something deeper, a mature affection quite devoid of the breathless ardor that he had felt for her sister, but somehow more fulfilling, as immutable as bedrock. Over the years, their relationship had settled with time into a comfortable détente, a very discreet, almost dispassionate involvement that they both accepted with equanimity. Helene knew he occasionally pursued other women, a fact she tolerated resignedly, not because she was too meek to stand up to him, but because she genuinely loved him, and knew that while he was capricious enough to crave the new, in the end he would always come back to her. As for Sikander, Helene was one of the few people he trusted implicitly and his only real confidante. With her, he was neither prince nor polymath, merely a man; she was the only person with whom he felt truly at peace, with whom he did not need to play a role, and it gratified him immensely to know that she was nearby, close enough for him to protect and keep safe from any threat.

Sikander was certain that he would find a safe refuge at the Imperial. He maintained a three-room apartment on the top floor, a pied-à-terre that was well staffed with a butler and an excellent private chef and a team of hand-picked bearers who made sure that the rooms were always aired and kept immaculately clean in case he decided to drop by. Best of all, a detachment of his personal guard were posted permanently on hand to watch over Helene, all of them highly trained and absolutely faithful, and Sikander knew that once he entrusted the girl's protection into their care, even the Superintendent would not be able to gain access to her without his express permission.

He cast a quick glance at Jane. Once more, she seemed to be in the deepest of stupors. Her face was as ashen as a ghost's, her breath so irregular that he was convinced he had lost her. Thankfully, when he touched her forehead, she let out the faintest of moans, reassuring him that it wasn't too late. Sikander sped up, driving the rest of the way to the hotel like a maniac. A dozen times, he very nearly ran people over, avoiding them only by the narrowest of margins. Twice he even came close to turning the car turtle, a pair of terrifyingly narrow escapes that ended up leaving broad scrapes on both sides of the Rolls' coachwork.

When he arrived at the Imperial, Madame Beauchamp was waiting in the foyer, having heard the car's droning approach from a great distance. As the Rolls rattled to a stop and Sikander leaped from behind the wheel, she came forth to greet him, hedged on either side by an entourage of four immaculately uniformed bearers. As always, Sikander's heart skipped a beat when he saw Helene. She was tall for a woman, taller than most Indian men, with an admirable posture that spoke volumes of her strong-willed character. The Maharaja's eyes flickered appreciatively over her figure. Even though she was wearing a simple high-collared black dress, cut in the Chinese qipao style, it was enough to emphasize the soft undulation of feminine curves hidden beneath.

Although Helene was nearing the ripe age of forty-five, it was fortunate for her that she been gifted with that rarest of qualities, a charm that seemed to deepen as she aged. And while she was not what most men would call beautiful, not in the traditional sense as her younger sister had been, with a mouth that was much too large and a jaw that was almost mannish, Sikander had always felt there was something startlingly arresting about her. It was her eyes, glinting in the afternoon sun like Ceylonese sapphires, sharp and level and unflinchingly frank, holding his gaze with an unblinking candor, filled with a vulnerability and still somehow a strength, a symphony of opposites which he had always found intoxicating.

"Your Majesty," Helene said, offering only the slightest of bows, a tremor of her hips so negligible that it was almost a calculated insult. Her mouth twisted into a mocking smile when she spied the girl lying limp in the passenger seat. "Your new friend seems very lovely," she commented, taking Jane to be inebriated. Those dramatic eyes flashed with scorn, unable to hide her obvious annoyance at Sikander's unannounced intrusion. "Although, I do fear she is rather underdressed, particularly for this weather, don't you think?"

"For God's sake, Helene," Sikander snarled, "the poor thing's been poisoned."

Immediately, the Frenchwoman's snide smile melted away, replaced by crestfallen regret as she realized that Jane was not drunk, but at death's door.

With a cluck of her tongue, she called to one of her bearers, a lanky dhoti-clad South Indian.

"*Jaldi karo*," she commanded urgently, "carry the girl up to the royal suite. And have someone go and fetch Dr. Roy immediately."

Sikander did not wait for the bearer to obey the French-woman's instructions. Instead, he snatched the girl into his own arms. Brushing aside the servant even as he tried lamely to help, he carried Jane into the hotel himself, dashing through the lobby and up the grand staircase towards the shelter of his private rooms, uncaring of the curious stares that his hasty progress drew from the scattering of diners enjoying a late tea in the atrium.

Helene hurried after him, finally elbowing past when they arrived at the top floor to unlock the door of his suite and hold it open for him, her face tense with concern. Sikander carried the girl within, past the richly decorated parlor and into one of the twin bedrooms beyond, where he laid her gently on the sumptuously brocaded bed, treating her as delicately as if she were made from porcelain.

"I will take care of her," Helene said to him sternly. "Go and get a drink, Sikander. You look a complete mess."

The Maharaja paused, huffing from the strain of having carried the girl up five floors. Unsure of quite what he ought to do next, he was about to argue with Helene, insist that he needed to stay with Jane in case she woke up, that he had so many questions that needed answers, but before he could voice a single word of objection, the Frenchwoman took one of his arms and steered him out of the bedroom, slamming the door in his face and shooing him away as if he were a mangy cat, not the ruler of Rajpore.

For a long time, Sikander stood motionlessly in the drawing room, gathering his breath. He could not help but feel quite helpless, a condition he never enjoyed. To his regret, there was little more he could do for Jane except wait for Dr. Roy to arrive, and pray that she made a quick recovery.

A sidelong glance at his reflection in a gilt-wood mirror that hung on a nearby wall told him that Helene had been somewhat kindhearted when describing him as a mess. The truth was he looked less like the King of Rajpore and more like a day laborer. Not only was his face streaked with dirt, his pugree in utter disarray, and the front of his doublet stained by rings of sweat, but when he caught a whiff of himself, Sikander realized he smelled as malodorous as a racehorse.

Squaring his aching shoulders, he limped over to the adjoining bedroom. Luckily, he kept an alternate wardrobe on hand at the hotel, for exactly such unforeseen eventualities. With a grimace, Sikander unwound his turban and shucked off his dank shervani, letting it fall to the floor. From one of the lacquered Chinese cabinets that lined the walls, he took a coat identical to that which he had discarded, except in crimson this time, with a delicate sprinkling of silver embroidery around the collar and large silver buttons enameled with the royal crest.

As he was shrugging it on, he heard a soft noise behind him. It was Helene, standing silently by the door, watching him with an intent look on her face.

"The girl, is she…?" he asked worriedly.

"Dr. Roy is with her now," Helene replied. Slowly, she moved towards him, reaching out to do up the front of the doublet, her nimble fingers grazing delicately against his chest as she carefully guided each button into its matching eyelet one by one.

"You have been neglecting me," she declared. Her eyes locked into his questioningly, her face remaining blank, but the Maharaja knew her temperament well enough to recognize the dangerous undertone of barely restrained exasperation in her voice.

"I have been busy lately, my dear. You may not realize it, but ruling a kingdom can be rather a lot more demanding that running a hotel."

He decided to try out his most winning smile on her, but Helene remained obdurately immune. "Don't you dare try your tricks on me, you vile man. I am sick and tired of your endless excuses."

"Helene," Sikander wheedled, "you know how I feel about you."

"Is that so?" She glared at him. "Then why, may I ask, have you not come to see me in over a week? Is that why you asked me come here, so that you could treat me with such disdain?"

Sikander sighed, knowing it was pointless to argue with her when she was in a mood as unforgiving as her current state. "Would it help if I said I was sorry?"

"Bah," Helene snarled, "*tu me peles le jonc!*"

Sikander smiled, enjoying the way she always seemed to lapse back into French when she was really worked up. Tentatively, he reached out to caress the nape of her neck just below her hairline, tracing the bluish outline of a soft vein which was barely visible through the translucence of her skin.

To his relief, Helene did not push him away.

"Let me make it up to you," he purred. "How does two weeks in Paris sound, this summer?"

"Really?" she exclaimed, as if she did not believe him. "You mean it?"

The pensive hopefulness in her voice caused a shiver of guilt to wrack through Sikander. *Poor thing*, he thought, overcome by guilt. In his preoccupation with matters of state and the like, he always managed to forget how difficult each day was for Helene, to be away from France, from her people, to miss the sound of hearing her native tongue being spoken. She never complained, of course; it was not in Helene's nature to grumble, but lately, he had sensed her homesickness deepening, particularly around Christmas-time, when she had seemed as morose as a widow.

"Of course!" he responded. "I give you my word. I shall have Charan Singh arrange the tickets forthwith."

This promise finally seemed to placate Helene. She leaned into his shoulder, nestling into the crook of his neck with practiced ease. She was as tall as him, but rather than being uncomfortable, this allowed the two of them fit together as perfectly as two pieces in a puzzle. An inexplicable sadness swept over Sikander, a wave of melancholia so intense that he couldn't help but shudder. Part of it was need, an anguish wracking through the pit of his stomach, an ache that was both enervating and thrilling at the same time. But another part was a sense of relief, a simple contentment.

Is this what love is? He thought wryly. It never ceased to surprise him, how strangely reassuring he found Helene's presence. As surely as a dose of laudanum, she soothed him, quelling his innate ennui. The Maharaja had known many beautiful women in his life, more than a few of them intimately, but he had never been able to bring himself to love any of them. It confounded him, this incapacity for any binding passion other than his abiding fascination with the criminal. What was the cause of this inability, he had often wondered? Was it perhaps because he had been cruelly robbed of the only woman he had even cared for, his mother? Or could it be that being a man of logic, he was suspicious of love, too cynical to accept that which he could not quantify?

Still, he thought with a sigh, *if I could find it in me to love, perhaps I would love Helene.* It saddened him to no end that he could never give her what she rightly deserved after all the years she had suffered silently as his paramour and his confidante, namely the affirmation of marriage. While it wasn't unheard of for a Maharaja to take a white woman for a wife, it was rare enough to be thought of as scandalous. No, there were far too many obstacles to permit him to make Helene his Maharani. Not only would such a union fly in the face of tradition, but he knew all too well that the English would never accept a Frenchwoman as the Queen of Rajpore.

And then there was Helene herself. She would never be happy, locked away behind the marble jallis of the zenana, relegated to living the invisible life of a purdahnashin. Sikander cared for her too much to ever do that to her, trapping her within a cage of duty and obligation, like an exotic bird doomed to slowly molt until all that remained was a tired wreck, once beautiful but now ruined.

Helene, ever sensitive, sensed the depths of his turmoil. Recognizing the torment in Sikander's expression, she arched one impeccably groomed eyebrow inquiringly. Her mouth broke into a gentle little smile and she leaned forward slightly, kissing him briefly on one cheek, letting out a sigh of complaint as his beard rasped against her delicate skin. She pulled away, leaving his nostrils filled with her intoxicating smell, that sweet perfume of Yardley's soap and Guerlain's Shalimar.

"Who is she?" Helene's eyes sparkled with barely contained curiosity. "Is she someone terribly important? She must be, because I have never seen you so concerned about a mere woman's welfare before, Your Majesty."

"She is nobody," Sikander replied, "the Resident's housekeeper, and as such, the only witness to his murder. That, my dear, is why she is important." He raised one hand and pretended to take a mock oath. "That and no other reason, I swear by my forefathers."

Helene's face stiffened, as if he had just slapped her. "The Resident," she said breathlessly, "do you mean Major Russell? He is dead…?"

"Yes," Sikander remarked, "his body was found earlier this morning. Hadn't you heard?"

Helene's reaction to this bit of news took him utterly by surprise.

"Good riddance," She spat, so heatedly that Sikander was taken aback. The unexpected acid in her voice shocked him. It wasn't like Helene to be so vehement. Ordinarily, she was kind-hearted to a fault.

"Heavens, Helene. It isn't like you to be so unkind."

The Frenchwoman puckered her brow. "He was a dreadful, unpleasant man. A real *connard, un pouffiasse! Imbécile!*"

Sikander stifled a laugh as this florid string of curses tumbled from her carmine lips. From her regal bearing and her refined composure, it was easy to forget that Helene's childhood had been spent on the streets of Paris, which had given her a vocabulary that was as colorful as a sailor's.

"I wasn't aware you knew the man quite so well," he said playfully. "Should I be jealous?"

Helene flared her nostrils, and a subtle, sphinx-like expression played across her face.

"He asked me to go to bed with him, you know."

"What?" The Maharaja sat bolt upright, stunned by this revelation.

"It's true. He was always making advances, the frightful man."

She looked at Sikander, her face ripe with expectation, waiting for him to react with some measure of asperity at finding out that she had been propositioned by another man, but he surprised her by letting out a strident laugh.

"Well, the man was certainly ambitious. And you can't fault him for having excellent taste."

Helene had hoped for indignation, even outrage, but to be confronted with such a callow dismissal infuriated her. Scowling murderously, she launched into another tirade of invective in French, most of which Sikander couldn't understand, but the few words he did recognize were of such coarseness that they would have made even the most seasoned of streetwalkers blanch. Trying to placate her, Sikander reached out to embrace her. Helene struggled to resist, snubbing this attempt at intimacy strenuously, but Sikander overpowered her easily. Clapping one palm over her mouth, he pulled her close to him, until at last, the torrent of profanity pouring from her lips dried up and with a wary groan, she let him rest his head on the soft pillow of her bosom, gently stroking his beard.

"Why didn't you come to me and tell me he was harassing you?

"I don't need you to fight every battle for me, Sikander. Besides, this isn't the first time a man has made a pass at me. I took care of it myself, just like I always do."

"And how exactly did you get rid of him?"

"It was simple enough. I warned him that I was spoken for,

and that I had no desire to dally with another man, not for all the money in the world."

"I am sure the Major was not pleased with such a curt rebuffal."

"Not at all. He said that I was a fool to refuse him, that my lover did not deserve me."

"He was right. I don't deserve you. You are much too good for the likes of me."

"It isn't funny, Sikander. Your Major may have seemed like a dolt but he had a frightening side." She pursed her lips. "He was much too forward, for one thing—always sniffing around, like a dog in heat. And such a pushy man, a bully, a real brute. There were times when he looked at me like he wanted to hurt me."

Helene trembled imperceptibly, a shiver that was transmitted to him, making him sit up worriedly as he realized just how distraught she was, and just how terrified she had been of the man. The Maharaja found himself dismayed by the depth of her reaction. It took a lot to scare Helene, after all that she had seen and endured in her youth. But the Major, he had managed to break down her defenses and scare her to her very core. Sikander could sense that much, even though she was very adept at concealing her feelings, even from him.

"When I told him I wasn't interested, he actually had the temerity to threaten me." Helene quivered with barely repressed indignity. "He said that I should watch out because he always got what he wanted." Her voice thickened. "The nerve of the *salaud!* Do you know what he called me? A whore. A royal whore."

The Maharaja's face hardened. Damn the man! He was lucky he was dead, because if he had still been alive, Sikander would have tracked him down and punched him squarely in the nose, never mind the political consequences. *The impudence of the bastard,* he thought bitterly. Even though Helene and he took great pains to keep their involvement discreet, it was almost certain that as the ranking representative of the English in Rajpore the Major had to have been aware that she was Sikander's mistress. But still, to have the audacity to threaten her, to call her a whore—it reaffirmed what Sikander had learned of the Major, that he had been a brashly presumptuous, extraordinarily egotistical man.

"Did he ever do more than just make advances? Did he ever try to actually accost you?"

"Of course not," she scoffed. "The man was full of hot air. A big windbag, that's all."

"I wish you had told me sooner!"

"The day I need help to handle a *connard* like your Major, *mon chéri*, is the day I join the nunnery." She snorted, "*Bah, morceau de merde! Fils d'une putain! Il peut brûler en enfer!*"

"I am sorry, my love. If only I had known!"

"You don't have to apologize for him, Sikander," Helene said. "I have met many men like that, pompous morons who think women are merely objects to be used to satisfy their basest needs and who refuse to take no for an answer."

"You should have had your bearers throw him out on his ear. That would have taught the cheeky bugger a lesson."

Helene's lips narrowed, the barest hint of a smile. "You would not believe how often I had the very same thought, how many times I was tempted to ban him from entering the Imperial, just so that I wouldn't have to endure his crude approaches week after week."

"Why didn't you do it then?"

"Well, for one thing, I couldn't afford to offend the Sahibs. Most of my customers are English, and you know how they already look at me with suspicion because I am French. Added to which, the Major was much too powerful to trifle with. If I had thrown him out, he would have made no end of trouble for me. You know very well that he was that kind of man."

Sikander nodded in understanding. Helene was perfectly right about that. It was obvious to anyone who had ever met him that the Major had been exactly the sort of person who felt no shame or reluctance in abusing his power to seek retribution against someone he felt had slighted him. No, she had made the smart choice by not pushing the issue until things came to a head. If she had, the Major would probably have gone out of his way to harass her even more.

"Maybe it is time we found you a husband, just to keep you safe."

Sadly, this jest misfired badly. Instead of being amused, Helene's mouth warped into an injured scowl. With a mercurial toss of her hair, she pulled away from him, but not before giving him a glare so imperious it could have fitted on the face of any empress.

"Do you think me so undesirable that there are no men who want me? I'll have you know, you cad, I have received three invitations of marriage just this last month, not the least of them being an overture from the Nawab of Deogarh."

It was obvious she was trying to make him jealous, but Sikander was too canny to rise to such blatant bait.

"Why don't you go ahead and accept?" he countered. "I am sure I could scratch up a suitable dowry for you, and Deogarh is a fine-looking fellow, if you like men with crossed eyes and horse teeth."

This remark only served to antagonize Helene even further. She shivered, and stood up angrily, stamping one petite foot down so hard he thought she was about to kick him.

"You know, Sikander Singh," she gasped, "you really are the most infuriating man."

With that proclamation, she turned and stormed away, slamming the door so hard behind her that it made Sikander's teeth ache in his jaw.

Shaking his head, he let out a frustrated sigh. As always, he had managed to put his foot squarely in his mouth. Why was it that he could deduce the most complex of mysteries from the most innocuous of clues, but when it came to saying the right thing to women, he still always managed to behave like a rank novice?

He was tempted to go after her, and try to apologize, but he knew Helene too well; in her current mood, any words of conciliation he tried to offer would merely be rebuffed, perhaps even violently.

Instead, Sikander lay back, using this lull to plan his next move. Closing his eyes, he went over a checklist in his mind. First and foremost, he had to parse what was rumor and hearsay from what was fact. For that, he guessed, he would have to pay a visit to Miller at the *Gazette* to see if could substantiate any of the information he had managed to gather about Major Russell.

Who else did he need to talk to? The elusive Captain Fletcher for one, the man who had last seen the Major alive the previous evening. He was said to be one of the Major's closest confidantes, but Lowry had cast a shadow on that relationship, with his hint that the Major and the Captain had lately been at loggerheads. What could have caused this rift? Sikander wondered. There was yet another answer he would have to uncover.

Then there was the brash Lieutenant with whom the Major had almost engaged in fisticuffs the very night before his demise. On the face of it, that meant the man had an immutable motive to want the Resident dead, but what was the real story? And what did his wife have to with the whole affair? The answers to both those questions, Sikander concluded, could only be found at the Rajpore Club, where the whole confrontation had unfolded in the first place.

Helene chose that moment to come back into the room. Like a whirlwind, she barged in to glower down at him with her hands on her hips, obviously still sulking.

"Changed your mind, have you?" Sikander said. Smiling, he leaned back on the bed and waggled one foot at her in lewd invitation. "I thought you might be back. I really am quite irresistible, aren't I?"

In response, Helene snorted, rolling her eyes. "Oh, get up, you pompous scoundrel, and put on some trousers. The funny little doctor, he wants to see you right away."

Chapter Twelve

Dr. Roy was waiting in the parlor, pacing back and forth impatiently.

At first sight, he seemed more a shopkeeper than a physician, with his rotund pot belly and a pair of thick spectacles that made him squint short-sightedly at everything and everyone. But appearances, as Sikander knew only too well, almost always conspired to deceive. Beneath this placid, unassuming exterior, Roy was rather an extraordinary fellow. Not only had he been one of the first Indians to graduate from the Imperial College in London, but he had been the very first to be invited to become a Fellow of the Royal College of Surgeons. Sadly, his reputation had become irrevocably tarnished when he became involved publicly with the National Congress, resulting in his being unfairly disbarred from practicing medicine and forced to return to Calcutta in disgrace. In Sikander's opinion, that had been a truly gross miscarriage of justice because, regardless of his political inclinations, Roy was the finest surgeon the Maharaja had ever met, better even than the twenty-guinea physicians whose clinics lined Harley Street.

When Sikander entered, the doctor's avuncular face broke into a wide smile, but he made no effort to genuflect, as was traditional for most people when the Maharaja granted them an audience. Curiously enough, Sikander did not press him to observe any formalities. After all, Dr. Roy had once pulled a bullet from his chest, and as Sikander saw it, that liberated the man completely from having to bow and scrape like a common khidmutgar.

"How is the memsahib?" Sikander asked. "Will she live?"

"You were quite lucky, Your Majesty," the doctor replied. "I managed to get here just in time to save her. I have administered an emetic of my own devising to induce vomiting, a concoction of ground charcoal mixed with a powder of root of ipecac. And I have pumped her stomach completely. Luckily for us the poison was mostly diluted."

"So she will recover?"

"I believe so, yes. She shall be weak for a few days, but after that, she ought to be as right as rain." Dr. Roy frowned. "She was very fortunate, this young lady of yours. By some miracle, the dose of poison she imbibed was too weak to be fatal. Still, it will be a few days before she is able to regain her strength. I advise bed rest and soup, I think, lots and lots of chicken broth, but no chillies, please. I find they create too much heat in the body to aid a patient's recovery."

"I shall have her taken to the palace. She will be safe there."

"I hope so, sir," Roy clucked. "The poor child has had a very narrow escape. The only reason she is still alive is because you found her when you did and managed to get her to me in time."

"Well done, Doctor! As always, you have managed to work a marvel."

Roy waved a hand dismissively, even though his grin betrayed that he was secretly flattered by these words of praise.

"Oh, it is nothing. A trifle, that's all." He gave Sikander a hopeful glance, his voice betraying an almost ghoulish eagerness. "Would you like my help with anything else…? I hear the Resident was murdered. I could dissect the body if you wish?"

"I tried, Doctor, but they refused to oblige. It seems they insist that Dr. Mason be tasked with that unseemly duty."

Roy winced, crestfallen by this bit of news. "That hack! For God's sake, Your Majesty, the man still believes in leechcraft."

"Nonetheless, he is the coroner of record, and we must strive to accommodate the English as best we can, yes?"

"Do we have a choice?" Roy rolled his eyes so sarcastically that Sikander could not help but chuckle.

"Thank you for your help, my dear fellow, but I am afraid that I must excuse myself. I think I shall go and have a few words with the girl now."

He spun, about to head for the bedroom, but Roy moved with a speed that defied his girth to obstruct him.

"It would be best if you waited for a while, sir," he said with a stiff shake of his head.

Sikander glowered at the man, his nostrils flaring with irritation. "I need to see her immediately. I have questions that need to be answered."

"I am afraid I cannot allow that. She is very weak, and needs to rest."

Sikander was not accustomed to being defied, and fond as he was of the doctor, this impertinence was pushing him perilously close to the edge. "Get out of my way, you damned fool!"

Roy's face fell at this rebuke. He opened his mouth to object but the forbidding look on the Maharaja's face warned him it would be pointless to insist.

"Very well," he said, shaking his head mulishly, "but if she takes a turn for the worse, you shall be entirely responsible."

Indicating that Sikander should be quiet, he eased open the door and tiptoed into the bedroom. Jane seemed to be fast asleep, tucked away in a large four-poster bed which dwarfed her diminutive form. Roy let out a theatrical cough to announce his intrusion, but she remained motionless, as still as a corpse. Other than the slight rise and fall of her chest and the barely audible murmur of her breathing, she could well have been a statue carved from cold marble, so peaceful that for a moment Sikander felt guilty disturbing her.

He waited patiently as the doctor approached the bed, reaching into one capacious pocket to pull out a vial of smelling salts which he fanned beneath Jane's nose with a practiced gesture. She came awake with a loud gasp. For one long moment, her eyes remained vague, unfocused, darting nervously around the richly decorated room, visibly taken aback by the splendor of her surroundings

"Who are you?" she gasped as her gaze came to settle on Sikander. "Where am I?"

"I am the Maharaja of Rajpore," Sikander explained with a slight bow, "and this is my suite at the Imperial Hotel."

Jane goggled at him, her face slack with disbelief, as if he was speaking a foreign language and she couldn't understand a word he was saying.

"Don't worry," Sikander said gently. "You are safe here, I promise you."

"I am…I am not dead."

"No, I am glad to say you are going be just fine. We managed to get to you just in time, but I am sorry to say that your employer wasn't quite so fortunate."

"The Major?" Her eyes widened even farther until it seemed to Sikander that they would split apart at the seams and turn inside out.

"He is dead," Sikander announced as solemnly as an undertaker.

This revelation made Jane wince, as if he had struck her, and then, her face crumpled. With a soft moan, she broke down. A torrent of voluble, voluminous gasps of sorrow poured from her lips, wracking through her willowy frame, a grand mal of regret.

"That's quite enough," Dr Roy exclaimed. "As I feared, the ordeal has been too much for her. Your questions will have to wait."

He tried to shoo Sikander away, but the Maharaja remained unmoved, offering Roy an indignant frown. "You may depart, Doctor. I shall send for you if you are needed further."

Roy flinched when he heard the inflexible note of finality in Sikander's tone. While Jane's welfare was uppermost in his mind, he was pragmatic enough to realize that he could not afford to offend his patron, the very person upon whose good graces he was entirely dependent. Besides, he was cognizant enough of the Maharaja's moods to know that it was pointless to debate with him when he was determined to have his way; no matter what words of dissent he might offer, in the end, once Sikander had made up his mind, he was as obdurate as stone.

"If you insist," he said reluctantly, beginning to bow before realizing what he was doing and then stopping in mid-motion, like a broken jack-in-the-box. "Please, I beg you, do not tire her too much, or it may be detrimental to her well-being."

With that warning, Roy beat a retreat, carefully shutting the door behind him to leave Sikander alone with Jane.

By then, she had managed to curtail her sobs and was warily watching the Maharaja over the rumpled edge of the quilt that enfolded her. Sikander pulled up a high-backed chair and sat down directly opposite the bed, leaving enough distance between them so that she would not feel hemmed in.

"Don't worry, Madam," he said in his most disarming tone of voice. "I am not going to hurt you."

Jane sat up, crossing her arms across her chest.

"The Major is really dead?" She fixed him with a suspicious glare, as if to suggest she did not trust him one bit. "You aren't lying to me, are you?"

Fiercely, she glowered at him, giving him a stern school-marmish look he might have found intimidating if she hadn't seemed so weak and pale that he was afraid she was about to faint once again. Sikander found himself studying her face, revising his first opinion of her age. She was older than he had guessed, nearer forty than thirty, and there was a hardness to her, particularly around the eyes and lips, that intractability which only a lifetime of adversity can evoke. She wasn't beautiful, he decided. Her hair was too short, almost ascetic, and her nose much too pert. In spite of that, Sikander found to his surprise that he thought her quite attractive. This realization shook him a little. He had never liked his women working-class, with rough skin and drab manners. No, he much preferred them primped and oiled and rouged like courtesans, clad in Parisian silk and smelling of the finest perfumes, but to his dismay, as he noted that Jane had a smattering of freckles on her cheeks, something tugged at his heartstrings and made him instinctively feel drawn towards her.

Sikander hesitated. How was he to treat her? Was she to be a suspect, someone to be interrogated rigorously? *No,* he thought, *if anything, she was a victim, the only true innocent in this whole unholy mess,* and he would behave with only equanimity, not suspicion.

"Why would I lie, Madam?" He said, holding her eyes with his own, trying to convey a sense of utmost sincerity. "What have I to gain from it?"

Jane clenched her jaw, considering his reply, and then, slowly, with immense gravity, she exhaled and averted her gaze, pulling the duvet up to her neck to swaddle herself, almost as though she was trying to conceal herself from his penetrating gaze.

"I have no wish to cause you any further anguish," Sikander said gently, "but I need your help, Madam, if I am to find who murdered the Major and very nearly took your life as well."

Once again those eyes turned back to settle on him contemplatively, their corners ringed with a startling umbra of gray that seemed to darken almost to purple as she nodded, gritting her teeth. "I shall try my best to accommodate you," she said bravely, her face so determined that Sikander felt an absurd flicker of pride.

"Thank you," he said, vastly relieved. "Let us talk then about the events leading up to last night." He fixed her with a hopeful smile. "Tell me, how did the Resident seem yesterday?"

"What do you mean?"

"When I spoke with him earlier, Mr. Lowry mentioned that the Major seemed rather sour-tempered yesterday. Would you happen to agree with such an observation? Was he behaving quite normally, or was he indeed out of sorts?"

"Oh, he was rude, aggressive, abrasive to the point of being intolerable, but no more so than usual." Her lips split into a tentative smile. "Or perhaps I had just become inured to his many unpleasant qualities. Like a blister on the heel of your foot, after a time, you forget exactly how painful it can be."

Sikander chuckled, glad to see that Jane was feeling a little better. "How about visitors? Did the Major have any callers yesterday?"

"Yes, he did, now that you mention it. He had three, if I remember correctly."

She wrinkled her brow. "The first was Mr. Lowry. He came by quite early, just after ten-thirty. I remember, I was in the garden pruning my roses at the time."

"Lowry," Sikander mused. "I didn't know that he and the Major were close."

Jane pulled a face, as if to signify her distaste for the Magistrate. "I doubt they were, sir. It struck me that Mr. Lowry was rather a thick-skinned man, in more ways than one. He often came by but always without being invited, inevitably seeking favors from the Major. In fact, the Major had me turn him away on several occasions."

"And yesterday? Did he refuse to see him yesterday?"

"Not quite. You see, when Mr. Lowry came calling, the Major had already departed for the City Palace. I asked Mr. Lowry if he cared to wait but he declined, saying he had only come by to leave Major Russell a belated Christmas gift."

"A gift? What manner of gift?"

"Oh, it was a bottle of wine, Your Majesty."

Sikander's eyebrows shot up. Could she mean the Oloroso? Could Lowry be the one who had provided the very bottle that Sikander had found in the dead man's bedroom?

"Was it wine, Madam, or sherry?"

"Aren't they one and the same?"

Sikander let out a vast sigh. Ordinarily a comment like that would have sent him right off the deep end, but he had come to quite like Jane, enough that he realized he could not fault her for her ignorance. The poor thing had endured a difficult life denied of the privileges he had always taken for granted. He understood that it was unfair to expect someone of her low background to have developed the same fine tastes he possessed.

"When you are in better mettle, my dear, remind me to explain the difference, but for now, let us return to yesterday and the Resident's other visitors. Other than the estimable Mr. Lowry, that is."

"Well, his Munshi came by at about one-thirty to deliver some letters." She frowned. "Actually, now that I think of it, he seemed in quite a temper."

"How so?" Sikander asked, his ears perking up.

"Well, ordinarily, the Munshi is a very quiet, well-mannered man, but yesterday I heard him arguing with the Major." She leaned forward, until her face was just a few inches away from his own. "He was shouting actually, which was very surprising."

Sikander frowned. That wasn't just surprising, but downright shocking. The thought of an Indian raising his voice to his master was unheard of. It could only mean that something irrevocable had happened between the two men, a break that had pushed the Major's assistant past the brink of reason.

"Do you have any inkling what they were arguing about?"

"Not really. I was making some tea, and all I overheard was their raised voices. I came dashing in to see what the hullabaloo was about before things managed to get really ugly, but they quieted down as soon as I entered the room. They insisted on acting like nothing was wrong."

"Hmm," Sikander mused, assimilating this snippet of information. How very fascinating! What could have been the cause of such a vociferous argument? Whatever it may have been, it had to be well out of the ordinary, especially if it had caused someone like the Munshi to lose his composure. When they had spoken earlier, he had struck Sikander as rather a harmless fellow. But if the Major had managed to push him to so flagrantly exceed the boundaries of acceptable behavior, it had to be something worth investigating further.

"Who was the third visitor?"

"Oh, it was Captain Fletcher. He was the one who escorted the Major back from the New Year's Ball last night."

"What time was that?"

"I...I am not sure, sir. I did not check the clock at the time. All that I can say is that it was very late, and that the Major, well, he was rather under the weather.

"You mean he was drunk?"

She nodded once, not willing to confirm this insinuation. "He was almost insensate, which is why Captain Fletcher had to accompany him, I imagine. Upon their arrival, I sent for Ghanshyam to help the Major to his room, but he was nowhere to be found, so I had to pitch in. It took some effort, but together the two of us managed to drag him upstairs to his bedroom."

"And Captain Fletcher left after that?"

"Yes. He offered to stay, but I certainly did not keep want to keep him here."

She faltered, just a momentary hesitation but it was enough to give him the distinct sense that she did not entirely like the Captain, that she was more than a little uncomfortable around him.

Sikander decided to pursue this intuition more closely. "Do you know the Captain well, Madam?"

"Well enough," she said guardedly.

"It seems to me that you have little regard for him. Why is that?"

Jane did not reply, instead pursing her lips until they were almost invisible.

"Did he ever make overtures toward you?"

She blanched, before giving him the faintest of nods.

"Only once. I rebuffed him quite strongly. He tried to press his suit but I made it clear I had no desire to be courted by him." She shuddered. "He is a rough man, sir, with coarse manners."

"I believe he and the Major were great friends, but they had a falling out some weeks previously."

She shrugged. "Yes, they had rather a heated argument. Right in front of me, in fact. I had the misfortune of bearing witness to the whole sordid mess."

"Is that so? Would it be indelicate of me to ask what caused this rift?"

"Frankly, I think it was the Major's fault entirely. From what I can piece together, he had made the Captain a solemn promise to help him gain his Majority, and I think he let him down quite badly. When this promised promotion failed to materialize, the Captain was understandably sore, and in his wrath, he threatened the Major."

"What kind of threat?"

Jane shivered involuntarily. "He said the Major would regret betraying him, and that he would get even with him, even if it was the last thing he did. Of course, I doubt he meant it. I think he was so angry he may have said rather more than he intended to, harsh words that I suspect he may have come to regret later, but sadly, it was too late for apologies. The Major was quite incensed with him. Before their quarrel, you see, the Captain had often joined him for supper, but that ended rather abruptly once they had words. In fact, I hadn't seen the Captain for the better part of a fortnight, not until he arrived in the Major's company last night. To tell the truth, that was why I was so glad when he left. The last thing I wanted was another uncomfortable scene that late at night."

Sikander sat back, lapsing into a disconsolate silence as he considered what Jane had just revealed to him.

"What happened after Captain Fletcher had departed? Did you go back to bed?"

"No, not quite immediately. Before I could retire, I heard the Major calling for me."

"He was awake?"

"Yes. He seemed to have recovered somewhat, well enough to tell me to fetch him some more wine." Jane shook her head disapprovingly. "I told him he had imbibed quite enough for one night. I offered to make him a cup of tea to calm his innards, even though the bawarchi had departed for the night. He refused, and insisted that I bring him something to drink, even if I had to go down to the bazaar to get it."

"Let me guess. That was when you remembered the bottle that Mr. Lowry had brought by as a gift."

"Yes, I did. When he demanded a drink, I fetched it from the larder for him."

Sikander leaned forward, finally beginning to understand what had happened to Jane. "Tell me, Madam, did you happen to open it first?"

"Of course! I had to uncork it before I took it up to him in his room, and decant it."

"Now be truthful, my dear. It is absolutely imperative that you do not lie. You poured yourself a glass, didn't you, before you took the bottle up to the Major?"

Her cheeks colored and he was certain that she was going to deny this accusation, but then, with a vast sigh, her head bobbed up and down.

"I did," she admitted shamefacedly. "I know I shouldn't have, but I just couldn't resist." She gave Sikander a guilty smile. "It has been years since I have partaken of harsh spirits, sir, but it was the New Year and I was damnably tired of the Major and his deviltries, and so I thought, what could one wee glass hurt, especially if I watered it down with a bit of lemonade…?"

Of course, Sikander thought. *That was what had saved her.* She had thought the sherry to be like arrack or some other raw liquor, in need of diluting, and while ordinarily, he would have thought it a cardinal sin to add lemonade to an Oloroso, this once, he was willing to forgive her such barbarity, considering it had managed to save her life.

Suddenly, like a scintilla of light sparkling in a dark room, it seemed to dawn on Jane just how deeply she was entangled in the Major's murder. "Oh, God, it was the wine that was poisoned, wasn't it?"

"I can't be sure of that," Sikander said, "not until I have done some chemical tests, but yes, it seems likely."

"You think it was Mr. Lowry who did it…?"

"It's possible," Sikander murmured. "I will have to investigate if he had a genuine motive to want to be rid of the Major, but yes, he has just become one of my prime suspects."

"He used me," she gasped, clutching at her chest. When added to the cumulative horror of the Major's death and her own close escape, it just too much for her to take. Something in those magnificent eyes wavered, an inundation of panic which she had hitherto managed to hold back by sheer force of will, now overflowed its banks like a flood.

"Oh, he's really dead, isn't he?" Jane let out an immense groan. She began to rock back and forth. Without even realizing what she was doing, she crammed one fist into her mouth, biting down on her knuckles wretchedly. And then, to his dismay, she began to keen, a shrill threnody which seemed to wrack through her like a fit, seemingly beyond her ability to control.

It frightened him, the intensity of this hysteria. Sikander tensed, gritting his teeth. He had never been comfortable with emotional displays, particularly from women. The problem was that he never knew quite how he was expected to react. He supposed he should say something to console her, but the thought of saying the wrong thing made him balk, leaving him unexpectedly at a loss for words.

"Don't worry, Madam," he said, trying not to seem too brusque. "Everything will be fine, I promise you."

"Why are you being so kind to me?" Jane said, uncertainty flaring on her face once more, like a tragic coating of rouge.

"Let's just say I cannot resist a damsel in distress," Sikander replied. "Why, often I find myself causing young ladies distress intentionally just so that I can rescue them later."

Sadly, this attempt at levity failed to find its mark. Jane remained somnolent, as cold as a cadaver. "What is going to happen to me now?"

Her voice was so barren, so empty it made Sikander flinch.

"As I said, Madam, everything is going to be just fine."

Forcing his lips into a smile, Sikander broke from habit and reached out to fold Jane's fingers into his own. She shrank away from him, trying to wrest free, but he refused to let go, holding on with a dogged tenacity.

"Don't you worry. I will take care of you. You have my word on that."

Chapter Thirteen

Once he was certain that Jane was settled comfortably, Sikander decided it was time for him to depart.

He bid farewell to Helene, but it was an uncomfortably cold parting. Though he made one last desperate attempt to kiss her in the hope that it would mollify her pique, she averted her cheek very deliberately. In the end, he had to settle for offering up an awkward profusion of gratitude for her help, to which she replied with a snort so thunderous that it compelled him to beat a hasty retreat.

Rather than returning to the palace for his customary afternoon nap, Sikander decided to make a quick detour to see if he could corner Captain Fletcher, who now seemed doubly suspicious to him, given what Jane had just revealed.

The Rajpore Gymkhana was situated at the very outskirts of the British town, bordered on one side by the Cantonment and on the other by the azure ribbon of the River Oona. It sprawled across nine acres, a panoply of carefully maintained lawns, at the center of which stood an expansive main clubhouse constructed in the mock Tudor style.

In Colonial patois, a *gymkhana* was the combination of the Hindustani word *gend* or "ball," and *khana*, Persian for "house," hence, a ball-house, or quite literally, the house for games. It was a uniquely British-Indian institution, one part gymnasium and two parts gentlemen's club, as parochial and exclusive as Boodle's or the Savage, a private sanctuary to which the Sahibs could retreat for a few hours each evening to partake of a *burra peg* or two while sitting on moldy wicker furniture and reminiscing about all they had left behind in jolly old England.

The gymkhana's actual origins were quite humble. It had begun as a sporting association, founded and funded thanks to Sikander's grandfather's enthusiastic largesse, when the old Maharaja had decided to donate some land and a yearly endowment of three hundred rupees to the English to build a place where they could indulge their leisure in manly pursuits like pig-sticking and polo and cricket.

But as time had passed, the club had evolved into something more. It had become a formidable bastion of English Colonialism, a testament to the British way of life, a veritable shrine to their bland passions. What had begun a humble tented pavilion had grown into an establishment that put Sikander's own palace to shame, with its three covered shuttle courts, four grass tennis courts, two swimming pools, a seven-table billiards room, a card room where bridge and whist were played, a private boathouse, and even a golf course, of which his grandfather had been a great patron. That was one passion of the Occidentals that Sikander had never quite been able to understand—the dubious lure of wandering around all day under the blistering sun wearing tweed and gaiters while assaulting a gutta percha ball with a stick.

For the memsahibs, there were two halfway decent restaurants, a well-cared for library which stocked the latest periodicals from Calcutta, a theater where the Rajpore Dramatic Circle regularly mangled Shakespeare's tragedies, and a formal dining room with a dance floor. Nonetheless, in spite of these many and diverse facilities, Sikander disliked visiting the club. Part of it was because he despised most of the members, thinking them precisely the sort of insufferable arrivistes he tried most to avoid. But beneath this innate snobbery, there was a far more pernicious reason he rarely patronized the gymkhana. In a typical display of English arrogance, it was decidedly whites only. The only natives permitted inside, other than Sikander, who was the sole Indian member, were the three hundred employees who ran the place with silently ruthless efficiency, the menials and the ayahs, the bearers and the groundskeepers, the ball boys and the cooks, that myriad of invisibles who made sure that the careful machinery of British leisure was never disrupted, not even for a solitary moment.

Perhaps that was why he had always felt out of place there, uneasy, surrounded by so many hostile white faces. Sikander had always prided himself on being rather a fearless sort, and he knew only too well that without his munificence to subsidize its operations, there would be no club at all, but that fact did not reduce the awkwardness that gripped him when he visited the place one whit. If anything, it made him even more self-conscious, cognizant that his membership was only tolerated because he was the one with the deepest pockets, and that most of the other patrons would always see him as a servant rather than a peer.

As the Rolls approached the gymkhana, Sikander took a long moment to contemplate turning back. A surge of trepidation ran through him, an uncharacteristic reluctance, but gritting his teeth, he reminded himself that he had no time to squander. He was experienced enough to know all too well that a murder was most easily solved within the first forty-eight hours of its commission. That was when the trail was at its freshest, while the body was still warm. Once it cooled, it became that much more difficult to find the killer, regardless of how talented the detective might be. After all, the human memory was a fragile, mutable thing. As time passed, witnesses changed their stories. Details that had seemed crystalline at first blurred in the mind, and with every wasted moment, every bit of evidence seemed less tangible, like smoke dissipating before a breeze.

Understandably, the Maharaja's advent at the club managed to cause quite a furor. Out on the immaculately trimmed greens, a polo match had just concluded its final *chukka* and a horde of brightly clad soldiers were cantering their horses back to the club paddocks, directly intersecting his path. When the Rolls thundered past them like a storm on wheels, the horses startled, whinnying and bucking with panic and nearly managing to unseat half the Rajpore Regiment polo team. Sikander grinned and waved one hand at them in apology, before rolling to a gradual stop outside the main entrance, throwing up a vast cloud of gravel in his wake, and managing to make an abominable racket.

Leaving the car idling, Sikander squared his shoulders and strode into the club. Past the wide arched entrance, a broad arcade ran the entire length of the gymkhana, a wide verandah whose parquet-tiled floor was dotted with an uneven arrangement of wicker tables and chairs. On his immediate left, a pair of French doors led toward the ballroom, which was adjoined by the bar and the formal dining room, next to which a dog-legged staircase led upstairs to the billiards room and card room and library.

Just inside the vaulted entrance-way, the Maharaja paused, sticking to the shadows so that nobody would notice him. He adjusted his gloves with an exacting fastidiousness, casting a rather jaundiced eye around to take in his surroundings. As always, the club's ostentatious décor made him cringe. It was like he had taken a wrong turn and stepped straight into one of Flora Annie Steel's dreadful novels, from the tattered tiger heads mounted on the walls to the muslin nets that swathed each table like spiderwebs in a futile attempt to keep mosquitoes at bay, not to mention the turbaned punkah-wallahs who stood at discreet intervals, pulling at ropes to keep the linen fans hanging from the roof creaking back and forth noisily.

It surprised him how seedy the club looked by light of day. When he had last visited just the night before, the place had been at its festive best, as gaily decorated as a temple, the walls festooned with bunting and shiny streamers, the grounds lit up by hundreds of Chinese lanterns, giving the place a delightfully Oriental decadence. But now, without the flattering cloak of night and the roseate glow of champagne to dull his wits, it seemed even more dilapidated than usual. A musty smell hung in the air, that ripe odor of mold and rancid cooking oil. The tiles underfoot were cracked and uneven, the oak-paneled walls crisscrossed with termite tracks, the paint on the ceiling peeling as a wide web of cracks spread outward like the lines on an old woman's palm. The wicker furniture was far too creaky, the potted ferns that lined the verandah were limp and listless, and there was a yellow tint to the tattered chintz tablecloths. All in all, it gave the gymkhana an air of weary decay, as if to illustrate that the grand days of the Raj were long past and all that remained was a tired echo of decrepit glory.

To his dismay, the club was rather too crowded for comfort. Sikander grimaced, barely able to swallow his distaste. He should have remembered it was a half holiday, and as a result, the place was packed to the rafters, every table in the verandah taken, by a multitude of unfriendly white faces, mostly local families, he guessed, complete with their grubby little children, running around screaming at the top of their voices as if they were possessed by demons. As he had dreaded, his entrance caused a minor sensation. It began with the table nearest the door where a knot of plump Englishmen sat enjoying a kettle of tea under the watchful eye of a white-coated bearer. As Sikander passed, they paused and turned to glower at him, their faces livid with annoyance, as if to suggest that he was just another unwanted interloper who had forced his way into their little haven of Englishness. And then, like a row of dominoes being knocked over, it spread from table to table, neck after neck swiveling to look in his direction, the hubbub of conversation slowly withering away to a gaunt silence until it seemed to him every single eye in the club was staring straight at him.

Ignoring the humid hostility thickening the air, Sikander raised a hand and beckoned at the Abdar, the head steward, who was standing rigidly behind a long serving table at the center of the verandah. The man came rushing, almost tripping over in his haste to respond. Sikander knew him very well. His name was Harpreet Singh, and he was one of Charan Singh's innumerable siblings, albeit a smaller, more rotund version of the Maharaja's faithful manservant. In fact, it was at Sikander's recommendation that he had secured this very position, and in exchange, it was his job to make sure the Maharaja was kept well supplied with information, passing on the rumors and gossip that he inevitably overheard from the Sahibs as they spent their evenings in the determined pursuit of relaxation.

"Yes, Huzoor?" Harpreet Singh inquired. Inclining his head, he performed a complicated salutation, raising one hand to his forehead to claw at his forelock.

"I was hoping to speak with Captain Fletcher."

The Abdar nodded and pulled out a battered fob-watch from his vest, gazing down at its well-worn dial with a frown. "I believe that he can presently be found in the card room. If you wish it, sir, I shall endeavor to fetch him for you."

"No," Sikander said, "Send a bearer. I need to have a word with you."

"Of course." Swiveling, the Abdar called for a nearby waiter, a gangly young teenager with barely the first scruff of manhood on his chin, and barked out a series of instructions in Punjabi, sending the boy hurrying away.

"I have told him to fetch the Captain immediately," he explained, turning back to the Maharaja. "How else may I be of service to Your Magnificence?"

"I wanted to chat about the Resident Sahib for a moment," Sikander started to say, but the Abdar forestalled him with a frantic bob of his head.

"Please, not here," he whispered, clearing his throat pointedly, as if to remind Sikander that a hundred hostile eyes were watching. "Would you care to step into the ballroom?"

Sikander understood the man's need for discretion all too well and obliged his request, following Harpreet Singh through the wide glass doors into the Grand Ballroom, a handsome oak-panelled room with a high, barrel-vaulted ceiling. Inside, he saw that the remnants of last night's festivities were still being cleared away. Nearby, a gaunt sweeper, as ancient as a wraith, hunched over on his haunches, slowly polishing the floor to a greasy luster with what smelled like a mixture of linseed oil and Murphy's soap. The Abdar hissed and immediately, the sweeper ceased his labors and retreated, leaving his work incomplete, as did the pack of servants who were folding away the tables and stacking wooden chairs against the wall.

"Forgive my rudeness, Sahib," Harpreet Singh apologized, "but after what has happened this morning, the English are on edge. Jardine Sahib has been making a fuss all day."

"Of course," Sikander commiserated. "I don't want to get you into any trouble. I just have a few quick questions about the New Year's Ball last night. I heard there was a bit of an altercation."

"Yes, indeed," the Abdar replied. "It was a real tamasha. The Major Sahib got into a heated argument with another officer. It almost brought the evening crashing to a premature halt."

"Do you by any chance happen to know what set the argument off?"

"Oh, I saw it all." Harpreet Singh smiled conspiratorially. "The Major arrived quite late and spent some time chatting with Fletcher Sahib, but then, a young memsahib approached him. Together, they retired to a discreet spot upstairs, on the back balcony, and, how shall I put this delicately, after a brief conversation, they began to kiss, Huzoor."

"Is that so?" Sikander said, trying not to let his excitement show. "Are you certain what you witnessed was entirely romantic? Couldn't the Major have been making an advance, forcing himself upon the poor girl?"

"Forgive my presumption for daring to contradict you, Huzoor," Harpreet Singh said with a leer, "but it was consensual, of that I am confident."

"Are you absolutely certain?"

"Oh, by golly, yes! The two of them were going at it like a pair of langurs in mating season."

"Describe this chaste young woman to me, will you?" Sikander tried to keep his voice businesslike, even though inside he was seething to get on with chasing down this mysterious memsahib who had inspired such drama at the Ball.

"Oh, she was a pari, Your Highness, one of the Apsaras come to life." The Abdar let out a low wolf whistle, squeezing a shrill breath through his front teeth. "Skin like silk, eyes as blue as a midsummer sky. Now that is the kind of woman a man prays will keep him warm on the coldest winter's night."

Sikander gave him an amused wink. "You have the heart of a poet, Harpreet Singh."

The Abdar laughed. "I appreciate beauty, Sahib, especially since I have been cursed with a wife who is as ugly as an ogre."

Sikander nodded his head appreciatively at this witticism. "Let us backtrack for a moment. You say you saw the Major and this memsahib kissing? What happened after that?"

"What always happens?" The Abdar gave a stoic shrug. "The pretty lady's husband showed up. A tall young lieutenant, built like a scarecrow with a face as ugly as a gargoyle's. I thought it was a tragedy that someone as delectable as she was wasted on the likes of him." He shuddered. "He was a real challah, Huzoor. The Resident Sahib was holding court out on the lawn, about a half hour after I saw him being amorous with the memsahib, when this Lieutenant just walked up to him in front of everyone, and actually slapped him across the face with a glove. Can you believe that?"

Sikander pursed his lips. "How did the Major respond to this challenge?"

"Oh, he looked ready to kill the boy, but thankfully, before they could come to blows, Fletcher Sahib jumped in and put a stop to it." He grimaced. "It was quite a scandal, let me tell you. Lowry Sahib came and dragged the young Lieutenant away, and expelled him from the club, along with the unfortunate memsahib."

"What about the Resident?"

"Oh, he didn't linger much longer either. He left about ten minutes later, in the company of Captain Fletcher," he said with a shrug. "That was about all the excitement for the night. The party went on for a little longer, until an hour or so after midnight. At the latest, it would have been around one-fifteen, give or take a few minutes."

A shiver of excitement ran down the Maharaja's spine. Thanks to Harpreet Singh, he now had the time-line of events he needed, and a halfway decent one at that. The Major had left an hour before the party ended, between eleven and eleven-fifteen. However, Sikander's examination of the crime scene had led him to believe that the Major had been poisoned between three and five a.m., which meant that whatever had killed him had to have been introduced into his system *after* he had departed the ball.

"Personally, I am convinced it was the Lieutenant who murdered the Resident Sahib, Huzoor," Harpreet Singh interjected. "What do you think?"

Sikander gave the Abdar a sour glare. He really had no interest in the man's opinions, and besides, it was much too early in the game to jump to such a wild conclusion, and certainly not without subjecting the errant Lieutenant to rigorous questioning first.

Just as he was about to recommend that Harpreet Singh stick to waiting tables and leave the detecting to him, he felt a knot in his stomach, a sixth sense warning him that he was being watched. Spinning around, he saw Fletcher standing framed in the glass doorway of the ballroom, staring daggers in his direction, his coarse features twisted into an expression of pure malevolence.

As their eyes met, the Captain turned and scurried away with great alacrity. Immediately, Sikander bid a rushed farewell to Harpreet Singh, and dashed after Fletcher, eager to stop him before he could slip away. Like a tornado, he stormed out of the ballroom, barging through the doors with such haste that one of the glass windows cracked right down the middle, only to crash headlong into the squint-eyed young waiter the Abdar had deputed to summon the Captain, very nearly bowling him off his feet.

As soon as the man managed to regain his balance, he greeted the Maharaja with a wary bow. "Your Highness, I regret to say, the Captain is not at the club at present."

Sikander scowled. "How can that be? I just saw him, standing right here," he started to say, but the boy gulped and interrupted him in mid-sentence.

"Forgive me, Sahib," he groaned with a sheepish look, "but you must be mistaken. He is not here."

A formless rage clenched inside Sikander's chest, so overpow-ering that it made his head throb. His face turned a startling shade of purple, and two livid veins pulsed in his temples. Before he knew it, he had clenched his fists and taken a half step forward.

"Do you take me for a fool?" He thundered, so loud that it was almost deafening. Immediately, in unison, fifty English necks swiveled to watch the Maharaja, their collective eyes gleaming with appalled curiosity.

"Sahib," the waiter yelped, "I am only the messenger."

With those words, he squeezed shut his eyes, preparing him-self to silently take whatever punishment the Maharaja chose to dish out. This hapless gesture of acquiescence was what made Sikander pause. He couldn't just vent his irritation on this poor fool. He was only a pawn, Captain Fletcher's catspaw, who had no choice but to do as he had been ordered.

It was the Captain who was ducking him, but why?

Why was he avoiding the Maharaja so assiduously, unless he had something to hide?

Chapter Fourteen

"Get out of my sight!"

"Oh, bless you, Sahib," the boy intoned, and backed away with a speed that would have put a rabbit to shame. As for Sikander, he spun on his heel and headed toward the exit, eager to get out of the club as soon as possible, away from the British half of Rajpore altogether and back within the borders of his own territory.

Sadly, before he could make good his escape, a large man who had been seated in one secluded corner of the verandah beneath the shade of a garish red and blue lawn umbrella leaped up and waved at him eagerly.

"Your Majesty! Yoo hoo!"

It was Miller, the local presswallah. In spite of his irritation, Sikander's mouth twisted into an involuntary smile. At first glance, the man cut a comical figure, the very epitome of a Falstaffian buffoon. He was extraordinarily corpulent, with three voluminous chins and a pink sweaty moon of a face, which when coupled with his propensity for rumpled white tropical suits, left him looking rather like a downed dirigible. Behind this bumbling exterior though, there hid a formidable intelligence. Like Sikander, Miller was a polymath, the sort of man who took an interest in anything and everything. Perhaps that was why Sikander had always had a soft spot for the acerbic Englishman. He was the only person in Rajpore the Maharaja could have an unrestrained conversation with, a marvelously erudite man whose company he had always found immensely diverting. Best of all, the presswallah knew all the local English gossip. He kept a vast network of informers—servants and bearers and ayahs and durjees and dhobis—on his payroll, and they kept him apprised of every little development happening in the English town, from the most mundane of conflicts to the most salacious of scandals.

As Sikander altered his path to approach Miller's table, the plump Englishman collapsed backwards into his chair with such violence that its wicker legs creaked alarmingly, as if to voice complaint.

"Forgive me, Your Majesty," he exclaimed. "This humidity, it saps me terribly."

Letting out an exaggerated groan, he removed his hat with one limp hand and began to fan himself desultorily. Sikander smiled as he saw Miller's foppishly long hair. It was another one of the presswallah's well-documented eccentricities, a mane of silken curls as golden as a sunrise, which he insisted on wearing in ringlets, like a Cavalier. On a woman, it would have been somewhat becoming, but on a man the size of Miller, all it accomplished was to render his appearance even more incongruous. And then of course, there was the perfume. In addition to his lamentable taste in haberdashery, Miller had a bizarre preference for cheap cologne. He seemed to bathe in it until the musk surrounded him like a fragrant cloud, but sadly it did little to disguise his smell, which was quite piquant, a rank odor of sweat and gin and printer's ink that made Sikander feel more than a little queasy.

"Well," Miller said as the Maharaja took the chair opposite him, pulling it as far back as he could to avoid being overcome by the miasma of the man's stench, "it seems we are finally rid of Major Russell, yes."

With an insolent flourish, Miller gathered up a glass and raised it in mock-salute. Sikander guessed it was probably filled to the brim with Gordon's gin. Even though it was not yet four o'clock, he could tell from Miller's ruddy cheeks that as usual the presswallah was already half drunk, well on his way to being truly pickled before the sun had even set.

"Here's to good riddance," he exclaimed recklessly with no regard for who happened to overhear him, "May the bugger rot in purgatory for all eternity."

With that declaration, he downed the glass' contents in one vast gulp, before slapping it back down onto the table with an unlikely vehemence.

"Why, Mr. Miller," Sikander said, taken aback by the acid in his voice, "I was not aware you felt so strongly against the Major."

"Ha!" Miller hissed. "He was an asinine jackass who seemed to believe that the independent press existed only to serve his whims and fancies. In fact, the last time we spoke, he promised me in no uncertain terms that he would have me locked up like a common criminal if I ever dared to slander him in print."

Abruptly, he leaned forward to fix Sikander with a penetrating glare. "Rumor has it that you think his death was a murder, not a suicide."

He peered at Sikander keenly, trying to deduce something from his expression, but the Maharaja was a past-master at keeping his emotions well hidden.

"I have heard another rumor that you are poking about trying to find the killer."

"Perhaps…I haven't quite made up my mind about it yet." He held Miller's stare with a level, poker face, offering him the slightest of smiles. "In fact, I was hoping you could help me with that."

Miller laughed, a great booming clamor of noise that made Sikander grimace, as if he had been struck physically. "I thought as much," he smirked. "How could I possibly help you? I am just a humble journalist."

"Come now, Mr. Miller, don't play coy. You have a rare talent for secrets, both for keeping and uncovering them."

Miller brushed this compliment away with a dismissive wave of one hand, but Sikander could see from his expression that he was inordinately pleased by this remark. He meant every word. In spite of his flaws, Ernest Miller was an extraordinarily useful creature. His position at the *Rajpore Gazette* coupled with his skill at poking about in other people's business made him a very valuable asset for the Maharaja. Not only was he an excellent editor who ran the *Gazette* with an iron fist but, for lack of a better phrase, Miller was a bloodhound, apt at sniffing out secrets. He had a unique propensity for finding usable information where most others only saw random and disconnected facts, and his files were as voluminous as they came, his intelligence sources second only to Sikander's own chief minister, the redoubtable Ismail Bhakht.

"What do you need from me?" Miller asked, frowning speculatively.

"I want to know whatever you can tell me about the Major's private life."

The journalist's mouth split into a cocky smile. "If I did happen to have such information, Your Highness, I might wonder what I have to gain by revealing it to you."

"I am sure we could come to some arrangement, provided of course that what you know is worth paying for," Sikander responded with an equally hawkish grin.

Miller's eyes narrowed until he seemed almost porcine, and he licked his lips greedily.

"Very well," he said. "Where would you like to begin?"

Sikander leaned forward, lowering his voice to a murmur. "When I spoke with Mr. Lowry earlier, he mentioned that he was at Cambridge with the Major, but Russell was sent down. Would you happen to know why? I imagine it must have been quite a scandal."

"I have no doubt it was," Miller said, looking rather embarrassed. He shrugged, a vast quiver that seemed to cascade through him in a cataclysm of loose flesh. "Sadly, sir, I must admit I do not know."

"Could you possibly find out?"

"I could certainly try, but it will take a bit of time." He sounded annoyed at being caught out, even vexed. "Let me see what I can dig up."

"Good! Meanwhile, tell me what you know about the Major's antecedents, will you?"

"Oh, now that I can help with! I wrote a biographical piece about him for the *Gazette*, you see, when he came out to take up the Resident's position. According to official records, he entered the Army when he was quite young, a purchased commission as an ensign in the Bengal Light Infantry. He was seconded to be one of General Prendergast's aides during the march into Burma, and acquitted himself particularly well, although there was some sniff of impropriety in the aftermath of the fall of Mandalay."

"What manner of improprieties?"

"Oh, he was accused of lining his own pockets. It was said that he took rather a handsome gratuity from a cabal of merchants when it came to disposing of some of the booty looted from the royal palace in Mandalay. Some may have called it a backhander, but I believe the Resident Sahib saw it more as a well-earned commission."

"Was it a large sum?"

"Large enough to show his true nature, but not so much that it got him into trouble. In either case, he got off clean and was rewarded with a Lieutenant's pips, after which he was seconded to the North Western Frontier.

"Since then, he has managed to make quite a name for himself, enjoying quite a meteoric rise there by all accounts. I believe he was one of the masterminds behind the Chitral Expedition and the Tirah Campaign, after which he was promoted and sent on to Sindh and then to Travancore, where he served until about six years ago, when he seems to have committed rather a large blunder."

"What sort of blunder?"

Miller tittered, and made a great show of rolling his eyes suggestively. "A woman, of course. There always is, isn't there? A native bibi came forward and claimed that he had made a promise to wed her and then betrayed her trust. Russell of course claimed he had done no such thing, but the ensuing scandal did quite a lot of damage to his prospects." He lowered his voice to a whisper. "If rumor is to be believed, she accused him of beating her, once so severely that it apparently caused her to lose their child."

Sikander's face hardened. As far as he was concerned, there was nothing quite as low as a man who raised his hand against a woman. Not only were the poor creatures too weak to fight back, defenseless in every way except with their tongues, but it took a particularly vicious breed of man to behave with such reprehensible savagery. Sikander found himself despising the Major even more. If only he had known, he would have never permitted the man to be appointed to so senior a post. But then, the Major had been careful never to allow the true brutality of his nature to show through. It had remained hidden behind a veneer of civility, but Sikander chastised himself for not realizing that the Major's aloofness had merely been a carefully cultivated mask. There was even a clinical condition that described men like that—*Manie sans delière*, or "mania without delirium," a scientific term propagated by Phillipe Pinel. It described the sort of unnatural moral insanity demonstrated by egocentric individuals who lacked both a conscience and a sense of morality and believed themselves to be above the rules that applied to normal humans.

"How is it that he was never brought up on charges?"

"Oh, I suspect it was hushed up. There was the fact that the victim in question was a native, and I believe the Major was most vociferous in his objections that he had not touched her. I suppose it was inevitable that he would get off scot-free. As it always proceeds in these matters, his word as a gentleman was thought to be solid, but the fallout did manage to damage his professional reputation quite irrevocably."

"Because of a woman? That seems excessive."

"Well, as it turned out, the woman in this case was the youngest daughter of one of the Maharaja of Travancore's most faithful retainers, who was understandably irate at the time. And he had friends in Madras, high-ranking connections who did not approve of a middle-aged officer philandering with a girl young enough to be his granddaughter. In either case, the

Major was given an early retirement and discreetly shunted out of Travancore and informed that there would be no further promotions on his horizon."

Miller pursed his lips disapprovingly. "If rumor is to be believed, he began to drink rather heavily and spent the next two and a half years languishing at a loose end in Calcutta before being granted his next posting, which happened to be here at Rajpore, a position which I believe he was offered only because he had considerable previous experience with the Afghans. Of course, even though it was a bit of a comedown after some of the exalted positions he had occupied previously, needless to say he jumped at the chance to be a pain in your neck, a job at which he excelled by all accounts."

With that, Miller sat back, looking very pleased with himself. Sikander waited for him to go on, but it seemed that was the gist of the information he had to offer at that time.

"Is that all?" Sikander said, somewhat disappointed. While the tidbit about the Major's misadventures in Travancore was certainly interesting, it gave him little insight into why someone would want to see him dead. "You're losing your touch, Mr. Miller. I was hoping for something more, well, salacious. Why, I learned more from Mr. Lowry, and he is not even a journalist."

The presswallah's face stiffened, visibly goaded by this jibe. "Ah, our eminent Magistrate! Now there's a man who is extraordinarily good at keeping secrets." Miller sniffed, his face souring with barely concealed distaste. "He isn't all that he seems, that one, let me assure you."

"What do you mean?" Sikander asked, intrigued by this comment.

"Actually, you may find this interesting," Miller gloated. "It just so happens that Mr. Lowry is a molly."

"A what?"

Miller gave Sikander a suggestive wink and made a rude gesture, waving one limp wrist back and forth. "A man's man, Your Majesty, if you know what I mean. He's a Margery. A Mary-Ann."

"What?" Sikander's mouth fell open in unmitigated surprise. It took him a minute to understand what the presswallah was insinuating, before comprehension dawned like a kick in the head.

"Are you trying to tell me that our Magistrate likes to indulge in the sin of the Greeks?"

Miller laughed, a staccato burst of glee. "Oh, there's nothing Greek about it, I assure you. If anything, he has a marked preference for Anglo-Indian telegraph boys, the younger the better."

Even though Sikander considered himself a man of the world, he found himself utterly stunned by this revelation. It was such a surprising bit of news that it managed to pierce even his ordinarily unflappable exterior. Like most people, he was all too aware that sodomy and buggery were common amongst the English, particularly soldiers of the lower ranks who were forced to spend years on campaign, far away from the company of any women other than the harlots who plied a brisk trade around the Cantonments. And of course, he had heard stories that such things were quite common in British boarding schools like Eton and Harrow. But never in his wildest flights of fancy would he have guessed that Lowry was an invert. There were no signs to suggest it, at least no apparent ones. The Magistrate wasn't an effeminate man, not in the least. Tiresome perhaps, and long-winded, but he seemed as red-blooded as anyone else. *For God's sake*, Sikander thought, *I even had him along on the annual battue last year, and he bagged a buck.*

His face tightened with barely repressed distaste. If what Miller was saying was true, if it wasn't just a scurrilous rumor, then that changed everything. This information about Lowry's sexuality, managed to cast an altogether different complexion on his relationship with the Major. Was he indeed an unwitting pawn after all, as Sikander had believed, or had he been involved with the Major in some darker, more twisted way?

"Are you sure of this, Mr. Miller, or is this just hyperbole?"

Appalled by such a blatant querying of his veracity, Miller let out a vexed snort. "I am unequivocally certain, Your Majesty.

In fact, I have a signed affidavit from a ball boy at the Calcutta Cricket Club. He approached me last year with rather a lurid tale to tell. It seems he and the Magistrate had a bit of a dalliance not long ago, and when they parted ways, he was left disappointed, feeling as though he had been taken advantage of." Miller smiled, as oily as a Turk. "In exchange for a small gratuity, he was only too happy to share the sordid details with me."

Sikander's brow furrowed, his mind ticking away like an abacus. So Lowry was a sodomite. That singular fact changed his understanding of the man completely. Was that what had caused the falling out between of the Major and him all those years ago? Sikander had a gut feeling he was on the right track. Possibly the Major had discovered Lowry's affliction and was repelled by him. Yes, that made ample sense. That would be more than enough to amputate a friendship irrevocably. And that would certainly explain what leverage the Major had possessed over Lowry, the dirty secret that had kept the Magistrate dancing to his tune, like an organ grinder's monkey.

"Excellent, Mr. Miller," he said, beaming at the presswallah, "now this is more like it. This I can use, by God Almighty."

Miller preened. "I am glad to see you are pleased, Your Highness. Is there anything else I could assist you with?"

"As a matter of fact, tell me what you know of this fellow Fletcher."

"Well, personally, I must confess, I simply can't bear the man. One of the most unpleasant people I have ever met, and I have encountered a few foul specimens in my time, let me tell you."

"Might I ask why you dislike him so deeply, Mr. Miller? Has he done you some personal harm?"

Miller scowled, not bothering to hide his obvious antagonism. "Fletcher's a bully, your Highness. The worst kind of Ajax, one of those overly sweaty, virile types who spend every waking hour on the playing field. It doesn't help, of course, that he has a natural propensity for violence, an ability that borders almost on being a gift, and like most brutes, he believes that his physical strengths make him far superior to those of us who prefer to indulge our energies in more sedentary, civilized pursuits."

His plump face colored, twisting into a grimace. "It's ironic, really. I imagine that this brutishness is the very quality that makes him such a fine soldier. The same traits which are so loathsome in peacetime, they are of such great value upon the field of battle, yes…?"

"Is he indeed as fine a soldier as they say he is?"

"I hate to admit it, but yes, there's no question about that. His record is beyond reproach."

"Perhaps I am expecting too much from your memory, but would you be able to recount his war record for me, at least in a cursory fashion?"

"I can certainly try. Let me see what I can recall," Miller took another generous sip of gin, and rubbed at his temple with one thumb and fingertip. "Hmm, numerous commendations for conspicuous valor, which suggests that he is as brave as Hector. He fought in Burma, at Minhla where he was decorated for gallantry, and the advance from Toungoo, and then in Afghanistan during the Tirah Campaign."

"Did he distinguish himself against the Afghans?"

"No, not quite. The Captain had a bit of unfortunate luck that kept him out of any real action."

"What happened?"

"I believe he had been picked to lead a relief column to Sarahgiri but two days before his troop was scheduled to depart, he took a dreadful tumble off his horse and shattered his knee while playing a rather spirited game of polo." Miller shrugged. "Still, one man's bad luck is another man's good fortune, or so they say. We all know how Sarahgiri turned out."

Sikander nodded. Sarahgiri was a debacle rarely talked about by the British military, one of the worst defeats they had suffered at the hands of the Afghans. Without warning, five companies of the 36th Sikh Regiment had been surrounded and trapped in a remote signaling post by an army of 10,000 Afridis. Rather than facing the ignominy of surrender, the gallant Sikhs had chosen instead to make a last stand. As bravely as the Spartans at Thermopylae, they fought to the last man, defending their posts even as they were overrun by a horde of Pathans bent upon bloody murder.

"Good Heavens, Fletcher had a very narrow escape there, didn't he? If he hadn't toppled off his horse, the Afghans would probably be wearing his guts for garters by now."

"Yes, he has the devil's own luck, but knowing the man, he probably thinks he could have won the damn skirmish if he had been in command."

"How did he happen to end up in Rajpore?"

"Oh, he was seconded here, against his choice, of course. He was one of Younghusband's guides during the whole Tibet affair, but the only action he saw was a musket-ball in the bottom early on the march to Chumik Shenko which became infected. It took him a while to recover, after which, the good Captain had the temerity to send a strongly worded letter to his superiors in Simla demanding that they promote him immediately and post him to Palestine."

"That was not what happened, I imagine."

"Of course not. The War Office does not take kindly to having demands made of it by lowly Captains. As a result, he was sent off here, to Rajpore, banished to finish out the rest of his career in quiet dudgeon."

"How unfortunate for him!" Sikander pursed his lips. "Isn't he rather old to be a mere Captain?"

"You don't know the half of it, Your Majesty. If rumor is to be believed, the poor bugger has been passed over six times."

"Is that quite a common occurrence, to be passed over so many times?"

"Not at all," Miller replied. "It's surprising really. If I were him, I would have taken the hint and put in my papers for an early retirement by now, but then, our friend the Captain has always been rather too tenacious for his own good."

The way Miller emphasized the word "tenacious" suggested to Sikander that he intended it as an insult, not a compliment.

"Did you know," the Englishman said with a florid grimace, "that he has won every single one of his promotions on the battlefield? Can you believe it?"

"Is that so?" Sikander said, impressed by this statistic in spite of his disdain for Fletcher.

"Yes, it seems very inspiring, doesn't it? But then, if you stop to think it over, what other choice does he have, the poor dolt?" Miller shook his head. "Our dear Captain is not quite as pukka as he likes to pretend, you see."

Sikander mulled over this statement, wondering what exactly it could portend. The word "pukka" was a very interesting one, uniquely Anglo-Indian in origin but with myriad vague meanings that depended entirely on the context in which it was used. In a positive sense, it could mean anything from reliable or trustworthy to admirable, but when used negatively, it suggested that someone or something was not quite legitimate or acceptable. Sikander frowned. It was the ultimate accusation, at least in British India. To be accused of being not pukka meant a man could not be trusted, and to have been saddled with a label like that, no wonder Fletcher's career had stagnated with a mere Captaincy. And there was nothing the Captain could have done to counter such a scurrilous accusation, he thought, because it was precisely the sort of backroom gossip that followed a man around, not specific enough to be forgivable, but just tangible enough to be damning.

"I am not sure what you are trying to insinuate, Mr. Miller. You will have to be more specific."

Miller leaned forward until his face was just inches away from Sikander, so close that the Maharaja could smell the fetid tang of gin on his breath.

"I have heard stories about his grandmother, sir. It is said that she was a native bibi, a Pahari woman taken by his grandfather to be his second wife. And the Captain, he is quite dark in complexion, is he not, which suggests that he may be a chee-chee, I suspect. There's definitely some brown in the mix. He's an octoroon at least, a minimum of one-eighth Indian, sir. I am convinced of it."

Sikander's eyes widened. This was a damning accusation indeed, and if it were true, it held nothing but the direst connotations for Captain Fletcher. The chee-chees, the half-and-halfs, the Eurasians—call them what you may—occupied a bewildering position in British India. Their skin color was as varied as their ancestry—some were as pale as ivory while others as black as charcoal, but regardless of their complexions, they belonged neither to the East nor to the West. Instead, they lived in the no-man's land between the India inhabited by Indians, and the white-washed cottages of the British Raj. It was tragic that an entire population should be doomed to be marginalized so completely and perhaps the truest example of the old saying that the sins of a father inevitably were visited upon his sons. The Indians despised the Anglos, thinking them as foreign as the white men who had spawned them, while the British shunned them equally, too embarrassed to acknowledge the outcome of two hundred years of heat and lust.

There had been a time when it wasn't unheard of for a man who was a half-blood to rise high in service of the Empire, particularly if he was gifted with uncommon military prowess. Take the case of Sir Robert Warburton, who had founded the Khyber Rifles, or Colonel Henry Forster who had raised the Shekhawati Brigade, or the most famous of them all, James Skinner, the founder of the Yellow Boys, who had begun his career as a mercenary but had retired ultimately as a Companion of the Order of the Bath. Why, one Anglo had even risen to become the Prime Minister of England, the redoubtable Lord Liverpool, whose mother had been half-Indian. But these cases were few and far between. The truth of it was that Anglo-Indians were not welcome in British Regiments. Most of them had to turn to native armies to make a career for themselves, and the few that did find a place in British service were often discriminated against, denied advancement because of their origins.

Sikander grunted as understanding dawned. That explained a great deal about the Captain and his uncommon valor. He would have had to be twice as brave as any other officer, twice as diligent, twice as dedicated to make up for having only half the blood.

"How sure are you of all this? How credible are your sources?" he asked Miller sternly, unwilling to use the information if it was simply gossip.

"I am willing to stake my reputation on it. To tell the truth, there is part of me that almost pities the poor bugger. By all accounts, he is a hell of a cavalryman. Why, if he had been born in Blighty, he would have been a Colonel by now for certain, but sadly, he is just an aging Captain."

With that pronouncement, Miller picked up the bell that lay atop the table and rang it shrilly, summoning a bearer and commanding him to bring a fresh bottle of gin. "Would you care for anything, Your Highness?"

Sikander raised one hand in curt refusal, waiting for the waiter to leave before he continued. "There is one more person I would like to know about. His name is Bates, I think?"

Miller's plump features hardened with loathing.

"Ah, the young Lieutenant." The presswallah wrinkled his nose in disgust. "A presumptuous little git, that one. He will not last long, not in India."

"What makes you say that?"

"He has great expectations, sir, and in India, great expectations are the death of a man. The only way to survive here is to learn that sooner or later life makes fools of us all. We have no control over the future. What is to be will be." He gave the Maharaja a mischievous smirk. "Karma, I believe your people call it. No matter how hard we try to evade it, fate always comes full circle to kick you in the arse when you least expect it."

Sikander smiled, amused by the man's colorful grasp of Hindu philosophy. "What can you tell me about the Lieutenant's background?"

"I don't know much, beyond the fact that he is the only son of a famous father," Miller said, "and as such, an utterly rotten little brat." He shuddered, barely able to contain his aversion.

"Perhaps you have heard of his father, The Right Honorable Major General Ernest Bates KCB DSO."

"I cannot say I have."

"Oh, it was a bit before your time, I imagine. The elder Bates was a true despot, an empire builder in the mold of Clive and Roberts of Kandahar. He did very well out of the Afghan War. Made quite a fortune plundering the Hill Tribes and settled down to a life of utter dissipation in Staffordshire, I believe. But of course, it didn't last. He squandered away all his wealth at dice and card-play, until he was drowning in debt, with his creditors clamoring for his neck."

"What happened to him?" Sikander asked solemnly, although he had some notion of what the answer would be even as he asked the question.

Miller mimed putting a gun to his head and pulling the trigger. "He chose to take the gentleman's way out. Sadly, his demise left his wife responsible for his debts. The poor woman barely had enough left after paying off his creditors to buy their son a commission with his old regiment, and even then, all she could afford was a lowly Lieutenant's posting.

"Since his arrival in India, the boy hasn't done much to distinguish himself. He was at Calcutta for a while but they sent him here, to get rid of his complaining, I suspect. He's a sour, bilious sort, very superior, fancies himself to be Wellington reborn. To the best of my knowledge, he doesn't mix much with the local officers and spends most of his time with rather a bad crowd, a ragtag of errant young rankers who are far too fond of drinking and carousing and gambling at cockfights. If my sources are to be believed, he has managed to amass quite a considerable set of debts himself in his short time here in Rajpore. Like father like son, I guess." An expression of utter contempt flashed across his avuncular face. "I must confess, I have a low opinion of the Lieutenant. He's a tyro of the worst kind, and his only redeeming feature happens to be that he has the good sense to be married to an absolutely charming creature."

"Ah, this must be the young lady who caused all the trouble between the Major and Mr. Bates at the New Year's Ball."

"Yes, poor thing!" Miller sighed, "You know, I don't blame the Major for taking a pass at her. She really is quite lovely." He smiled, as if the thought of admitting that a woman was beautiful embarrassed him. "Utterly wasted on young Bates of course. The boy hasn't the class or the character to do her justice. Poor thing, she deserves a real man, someone like you, Your Majesty, a man to be reckoned with."

Sikander dismissed this blatant attempt at sycophancy with a snort.

"Tell me, in your opinion, is the Lieutenant the sort of man who is capable of doing another man any real harm?"

Miller stifled a giggle, shaking his head like he could not believe his ears. "Oh no, he's as weak as milk, that one. That is why I am sure he has no future here in India. This is a place for men with stern wills and strong stomachs who aren't afraid to take risks, but poor Bates, he has no backbone. He expects to be rewarded because of who his father was, but what he fails to realize is that in India reputations have to be earned. A man must make a name for himself, or that is the end of his career."

"So you don't think him capable of murder?"

"I...I really can't say, sir. We are all capable of murder, given the right circumstances."

Sikander gave him an inquiring look. "Even you, Mr. Miller? I always took you for a pacifist."

The plump Englishman shrugged, a shudder that quivered through him like a grand mal. "Who can tell, Your Highness? By nature, I am a peaceful man, but in my chest there beats the heart of my Celtic ancestors. Who knows, if I were pushed far enough even I might be compelled to do something drastic."

"But not Lieutenant Bates?"

"I think not, no. He is a poltroon, sir, and as such, I believe he lacks the determination to take a man's life."

Sikander clenched his jaw, trying not to let his frustration show. "But he had ample motive," he argued. "In front of more than five hundred witnesses, he made dire threats towards the Major, and the man was trying to seduce his wife."

Miller grunted. "Perhaps, I guess it is possible, although I doubt it." He lowered his voice once more. "From what I have heard, our friend the Lieutenant prefers his meat somewhat darker. In fact, he is quite a regular visitor to the journeyman's brothel in the old city."

Sikander did a double-take, genuinely surprised. "Really?"

"Indeed, sir. As it happens, the young lady he visits has offered on several occasions to sell me an affidavit that could definitely put an end to our friendly Lieutenant's career." Miller exhaled noisily. "Oh, his poor wife, to be trapped in such a loveless marriage! What a damnable waste!"

"What is her name, this paragon of female virtue with whom you seem so smitten?"

Miller grinned like a lovelorn schoolboy. "Grace," he intoned reverently, "her name is Grace." He laughed. "It is quite appropriate really, and suits her well. You will see what I mean when you meet with her."

"Grace Bates," Sikander said, grimacing. "Poor thing indeed! She sounds dreadful, like one of Miss Austen's caricatures."

"Oh, appearances can be deceiving, I assure you. The lovely Mrs. Bates may seem fragile when you first encounter her, as delicate as Sevres crystal, but personally, I believe the young lady is a lot stronger than she likes to let on. If anything, I think she is probably more capable of murder than her tiresome husband."

"What makes you say that?"

"I suspect the young lady has hidden depths, Your Highness. If you only knew her story." Miller's voice wavered, tremulous with sympathy. "She is an orphan, you see. She lost both her parents to consumption when she was just a wee bairn and spent her childhood in an orphanage. I imagine she would probably have ended up as a housemaid or a parson's wife, but the girl ran away and came out to India looking for a husband."

"Is that how she found Bates?"

"Yes, she was a sea bride. They both sailed out on the same ship, and poor man, he became utterly besotted with her. But why she agreed to marry him, I will never understand. I can only surmise she never realized that he was just as penniless as she was. But then you know what the bard said, 'Love is merely a madness'!"

Sikander listened to this story with great interest. Miller's account of the Lieutenant's wife intrigued him. The presswallah's description of Mrs. Bates certainly did not match up with the mental notion of the wilting violet that the Maharaja had conceived in his mind. Up to that moment, he had imagined a weak, easily malleable woman whom he had assumed to be a victim. But this portrait that Miller painted of her suggested quite the opposite, depicting her as a woman of some strength and determination, who had demonstrated the courage to come to India to make a life for herself.

"I would love to speak with Mrs. Bates," he said. "Perhaps you could arrange an introduction for me, Mr. Miller."

"I would if I could, Your Majesty," Miller said apologetically, "but we move in different circles. However, I am certain you could catch her at Mrs. Fitzgerald's garden party tomorrow afternoon."

Sikander groaned, an exclamation that made Miller grin. Mrs. Fitzgerald was the most determined and relentless social climber in Rajpore. Each month, she held the most abominable of garden parties on the second weekend, and made sure to invite the most influential people in Rajpore. Of course, she made it a point to send the Maharaja an invitation each time, but he always declined politely. The last thing he wanted was to spend a day at some parvenu's soiree being gawked at as if he were some sort of exotic peacock.

Sikander frowned. He had assumed the party would have been canceled given the Major's untimely demise, but it seemed that Mrs. Fitzgerald was determined to brazen it out and had decided to soldier on in spite of the unfortunate timing, a development which in hindsight was perfectly in character for a creature so tiresomely jejune.

Miller chose that moment to lean forward and say, "If it isn't too forward of me, might I give you some advice?"

"And what will this cost me?"

"Nothing at all," Miller responded, "This once, my services are for free. All I ask is a moment to say my piece."

"Very well! Go ahead."

Miller paused, as if he were carefully considering his words before articulating them into vocality. "I think it would be best for you if this once, you just let things lie. Walk away. Permit the dead to rest in peace. There is nothing to be gained here, no clean endings. And nobody will thank you for your efforts or your troubles, I promise you."

Sikander fixed him with a disapproving sneer. "Is that what you intend to do? Print the Major's death was a suicide, and leave it at that."

Miller returned his stare with an almost Buddhist composure. "Yes, if that is what they tell me to do." He winced. "Frankly, I don't know why you care. The Major will not be missed much, now will he?"

"That's just it, Mr. Miller. I don't care about the Major. What I care about is the truth."

Miller laughed. "The truth! Surely you can't be that naïve, sir. The truth is a mutable thing. It changes, depending to how you choose to interpret it."

"Perhaps you are right," Sikander said coldly, "but regardless, I still intend to track down the man responsible for the Major's death."

"And what are you going to do once you find the culprit?"

"Do, Mr. Miller!" Now it was Sikander's turn to snort with derision. "Why, I am not going to do anything. Justice is best left to the proper authorities. All that I intend to *do* is solve this mystery before anyone else can."

"But why?" Miller asked, as if he just couldn't understand Sikander's motivation. "Why is this so important to you? To the best of my knowledge, you despised Major Russell even more than I did."

"Yes," Sikander replied, "I disliked him. But that will not stop me from moving heaven and hell to find out who killed him." He smiled, a narrow twist of his lips that was almost a sneer. "You see, I cannot bear to leave things unfinished. It just isn't in my nature.

"Besides, my dear fellow, this is the most fun I have had in months!"

Chapter Fifteen

It was dark by the time Sikander returned to the Raj Vilas.

His disposition, which had been so exuberant that morning, had taken a decided turn toward the grim. The initial enthusiasm that had so consumed him when he embarked upon his investigation had long since dulled, replaced instead by a sense of fatigue, as if somehow his very bones had turned to rubber.

Bringing the Rolls to a halt, wearily, Sikander dismounted. For a change, rather than using the front door and having to put up with the usual ceremonies of foot-washing and abject prostration from his underlings, he decided to enter the palace through a private entrance at the back of the building, very near the stables.

The Raj Vilas was immense, a fully contained world in itself. Spread across twenty-six sprawling acres, it comprised two wings with a total of eighty-four rooms, amongst which were six throne rooms, five banquet halls, seven temples, a grand ballroom with a domed skylight made of Belgian crystal, a well-stocked armory, a viewing room and a theater with a full-sized stage, a heated swimming pool, a gymnasium, a greenhouse, a terrarium, an observatory with a modern telescope, and what was widely considered one of the finest libraries in India.

Sikander himself occupied the entire top floor of the west wing, an opulent suite of six rooms that were his private domain. To his surprise, as he entered his chambers, he found Charan Singh waiting for him, looking even gloomier than was usual.

"Forgive me, Huzoor," The big Sikh greeted Sikander with a grimace so despairing it was almost comical. "I warned him you had forbidden it, but Jardine Sahib would not listen. He has taken possession of the Major's body."

Sikander let out a voluble curse, and shot Charan Singh a deeply irate look.

"Blast it! That was the only evidence we had!"

Unable to meet his accusing eyes, the big Sikh stared fixedly down at the floor, too afraid to face his master's wrath.

"There was nothing I could do, Sahib. He had a warrant signed by the Magistrate."

Sikander bit his tongue, choking down the torrent of recriminations threatening to bubble forth. It would be only too easy to vent his rage on Charan Singh, but the truth was it wasn't his fault at all. Bloody Jardine! Sikander hissed with irritation. He could guess exactly what the bumbling oaf's next move would be. No doubt he intended to go after Jane to take her into custody, but Sikander was too smart to be outmaneuvered so easily, not without putting up some semblance of a fight.

"Go to the Imperial Hotel immediately," he commanded the big Sikh. "Take an escort of a dozen men. Once you get there, I want you to bring the English memsahib back here. Use a covered carriage, and under no circumstances are you to allow that silly donkey of a Superintendent anywhere near her, do you understand?"

Charan Singh's morose expression receded, his face lighting up with the faintest hint of self-satisfaction. "I foresaw that is what you would desire, Sahib. The memsahib is already here, in the east wing, under close guard. I took the liberty of fetching her earlier this evening."

Sikander breathed a sigh of relief. "Thank the heavens! Perhaps you aren't quite useless after all!"

Charan Singh responded with a mordant sniff, and made a great show of bowing to the Maharaja. "Will that be all, Sahib?"

"Yes, you may go," Sikander started to say, but then he recalled there was one other piece of business that had quite slipped his mind. "Wait! Tell me, have we had an invitation from that dreadful Mrs. Fitzgerald this month?"

"Indeed, we have. It arrived a week ago, requesting your presence at a soiree that is being held tomorrow afternoon. I took the liberty of having a rather curt refusal penned by one of the royal scribes, and intend to dispatch it in the morning."

"Cancel that," Sikander said. "Instead, send a message telling her that I will be pleased to attend."

This announcement elicited an effusive sneer from the old Sikh, his upper lip curling with such distaste that he looked like he had bitten into a particularly bitter lemon. "Surely you are not serious? It is…it is beneath your dignity, Your Majesty. Think of what people will say!"

Sikander rolled his eyes. In some ways, the old Sikh was an even bigger snob than he had ever been, and inevitably, that meant that he was always more concerned about the Maharaja's social standing than Sikander was himself. "Oh, for once, just do as you're told, you fat lump!"

Charan Singh responded to this rebuke with a rigid scowl. Muttering to himself, he left, but not before giving Sikander one last glare and then slamming the door shut behind him to illustrate his disapproval.

Once he was alone, Sikander shucked off his rumpled clothes, and changed into a pair of velvet trousers and a silk smoking jacket before making his way to the room directly beneath his suite. Once this had been part of his grandfather's sprawling harem, that secret world of the zenana hidden away from prying eyes, but upon taking the throne, Sikander had retired all of the Burra Maharaja's aging concubines with handsome pensions, and spent a small fortune to turn the vacated space into a haven dedicated to the pursuit of his diverse and often esoteric interests. Now, half the area was taken up by his library, a vast collection encompassing a truly bewildering array of subjects, as diverse as zoology and anthropology and of course, his passion, criminology. Next to the library was a fully equipped scientific laboratory and his private study, and beyond that, his favorite place in the palace, his music room.

It was to this sanctum that the Maharaja retreated. To his satisfaction, he saw that Charan Singh, as efficient as ever, had preceded him and foreseen to his needs. In one corner, atop a Venetian marble side-table that abutted his favorite wingback armchair, a golden salver awaited, upon which were arrayed a slender bottle of absinthe, a *pâté de verre* carafe of chilled water, a small bowl of granulated sugar, and a Murano aventurine goblet. Sikander sank into the welcome embrace of the armchair with a sigh. Reaching for the bottle, he proceeded to pour out a measure of absinthe into the accompanying glass. Then, he took a silver slotted spoon and gently scooped up a tiny amount of sugar, before placing it atop the rim of the glass, almost like a sieve, through which he then carefully distilled a generous quantity of chilled water. Finally, he stirred the resulting mixture quite vigorously until it turned whitish and opalescent. This was the *louche*, when absinthe bloomed and turned cloudy and released its hidden herbal flavors.

Eagerly, Sikander swept up the goblet and guzzled down its contents, groaning gladly. It was a habit he had picked up while in Paris, a preference for absinthe and its uniquely anise and fennel flavor. Most of his peers preferred port or champagne, but in France, absinthe was a way of life. There was a time set aside each day for what the Parisians called *l'heure verte*, the green hour, when everyone, from the wealthiest of the bourgeoisie to the poorest of laborers, flocked to bars and cabarets to indulge in its soporific delights. Of course, there were those who argued that it promoted criminal tendencies, not to mention epilepsy and tuberculosis, a belief that was fast gaining ground especially after the gruesome Lanfray murders, when a Swiss farmer had murdered his family and tried to take his own life while under the influence of absinthe, but Sikander scoffed at such stupidity. As far as he was concerned, it was humankind's inner bestiality that led to acts of such wanton savagery, and absinthe, like any other substance, whether it be opium or laudanum, was merely a much maligned catalyst.

As the thujone in the wormwood calmed his nerves, slowing his heartbeat, Sikander moved over to the piano that stood in one corner of the room, its boxy varnished shape gleaming like a chitinous insect. It was a work of art, a one-of-a-kind instrument made expressly for Sikander by Steinway and Sons, a concert grand wrought from the finest cherry wood, its case gilded with real gold and its feet carved into lion's paws, its sides painted to represent the Muse Terpsichore playing a harp while a quartet of dryads pranced through a sylvan glade.

Sikander sank down on the piano's bare bench, eschewing as always the comfort of a cushion. He spared a brief smile for the alabaster vase that sat atop a pedestal nearby, a handsome Bartolini from Tuscany, wrought of the purest white stone veined lightly with gold, within which were contained his mother's ashes. Raising the piano's lid, atop which the seal of Rajpore was enameled in iridescent mother of pearl, he stared down at the keys silently. Flexing his knuckles, he lowered one slim finger to run it hesitantly across the smooth expanse of ivory, as if he were caressing a long lost lover. A discordance of conflicting chords echoed through the air, dispelling the silence that had begun to weigh on him, the implacable dolor that seemed to saturate the closed confines of the room, making the air feel dense somehow, claustrophobic. A more poetic man might have said it sounded like the piano was groaning, glad at last to be played after all these months, and Sikander let out a sympathetic sigh of his own, closing his eyes, his expression nearing rhapsody.

Hunching forward, he began to play in earnest. The piece seemed to choose itself, not at all what Sikander had expected. He had wanted something soothing, Chopin, perhaps, or Mozart, but instead, what sprang forth was a complicated, difficult arrangement, Liszt's *Transcendental Etude no. 4*, the Mazeppa, a haunting progression of melancholic arpeggios and despairing octaves that framed his dour mood perfectly.

Sikander took no particular pride in it, but he played the piano with consummate skill, as effortlessly as a virtuoso. It was his mother who had taught him to play—he had learned his first few notes sitting atop her lap, and after her death, he refused to play for anyone but himself. Now, he only sought out the comfort of the piano when he was particularly confused. In a way, it was a refuge for him, a safe place to which he could retreat and find the peace of mind that he remembered having cherished as a child, that elusive sense of calm which he had struggled to find ever since the death of his parents and the inheritance of his title.

By now, a warm drowsiness had begun to seep into his body, that roseate glow only the finest absinthe could induce. A numbness gnawed at the extremity of his senses, a pleasant fugue where the sensation of time seemed to slow down, every moment, every perception becoming painfully palpable, as though he were alive and dead at the same time, somehow caught in a waking dream. Sikander exhaled wearily. As he had explained once to Charan Singh, the absinthe was a key, a device he used to try and unlock his subconscious mind. Coupled with the piano, it served to calm him, pacifying the innate turbulence of his mind, and with that serenity came a heightened ability to make sense of the intangible, to finally see those subliminal connections between dissonant incidents which his liminal mind had taken note of but was unable to comprehend. It would be easy to describe it as a trance, but that was less than accurate. It was more like an enhanced state of awareness, not unlike that mental state that the Japanese called *mono na aware*, which roughly translated meant "an empathy toward things," that rare condition when a man became aware of the impermanence of the world. This allowed his vestigial senses to come awake, giving him what could best be described as heightened perception.

Sikander had always been fascinated by such vivid examples of mysticism. Inevitably, every culture in the world had descriptions of some form of spiritual transcendence or the other, and he had spent much time making a study of a great many of these exotic systems—from what the Tibetans called *gom*, to what the Sufis described as *muraqaba*—meditative states that could be achieved only through intense concentration and careful introspection.

And of course, he had dabbled equally with artificial ways to achieve such heightened consciousness, such as the shamanic dream-walking practiced by the Navajo tribesmen of America, whose medicine men were known to imbibe peyote under whose narcotic spell it was said they could break free of the mortal realm and cross over to the realm of spirits.

It had taken Sikander years of devout experimentation to find the correct formula that worked for him. Instead of peyote, it had turned out that it was the combination of music and alcohol that was his catalyst, these two diverse strands, one corporeal and the other ethereal, coming together to induce a temporary detachment from the realm of the physical, granting a brief respite where he could seek refuge in the world of pure thought and find a few moments to organize the cluttered miasma of his mind into some semblance of structure.

Given the dissonance of his current mood, Sikander was only too happy to surrender himself to the music. It washed over him, drowning him in its euphony, until all that remained was a sense of disconnection, an emptiness of the kind the Buddhists called Sunyata. Beneath his supple fingers, it swelled towards a crescendo, and with each delicate note, Sikander thought he felt it, that sundering of mind from flesh and with it, that rare flicker of insight for which he had been waiting so patiently. A tremor shivered though his lean frame, not quite an epiphany, but something close enough. He thought he could see it at last, a faint but distinct pattern coalescing from the bewildering array of evidence and suppositions he had aggregated over the day's investigations.

Sadly, at that very moment, just as he was on the very brink of making sense of it all, a quiet knock on the door shattered his reverie. Abruptly, Sikander's eyes snapped open, widening with fury. His hands clenched into fists, causing the music to come jarring to a premature end, leaving one last, lonely note hanging crystalline in the air, as sharp as a shard of broken glass.

Clenching his teeth, he whirled around to see who it was that had dared to disturb him. To his surprise, it was Jane, standing framed in the doorway, watching him with a mixture of distrust and trepidation. She seemed as pale and insubstantial as a spectre, her slender figure hunched over, clad only in a thin, silken robe which she held tightly closed, her arms folded around her as if she were afraid she would fall to pieces if she loosened her grip.

Ever the gentleman, Sikander rose, stifling a frown. His servants knew better than to intrude upon his solitude, but Jane was a stranger, and he had no choice but to bear her presence, even though he would have preferred dearly to be alone.

"Forgive me, Madam, I did not mean to disturb you," he said stiffly, giving her the briefest of bows.

"Oh no!" Jane offered him a shy smile. "Please, don't stop on account of me." She waved one listless hand towards the piano. "That was quite beautiful. You play very well."

Ignoring this compliment, Sikander shut the piano's lid with a thwack so livid that it made Jane wince. "How can I help you, Madam?"

"I just wanted to thank you," she whispered, taking a half step back, as if he had managed to scare her with his brusqueness.

When he saw her fear, Sikander's rage leached away. "Please, come in," he said, by way of apology. "I was just about to have a drink. Won't you join me?"

Jane hesitated. He could see she was tempted to decline his invitation, but then, with an admirable grace, she took one tentative step into the room. Together, they moved over to occupy a pair of Victorian etoile armchairs that stood in one corner of the music room, on either side of a small ivory-topped pedestal table.

"Madam, shouldn't you be in bed?" Sikander inquired as Jane sank down wearily, as if this simplest of motions had taken every ounce of energy she could summon. "The doctor was quite insistent that you needed to rest."

"I find that I can't sleep, sir," Jane replied. "To tell the truth, I don't know if I will ever be able to sleep after what happened last night."

Sikander found himself empathizing with her. "In that case,

since I am unable to fall asleep either," he said gallantly, "let us enjoy a glass of champagne, shall we?"

He motioned toward the table, where a bottle of Pol Roger was waiting patiently in its silver bucket.

Jane blushed, and then, with a bashful smile, she leaned forward, perching on the end of the chair like a curious bird. "I have never tasted champagne before," she murmured.

"No?" Sikander exclaimed, unable to disguise his disbelief. "That is a shortfall that we must remedy with the utmost haste."

Picking up the bottle, he half-filled a tall silver flute, letting the bubbles fizz away before offering it to her. Jane gave him a suspicious look, as if she was unsure of what to do. Biting her lip, she took the glass doubtfully, her hand wavering as she brought it to her mouth for the most cautious of sips.

"Oh!" Her face crinkled into a grimace. "That's absolutely dreadful."

Sikander laughed. "Give it a moment, Madam, and try it again."

Jane raised one questioning brow, before doing as he urged. This time, rather than disgust, her eyes widened with pleasure. She let out a surprised little chuckle. "I have changed my mind," she said conspiratorially, "Champagne is marvelous." With those words, she downed the rest of the glass, gulping it down in one eager gasp. Sikander watched her bemusedly, leaning forward to immediately refill her glass, ignoring her abject refusals.

"I really shouldn't, sir. What if goes straight to my head?"

"Nonsense! Just think of it as overpriced grape juice."

Jane laughed and accepted the glass with a graceful tilt of her neck. "Might I ask you a question for a change, sir?"

"Of course," Sikander replied expansively, taking a sip of champagne himself.

"Have you made any progress in uncovering the Major's killer?"

The Maharaja hesitated, reluctant to reveal any details of his investigation, particularly given his spectacular lack of success in making any real headway, but as he peered at her over the rim of his glass, noting the brittleness of her manner, he sensed

Jane desperately needed some measure of reassurance to make her feel safe.

"Don't you worry, my dear! I will find the murderer, you can be certain of that."

Jane shuddered, as if to suggest that his words, while kind, had done little to encourage her.

"I am glad he is dead," she blurted out, before clapping one shocked hand to her lips. Her eyes widened with horror as she contemplated the magnitude of what she had just said. "God, does that make me a bad person?"

Sikander did not quite know how to answer this question. Her candor had managed to surprise him, and once again, he was struck by the uncanny feeling that he was missing something, that there was a deeper connection between the Major and Jane that he hadn't quite been able to apprehend.

"If you don't mind my asking, Madam, however did you happen to end up here in Rajpore? I mean, it is rare for one to find an Englishwoman in menial employment. Most often housekeeping positions are filled by Anglo-Indians or the like, at least in the Punjab."

Jane did not reply. Her face hardened, but not before a brief flicker of pain had managed to distort her features, just the slightest shadow of some half-forgotten tragedy that she had learned to conceal well enough but whose memory couldn't help but betray her just for the blink of an eye. Sikander recognized it all too well. He remembered having felt something familiar, an abject despair that had all but consumed him when he had lost Camille. *A man! There had been a man*, he thought. That was what had bought her to Rajpore.

"What was his name?" he asked gently.

Jane winced, as if he had struck her a physical blow.

"Michael," she said, "his name was Michael." Her eyes were bleak, brimming with pain, as if it hurt her just to think of the past, much less articulate it into words. "He was tall and very shy, and…"

Her voice caught in her throat, and she gave the Maharaja a lugubrious smile. "Oh, for the life of me, I cannot remember what he was like at all."

Sikander knew exactly what she meant. There were times he could barely summon up more than a shadow of a memory of Camille, a vague suggestion of laughing eyes and an elfin smile, as if she had become little more than an insubstantial ghost. But the pain, that worn ache in his heart whenever he thought of her, it was still as palpable for him as the day that she had died.

"Why don't you start at the beginning?" He suggested.

Jane gathered her breath, and let out a vast sigh. "I never knew my father. He departed before I came into this world, and my mother followed soon after. My poor mother, what a fragile, brittle thing she was!" Jane pursed her lips sadly. "She chose to take her own life when I was just a few months old, leaving me orphaned.

"Poison," she said blankly. "Just like the Major. Isn't that curious?" Her voice wavered, and she gritted her teeth, gathering her strength before continuing. "I was fortunate enough to be raised by my uncle. He was unmarried, a missionary with no children, but he reared me as if I was his own and ensured that I had a fine education. A wonderful man, my Uncle Roderick, with a truly kind soul. He was an abolitionist, and traveled frequently to Africa to bring the word of our Lord to the wild Bushmen of the Namib.

"Have you ever been to Africa, Your Highness?" she asked. Sikander nodded no, and Jane gave him a shy smile, a grin of such genuine pleasure that he felt a pang of unanticipated desire. "It is a wonderful place. A land of great and simple joy, of such potent and miraculous mysticism that you find yourself humbled time and again, the sort of place that makes you truly glad to be alive.

"Is it strange then that I felt more at home on the veldt surrounded by the wilderness than I ever did in England, mingling with boys my age?" She flinched, a forlorn little twist of her mouth. "I suppose there was something wrong with me, but I never felt the desire to marry, although there were a few offers. And my uncle, he was kind enough to leave the choice to me, but after what had happened to my parents..." She shrugged, letting her voice taper away to a choked murmur. "Sadly, my uncle passed when I was twenty-five, but not before he had managed to secure a position for me as a governess for a gentleman in London who had two young daughters who required instruction. And that was where I met Michael, just a few weeks after my twenty-ninth birthday."

After her earlier reticence, she seemed glad, almost eager to tell her story, as though she had been waiting for a chance to unburden herself for years.

"He was a clerk with my employer's shipping company, and I met him only once. But sometimes even one encounter is enough, particularly when you meet the person who is made just for you, someone who fits with you perfectly. It's ironic, really. I spent my youth being exceedingly cynical, scoffing at people who talked of love, and then, in one fell swoop, when I saw Michael..."

She glanced at Sikander hopefully.

"Do you know what I mean, Your Majesty? Have you ever had someone like that?"

Sikander nodded imperceptibly. "Once, a long time ago," he murmured, "I did, for a very brief time."

"What happened to her?"

"She died, Madam," he said, with great finality, as if to declare he had no further desire to discuss the matter with her, or anyone else

Jane gave him a sad look of commiseration, before resuming her story. "Then you know exactly how I felt, sir. I had given up on ever meeting someone like Michael, but when he began to court me, it was like a fairy tale had come to life, and I was its heroine. He swept me away. It began with him asking permission to correspond with me, a request I accepted warily enough, but then those letters, oh, those letters, how they made my heart leap each time I received them!

"It wasn't long before Michael and I came to care for each other deeply. Even then, I was so surprised when he asked for my hand. I had always considered myself too old for him; I was nearing thirty, for God's sake, almost an old spinster, and I had no dowry to speak of. And so, I refused him. But he was so persistent, the dear, sweet boy. He kept pestering me, time after time, until, in spite of my fears, I finally decided to accept his proposal."

"What went wrong?"

"Oh, it was fate, I guess. Fate always puts an end to dreams, doesn't it?" She shook her head, stiff with sorrow.

"Michael had our future together all planned out. He was to travel out to Calcutta where he had managed to secure a sinecure with an indigo trader, and I was to join him after some months, once he had made the requisite arrangements for us to be wed. After his departure, I waited and waited for almost seven months for him to send for me, but instead, one day the letters just stopped. Naturally, when I did not hear from him, I started to worry and decided to follow him out to India. My employer, while sad to see me leave his service, was kind enough to arrange passage for me to come out to Calcutta. Why, he even provided me with a modest dowry, just a few pounds, but it was a princely gift for someone as impoverished as myself, a veritable fortune."

She shivered; no doubt recalling the rigors of the journey out, those dreadful weeks spent sweltering through the tropics in a tiny cabin in steerage, being dreadfully seasick each time the ship wallowed through the waves.

"When I got to India…" she swallowed a groan, the strength to speak suddenly deserting her.

"Let me guess," Sikander said softly, finishing her sentence for her. "You found that he had married someone else."

Jane nodded dully, as mechanical as an automaton. "Yes, some grasping little ninny he met here. She was the nineteen-year-old niece of the planter with whom he was employed. He had jilted me for her without a second thought, and when… when I confronted him, he laughed at me."

Her slender frame shook with a barely repressed outrage that was still potent even after the time that had passed. "After all his promises, all his declarations of undying affection, the only apology he was willing to make was the offer to pay my passage back to England if I left quietly, without making a scandal."

"You could have taken him up on his offer," The Maharaja countered, "gone back and started anew. Perhaps found another suitor."

But even as he said those words, he knew that she could never have done something like that. She was too proud. Even though he had spent barely a few minutes with Jane, he could not imagine her playing the broken-hearted lover, or the tragic spinster. No, just like Helene, she was a survivor, the sort of person who had to make her own way in the world, even if it meant having to work as a servant.

"There was nothing for me back in England." Jane's face sagged with barely subdued anguish, confirming his suspicions, as if she could tell exactly what was going through his mind. "Besides, I had felt a higher calling."

"You mean to say…?"

"Yes," she intoned reverently. "I decided I would give myself up to the service of the Lord and take the most solemn of vows. I was lucky enough to find a place with the Institute of the Blessed Virgin Mary. You may know us by our common name, the Sisters of Loreto."

Sikander nodded, recognizing the name. They were an old order known particularly for their fine English-language schools for girls.

"Once I had completed my novitiate, I was sent out to teach, first at Darjeeling and then at Tara Hall in Simla, where I resided until last year, when I was selected to accompany a group of sisters here to Rajpore to attempt to establish a parish school."

Sikander recalled the mission. The Sisters had petitioned Ismail Bhakht to fund an English school for orphans in Rajpore, but the proposal had floundered when the Major had interfered, as usual, and insisted the school be only for white children, as a result of which the blessed sisters had been forced to return to Simla empty-handed. *All except Jane it seemed*, he thought, *who had decided to break with her vows and stay on in Rajpore.*

"What happened to make you decide to leave the convent?"

Once again, Jane seemed reluctant to answer him. Instead, she blushed, unconsciously beginning to rub at her arm, an instinctively habitual gesture, kneading the flesh of her wrist with one calloused thumb. Sikander's eyes could not help but be drawn to this absent-minded motion. He noticed an old scar on her forearm, a jagged cicatrice that curled around her bony wrist like a snake devouring its own tail, and suddenly, it became clear to him why she had left the Church. She would have had no other choice if she had tried to take her own life. The Catholics frowned mightily upon attempted suicide, and they would have forced her to leave.

"Let us just say the Mother Superior suggested I would be happier elsewhere pursuing another vocation," she said, noticing the direction of his gaze. Self-consciously, she pulled down the sleeves of the nightgown to hide her scars. "They felt I was not suited for the cloistered life. Conveniently enough, while we were here in Rajpore, I was lucky enough to be apprised of the Major's need for a housekeeper, and when I met with him, he offered me the position very readily. Personally, I thought Rajpore would be a pleasant change, and thus I accepted his offer. I had nothing to go back to really. I had grown weary of teaching, and Calcutta reminded me too much of Michael. As for England, well, all that was left of England was a faint and half-forgotten dream."

With that avowal, she lapsed into a pensive silence. Sikander sat back and considered Jane's story. It seemed believable enough, but his inner cynic refused to be silenced, thinking that somehow it was half-hearted, filled with far too many holes. His earlier intuition that there was far more to her relationship with Major Russell than she was admitting now returned ten-fold. Could their involvement have been more intimate than that of an employer and a housekeeper? Or was this a case of unrequited affection? It was an old enough story—a broken-hearted spinster with no prospects fastens onto to an aging and lonely bachelor like a limpet, with the intent to wed him. Yes, that made far more sense. To the untrained eye, Jane did not seem the cold, grasping sort, but Sikander could tell there were hidden depths beneath the hapless facade, a ruthless reserve, a streak of steel beneath her fragile exterior.

Sadly, before he could explore these suspicions in any depth, Jane raised one weary hand to rub at her temples, stifling a yawn.

"Forgive me, Madam," Sikander apologized, reminded that she was unwell. "I did not mean to tire you unduly. Perhaps it would be best if you were to retire for the night."

Jane shook her head. "Oh no, Your Majesty, this exchange has been most therapeutic. I was feeling exceedingly melancholic, but speaking to you has quite lifted my spirits."

"I am glad to be of service."

She gave him a hopeful smile. "If I may, can I beg one more favor, a minor imposition?" Eagerly, she beckoned toward the piano. "Play me something happy...Please!"

Sikander very nearly refused. It had been years since he had played for anyone but himself, but as he glanced at Jane, he felt an inexplicable affinity towards her, an empathy which made him decide to break from habit. Wordlessly, he crossed to the piano. Closing his eyes, he began to play, a simple but extraordinarily moving piece that had been one of his mother's favorites, Chopin's *Nocturne in C Minor*. He knew it so well it came to him almost effortlessly, his fingers dancing back and forth as if they had a life of their own.

As always, he lost himself in the ebb and fall of the chords, until Jane chose to let out a soft moan. His eyes snapped open, Chopin's ephemeral spell broken, to find that she had come to stand uncomfortably near him, poised just behind his seated form, so close in proximity that he could smell the soap on her skin, a fresh, almost virginal odor that made his stomach seize up in knots.

"That was breathtaking," she murmured, arching her slender neck as gracefully as a swan. That was when he noticed the bruises, a ring of old welts, already blue, surrounding her slim neck like a macabre necklace, as if she had been choked recently.

"Did the Major do that to you?" Sikander gasped, shocked.

Even as he whispered those words, a shudder wracked through Jane's slender frame. Her fingers scrabbled desperately at her robe, plucking at its collar, eager to hide her wounds from sight. Abruptly, something seemed to splinter inside her, a vital mechanism coming awry, and to his chagrin, she began to weep, a brittle paroxysm so inexorable that it seemed as if she were having a breakdown.

Sikander found himself rendered entirely helpless by such an effusive display of grief. He would have liked to reach out to try and comfort her, but his dislike of physical contact made him cringe with embarrassment. Instead, he clenched his fists, digging his nails into his palms so hard he thought his fingers would snap apart.

"Come on," he said, trying his best to seem diffident, "let us go and have another drink, shall we? That should make you feel better."

Jane's only reply was a groan. "Oh, what's the point of it? What have I left to live for?"

"That's the thing about life, my dear," Sikander said, giving her a tragic smile. "Just when you least expect it, something interesting always manages to turn up."

Chapter Sixteen

In spite of Sikander's best efforts to cheer her up, Jane's mood remained persistently dolorous.

He tried in vain to convince her to accept another glass of champagne, hoping it might dispel the morbid humors that seemed to have her in their grip, but she declined, begging instead to be allowed to retire for the night. Ever the gentleman, Sikander found that, in spite of his fears for her well-being, he really had no choice but to oblige. However, he did insist on escorting her up to her suite personally, paying no heed to her objections.

Once he had ensured that she was settled in comfortably, he bid her good night, and returned to his study, where he helped himself to a fresh draught of absinthe. It had been his hope to try and rekindle that transcendent state of clarity to which had been so close before Jane had intruded upon his contemplations, but this time around, regrettably, the rhapsody proved elusive. One glass became two, and two four. Slowly, the level of spirit inside the bottle dwindled, but still the answers he so fervently desired continued to elude him.

Finally, Sikander could bear it no longer. His patience at an end, he staggered to his feet and tugged sharply at a nearby bell-pull to summon Charan Singh.

The Sikh took some time to appear, and when he did show up, his turban was in disarray, his beard sticking up in untidy clumps.

"It is the middle of the night, Sahib," he said with weary indignation. "Why aren't you in bed, like a normal person?"

"Stop complaining, you dozy old fool, and have a carriage made ready. Nothing ostentatious, just a one-horse calash, and I will not be requiring a driver. And before you insist, no honor guard either. I am going incognito," he explained with a suggestive wink. "Today, I am not the Maharaja of Rajpore. I am just another punter looking for a bit of a good time, that's all. No tamasha and no fuss, do you understand?"

"And pray tell, Sahib," Charan Singh retorted with a scornful sneer, "where exactly is it you are intending to go at this ungodly hour?"

"As it happens, my good man," Sikander replied, unfazed by the Sikh's priggishness, "I have decided to pay a visit to Mrs. Ponsonby."

Charan Singh let out a mortified gasp. Most everyone in Rajpore had heard of the infamous Mrs. Ponsonby, although the majority of well-mannered people preferred to pretend that they had not. She was, for lack of a better term, the city's most renowned procuress, as much of a Rajpore institution as Ismail Chacha himself. Predictably, this announcement that Sikander intended to call upon such a notorious madam left Charan Singh, who was as straitlaced as a Brahmin, utterly perturbed, causing his bushy eyebrows to rise upwards so far that they seemed to disappear entirely, crawling under the hem of his turban in barely restrained shame.

"It is not proper for you to patronize an establishment of such low repute," he said primly. "If it is female companionship you desire, I can make more discreet arrangements."

Sikander interrupted him in mid-rebuke with a curt wave of one hand. "Enough! Just go and get my carriage ready."

As he had expected, Charan Singh chose to illustrate his disapproval by taking an abominably long time to carry out this simplest of chores. More than an hour trickled by before suitable transportation was ready, an expanse of time which Sikander spent pacing back and forth restlessly, halfway to wearing a hole in the Abusson carpet underfoot. In the end, it was nearing dawn by the time he finally managed to embark from the killa, not in an unremarkable calash as he had requested but rather atop a sleek two-horse phaeton so conspicuous that it rather defeated any hope he harbored of maintaining anonymity.

Overhead, the first frigid rays of daylight had just begun to discolor the gloom of night. Rather than taking the Hathi Darwaza, the Maharaja decided to take the Kashmiri gate to the east, and skirt the native town altogether, thus avoiding the rush of the early morning vegetable mandi. His destination was some five kilometers distant, near the northern edge of the Silent Lake, a handsome estate whose boundaries were lined by a towering stone wall. Beyond this imposing fortification, which could only be entered through a massive twelve-foot iron gate topped with wickedly curved spikes as sharp as scimitars, a winding gravel driveway led to an imposing Georgian mansion that would have been more at home in Lincolnshire than amidst the desolate backwoods of Rajpore.

From a distance, Mrs. Ponsonby's Academy seemed to be the residence perhaps of a prosperous boxwallah with more money than taste. The truth was somewhat more picturesque. The academy was, for lack of a better phrase, Rajpore's most exclusive brothel. Although to call it a mere brothel, Sikander thought with a wry smirk, was to do it a grave disservice. There were cathouses aplenty in the red light district that bordered the Cantonment, from the cheapest chaklas frequented by laborers and sepoys who fulfilled their carnal itches with hennaed, syphilitic one-anna whores in the shadows so that they did not have to gaze upon each others' weary faces, to the Anglo-Indian bordello near the Railway Station where visiting boxwallahs stopped for a few moments of carnal pleasure with mulatto courtesans well versed in the ways of love. But Mrs. Ponsonby's was special, its fame so widespread that patrons came from as far away as Lahore to enjoy the rare treasures it offered. Compared to the lowly tawaifkhanas of the old city, it was a veritable palace of pleasure, Elysium, Swarga, and Jannat all rolled into one, populated only by goddesses so delectable they put celestial houris to shame, and from whose seductive eyes a single wink could break a man's heart, not to mention his bank account.

What made the academy so singularly irresistible? It was the fact that Mrs. Ponsonby's was the only place north of Bombay where a man could go in search of that rarest of things in British India, the brief and fleeting taste of pearlescent white flesh for sale. Here, for the right price, the eager angler could find English girls who had come to India searching for fortunes only to have their hopes dashed, and green-eyed Irish widows whose husbands had died fighting the Boers, tall Russians who had strayed south of the border and French runaways from Chandernagore, silver-skinned Circassians from Armenia and pale Jewesses from Damascus and, if rumor was to be believed, even a sloe-eyed courtesan from the Middle Kingdom, with feet as tiny as rosebuds.

All these exotic creatures had one thing in common—they were all exceedingly exquisite and excessively expensive. In Madame Ponsonby's stable, there wasn't a single flower whose attentions could be purchased for less than fifty guineas, a veritable fortune to most of India's citizenry.

As a result, her clientele was very, very exclusive. There were no journeymen at the academy, no boxwallahs looking for a quick romp, only the crème de la crème of British India, lured by the promise of white flesh, coming in eager droves to sample the wares on offer and only too willing to pay whatever exorbitant prices Mrs. Ponsonby chose to charge.

Amongst her regulars, she counted no less than six Maharajas, a dozen peers of the Empire, and even an ex-Viceroy, not to mention the assortment of well-heeled zamindars who saved for years to earn a single night in the arms of any of her wards. Why, Sikander's own grandfather, the Burra Maharaja, had been one of the place's most fervent patrons, and it was right here that he had come to an unseemly end, suffering a ruptured ventricle while enjoying the company of a trio of acrobats from Rangoon.

It was to the portals of this fabled institution that Sikander directed the phaeton, bringing it rattling to a halt outside the front foyer, a pillared portico with ornate cornices that was vaguely Greek in origin by way of Calcutta Revivalist. The durban, a shaven-headed wrestler by the looks of him, came scurrying forward, no doubt to tell him to move along. Sikander leaped down, flinging the reins at him with indolent nonchalance.

"Keep it nearby," he said, tipping the man with a handful of coins he pulled randomly from one pocket. "I will be back shortly."

It must have been a handsome gratuity indeed, because the durban almost fell over in his haste to reverse direction so that he could hold open the door for Sikander.

Inside, the Maharaja found himself amidst a parlor so sumptuous it would have put most palaces to shame. Everywhere he turned, he was greeted by an excess of brocade and tuile and gilt, an inundation of French Baroque so garish it was almost blinding. On the left, a gilded arch bordered by ornate pilasters revealed a sweeping mahogany staircase that led upwards to the upper floors. On the right, another arch led to a vast banquet room, teeming with gentlemen gamblers come to try their luck at the multitude of games on offer. Of course, the dog races or cockfights which were so popular in the Cantonment were not to be seen here. No, Mrs. Ponsonby only offered the most refined games of chance, from the long standing *Vingt-et-un* table where fortunes were won and lost with each hand, to baccarat and hazard, and even that most American of pastimes, five-card stud.

Amidst this hubbub, at strategic positions around the banquet room, arrayed so as to always arrest the eye line, a bevy of beautiful women waited, clad scantily enough to cause a moral man heartburn. Sikander spared barely a glance for the exquisite favors on offer. He knew only too well, that beautiful as these specimens were, they were only second-string courtesans. The real beauties entertained their patrons upstairs, accepting visitors by appointment only in their first-floor boudoirs, while on the second floor, the most celebrated of Rajpore's concubines resided in absolute privacy, kept in regal style in richly appointed suites paid for by their lovers, like birds of paradise locked away in velvet-lined cages.

As Sikander paused for a moment, trying to get his bearings straight, the majordomo of the house, an impeccably dressed old South-Indian with skin as tough as leather, sidled up.

"May I help you?" He inquired, eyeing Sikander's dusty clothes down the not-inconsiderable length of his beaky nose.

How typical! Sikander thought with a wry grin, Mrs. Ponsonby's was so posh that even the servants had a sense of jaded entitlement, an observation which would ordinarily have rankled him if he hadn't been having quite so much fun.

"I am here to see Madame Krasnivaya," he said.

"That is not possible," the majordomo started to object, but Sikander cut him off with a grin.

"Let's not do this song and dance, shall we? Surely you recognize me?"

The man sniffed frostily, choosing to delay just a whisker too long before offering him a curt bow.

"Of course," he said. "If you would care to follow me."

Pivoting on his heels as gracefully as a dancer, the majordomo ushered Sikander toward a side door so that the Maharaja would not have to walk through the parlor and be subjected to the eyes of lesser guests. Sikander trailed after him at a dilatory pace, his eyes widening as a particularly buxom young blonde dressed only in a French maid's outfit blew him a very suggestive kiss. He offered her a wink as the majordomo carefully unlocked the door and urged him through it like a sheepdog herding a recalcitrant sheep, before pausing to ensure it was securely bolted once more behind them.

Beyond, a wrought-iron staircase spiraled up to the second floor, where the majordomo directed the Maharaja down a narrow corridor, leading him past a sequence of apartments from within which the muffled sounds of pleasure emanated, muted but still audible enough to make Sikander turn positively scarlet. At the end of this passageway, they came to a stop before a nondescript-looking door painted a dull white. Rather than waiting to be announced by the majordomo, whose solicitousness was starting to aggravate his nerves, the Maharaja shoved the old man aside and barged straight in. He found himself standing in a small, cramped room that seemed more like a company clerk's office than the private chambers of Rajpore's most notorious madam. He had been expecting gauzy curtains and brocade walls, with overstuffed divans everywhere within swooning distance, like a Turkish harem, but instead Sikander was greeted by bare floors and a drab utilitarian row of shelves stacked high with musty ledgers.

At the center of the room, perched in a tall wicker-backed wheelchair, an ancient woman was engaged in heated negotiations with an oily looking Englishman, ostensibly making the final touches to a transaction acquiring the services of a gamine courtesan who stood close by, a pert-nosed little filly he guessed was probably a Slav, judging by her cheekbones.

However, the moment Sikander made his dramatic entry, the old woman's wrinkled face broke into a smile and she paused in mid-sentence, dismissing the Englishman with one flick of her hand.

"Come back later," she said. "Something more important has just turned up."

The Englishman started to object, but one poisonous look from the madam was quite enough to quash his complaints and send him scurrying for the door, the girl following close behind, but not before pausing long enough to favor Sikander with a very saucy grin.

The Maharaja smiled back appreciatively, admiring her beauty for what it was, that effortless charm of innocence untainted by the hardship of time. With a sigh, he shook his head and sank into the chair so recently vacated by the Englishman.

"They seem to grow younger and younger, don't they?"

Madame Krasnivaya let out a cackle of delight.

"Why, bless my lonely heart! I never thought I would see the day when such a celebrated lothario such as yourself would visit my humble establishment. What brings you to us, your Highness? Have you lost your fabled touch?"

Sikander refused to respond to this jibe. Instead, he let his eyes play across the ravages of the old hag's features. The name was a *nom de guerre*, of course. He knew enough of Russian to know that Krasnivaya meant beautiful, a sobriquet which seemed almost ironic when applied to the withered creature who sat before him. She was very tiny, just over four and a half feet tall, not a midget or a dwarf, but somehow a woman in miniature, perfectly formed, from her hands and feet to her face, exactly two thirds the size of most women. Sikander had read once that there were tribes near the far reaches of the Caspian Sea who never grew taller than five feet high, and he guessed she hailed from one of those remote valleys, beyond the Caucasus Mountains. She made up for this lack of height however with an immensity of girth. Madame Krasnivaya was almost as perfectly round as a ball, with stubby little legs and knees so weakened by gout that she could barely walk, which explained the wheelchair.

As Sikander studied her, she gave him a coy smile, and he saw that her teeth had long since rotted and fallen out, to be replaced by dentures made from the purest gold which gleamed and glinted blindingly in the gloom of the room's gas lamps. Looking at her, he guessed she could have been anywhere between seventy and eighty, but he could not be sure. Even though her back was bent and her skin as desiccated as parchment, her face was still youthful, caked heavily with powder to give her a somewhat incongruous appearance, which was only made even more ludicrous by the preposterous wigs she liked to favor. In this case, it was an enormous construction of tiered curls so bulbous that it would have given Marie Antoinette nightmares. And if that wasn't striking enough, she wore a large *mouche* pasted on one wrinkled cheek just beside her lip, a taffeta *la coquette* shaped like a shiny heart.

The Maharaja spared a moment to meditate on what he knew of her history. If rumor was correct, she had been born in Georgia, one of the descendants of ancient Colchis. As the story went, an Amur Cossack, one of the Tsar's boyars who had been mapping the far reaches of Transcaucasia, had come across her one day, and had been so enchanted by her beauty that he had carried her away to become his wife. But then the Crimean War had come, and the Cossack had died in a hail of gunfire at Chernaya, leaving her to be sold for three guineas to an English officer named Lieutenant Ponsonby, who had brought her to Rajpore with him, only to die four years later of the bloody flux.

With his death, Madame Krasnivaya found herself widowed for the second time, stranded far from her homeland, with no means of support other than her husband's meager military pension. Most of the people who knew her had expected her to seduce a boxwallah and become his mistress, or perhaps sink her claws into some naïve officer and marry him next, but Madame Krasnivaya had surprised everyone. Instead of taking another husband, she had decided to gather together a troupe of the most beautiful whores she could find, and go into business for herself. Thus Mrs. Ponsonby's Academy had been born.

"As it happens," Sikander said, reciprocating her smile with one of his own, "I have come to see you, Madame, not your wards."

"Come to see me!" Madame Krasnivaya's rheumy eyes lit up, twinkling with delight. "How very flattering, although I fear I am too much woman for even a strapping young buck such as yourself…!"

Sikander feigned a small laugh, pretending to be amused by her flirtatiousness. "I do believe you're right. Isn't it fortunate then that I am here only to speak with you?"

As he made that declaration, the old woman's demeanor changed. The playfulness vanished, replaced by suspicion, a canny wariness. "Speaking with me is an even more expensive proposition than the other services we offer."

Sikander raised one acerbic eyebrow. "I am sure, Madame, that whatever the price may be, I can afford it."

"And why would I talk to you? My clients pay me well for maintaining their confidentiality."

"It would be sad, Madame, if you were forced to shut down this establishment and leave Rajpore." Sikander fixed her with a cold stare. "I am sure it would be exceedingly difficult, having to start again, particularly given your age."

"Are you threatening me?" Her eyes flashed fire.

"Indeed," Sikander replied, unflappable, "I most certainly am."

Madame Krasnivaya held his gaze for a long time, as if trying to test his resolve, to see who would be the first to blink. A lesser man might have found this exhibition intimidating, but Sikander remained entirely unmoved. It was quite obviously a display designed expressly to get a rise out of her visitors, and he refused to give her the satisfaction of letting her see that she had managed to perturb him in the slightest.

Finally, after what felt like hours, she nodded, her wrinkled features settling into a well-practiced frown. "Very well, what is it you wish to speak of?"

"The Resident of Rajpore, Madame. I believe he was a patron of your fine...academy."

At this mention of Major Russell, something seemed to flash across the old woman's face, a hint of nervousness so palpable that it aroused Sikander's curiosity.

"Indeed he was. He visited us every few months, as regularly as clockwork." A grimace played across her desiccated lips." And he had very particular and very expensive needs."

"What exactly do you mean, Madame?" Sikander straightened up, intrigued by the faint tone of disapproval in her voice. Whatever the Major's interests had been, they had to be exceedingly depraved to have managed to offend someone who had seen as much immorality in her time as Madame Krasnivaya.

The old woman let out a faint sigh, and fanned herself with one withered hand. "Well, for one thing, he insisted on my complete discretion, that I close my doors to my regular patrons whenever he chose to call on us. For another, he desired only young girls, the younger the better, and never the same girl twice."

"Is that all?" Sikander felt rather disappointed. He had expected something particularly salacious, given Madame Krasnivaya's obvious reluctance to discuss the Major's private affairs. While his proclivity for young girls was somewhat shocking, he knew only too well that such wickedness was all too common amongst men of a certain age, who saw the conquest of childish virtue as a way to regain some of the fervor of the youth that they had themselves left far behind.

"Not quite." She paused, seemingly struggling to find the right words. "The Major was, for lack of a better phrase, a man with a marked excess of anger."

"Really?" Sikander leaned forward, his interest piqued once more. "Do you mean to suggest he was the sort of man who enjoyed inflicting pain?"

The old Russian nodded, her face stiffening with barely repressed revulsion. "He was a great believer in the teachings of the Marquis de Sade." Her bony shoulders shuddered. "He liked to beat my girls, often with a horsewhip, until they bled."

Sikander frowned, taken aback. He had expected some hint of scandal, but this…it was just too prurient to swallow. Madame Krasnivaya had managed to surprise him, which was not an easy thing to do. Sikander prided himself on being a man of the world, familiar with many strange notions and outlandish habits that most ordinary people would have found deplorable, even degenerate, but the thought of the straitlaced Major secretly being a sadist—that was something he had not, could not have envisioned, not in a hundred years.

Though his mind was racing frantically, Sikander made an effort to maintain his outward appearance of calm. Tenting his fingers beneath his chin, he made himself sit back. "I was not aware that your establishment offered such exotic services."

"As a rule, we do not, but for the Major, I was forced to make an exception." Madame Krasnivaya bared her gilded incisors, as if to convey her immense dislike of the man. "At first, I suggested he take his patronage elsewhere. There is a woman in the old city, I believe, who does not care what is done to her girls. I recommended he try her establishment, but he insisted. He was very particular about discretion, and as you know only too well, there is no discretion in the native town. Frankly, I think he was afraid of getting caught in a scandal."

Sikander nodded. It made ample sense. The Major had obviously been a cautious man, given that he had managed to keep his proclivities hidden so far, and undoubtedly he was quite aware that if even a whiff of his demented passions was to get out, the ensuing scandal would have been the end of his career for once and for all.

"I had no choice, I assure you," she continued. "He was a powerful man, and I could not afford to get on his bad side. Besides, he paid us exceedingly well to accommodate his exotic preferences, and so, I let him indulge his passions on the mountain girls. They are as strong as oxen, and really, a little pain never hurt anyone, did it? I never allowed him near the white girls, of course. They are much too valuable."

A swirl of rage unfurled inside Sikander like a red flag. It infuriated him to no end to hear the old crone to speak of people with such cold disdain, as if they were little more than objects to be used and thrown away. Through a great force of will, he held his tongue in cheek, knowing he could not afford to alienate Madame Krasnivaya, not until she gave him what he needed.

"When was the last time he visited you, Madame?"

"Oh, about four months ago. I was willing to accommodate him, in spite of his special requests, until then."

"What happened to change your mind?"

The old woman did not reply at first, watching him sullenly, as if she did not trust him. Sikander waited her out patiently, until she let out a feeble sigh, and said, "I had a new girl, a pretty little thing, as fresh as a flower just in bloom. The sick bastard almost killed her. He broke her cheekbones and blinded one of her eyes." She clucked her tongue insincerely. "Poor thing, she will never be beautiful again."

Sikander shot her a disgusted glare, but it may as well have been wasted on the old woman, who barely even noticed.

"Why didn't you go to the police, Madame?"

"As a matter of fact, I did. I went to see the English Superintendent, the one who sweats too much and smells terrible. I knew him vaguely, from past experience, so I thought he would help me. He visited us occasionally, you see, and I always let him take his pleasure on the house." She touched her nose suggestively. "Of course, none of my young ladies were particularly eager to please him. It seems the fat man is the victim of God's most unfortunate injustice."

She winked one rheumy eye, and held up her finger and thumb exactly an inch apart, as if to suggest that Mr. Jardine was somewhat under-endowed, a gesture which caused Sikander to smirk, in spite of his mounting outrage.

"Didn't the fat man take any action?"

"Oh no, nothing at all. He heard me out, and then told me to pay the girl off and forget anything had ever happened, if I knew what was best for me."

Sikander's lips thinned, compressing until they were almost invisible. He had already had a fleeting prescience that he would receive just such an answer, that Jardine had hushed it all up, but in spite of his innate cynicism, some part of him had hoped that would not be the case. He had always believed that Jardine, in spite of his pungency and pugnacity, was ultimately an honest man, but now it was more than apparent that he was just as corrupt as the rest of the bloody Angrez.

"I banned the Major, of course, from making any further visits to us. Honestly, that was the best I could do."

"How did he react to such a restriction?"

"Oh, he was not pleased at all. He threatened to have me shut down, and stormed out of here, ranting like a madman."

"Weren't you afraid he would follow through with that threat?"

She laughed, a shrill birdlike twitter. "Afraid? Of that fool? I think not. I have faced down far more dangerous men than him. Besides, what can he do to me? I am an old woman, my boy. I have lived for far too long and seen far too much to be scared of an upstart like him."

"What about the girl? What happened to her?"

"I paid for her hospital bills, of course, to have a doctor stitch her up, for all the good it did. Sadly, the Major had ruined her for the business, so I gave the poor child some money and sent her to Hyderabad to an acquaintance of mine who serves the Nizam. I thought he could teach her how to be a housemaid, and that would be the end of it."

"But it wasn't?"

"No," Madame Krasnivaya shook her head sadly. "A few weeks later, a boy showed up looking for her."

"Her lover..?"

"Her brother!" she exclaimed with a snort. "Understandably, he was really quite livid when I told him what had happened."

"Let me guess. He swore to have revenge on the Major."

"Oh, not just that! He took an oath he would make him suffer first, like his sister had, and then kill him slowly."

Sikander sat up. Now this was more like it!

"Do you happen to recall this angry young gentleman's name, Madame?"

"No, I'm afraid not. It was some time ago, and sadly, I am not as young as I once was."

"Of course," Sikander said, trying not to look crestfallen. *It would have been too easy*, he told himself, *if she had the name.* Still, it was better than nothing. He had a starting point, and with Ismail Chacha's network of informers, it should not be too cumbersome a task for him to track down this girl and her brother, whatever remote corner of India they may have disappeared to.

"Is there anything else you can tell me, Madame?"

The old crone wrinkled her brow thoughtfully. "Perhaps... there is one other thing. The boy was a Gurkha, I think."

Sikander gasped. Like two pieces of a puzzle fitting together, suddenly something seemed to click into place in his mind. A saturnine visage flashed across his eyes, the remembrance of a Nepali face he had seen just a few hours earlier.

"Are you sure that he was a Gurkha, Madame?"

"Yes," she said, ambivalent at first, but then with strengthening confidence, "I am certain of it. He had one of those odd knives, I remember. It was almost as long as my arm. Only Gurkhas carry them, don't they?"

Sikander leaned forward, his excitement threatening to overpower him.

"Tell me, this Gurkha, did he have a scar on his face, shaped like a question mark?" he asked eagerly, his voice trembling as he mimicked a line jagging from his eye to his lip.

"Yes, that is the man!" Her wrinkled eyes widened with surprise. "He did have a scar, just as you described it."

Sikander bit back a curse. That clinched it. It was the syce, there was no doubt of it. After all, how many Gurkhas with disfiguring scars were wandering around Rajpore?

Hastily, he sprang to his feet. "Well, Madame, this has certainly been most enlightening, but I must leave now."

The old woman responded with another lustrous smirk, as lascivious as a teenager.

"Why don't you stay a while longer, Your Majesty? I have a few young ladies in my coterie who could make your visit even more interesting. There is a very lovely young Malay who has just joined us who does things that would make you weep."

She looked at the Maharaja expectantly, but Sikander shook his head.

"While that is a very tempting offer, Madame, I am afraid that I must decline. Perhaps another time." He gave the old woman a contrite smile. "*Dosvidaniya*, and thank you for your time. I wish you the very best."

"And you, my dear boy. May the gods give you wisdom, and may you always find shelter in a storm."

Barely had she finished mouthing that benediction than Sikander offered Madame Krasnivaya a brisk bow, and bolted for the door. Shouldering it aside, he broke into a run, very nearly bowling over the majordomo, who had been kneeling just outside, trying to eavesdrop on their conversation with his ear pressed to the jamb.

Impatiently, he dashed down the spiral staircase, taking three steps at a time, trying not to trip over his feet.

At last, he had a proper suspect. *The syce, of all people,* Sikander thought. To think that the man had been firmly in his grasp, and he had just let him walk away. What was happening to him? First he had missed Lowry's obvious duplicity, and now this… He shuddered, recalling Charan Singh's unkind jibe.

Maybe he really was getting old!

Chapter Seventeen

The trip from the Sona Killa to Mrs. Ponsonby's Academy had taken Sikander a little over an hour. He made the return journey in record time, covering the distance in just under half that duration.

Upon arriving back at the Raj Vilas, the first person he sent for was his manservant.

"Back so soon, Huzoor?" Charan Singh exclaimed, taking in his master's bedraggled appearance. "Well, wasn't that quick? Perhaps it is time I introduced you to my hakim. He has a fine reputation for helping a man whose spirits are, ahem, flagging."

"Stop playing the fool, you old goat!" Sikander growled. "Get a flying squad together immediately, and go arrest the Gurkha!"

Charan Singh obviously had several even more ribald comments up his sleeve, but faced with such barely repressed urgency, his face stiffened, his manner changing from playful to serious.

"Gurkha, Sahib?" he echoed, bewildered.

"The Major's syce, of course! What other Gurkha could I possibly mean?"

"You wish me to arrest this man?"

"Yes! Have him picked up immediately. I don't want too much of a tamasha, and make sure that no word leaks out to the English, especially that buffoon Jardine."

"I shall take care of it myself, Your Grace."

"Good! Now get out of my way, you elephant. I need a large drink, and quick."

"Hold on, Sahib!" The big Sikh interjected. "Your drink will have to be postponed. The chief minister is waiting for you. He insisted you see him as soon as you return."

This announcement caused a frisson of unease to ripple down Sikander's spine. His weekly meeting with Ismail Bhakht wasn't scheduled until the day after tomorrow, and this unannounced appearance was unexpected, to say the least. What was Ismail Chacha doing here? What crisis could have compelled him to come calling this early in the morning?

"Would you like me to ask him to come back later?"

"No, I shall see him now. Where is he?"

"In the Miniature Gallery, Huzoor."

"Very good," Sikander said. "Now go and take the Gurkha into custody. I will interrogate him later, once I have met with Ismail Chacha."

"As you wish." Charan Singh offered Sikander a curious look. "Might I inquire, what was his crime?"

"That is none of *your* business. Now, off with you, you orangutan, go make yourself useful!"

The Miniature Gallery was on the second floor of the palace, very close to the Observatory. Ironically, the name was quite a misnomer. If anything, it was one of the largest rooms in the Raj Vilas, an amalgamation of three sitting rooms that had been merged together to create a vast vaulted space the size of a barn. This had been Sikander's father's most favored refuge, the sanctum to which he retreated to indulge his favorite pastime, which had been the recreation of miniature models of famous battlefields. Hence the name, the Miniature Room, for every inch of space within was crowded by more than a dozen exactingly produced dioramas. There was a precise replica of Leonidas' stand at Thermopylae, with each of the Spartans wearing cuirasses wrought from real gold, and a scale model of the Battle of Actium, with a line of galleys afloat amidst a miniature lake filled with actual water. In the distant corner stood the diorama his father had been working on when he died, a incomplete rendering of Waterloo, with a variety of half-painted hussars and bare metal horses lying scattered messily across a denuded field made from real grass and dotted with tiny trees. Next to it was Sikander's personal favorite, a mechanical myriorama of Sevastopol and the infamous Charge of the Light Brigade, complete with horses mounted on rails that actually moved at the flick of a switch and miniscule cannon that shot miniature grapeshot accompanied by puffs of smoke and tiny bursts of black powder.

Even though it had been years since he had found the time to visit the place, Sikander had exceedingly fond memories of this room from his childhood. He paused in the doorway, smiling as he recalled the hours he had spent there watching his father line up his lead soldiers and knock them down, mimicking the roar of cannons and the rattle of guns with his lips as he told Sikander of these legendary battlefields, like a child playing with his favorite toys. Why, if he closed his eyes, it was like he could almost smell the pungent scent of paint and glue hanging in the air, evoking a pang of nostalgia that ached like an old wound.

Sikander halted beside the myriorama of the Light Brigade, and lifted the cloth cover draped over it, folding it back reverently. A cloud of dust swirled up to assail his nostrils, making him cough. Underneath, the diorama was in sad state. The baize landscape was tattered and several of the papier-mâché hillocks that made up the Crimean Peninsula had collapsed into themselves. Most of the Light Brigade's mounts had toppled from their rails, and Lord Cardigan seemed to have lost his head. As Sikander wound the crank on the side of the diorama, and released the lever that activated the mechanism, his only reward was a dull clank and a resounding groan as if to suggest the springs had long since reached their demise.

"Such is the way of life, my boy," a reedy voice cackled. "Whether man or machine, we must all break someday. "

The Maharaja turned to find Ismail Bhakht watching him, seated in a high-backed chair atop the raised proscenium at the far end of the room. At first glance, he seemed an unassuming man, more like a doddering old teacher of Urdu shayari in his woolen sherwani and Kashmiri Karakul cap than a senior statesman. But it took only one glance into his eyes to see that this was a man cast from the same mold as Kautilya or Machiavelli, with a mind as sharp as a saber of Toledo steel. Sikander gazed up at his wizened face, trying as he always did to guess exactly how old Ismail Chacha was. He had to be somewhere between eighty and ninety, but try as he might, Sikander had never been able to ascertain his exact age. In fact, in spite of his most assiduous investigations, he had been entirely unable to unearth a single fact about Ismail Bhakht's antecedents before he had come to Rajpore and taken up service with his grandfather.

There were, of course, countless stories about his past, largely rumors cloaked in hearsay wrapped in legend. One persistent myth insisted he was really the Burra Maharaja's bastard brother, the illegitimate offspring of an illicit affair Sikander's great-grandfather had with a Lucknowi courtesan. Another legend claimed that he had once been a holy man, a learned Hafiz who had lost his faith and thus turned away from the path of the devout. And then of course there was Sikander's favorite, the story which he had always felt summed the man up best, that he was an orphan who had once pick-pocketed Sikander's grandfather, only to be adopted by him when he was apprehended. There was some proof to support that at least, considering the loyalty with which he had served three generations of Sikander's family. Sadly, most of the people who could have corroborated any of these rumors were long dead and buried, and the few that were still alive, like Charan Singh, refused outright to speak a word of ill about the chief minister.

Sikander guessed that this reticence came not from fear, but rather from a deep and abiding respect, an emotion that he felt himself, along with an immense affection for the old man. He could count the people he trusted implicitly on the fingers of one hand, but beyond a doubt, Ismail Bhakht would be among the top of the list. In that respect, he had much in common with Charan Singh. The giant Sikh and the ancient Mussulman were both loyal to a fault and lived only to serve the Maharaja. But unlike Charan Singh, who indulged his every whim as obediently as a dog, Ismail Chacha preferred to treat Sikander like a favored student whom he was tasked with educating in the ways of the world. While occasionally this attitude could be condescending, Sikander was wise enough to know that everything Ismail Chacha did was not just in his best interest but also for the ultimate welfare of Rajpore, and that he was genuinely fortunate to have someone of the old man's wit and dedication in his service.

"I see you have had rather an eventful night," the old man said, with one of his trademark grins, more suited to the lips of a ruffian than the first minister of a princely state. With a flick of his wrist that was more a command than a request, he invited Sikander to take the armchair opposite his own, a tall *directoire*-style *bergère*. "Forgive me if I do not rise and bow, Majesty. I am an old man, and my knees are not as limber as they used to be."

"That's fine," Sikander said, taking the proffered seat. "You look in fine form, if I may say."

"I wish I could say the same about you," the old man said with a twinkle in his eyes. "Frankly, I am surprised to see you awake this early. Has the world turned upside down? Can it be the sun has risen in the west? Is north now south and day now night?"

"Oh, I have been a busy boy this morning. I presume you have heard about Major Russell being poisoned."

"Indeed, I have." The minister let out a knowing sigh. "I have also heard that you have taken it upon yourself to investigate this tragic affair. "

"Someone has to," Sikander said, bracing himself for yet another lecture about propriety. "Charan Singh thinks it is unsuitable for me to go poking about in such matters, that it is beneath my dignity. Do you intend to say the same thing?"

"You have always had a fine idea of what is beneath you, my boy, and you have always made it a point to do exactly as you please. Frankly, I have neither the desire nor the patience to correct you. As you can see plainly from my wizened countenance, I am not your mother." Ismail Bhakht cackled, inordinately pleased by this brocard. "I should warn you, though, that Simla has dispatched a man to look into this mess, a special investigator named Simpson. I received a telegram confirming that he will be here very soon, perhaps even as early as tomorrow."

"Is that so?" This bit of news threw rather a large spanner in the works. The last thing Sikander needed was another amateur obstructing his investigation, causing it to grind to a halt. Jardine was tiresome enough, but a glorified accountant from Simla, with the full backing of the Burra Sahibs in the India Office, no doubt he would be even more obstructive. "Do we know anything about this Simpson? "

"I have heard rather ominous things. The British like to send him out when they want to teach native princes a lesson for step-ping out of line. Your friend Jagatjit endured his company most recently when he was assigned to Kapurthala last year to audit his spending habits. I believe Simpson made quite a nuisance of himself. By all accounts, he is a very tedious sort." The old man smiled wanly. "If rumor is to be believed, he is said to be entirely incorruptible."

"Good heavens!" Sikander exclaimed. "Whatever are we to do with such a creature?"

Ismail Chacha offered him an apologetic shrug. "Do not lose heart, my boy. There is time still before he shows up, more than enough for you to work your particular magic. Come on then, tell me, have you any theories yet about who may have killed our beloved Resident?"

"I have a few notions." Sikander could not help but emit a frustrated sigh. "This case…it's a difficult one. It's surprising really how many people abhorred the Major."

"Who have you spoken with so far?"

"Quite a few people! Lowry for one, and the Major's servants, and of course, your old friend, Madame Krasnivaya."

"Ah, the lovely Russian! How is she?" Ismail Bhakht's mouth split into a moonstruck grin that belonged on the face of a love-lorn teenager rather than on his ancient visage. His eyes gleaming, he leaned forward, his nostrils flaring slightly, as if he detected the scent of impending gossip. "What did she have to say?"

"Well, if she is to be believed, it seems our dear Major liked to hurt women, especially girls of a tender age."

Sikander had imagined Ismail Bhakht would be at least as shocked as he had been when he had first learned of the Major's sordid inclinations, but to his surprise, his reaction was quite the opposite of what the Maharaja had expected.

For a long minute, the Chief Minister remained silent, close-mouthed, before offering the Maharaja a grave nod. "I fear, Your Majesty, that I have not been entirely honest with you. You see, I have been aware of the Major's…ahem…peculiarities for quite some time now."

"You have?" Sikander exclaimed, astonished. "For God's sake, why did you not tell me?"

"What good would it have done? Like yourself, I was under-standably irate when I found out about his deviant tendencies, but when it comes to matters in the English hemisphere, we are as powerless to intervene as eunuchs. And frankly, if I had breathed a word to you, you would have gone off half-cocked and caused a tamasha, and the Major would simply have denied everything and made us look like fools."

The blunt veracity of this statement rankled intensely. The old man was correct, of course, as always. There was damnably little Sikander could have done to stop the Major. True, he could have tried to smear the man using Miller, but that would have left him open to libel, and knowing the Major, he would have pounced at a chance to come after Sikander personally. Perhaps he could have tried to bring pressure through his contacts in Simla, but the truth of the matter was that as the Resident Officer, Russell had been pretty much inviolate, impervious to any challenge he could have made. A more reckless prince might have decided to have the man murdered, but Sikander was not bloodthirsty enough to resort to such an extreme solu-tion—although, the same, he realized with a shiver, could not be said for Ismail Bhakht.

"You didn't have anything to with this, did you?"

Part of him expected a confession there and then. Sikander knew the Chief Minister well enough to realize that the old man would not think twice about taking the law into his own hands. He was as cold-blooded as a cobra, and wouldn't miss a wink of sleep over having a man murdered. And poison was definitely his oeuvre. Ismail Bhakht had always been an exceedingly subtle man, and what more subtle way was there to remove someone from the picture than by feeding him half a pint of strychnine?

To his unmitigated relief, rather than confirming his worst fears, the old man burst into a gale of reedy laughter.

"Oh, very good!" he cackled. "I was wondering how long it would take for that macabre mind of yours to arrive at that conclusion." The old man shook his head, fixing Sikander with shiny eyes. "In reply to your impertinent question, I should hope, my boy, that you have better suspects than me."

"Actually, I believe I do," Sikander replied. "In fact, I believe I know exactly who killed the Major."

"Who?" The old man sat up, intrigued. "Is it one of the Angrez?"

"No, I think it was the Major's syce."

The old man's eyebrows lifted imperceptibly, but for someone as poker-faced as Ismail Bhakht, it was as good as a gasp. "The syce? What does he have to do with anything, Huzoor?"

"Actually, as it turns out, it seems that his sister was one of Madam Krasnivaya's whores, and the Major beat her half to death."

Sikander quite enjoyed the look of astonishment that crept across Ismail Bhakht's face when he disclosed this revelation. "He is a Gurkha, by the way, a thoroughly dangerous-looking specimen."

Ismail Chacha arched one doubtful brow. "I think that you are grasping at straws. I do not know the man personally, but I doubt any Gurkha would stoop to using poison. As a breed, they prefer to face their enemies head-on. If he did indeed have a vendetta against the Major, then I am sure he would have tried to hack his head off with a kukri. But poison, no, I think he is not your man."

The conviction with which he made this declaration caused Sikander to frown. Ismail Chacha's words were, as always, brutally logical, and had managed to steer uncomfortably close to his own doubts. Could the old man be right? Was there more to the case than it seemed? Was the Gurkha just another false lead?

"What do you suggest my next move should be?"

"You never were much of a chess player, my boy. If you were, you would know that you must always look to the rook. There is one man who was privy to all the Major's secrets, one person who he trusted implicitly above all and who had both the access and opportunity to easily administer a dose of poison. Honestly, if I were you, I would take a good long look at the Major's vakeel."

It took Sikander a minute to grasp exactly who the old man was talking about. Surely he could not mean Munshi Ram? What earthly reason could Ismail Bhakht have to point a finger at him, of all people?

"I have already interviewed the Munshi," he responded, not bothering to conceal his doubts. "He seems harmless enough."

The old man let out a sniff, the briefest of exhalations that managed to speak volumes.

"There is an old pahari saying, Huzoor. You can always trust a villain to be villainous, but never trust a man who seems innocent at first glance."

This cryptic comment only served to rouse Sikander's curiosity even further. "What are you not telling me?" he groaned. "And do stop trying to be so mysterious."

The old man rolled his eyes, annoyed that Sikander was refusing to play along with his little game. "The Munshi is not, as they say, *pukka*," he said rather stiffly. Ismail Bhakht pursed his ancient lips, until they were almost invisible. "From what I have heard, he is in the habit of taking *baksheesh*."

Sikander scowled, mirroring the old man's disapproving expression. Baksheesh was a peculiarly duplicitous practice imported to India from Persia. In layman's terms, it quite simply was a bribe, or rather, if one wished to be more polite, a gratuity, a gift to ensure that certain favors were performed. As a practice, he knew all too well that it had become endemic to British India, particularly in the Princely states. Personally, Sikander took a poor view of such rampant corruption. He was a sincere believer in the enlightened state, and had always felt that the role of civil servants was to serve the populace, not fleece them to line their own pockets. As a result, he had tried his best to discourage the practice, but in spite of his most assiduous efforts, it continued to flourish in the English quarter, to his dismay.

"I understand your disdain for such things, Chacha, but surely the willingness to take a bribe or two does not make a man a murderer?"

"Tell me, my boy, how much do you know of the Munshi's past?"

Sikander furrowed his brow, trying to recollect what he could, which turned out to be abysmally little.

"Not much, other than the fact he was employed here at the palace some years ago, wasn't he, when Lal Singh was on the gaddi?"

The old man dipped his head, a stork-like gesture of affirmation. "Yes, he was indeed a clerk for some years, until I was forced to adjourn his position due to an excessive display of moral ambiguity."

"You mean he tried some sort of fiddle, but you caught him with his hand in the kitty?"

The old man shot Sikander a look of profound consternation, as if to chastise him for interrupting. "Of course, I made it a point to keep a close eye on the man, especially when he entered British service. Let me just say that this very moral ambiguity is a quality that has served the Munshi exceedingly well while working for Major Russell. Since his promotion to the Resident's vakalat, he has made quite a fortune for himself."

"Is that so?" From his dress and demeanor, Sikander had not taken the Munshi to be particularly well off, little more than an average government employee. If what Ismail Chacha was saying was true, then that was a sham, a carefully orchestrated mask.

"Yes. From what I have been told, he is quite well known for being a speculator." The minister's voice hardened as he said the word speculator, crisping with contempt.

"What sort of speculations do you mean?"

"Land mainly," Ismail Chacha replied dourly. "Some years ago, during your dear departed father's tenure, the English asked us to grant them some acreage south of the city so that it could be allotted to widows who had lost their husbands in the Afghan Campaigns. As I recall, your father was exceedingly generous, and signed over close to four thousand hectares."

Sikander let out a low whistle. That was a handsome allotment indeed. Generally, one hundred hectares was the equivalent of one square kilometer, and four thousand, that was a piece of land roughly the size of the old city, if not larger.

"Sadly," Ismail Chacha continued, "the widows never actually received their grants. Instead, even as the awards were delayed interminably by the Resident's office, the hapless women in question were approached by intermediaries and offered small settlements if they agreed to sign the land over to another agency. Can you guess who was in charge of making the allotments, and who was no doubt sending out these middlemen?"

Sikander gave the old man a sour grin. It was the oldest bundle of them all, a good old-fashioned land grab. In Rajpore, given its prime location and abundant harvest, every hectare was as good as gold, and whoever it was that had appropriated the land in question, he was bound to end up as prosperous as a zamindar.

"It was the Munshi, wasn't it?"

"Yes, I am sure of it," the old man said with a scowl. *No wonder he was offended*, Sikander thought. Not only had the Munshi been derelict in his duty and tried to use his position for profit, both of which were anathema to a man as unimpeachably honest as Ismail Bhakht, but then he had compounded his sin by preying on the helpless.

"Why didn't you intervene, Ismail Chacha?"

"Surely you are joking, Huzoor. It was an English matter, and as you well know, we have no jurisdiction in the English town."

Sikander nodded. He was right, of course. If he had tried to make a complaint, he would only have been rebuffed, a polite refusal no doubt, but a rejection nonetheless. The English were sticklers when it came to keeping Indian noses out of what they perceived as their business. It wasn't just a matter of ego; it was unsubtle racism at its worst. The gora Sahibs believed themselves to be far superior to the natives, even though the culture of the Indus had been flourishing while they were running about, painting their faces blue with woad, and beating each other on the heads with clubs made of bone.

So, it seems the Munshi was building a handsome little empire of his own, Sikander thought, furrowing his brow. But why would that compel him to kill the Major? No, he was missing something. The scenario just did not make sense, unless...remembering what Jane had revealed about their squabbling, suddenly, Sikander saw it as clearly as one of Fibonacci's hidden patterns.

"I think that perhaps we have this backwards," Sikander said. "What if it was the Major who was the brains behind the whole operation, the puppet-master pulling the Munshi's strings?"

Ismail Chacha mulled over this proposition for a minute before offering the barest of nods. "It is possible, yes."

"In that case, would that not provide a fine motive for murder? What if the Munshi was afraid that the Major intended to make him his scapegoat, that he planned to throw him to the wolves to cover his own nefarious tracks? Would that not be enough of a reason to want someone dead?"

Another, even longer pause ensued while Ismail Chacha considered this hypothesis, before he let out a low whistle, as if he was impressed.

"By the stars," he cried, "I think you might just be onto something."

Chapter Eighteen

As he emerged from this rather perplexing encounter with Ismail Bhakht, Sikander nearly crashed headlong into Charan Singh. The enormous Sikh was lurking behind a nearby pillar, doing a terrible job of trying to seem inconspicuous. When he rushed forward to accost the Maharaja, Sikander couldn't help but take note that the man had a real beauty of a bruise beginning on one cheek, a florid lesion that made him look like he had just gone fifteen rounds with a prizefighter.

Sikander hid a smile. His instincts had been dead on, it seemed. The little Gurkha had turned out to be a handful after all. "Did you get your hands on the syce?"

"Yes, Sahib." The big Sikh's fingers reached instinctively for his cheek, caressing the bruise. "He is awaiting your arrival, in the dungeon."

In truth, the dungeon was rather a grandiose name for what was little more than a guardhouse abutting the barracks of the Royal Guard. In Lal Singh's time, there had been a proper bastille deep within the bowels of the killa, an ominous place where his enemies had been locked away, even tortured, but Sikander had made it a point to brick the place up the instant he came to power. Now, the kotwali was housed in a tall turreted tower at the distant corner of the east wing, used mainly to detain soldiers who had enjoyed rather too much to drink for their own good, and the occasional servant who decided to be a little too light-fingered. Even the interiors were more like an inn than a prison—instead of cells with chains and bars, the dungeon contained a number of neatly decorated rooms, simply furnished and kept immaculately clean. The only visible hint that this was a place of detention was the fact that each room was protected by a thick door reinforced with metal bands, and guarded by a sizable contingent of handpicked soldiers, who took turns patrolling the tower's immediate environs in pairs.

The Gurkha was being held in a cell at the base of the tower. His hands and legs were manacled, and he was being watched over closely by a Daffadar Sergeant, a fit-looking young Sikh who resembled Charan Singh so much that Sikander guessed he was yet another of his innumerable sons.

"Leave us," Sikander commanded. "I think your father and myself can handle this fellow."

With a bow so sprightly that it nearly decapitated the Maharaja, the boy hurried away. Sikander nodded at Charan Singh, who shut the door and latched it securely, before crossing to stand behind the Gurkha, folding his arms across his chest and glowering down at the smaller man. Meanwhile, Sikander retreated to a narrow bench at the opposite side of the room and sat down, taking his time to dust his trousers and to carefully smooth back his hair before finally fixing his undivided attention on Gurung Bahadur.

How was he to break the man? Beyond a doubt, he would be a tough nut to crack. Gurkhas had a formidable reputation, not just as soldiers, but for personal toughness. There was a saying they were said to revere—*"Kaphar hunnu bhanda marnu ramro"*—"Better dead than live like a coward." No, it would take a lot more than the mere threat of violence to loosen the syce's tongue. One only had to cast a glance at his face to confirm that suspicion. Sikander had seen dockyard brawlers who looked less battered. If Charan Singh seemed knocked about, this fellow looked even worse for wear. His scarred face, already ugly to look at, was now positively villainous, like something from a nightmare, with one eye swollen almost shut and a nose so caked with blood that Sikander suspected it had been broken. Still, he looked uncowed, watching the Maharaja defiantly, without missing a blink.

Perhaps that was where the key to interrogating him lay, Sikander thought, and with this flash of insight came the realization of what approach he needed to adopt. If he was going to get to the Gurkha to talk, he would have to turn his very strength, his toughness, into a weapon and use it against him.

Sikander leaned forward, fixing the man with a stare that was nothing short of baleful. "I am very disappointed in you, Gurung Bahadur. I thought that your people were famous for their honor, but you are no true Gurkha. You have no honor, I see that now."

As he had expected, this castigation made the man flinch far more readily than any blow could ever have. "Why do you say such a terrible thing to me, Sahib?" Gurung's outrage was palpable with each word.

"You ate the Major Sahib's salt. You swore an oath to him, did you not?"

"I did, and I obeyed it."

Sikander let out a theatrical snort. "Lies! The first chance you had, you betrayed him. You betrayed your oath!"

"I did not." The Gurkha clenched his teeth, rising to the bait, exactly as Sikander had hoped. "I swear it, by all that is holy."

"Did you think I would not find out about your sister?"

Even as Sikander asked this question, the Gurkha's demeanor changed. In the blink of an eye, his diffidence vanished, his face growing cold, so relentlessly adamant that Sikander felt a shiver run through him. At that moment, for the first time, Gurung Bahadur looked truly dangerous, the sort of man who could kill in cold blood and not lose a moment's sleep over it. A quick glance to his right told him Charan Singh, who had drawn in his breath imperceptibly, had seen it too. This was it then, the tipping point, the crescendo of any interrogation. The next moments were make or break—would the man crack, or would he try to bluster his way out?

"Very well, Sahib." The Gurkha offered Sikander a curt nod. "I confess. I am guilty."

It was that simple, an admission so direct and unadorned that it managed to leave Sikander at an utter loss for words. While the Maharaja had certainly been hoping for a confession, what he had not expected was for it to be so forthright, so very straightforward. It was unsettling, to say the least.

"You would have liked my sister," the Gurkha murmured. "She was very beautiful. Not just pretty, but as lovely as the moon on a winter night. And so innocent, barely more than a child." He smiled wistfully. "When I was a boy, I always tried to protect her, to keep her safe, but then, when I came of age, I joined the Regiment, and had to leave her unguarded." He let out a muted groan, a sigh so heartfelt it was almost a sob. "It is my fault, Sahib. I am responsible for what became of her. I do not deny my sister was a whore, but it was not her choice. My father sold her into servitude to the zamindars to pay off his debts. They forced her…they…"

His voice tapered away, too thick with sorrow to continue. Sikander watched the man silently, more than a little taken aback by such an open display of emotion from such a taciturn man. To his astonishment, he realized that some small part of him could not help but sympathize with the Gurkha. He had heard such stories before, of landlords taking possession of the children of serfs when harvests failed. It was little more than indentured slavery, and he had done everything in his power to stamp out such lamentable practices within the domain of his own kingdom, but outside Rajpore, he knew only too well that such things were woefully commonplace.

"You should have brought her to me. I would have helped you find justice."

The Gurkha let out a sarcastic snort, halfway between a laugh and a gasp. "Justice, Sahib! Surely you are too wise to believe in something quite so naïve. There is no justice to be had against an Angrez of the Major's standing, especially not for beating an Indian whore half to death." He fixed Sikander with a mournful sneer, a grim deaths-head of a grin that looked like it belonged on a skull. "Besides, it is too late for my sister to hope for justice. She took her own life," he explained. "She threw herself into the gorge not six weeks after that bastard ravaged her."

This piece of information shocked Sikander. *No wonder the Gurkha had been so eager to see Major Russell dead.* He found himself at a loss for words, struggling to offer the man some measure of reassurance, but what could he say? What would it be but little more than cold comfort? No platitudes could make up for the loss of someone you loved, no matter how heartfelt.

The Gurkha seemed to sense his hesitation, and his lips split into a bitter grimace. "There is a story my mother told me when I was but a boy. Once there was a village that was being threatened by a savage monster. Each night, it would come and steal away their children, and eat them, leaving the bones behind to be found the next morning. The villagers were too scared to stop the monster, except for one boy who dreamed of being a hero. 'I shall slay the beast,' he announced, 'and save all of you.'

"The villagers were overjoyed, and they gave him three gifts, a spear made of silver and a shield made of glass, and a rope made from the hair of a hundred virgins which would never break.

"The boy was scared, but he marched deep into the lair of the monster. 'Come forth,' he shouted a challenge, 'and face me,' brandishing his spear and clapping it against his shield to hide the sound of his knocking knees. In reply, the monster descended upon him, roaring with rage. It was horrific, a nightmare come to life, with the head of a lion and the body of a snake, and a mouth filled with teeth like glinting scimitars.

"'You dare to challenge me, foolish boy,' the beast roared. 'I shall kill you slowly, until you beg me to die.' With a growl, he swooped down, but before he could bite, the boy threw up his glass shield, and the sun reflecting from its shiny face blinded the beast, making him blink. Immediately, the boy leaped forward and quickly looped his rope around the beast, binding him up in knots that he simply could not break. The beast was stunned.

He roared and raged, fighting the knots, but try as he might, he simply could not escape.

"In the end, he fell to the ground, exhausted. As he lay there, the boy raised his silver spear, and said, 'I shall do to you what you wanted to do to me. I will kill you slowly until you beg for death.'

"And that is what he did. He took six days to kill the monster, cutting him a thousand times. And each time the beast screamed with pain, the boy laughed, louder and louder until at last, the monster begged him to end its misery. In the end, the hero cut off the beast's head from which he made a helmet, and flayed its skin, from which he fashioned himself a cloak. Wrapped in this gruesome prize, he headed back to the village, dreaming of how the villagers would greet him, with an ovation of joy, and salutations aplenty praising his valor.

"As he reached the outskirts of the village, he saw a pretty girl, working in the field. 'Hallo,' he said, 'it is I, the hero. I have returned triumphant. The monster is dead.' He had expected the girl would laugh and embrace him, perhaps even give him a kiss, but instead, she let out a wail and ran away, leaving him behind.

"This happened again and again. 'Wait,' the boy said, 'it is I, the hero who slayed the monster,' but whoever he tried to approach fled from him, screaming with fear. Naturally, the hero was perplexed. *Why are they afraid?* he wondered. *Did I not slay the beast and save them? Why do they run away from me?*

"He found the answer to that question a few moments later. At the center of the village, there was a well, and as he paused, leaning thirstily over its rim to draw a bucket from which to drink, he realized why the villagers were avoiding him. What he saw was that the helmet made from the monster's head and the cloak of monster skin had merged with his own flesh, and he had become a monster, just like the beast he had set out to slay."

The Gurkha gave Sikander a level frown.

"I do not claim to be a good man, Sahib. I have done terrible things in battle, but whatever sins I may have to my name, they were accrued in the name of duty and honor. I am a warrior, from a clan of warriors. From childhood, we are taught to live according to a code. Protect the weak. Face your enemy and never retreat. Never harm those who cannot fight back, and never let a wrong go unavenged. I may not be rich or powerful, but these are my beliefs, and I have tried to adhere to them for one simple reason, because without honor, a man is just an animal.

"Unfortunately, Your Majesty, we live in a time when it is difficult to tell monsters apart from men. They hide amongst us, often in plain sight. That Angrez, he may have been the Resident, but for any man to inflict such horrors on a helpless woman; it is clear to me that he had no honor. Did I wish to take his life? More than anything, yes."

Gurung Bahadur scowled. "I gave up everything, Sahib. I resigned my commission. I sold what little property I had, and came here. I was convinced at first that the old woman was the one who was responsible, but when I confronted her, she told me what the Major had done to my sister. I confess, I found it hard to believe that a Sahib with such a famed reputation would behave in such a barbaric way, and so I decided I would seek out the Major and discern for myself what kind of man he was.

"It was not easy getting close to him, Your Majesty. Not only was I a native, which made egress into the English town difficult, but also, I could not reveal my military past, because I did not wish the man to peg onto my true identity. Instead, I was forced to seek out an old friend who had served with me in Tibet, who was able to help me secure a sinecure at the Residency." He frowned. "I had to use most of my savings to pay a hefty bribe to the Major's Munshi, who ensured that I would take up position as his syce, even though such menial labor was beneath a man of my military experience. All so I could watch him, Sahib. I watched the Major and waited, for months, and everything I saw only made me sure that he was an evil, rabid man, fully deserving of what was coming to him."

"So you poisoned him, you admit it?"

The Gurkha shook his head.

"Oh no, I only wish I had! I had every intention of killing the Major, but, to my chagrin, I did not have a chance to put my plan into action. Someone else beat me to it."

"You truly expect me to believe that?" Sikander retorted with a snort.

"I do not care what you believe, Sahib. All that I care is that he received his comeuppance. My only regret is that he died so easily. If I had had my way, I would have taken my time, made sure he suffered the way he made my sister suffer. I would have made him endure the same pain, the same agony." He pursed his lips, watching Sikander proudly. "I am willing to accept whatever fate you may choose for me. Put me on trial. Hang me, I will go to my death willingly now that that bastard is in hell."

With that, the Gurkha fell silent. His words, albeit brutal, had managed to touch something primal in Sikander's heart. *If I were in his place*, he found himself wondering, *would I have acted any differently?* Much as Sikander prided himself on being a rational man, he knew only too well the answer to that question was a resounding no. If anyone had dared to harm a single hair on Helene's head, he would have had them beaten to death in plain sight, regardless of the political or legal ramifications.

This realization left him rather discomfited. How could he condemn a man for doing what he would have done himself, had their places been reversed?

"What do you think?" He turned to Charan Singh who had been listening to this exchange silently. "Should I believe him?"

The big Sikh frowned, looking as confused as his master. "I cannot say, Huzoor. He is a killer, of that much I am sure, and he had plenty of reason to hate the Major Sahib, but ...I do not think he is the one who poisoned him."

Sikander scowled. Part of him wanted to disagree, to have the man arrested on the spot, but another, more logical part saw that Charan Singh was right. There were just too many lingering doubts to dismiss outright, far too many more enticing trails to follow. Granted, he could have Gurung Bahadur locked up anyway. The Gurkha was still an excellent suspect, and while his story was tragic, there was enough circumstantial evidence against him to guarantee prosecution in any assizes.

While that was certainly a tempting proposition and one at which a more ruthless prince might have leaped, Sikander was neither cruel nor unscrupulous enough to consign an innocent man to the gallows, not without overbearing proof. Besides, it was still early in his investigation. He had a list of suspects still to interview, all of whom had motives as compelling as the Gurkha's, if not more so.

"I am not sure what I should do with you," he said to Gurung Bahadur. "For now, you shall remain in my custody until I make up my mind.

"He stays here," Sikander commanded Charan Singh. "Keep a close eye on him. Feed him, and have a doctor take care of his injuries. And one other thing..." The Maharaja fixed the big Sikh with a glare. "If I find even one more bruise on him when I return, it will not bode well for you. Do you understand?"

"I live to serve," Charan Singh responded, but the petulant look on his face spoke volumes. He was not at all happy being denied a chance to avenge the unseemly welt the Gurkha had so recently given him.

As Sikander left the dungeon, another even more disturbing thought occurred to him. If Jardine were to somehow find out about the Gurkha and his connection to the Major, he would throw a proper fit! Sikander reminded himself to have a word with Charan Singh to ensure that there were no leaks from the palace staff. The last thing the Maharaja needed was for the Superintendent to show up with half a dozen constables pushing to have the Gurkha turned over to his custody. It would certainly satisfy the English to have a convenient scapegoat to blame, particularly a native who looked quite as obviously villainous as Gurung Bahadur.

If anything, that made it even more imperative that Sikander bring an end to the case as expeditiously as possible. But where was he to begin? By his reckoning, he had several possible suspects still left to interrogate. Chief amongst them was Fletcher, who had been avoiding him as diligently as a gambler evading a debt-collector. Then, of course, there was Lieutenant Bates, who had scuffled with the Major so publicly at the New Year's Ball just hours before his death, and of course his mysterious wife, the young lady who had been the cause of that furor. And now, after what Ismail Chacha had revealed about the Munshi, it seemed he had to add him to the list as well, even though Sikander had grave doubts about his capacity to commit murder. Granted, he had the means and the opportunity, but as a motive, the notion of profiteering seemed tenuous at best. Still, Sikander knew from experience not to dismiss even the wildest probability without first investigating it.

Unfortunately, all of that would just have to wait, he told himself. First he needed a bath and shave, and then it was time to change into his Sunday best.

After all, Sikander thought, trying not to cringe, *I have a garden party to attend.*

Chapter Nineteen

At the stroke of noon, the Maharaja's convoy embarked from the Sona Killa.

Charan Singh had wanted to go the whole nine yards, insisting upon a proper royal procession with trumpeters and chobdars and the Rajpore Regimental Bagpipers accompanying a full paltan of the Palace Guard, dressed resplendently in their russet tunics and bright blue pugrees. Why, he had even tried to get his master to ride atop one of the royal elephants, but Sikander had flatly refused. Instead, he had insisted on keeping his entourage discreet, just himself and the old Sikh accompanied by a dozen handpicked retainers.

For a change, Sikander found himself relegated to the passenger seat, fidgeting impatiently while Charan Singh's eldest son, Ajit, a handsome young man who was the spitting image of his father, except a half-foot shorter, deftly maneuvered another of the Rolls-Royces, the blue one this time, downhill towards the British Lines. Outside, it was shaping up to be an extraordinarily humid day. The promise of rain hung in the warm air, like a waking dream, making Sikander sweat profusely. As if that wasn't bad enough, his already foul mood was only worsened by the fact his ornamental turban felt too heavy and the neck of his ornate achkan was choking him to the point of dizziness.

The venue Mrs. Fitzgerald had chosen for her abominable affair was the Ross Common, the smallest of Rajpore's three hotels. It was located near the margins of the English Town, at the peripheries of the Cantonment. Before the Great Mutiny, this was where the small Company contingent had been picketed, but after 1857 and the establishment of a permanent English Mission in Rajpore, a new fortified camp had been erected near the Railway Station, a long row of barracks and stables to house three regiments permanently, two infantry, one Sikh and one Dogra, and a light horse regiment which specialized in frontier warfare, not unlike the Guides.

At about the same time, a retired Army officer named Herbert Ross had purchased the abandoned Company complex and renovated the cottages, turning them into an outpost where the many travelers passing through Rajpore could seek a night of shelter. There were twelve bungalows in total, spread out over one and half acres, surrounding a small landscaped rose garden and a two-storey lodge that hosted a restaurant and a ballroom. Sikander had never been there before, but from what he heard, it was rather a dusty, drab establishment, certainly not as luxurious as the Imperial, targeted more at tradesmen and civil servants rather than patrons of Sikander's status and refinement.

As he had dreaded, his arrival, although greatly reduced in spectacle, still managed to cause quite a hubbub. Hoping to arrive quietly, he had planned to make an entry well after the soiree's start. However, judging by the curious crowd that spilled out to watch his automobile approach the Ross Common, Mrs. Fitzgerald must have spent half the morning boasting to all and sundry that the Maharaja of Rajpore had finally decided to attend one of her events.

Barely had the Rolls clattered to a halt, that Charan Singh sprang out, his martial bearing and spotless uniform drawing a number of approving looks from the retired soldiers in the crowd. His back ramrod straight, the giant Sikh gave his son a haughty nod, who responded by sounding off the Rolls' horn thrice in quick succession, three strident squawks substituting for the traditional trio of drum rolls that ordinarily announced Sikander's arrival.

Even as these raucous notes reverberated through the air, Charan Singh cleared his throat, and with stiff hauteur, announced, "All Hail His Highness Farzand-i-Khas-i-Daulat-i-Inglishia, Mansur-i-Zaman, Amir ul-Umara, Maharajadhiraja Raj Rajeshwar, Maharaja Sikander Singh Bahadur, Yadu Vansha Vatans Bhatti Kul Bushan, Maharaja of Rajpore."

Embarrassed, Sikander waited restlessly until his manservant was done extolling his many and varied honors before dismounting from the automobile. It took all his strength not to let his discomfort show, and he gave Charan Singh a poisonous glare before fixing a cool smile on his face and striding into the hotel's foyer. The usual array of frosty faces greeted his advent, bearing expressions of barely disguised contempt as they watched his every move warily. Sikander nodded regally at them, striking a posture of relaxed nonchalance. Wrinkling his nose, he gazed around him, shuddering inwardly as he took in Mrs. Fitzgerald's attempts to create a festive atmosphere. Half the place seemed to have been bedecked gaily with enough red and white bunting to put a victory parade to shame. As for the rest, it had been hung with gauzy silk and brocade, in an attempt perhaps to create an exotic, even Oriental atmosphere. The end result was truly dazzling, a monument to poor taste that would have made even the most relentless of parvenus blanch.

The Maharaja tried not to dissolve into laughter. Behind him, Charan Singh let out an astounded gasp. The theme of the afternoon, it seemed, was the *Arabian Nights*, judging by the costumes that Mrs. Fitzgerald's guests were wearing, ranging from a very overweight Ali Baba with a pendulous belly bulging from beneath a tiny waistcoat, to a haughty looking Scheherazade with a truly admirable bosom barely constrained by her Lucknowi bodice. Sikander turned and gave his manservant an inquiring look. Predictably, the big Sikh had failed to mention that this was a *bal masqué,* no doubt because he was well aware that his master despised such affairs. As far as Sikander was concerned, costume balls were unequivocally the tattiest kind of gatherings, and most of these people, evidently willing to make fools of themselves in public, had far too little self-respect and even less taste. Unfortunately, his own attire, comprising a carmine brocade Achkan with enough golden embroidery on its bodice to put a Hussar to shame, was quite vulgar enough to fit right in, a fact that caused him no small distress.

To his chagrin, there seemed to be rather a preponderance of overdressed rajahs dotting the crowd. Sikander's face reddened as he moved forward, turning a bright scarlet to match his tunic, and he found himself wishing he had a mask to hide behind. Thankfully, most of the people he encountered stepped hurriedly out of his way, unwilling to engage him in conversation. Not that Sikander was concerned by such snubs. He had braved Mrs. Fitzgerald's revelry for a very specific reason. Beyond that he had no desire to socialize, and those few who hesitantly tried to greet him, he pointedly ignored.

Making a slow circuit of the foyer, Sikander concentrated on searching for his quarry. He paused only to watch the jongleurs and contortionists that had been hired to entertain the guests, smiling as he passed a slender girl who was bent over backwards, clapping appreciatively as she eased a sword down her gullet, swallowing a twelve-inch blade with effortless ease, all while upside down.

Finally, he spotted the first of his targets. Dr. Mason was exactly as Roy had described, a tall, well-proportioned man, almost Dickensian in appearance, as rotund and shiny-faced as Mr. Micawber. Even though their paths had never crossed before, Sikander felt he could make several educated guesses about the man's personality and character just from his appearance. His complexion was sanguine, which told him that Mason was the sort of man accustomed to having his own way. His posture, and the way he shifted from foot to foot every few moments, suggested he had a touch of the gout, and the old-fashioned mutton-chop whiskers he favored made him look somehow dogmatic. A few other sundry details caught Sikander's eye—the Masonic pin he wore in his lapel, and the Regimental Ascot around his neck, both indicated an Army background. And then of course, there was his choice of accoutrement, a tartan kilt and doublet, complete with a furred sporran. Clan Munro, judging by the interwoven pattern of red and black, if Sikander remembered his *Vestiarium Scoticum* correctly, which meant the doctor's origins lay in the Highlands. Of course, he might merely have come in fancy dress as a Scotsman, in which case, the kilt indicated that he was a bit of a dunce.

Ordinarily, Sikander would never have resorted to something as boorish as accosting a stranger in public without an introduction. No, in the normal course of events, he would have sent an invitation to Mason, requesting him to call upon the Maharaja at his earliest convenience, so that he could interview him in private. However, since time was of the essence, for once, he decided to do away with social nicety. Putting on a convivial expression, Sikander approached the doctor rather brazenly, tapping him gently on one shoulder.

"Dr. Mason, isn't it?" He held out his hand when the man swiveled to face him. "I am Sikander Singh, the Maharaja of Rajpore, and I would like a quick word, if you would be so kind."

To his dismay, in spite of this attempt at politesse, the man's face remained as wintry as a glacier, and he made a point of ignoring Sikander's outstretched hand, glaring down at it disdainfully, as if it were leprous.

"I don't treat natives."

"I am not here seeking treatment. Actually, I was hoping to request a small favor."

"What manner of favor?" The squint he gave the Maharaja suggested that he did not care for him, even though Sikander's rank compelled him to remain courteous.

"I want your medical opinion, that's all." Sikander raised his hands and shrugged. "About Major Russell, as a matter of fact, and his unfortunate demise."

"Oh no." Mason shook his head, letting out a florid snort. "Superintendent Jardine warned me you would come sniffing about, and he was really quite adamant that I am not to tell you a thing."

Sikander had to make a real effort to remain smiling. "You seem like a pragmatic man, Doctor. Perhaps we can come to an arrangement."

As he had hoped, this overture made Mason hesitate. "What exactly do you have in mind?"

Sikander let out a sigh, relieved that this gambit had not been rebuffed. "Tell me, Doctor, do you enjoy the water of life?"

"I beg your pardon."

"Whiskey, Doctor! Are you a whiskey man?"

At the mention of whiskey, Mason's face gleamed with a sudden flush of desire. "I may have been known to enjoy a drop or two," he said guardedly.

"Excellent!" Sikander tried not to gloat that he had guessed the doctor's weakness accurately. He was a Scotsman after all, and what Scotsman could resist the lure of a fine cask? "It so happens that I have a case of Laphroaig 1898 sitting in my cellar, but sadly, I prefer champagne myself. Perhaps you would be so kind as to take it off my hands."

Without even realizing it, Mason licked his lips. A medley of opposing expressions flashed across his features, greed battling against antipathy. To the Maharaja's unmitigated delight, it was greed that ultimately seemed to win out.

"Very well, I don't see what harm could come from answering a few questions, as long as they are reasonable."

"Marvelous! Tell me, did you know the Major well?"

"Not really," Mason frowned. "We moved in different circles. He was a bit of a high flyer. I, on the other hand, am a simple man, a humble country surgeon."

From the disapproval in his tone, and the wrinkling of his nose as he uttered the phrase "high flyer," it was only too apparent to Sikander that Dr. Mason had harbored exactly the same low opinion of the Major that he possessed. "I take it you disliked the man."

"Well, I have no desire to slander the dead, but Russell was, in my opinion, a bit of a chancer."

"In what way?"

"There were stories," Mason said with a noncommittal shrug, "the usual rumors. Also, the man was poxed, can you believe it?"

"Poxed?" Sikander said, visibly shocked.

"Yes, it is said he was quite a rake in his youth, a regular patron of the bordellos in Madras. Sadly, those youthful misadventures left him with a chronic case of the sailor's disease, the poor bugger. It flared up last year and he came to me seeking a cure. I prescribed mercury, of course, and told him to stay away from women." He rolled his eyes disapprovingly, nonplussed by the fact that he had just broken the medical profession's oldest oath and betrayed a patient's confidentiality.

"Syphilis," Sikander intoned, "are you absolutely sure?"

"Of course I am," Mason snarled, annoyed by the presumption that he could be anything but correct. "I have seen more than my fair share of such cases, trust me."

Sikander was unsure whether to be bewildered or delighted by this latest revelation. The Major had been syphilitic. That unexpected fact put an entirely different cast on the whole situation. Like most red-blooded men, the very mention of the French disease was enough to make Sikander shudder with revulsion. It was the main reason he had made it a point to always be exceedingly careful with his assignations, making certain to ensure that the women he slept with were clean, especially during his sojourn as a student in Paris. *Poor bugger indeed*, he thought, shivering involuntarily, As diseases went, syphilis was a particularly pernicious malady, a malaise that didn't just cripple a man physically but attacked the very core of his being, stripping him not just of his health, but ultimately also of his faculties for reason.

It explained a lot though, Sikander thought, certainly clarifying why the Major had been acting erratically, not to mention his delusions of grandeur and his high-handed behavior. Dementia was a common enough symptom, especially of neuro-syphilis of the tertiary variety. *Yes*, he thought, *the more he considered it, the more it fit*. He had already verified that the Major frequented Mrs. Ponsonby's with some regularity, which suggested a pattern of behavior. Men who patronized brothels were generally habitual about it, and in India in particular, that was a very dangerous habit to indulge. Soldiers' brothels, or chaklas, as they were commonly known, were a breeding ground of venereal diseases. In spite of the Cantonment Act of 1895 and the Contagious Diseases Act, the British Establishment still took a very duplicitous stance when it came to prostitution, especially in army Cantonments. On the face of it, all such trade was condemned, but the Burra Sahibs were only too happy to turn a blind eye to the dozens of cathouses near the Railway Lines, all of which were regularly patronized by the lower ranks. In fact, Sikander recalled a report he had read a few years ago published by the Abolitionists that described how common syphilis had become amongst the rank and file of the Indian Army, citing that at least one in six soldiers suffered from it.

"If you have no further questions," Mason declared impatiently, glancing pointedly at his fob watch, "I really should be getting back to my wife."

"Just a moment longer, Doctor," Sikander insisted. "I was wondering, did you perform an autopsy on the corpse when it was brought to you?"

This question made Mason bridle. "I most certainly did not." His nostrils flared with distaste. "I am a physician, Mr. Singh, not a butcher."

Sikander ground his teeth. Dr. Roy had warned him about Mason's retrogressive fustiness when it came to modern surgical techniques, but to be greeted by such overt hostility… the man's marked lack of common sense was enough to set him on edge.

"But Doctor, doesn't Virchow say that pathological necroscopy is absolutely essential, the key to deducing the solution to any violent crime?"

Mason glowered at him, obviously displeased by Sikander's gall at daring to question him so blatantly. "I viewed the body, and frankly, as far as I could tell, there was no need for a postmortem. The cause of death was only too obvious. The Major had been poisoned."

"Yes," Sikander groaned, trying to keep his frustration in check, "but which poison, and in what quantity? That is what I need to know."

"Why does it bloody well matter?" Mason shrugged, as if to illustrate his utter disinterest in Sikander's investigative process. "I followed the rules to the letter. The inquest is done and dusted, and the case is as good as closed. As far as I am concerned, this was undoubtedly an episode of death by misadventure."

"In that case, Doctor, I would like very much if you would permit my personal physician to examine the Major's body."

"Why on Earth?" Mason exclaimed, visibly affronted by such a suggestion.

"While I am certain your conclusions are spot-on, I need him to ascertain two things for me. First, to corroborate that it was indeed strychnine that killed Major Russell, as I suspect, and secondly, in what quantity the said poison was administered. For that, I will require two samples, one of the stomach contents to see what the Resident consumed last night, and the other a section of his liver to determine the level of toxicity in his system."

Sikander's excitement bordered on the ghoulish as he launched into an enthusiastic explanation of the intricacies of tissue sampling to Mason, but just as he was warming to the subject, the doctor interjected brusquely, "I cannot help you."

"I beg your pardon?" Sikander was taken aback by being dealt such a curt refusal. He had expected Mason to play hard-to-get, thus resulting in another, more protracted bargaining session during which he would have to offer a more generous bribe, but to be faced with such a blunt dismissal…it was disconcerting, to say the least.

"It just isn't possible. You see, the Major has already been cremated."

"Cremated?" Sikander exclaimed, stunned.

"Yes, the body was claimed this very morning."

"By whose order?"

"Why, the Magistrate's, of course," Mason replied. "I received explicit instructions from Mr. Lowry himself. He came to see me late last evening."

"Lowry," Sikander echoed. "Lowry told you to cremate him?"

"Yes," the doctor said. "He was most adamant. He informed me it had been Major Russell's express desire to be cremated when he passed, since he did not wish to be buried in Indian soil, and that he had been tasked, as one of his closest friends, to ensure that these wishes were carried out." He squared his shoulders and gave Sikander a self-satisfied glare. "What can I say? It struck me as a perfectly sensible request."

This unforeseen development left Sikander flabbergasted. Any form of initiative from Lowry was surprising enough, but to directly contradict the Maharaja's specific instructions that he wished to examine the corpse, and that too after promising Sikander that he would try his best to pressure Mason into letting him make an autopsy, it just didn't make a whit of sense. The Maharaja wrinkled his nose. Whatever game the Magistrate was trying to play, it stank like rotten fish. In fact, everything about Lowry was beginning to deeply offend his finely tuned olfactories. The man had far too much of a stench attached to him to be nearly as innocent as he liked to pretend.

Without a body, Sikander had nothing. All that he could manage was conjecture and hearsay, and neither of those would hold up in a court of law, not for a minute.

"Tell me, Doctor," he said in a voice as corrosive as acid, "don't you think it would have been infinitely more sensible for Mr. Lowry to have waited a few days to carry out the Major Russell's request, until an officer of the Major's stature had received the public funeral that a man of his rank is entitled to? And for that matter, the Major was a Catholic. Didn't it strike you as at all odd that a gentleman of the Catholic persuasion should ask to be cremated?"

Mason's brow wrinkled as he considered these questions. Judging by the expression of growing doubt writ upon his face, it was patent the justifications he had been offered by Lowry no longer seemed quite so compelling in hindsight.

"Look," he snarled, as belligerently as a bulldog, "I am not a bloody policeman, am I? Why don't you go and speak to Lowry directly?"

It was quite obvious from his truculent demeanor that his patience, already tenuous, had finally come to an end.

"Frankly, I have said all that I am willing to. Now kindly excuse me."

The finality in his voice suggested that no amount of whiskey, however expensive, would compel him to brook any further inquiries. "And might I suggest," he added, "if you feel any further desire to speak with me, next time call at my office. And be sure to make an appointment first!"

Chapter Twenty

With that high-handed rebuke, Dr. Mason gave the Maharaja a thunderous scowl and strode away. Frowning, Sikander turned to Charan Singh, who had been shadowing him while keeping a respectful distance as was his habit. "I have a task for you, old man. Speak to the servants, and see if you can locate a young memsahib for me."

"Is that wise, Sahib?" The old Sikh said, raising one disapproving brow. "Wouldn't it be better to behave just this once?"

"Oh no, you dirty-minded ape!" The old fool thought he was seeking an assignation, of all things. "I mean a specific memsahib. Her name is Mrs. Bates, and she is the main reason I have come to this deplorable gathering. She is the one I need to question."

Charan Singh gave his master a toothy grin, as if to suggest that he did not believe Sikander's motives were quite as platonic as he was pretending. "I will try to locate her, Huzoor."

Even as he spun on one boot-heel and marched away, Sikander retreated in the opposite direction, suddenly desperate for a breath of fresh air and a few solitary moments to gather his thoughts. Unfortunately, out on the Ross Common's lawns, things were even more hectic. A massive striped tent that looked like it had been stolen from a circus had been erected right in the middle of the rose garden, surrounded by rows of trestle tables bearing a buffet lunch at which an innumerable horde of Angrez foraged, like pigs at the trough, while a few feet away, a six-piece orchestra sat atop a raised stage, murdering what sounded like Debussy with glib enthusiasm.

Unfortunately, before he could find a quiet corner, he saw his hostess, bearing down on him like an unstoppable juggernaut. Lady Fitzgerald, as she liked to style herself, was hard to miss. The best word he could devise to describe her was "redoubtable," in recognition of that stolid beam and stately prow, so reminiscent of one of Bismarck's battleships. On the face of it, she made a fine picture of English gentry, with an upper lip so accustomed to being stiff that it could have cracked a block of cement and that supercilious superiority of manner that came only from inherited wealth.

But the truth about her, as Sikander knew, was somewhat more picaresque. He had the real scoop from Miller. The lady in question was neither a Lady, nor a member of the gentry at all. She had begun her life as a greengrocer's daughter in Manchester, but at the tender age of fifteen, had run away and made her way to London to become a draper's assistant at one of the high-priced establishments near Bond Street. That was where she had made the acquaintance of one Malcolm Fitzgerald, a cad and a bounder who had a reputation for being a procurer of women for gentlemen of the sort possessed of an excess of income and a taste for the gutter. It was this Fitzgerald who had introduced her to the elderly Nawab of Malerkotla, who had become quite smitten by her, most likely since he was a keen connoisseur of horseflesh and Mrs. Fitzgerald in her youth had borne a striking resemblance to that particular year's Derby winner. In either case, they had begun an affair that had culminated with the Nawab bringing her out to India and installing her as his mistress in a luxurious palace amidst the dun fields of rural Sangrur.

Quite obviously, Malerkotla, a dusty hellhole of a town amidst the vast plains of Punjab, as far from civilization as Hades itself, had been entirely unsuitable to Mrs. Fitzgerald's taste for the good life. Within months, her high-handed behavior had made her increasingly unpopular, not just with the populace, but also with the Nawab's family, who had recognized her for what she was, a grasping gold digger of the most shameless sort.

Less than a year after her arrival in Malerkotla, the old Nawab had passed away, rumoredly during a particularly energetic session of lovemaking. Mrs. Fitzgerald, ever the survivor, had been quick to comprehend that her days of regal repose amidst the Doaba were at an end. Even as the Nawab's body had cooled, she had decamped from Malerkotla with breathtaking dispatch, but not before helping herself to a trunkful of the choicest jewels she could gather. A year later, she had arrived in Rajpore, and begun her career as the *grande dame* of local society. Over time, her soirées had come to be the highlight of the Rajpore season. Personally, Sikander had always dismissed her efforts as garish, but to the staid denizens of the Civil Lines, Mrs. Fitzgerald's parties seemed as glamorous as anything that was happening in Simla, if not Calcutta. As a result, her invitations were keenly sought, even fought over, with the younger officers willing to go to any lengths to make it to her list.

It embarrassed Sikander to be seen at one of her gatherings, and though he knew that he was only there because of the Major's murder, it aggravated him to no end to think he had given her just what she had craved for so long—the added glamor of having a native prince adding color to her deplorable spectacle, like some sort of trained monkey.

This embarrassment intensified to panic as Mrs. Fitzgerald picked up speed. Mortified, Sikander lost his nerve. Turning on his heels, he decided to flee before she could catch up with him. It was a close run thing, the Maharaja scurrying along frantically like a hare, Lady Fitzgerald coursing after him like a rather dumpy hound, but he was finally able to shake her by seeking refuge behind a particularly bushy potted Grevillea.

As he recovered his breath, trying his level best to seem unobtrusive, Sikander was accosted by Miller, who had been watching the whole chase unfold with a sardonic smirk. The presswallah looked a righteous fool, all dressed up like a Turk, from his pointy slippers right up to the silver embroidered fez he wore perched jauntily upon his head. And judging by the bright coloring in his cheeks, he had already enjoyed more than a drink or two, which explained the uncharacteristic expression of *joie de vivre* sparkling on his ordinarily sullen face.

"My God, Mr. Miller, what on Earth are you supposed to be?"

The presswallah let out a vast chuckle. "Just something picked up while I was in Egypt, Effendi. I think it makes me look quite dashing."

Clasping his hands to his hips, he tried to affect a flamboyant pose, as fitting a rake on stage, but sadly, the best he could accomplish was the look of a rather careworn duck, given his rotund body and long neck bobbing up and down comically.

Sikander rolled his eyes. "Tell me, were you able to track down the information I asked you to investigate—about the Major and why he was compelled to leave Cambridge?"

"I'm afraid not," Miller said, sobering up so quickly that Sikander found himself wondering if the man had been play-acting all along, acting the fop on purpose. "I have put out some feelers, but I am sad to say that none of my sources have gotten back to me yet."

Sikander let out an involuntary curse so colorful that it made Miller wince. The journalist's face fell, obviously thinking that the Maharaja's ire was directed at him. "I am sorry that I have not been more helpful," he apologized sheepishly.

"Not at all, Mr. Miller," Sikander murmured. "Let me know directly when something turns up, will you?"

"Of course!" He gave Sikander something between a nod and a hop. "Would you care to join me for a drink?" He held up his glass, wrinkling his nose. "Rather dreadful swill, I'm afraid, but at least it *is* free."

"Thank you, but no! Sadly, I really must track down the Magistrate and have a quick word with him."

"Well, good luck with that," Miller snorted. "You will find him in the main dining room, holding court to the usual crowd of sycophants. I can only hope that the high and mighty Mr. Lowry can spare the time to speak with you."

"What makes you think he will not?" Sikander asked, smelling more than a hint of recrimination in the presswallah's tone.

"Oh, the man seems to have been infected by a strange malaise, Your Majesty. A more dreadful case of *caput turgidum* I have yet to see." Miller smiled, overly amused by this feeble witticism. "His fat head has gotten so large, I am surprised the odious fellow can stay upright."

"Well, I will just have to cut him down to a manageable size, won't I?'"

"Much as I would dearly love to see that," the presswallah tittered, lifting his fez in salutation, "I have rather a pressing engagement to keep." He offered Sikander a mock bow, then staggered away, somehow managing to keep his balance as he made a beeline for the nearest bearer he could spy with a tray of champagne.

Shaking his head indulgently, the Maharaja wasted no further time in setting out to confront Lowry. The Ross Common's dining room was an ornate enclosure, accessed from the main foyer by a pair of arched Venetian doors. It was decorated in that grim Victorian style that always caused Sikander to gag, with dreadful Acanthus-papered walls and an excess of Rococo furniture that had been buffed to the sheen of old ivory, no doubt by a legion of long-suffering servants. Inside, rather than one large open space, the interior was partitioned into small alcoves, within which nestled damask-covered tables, thus permitting diners some semblance of privacy.

Rather than barging in, Sikander opened the door just enough so that he could peer inside. Lowry was in the last alcove on the left, surrounded, as Miller had described, by about a half dozen hangers-on, mostly traders and boxwallahs by the look of them. Instead of approaching the man directly, Sikander decided to take a circuitous route, careful to ensure that he was not spotted, until he managed to fetch up behind the leafy cover of a large potted acacia, close enough so that he could eavesdrop on Lowry's conversation without being detected.

"Have you heard from Simla yet, about who is to be our next

Resident?" This from one of the boxwallahs, a gaunt, bespectacled fellow dressed as a Cossack.

Lowry, who had chosen to attend as a Roman senator, it seemed, done up in a toga that looked to be fashioned from a bedsheet, replied to this question with a self-satisfied smile. "It is only a matter of time. I have been informed that a special investigator has been dispatched to look into the Major's death and is expected to arrive as soon as tomorrow. I have no doubt he will come bearing orders confirming my appointment to the post."

"About damn time!" Another of the men exclaimed, a slippery-looking fellow with a thin mustache who gave Lowry an ingratiating smile. "I hate to speak ill of the dead, but it will be good to have a pukka man at the reins for a change. While Major Russell, God rest him, was a decent enough sort, he let that damned Maharaja have too much latitude, I must say."

"Hear hear!" This from a man Sikander recognised, an abrasive Scotsman named MacGregor who happened to be the head of the jute cartel, and was forever petitioning the palace to privatize royal land. "That fellow gets far too many liberties for an Indian. Simla should just have him off the throne and take over themselves, like they did in Oudh. Now that would be good for business!"

Lowry puffed out his chest. "Don't you worry, my friends! Once I take over, things will change soon enough. I have the Maharaja of Rajpore firmly under my thumb, I assure you of that."

"Is that so?" A silken voice hissed from behind him.

With a start, Lowry spun around. A flare of panic seized him when he saw Sikander advancing toward him, an anxiety he only just managed to keep in control. "Your Highness," he squawked, making a monumental effort to force his mouth into a smile, "what are you doing here?"

Sikander ignored him, though his veiled eyes never left Lowry's face, his gaze so piercing that the Magistrate struggled not to flinch before its intensity. As for his companions, they watched the Maharaja as warily as if he were a tiger about to pounce.

"Make yourself scarce, won't you?" Sikander snarled with the sort of effortless rudeness that only a man of unimpeachable quality can manage. "Mr. Lowry and I would like some privacy."

The boxwallahs reacted as if he had just slapped them. En masse, they leaped to their feet and bolted away, with all the haste they could manage without causing a stampede.

Sikander still did not say a word to Lowry, letting him sweat. He held his tongue, waiting until a porter had pulled up a chair for him. Tipping the man with a gold mohur and waving away his grateful salutations, he sat down and crossed one leg over the other with languorous grace before offering the Magistrate a nonchalant smile. "Under your thumb, am I?"

Lowry reddened. "It was just talk," he started to apologize, but Sikander cut him off abruptly.

"Do you think me a fool?"

"No," the Magistrate replied, bewildered by this unexpected question, "of course not!"

"Then why must you persist in treating me like a clown?" Sikander's face hardened. "Tell me, why did you order the Major's corpse to be disposed of with such alacrity?"

To his credit, Lowry managed to keep his composure, rolling with this barrage as adroitly as a veteran prizefighter. "It was his most fervent wish," he explained. "The Major told me often that he did not wish to rest for eternity in Indian soil, and that he had always wanted his ashes to be scattered across the lakes in Windermere."

"Is that so?"

"Yes, I swear it."

"Don't lie to me," Sikander hissed, slapping one palm down on the table so hard it wobbled, threatening to give way. Lowry recoiled, shocked by such an overt show of ferocity. His features suffused with terror, his mouth flopping open and shut, like a beached fish.

"I did not…I have not lied." He tried to bluster, so ineffectually that it could not have fooled a child, much less a man of Sikander's acumen.

"Don't waste my time, Mr. Lowry," Sikander snarled. "For your information, I know all about the wine."

"The wine?" This time, the Magistrate's bewilderment was much more real. "What wine? What in God's name are you talking about?"

"The Oloroso, you fat fool! You delivered a bottle to Major Russell as a New Year's gift, didn't you? I have tested it, and it was undoubtedly laced with strychnine."

Lowry's mouth sagged open, his eyes growing as wide as a deer caught by a hunting lamp. For one brief heartbeat, Sikander thought he had managed to corner the man, that he was going to break down and confess everything, but instead, the Magistrate made a strange noise, something between a snort and a chuckle.

"Oh, that's just grand!" he gasped. "You have the wrong man, Mr. Singh."

Sikander grimaced, surprised by the self-assurance of this denial. "I think not! I have it by your own admission, one that Miss Jane will only be too happy to corroborate, that you brought the wine to Major Russell. Or do you deny that?"

"Oh, no, not at all. I am indeed the person who brought Major Russell that particular bottle of wine."

"Then you are definitely the one who poisoned him!"

"Not quite," Lowry offered him a cherubic grin. "I am sad to say, Mr. Singh, that on this occasion, you are utterly mistaken. You see, Captain Fletcher is the man you are looking for. He gave that particular bottle to me and asked me to deliver it to the Major, just last week."

With that declaration, he sat back, folding his arms across his ample chest to watch Sikander with rather a pompous expression, as if he were waiting to see precisely how the Maharaja would react, now that the theory of which he had been so certain had been so decidedly unraveled. Sikander's mind raced to assimilate this surprising turn. Was Lowry telling the truth? Was the Captain indeed the one responsible for the poisoned Oloroso? Or was this a feint, a barefaced attempt by the Magistrate to deflect suspicion away from himself towards another?

Before Sikander could make up his mind, Lowry swaggered to his feet. "I have given you all the time I can spare," he said, rather too self-importantly, as if he had suddenly discovered he possessed a spine. "This interview is at an end. If you have any further questions, I suggest you make an appointment at the Residency."

The Maharaja raised one sarcastic eyebrow, not at all antagonized by such cavalier brusqueness. "Good heavens, I almost forgot. You are now the senior man in Rajpore, aren't you?"

"Indeed, I am," Lowry said, as pompous as a pasha, "and while I would dearly love to sit here chatting with you, I have a great deal of work to do."

"Well," Sikander countered, "at least until Simla sends out a more suitable replacement."

This comment brought Lowry juddering to a halt. He gave Sikander a sidelong look, inquiry mingling with trepidation and not a small amount of befuddlement. "I have every certainty, Mr. Singh, that I shall be the one to be confirmed as the new Resident of Rajpore."

"Perhaps," Sikander said coolly, examining his fingernails with an expression of utter disinterest. "Of course, I might have some say in the matter."

"I beg your pardon?"

Sikander leaned back, and stretched his arms lazily. "Nothing is certain in life, Mr. Lowry." He shrugged, a theatrical shudder of his shoulders. "Who can tell what the future holds? Besides, I have to wonder how Simla would feel about confirming your temporary assignment if they knew your secret?"

This question caused the man to shudder visibly. The panic which had so recently receded now returned two-fold. "This is preposterous! I have no secrets."

From the subtle tremor in his voice, Sikander sensed he had backed the man in a corner. "Let me paint a hypothetical picture for you, Mr. Lowry. Imagine a man who has a closely guarded infirmity, one that is shunned amongst men of quality, which if uncovered could be damning not only to his career, but also to his reputation. And then imagine that someone should discover this most closely guarded of secrets, which he then holds over that unfortunate man's head, forcing him to do things against his will, dreadful insidious things. Tell me, how would that man react?"

He fixed the Magistrate with an unblinking glare. "The Major discovered your secret, didn't he?"

Lowry winced, his face going as pale as chalk, and he averted his eyes, unable to bear such a candid scrutiny. "I don't know what you're talking about," he objected weakly.

"Come now." Sikander lowered his voice until it was just a whisper. "He found out that you are a sodomite. I am sure of it."

Lowry gasped, feigning outrage at such a damning accusation, but his fury was much too brittle, too practised to be anything but artificial. It was like he had spent hours in front of a mirror rehearsing this denial, until it seemed more like an actor mouthing lines from a script rather than genuine indignation. "How dare you try and besmirch my good name! This is untenable."

"Shut up!"

"Mr. Singh! I will not tolerate being spoken to with such crude contempt...."

"Shut your damn mouth," Sikander said cruelly, "or I will shut for you."

The Magistrate's face stiffened. For a heartbeat, Sikander thought he had pushed the man too far, that perhaps he had managed to uncover some hidden reservoir of strength that would compel him to resist such brash harshness, but then, in the blink of an eye, all the fight seemed to go out of Lowry. With a vast groan, he collapsed back into his chair, as limp and nerveless as a rag-doll.

"What is going to happen now?" he asked in a small, dead monotone.

"Let me make this clear." Sikander's tone was almost sympathetic. "Frankly, I could not care less how you live your personal life. However, I suspect the Major was not quite as charitable as I am." He fixed Lowry with a knowing look. "How did it happen?

Did he walk in on you, all those many years ago, in *flagrante delicto* perhaps, with another man? Is that what caused your falling-out?"

Lowry gave him the briefest of nods, so slight that it was almost imperceptible.

"I can only imagine your surprise when you heard from the Major after all this time. When he offered you such a plum posting, no doubt you thought he had finally forgiven you, but that was not the case, was it?"

The Magistrate let out a low moan, as if every word was a wound.

"Did he blackmail you, compel you to do his will, or else threaten to expose you? Is that why you killed him, Mr. Lowry?"

The man finally found the strength to look at Sikander, staring at the Maharaja stonily. Abruptly, he seemed very different from the bumbling creature from a moment before. Now he seemed older, so tired that it brinked upon exhaustion, a broken wreck of a man. It was like Sikander was seeing him for the first time, now that his carefully maintained mask had wavered, like a changeling revealing its true face, a lonely, deeply unhappy creature who looked like he barely had enough strength to go on.

"I didn't kill him," Lowry whispered. "God knows I thought it often enough, but I did not do it, I swear by all that is holy."

"Why should I believe you when you have lied to me in the past?"

"I have a great many flaws, Your Majesty, but I could never take a life, and especially not Will's." He grimaced. "You have to believe me. He meant too much to me."

As he said those words, his face was wracked by a tremendous sorrow, and suddenly, Sikander realized how wrong he had been about Lowry's motives. He sat back, abruptly seeing everything very clearly. "You loved him, didn't you?"

The Magistrate's only reply was a gaunt groan.

"He was the one person I cared for more than anyone else. When he left Cambridge, I thought I had lost him, but then, when he sent for me after all this time, I felt that most dangerous of things, Mr. Singh. Hope. I let myself feel hope.

"That is why I came to Rajpore when Will asked, because I thought at last we could be together!" He glanced up at Sikander with that woebegone gravitas that only a man who has known love to be unrequited can feel. "And even though it did not take me long to realize that he did not reciprocate my ardor, I stayed, if for no other reason than to be near him.

"You think I killed him?" Lowry chuckled. "You really believe I could do that, murder the one person I loved more than life itself? Why, I assure you, it would be easier to kill myself!"

Chapter Twenty-one

This confession hung lugubriously between them, as immovable as a monolith.

Obviously, now that his deviant preferences were out in the open, Lowry was much too embarrassed to even meet the Maharaja's eyes. "If you will excuse me," he said awkwardly, "I really should be getting back to the others."

With a small nod, he rose and hurried away. Sikander did not impede him, even though he was unable to quell his misgivings about the man. It had been a convincing little monologue, so credible that he was tempted to fall for it, except for his reluctance to accept anything Lowry said at face value. The Magistrate was undoubtedly a liar *par excellence*, not just because he had a glib tongue, but also because he had spent so much time hiding the truth about his sexuality from the world, becoming as adept at playing a role as any thespian.

Still, a nagging voice in Sikander's head insisted that Lowry was telling the truth. And if he had indeed cared for Major Russell as deeply as he claimed, then that left him with no motive at all to want him dead. Abruptly, Sikander was assailed by an unbearable weariness. It was more than mere ennui, an unexpectedly vertiginous dizziness that made him feel faint for an instant. Fighting this unexpected exhaustion, he retreated from the dining room. Shying away from the crowd, he staggered in the direction of the guest bungalows, searching for a secluded spot where he could gather the tatters of his composure around him and take a moment to regain some measure of equanimity. To his relief, he spotted a gazebo nearby, behind a manicured privet hedge, an island of relative privacy that seemed deserted. With a groan, he made a beeline for its refuge, glad to be away from Mrs. Fitzgerald and her guests.

Once inside the gazebo, he let out a vast sigh. *What a fool's errand the whole expedition had been!* Sikander thought, giving vent to his frustration by rattling off a string of expletives so colorful they would have made a lascar blush.

He had thought himself alone, but a dim susurration behind him informed him he was not. He heard the briefest whimper of indrawn breath, as if to chastise his rudeness. Surprised, he turned to find he was being watched by a very lovely young woman. She was seated on a wrought-iron bench in one secluded corner of the gazebo, partially obscured by a large fern, which was why he had missed her.

Sikander's first impression was of fragility, of enormous Dresden blue eyes that stared at him with great apprehension and cheekbones so prominent that they looked like they would rip through her skin.

It surprised him to be confronted by such unbridled beauty, and he found himself a little staggered. To his dismay, the memsahib took this hesitation to be surliness. Thinking that he wished to be left alone, she rose to her feet. Almost without realizing it, Sikander took a step forward, moving to stop her before she could escape. As he came closer to her, he realized that she was very small, just under five feet tall, as tiny and delicate as a doll. He let his eyes flicker down from her face, playing across her body with an uncharacteristic lasciviousness that made the young lady turn a vivid shade of carmine that perfectly matched her russet hair. Sikander smiled, and continued his appreciation shamelessly. It pleased him that in spite of her slenderness, there really was nothing lacking with her figure, which was quite well rounded in all the right places—apparent in spite of the fact that she was dressed demurely, in tatty dark green drapery that was vaguely Greek in style

"Hera, Madam?" he observed, raising one brow.

The young lady in question brightened, letting out a delicate laugh that made her even more comely. "Oh no," she replied. "Andromache, and my husband has come as Hector."

Sikander tried not to groan, not just because of the afore-mentioned husband, but also because it was just so typical. The husband had to be a soldier, and a young one at that, for Hector was the choice they always made, those witless boys trying to play at being men, choosing heroes without ever realizing what they symbolized. Hector was a poor choice for any warrior, heroic enough certainly, but slain at the hand of Achilles, and a bad death at that. No, Odysseus would have been a better choice, and this delectable creature, what a Penelope she would have made, with no shortage of suitors trying to keep her bed warm.

"I am the Maharaja of Rajpore," he said, "but you, my dear, can call me Sikander."

With that cheeky introduction, he offered the memsahib a fine leg, taking the opportunity to try and glance down the front of her dress.

"Oh, I know who you are," she croaked diffidently, and to his surprise, reciprocated with a perfect curtsey, so reminiscent of a schoolgirl that it made him break into a smile. Abruptly, it occurred to him that he had seen her before. Hadn't she been at the Resident's bungalow the previous morning, the pretty little thing who had caught his eye in passing?

"I regret to say, Madame, that puts me at a marked disad-vantage. I thought I knew most of the people in Rajpore, but… Might I be so bold as to ask your name?"

It occurred to him that he was being impertinent, transgress-ing well past the boundaries of politeness by engaging her so overtly, but he found himself quite disarmed, not just by her obvious beauty but also by the air of innocence that emanated from her like a sweet perfume. She seemed the very epitome of purity, unsullied, untainted by the cynicism of life that had turned people like Sikander into old men before their time. But was it real, or was it just a façade? Too often inexperience and ignorance masqueraded as innocence, particularly in the youthful, but in this case, could this young lady be that rarest of creatures, a genuine ingénue, utterly unaccustomed to the ways of the world?

"Grace," she blurted out, before realizing her mistake, that offering her Christian name to a stranger might be thought to be forward. A roseate blush spread across her cheeks with a delicacy that no amount of rouge could ever achieve. "I mean, Mrs. Bates. My husband is a Lieutenant in the Cavalry."

At last, Sikander thought, delighted, *a stroke of luck!* Here she was, the very person he had come to see, the object of the Resident's romantic attentions. And now that he had met her face to face, he could see what had drawn the Major to her, like a moth to a flame. Mrs. Bates was every bit as enticing as he had been told, truly a breathtaking specimen, not a Penelope after all, but rather a Helen, the sort of creature for whom men sank ships and started wars.

"How fortuitous, Madame! I was hoping our paths would cross. I have been quite eager to speak with you."

In spite of his most charming smile, a flicker of alarm darted across her face, one flawless wrinkle marring that matchless brow. "I really should get back to my husband. He must be worried about me."

"Please, Madam," Sikander smiled, "can you not spare me just a few moments?"

This plea caused Mrs. Bates to hesitate. Like most women, she was weakened by the thought of having a powerful man in her debt. After taking a moment to make up her mind, she nodded, one curt shake of her head before she returned to the bench and sank back down, crossing her legs neatly and smoothing her robes. "What did you wish to speak about?"

Sikander realized he was staring at her again. *Stop being such a dunce*, he chastised himself. This behavior was most unlike him, to ogle at a woman as fervidly as a schoolboy. "Actually, I was hoping we could talk about Major Russell."

She reacted exactly as he had expected, by turning white as a ghost. "Excuse me," she said, leaping to her feet so hurriedly she almost toppled over, "I really ought to go."

"Sit down!" Sikander hissed. The steel in his voice took her by surprise, and almost meekly, she obeyed, watching him as nervously as a mouse being cornered by a cat.

"I am afraid I cannot help you," she groaned. "I barely knew the man."

It was a lie, and a feeble one at that.

"It is useless to deny it, Madame. It is well known that you and the Resident were, to put it politely, involved."

Of course, Sikander knew that she would deny this accusation, but this was only his opening gambit, and exactly as he had expected, Mrs. Bates countered by trying to bluster her way out.

"How dare you?" she said with an outraged gasp. "I will have you know, I am a happily married woman."

"Are you, Madam?" He said, leaning forward. "That is not what I have heard." Sikander fixed her with a level frown. "Let me be blunt, I believe you are involved in Major Russell's death. All that remains is for me to find out exactly how, and to what extent."

Faced with such a forthright accusation, Mrs. Bates recoiled. Her lips parted in a gasp, her mouth falling open into a rictus of pure indignation. Those scintillating eyes widened, filling with tears so distraught that Sikander was hard-pressed to believe that she was faking them, not unless she was as fine an actress as Sarah Bernhardt herself.

"How can you accuse me of such a heinous deed?" she whispered with a glare so accusatory that he almost felt a pang of remorse for suspecting her. "Why are you being so cruel?"

It was a breathtaking performance, right down to the perfect sob that escaped from those soft lips, touched by just the right amount of abject despair. For a moment, she seemed so vulnerable that Sikander was almost convinced. But then, he saw those eyes, watching him with a wary gleam, and he knew at once it was all a pretence. *He had been correct to doubt her*, he thought sadly, feeling somewhat betrayed. The innocence he had found so beguiling was just a veneer. And it was quickly becoming apparent to him that Mrs. Bates was most accomplished in using this distressed damsel act to manipulate men into getting her own way.

Now that he could see the truth of the woman, Sikander was relieved. No longer was her beauty quite as intoxicating as it had been just a few minutes ago. At last, he felt he had the measure of Mrs. Bates. She was a temptress, a siren. Like Mohini, she used her beauty to beguile and enslave men, charming them into doing exactly as she desired. But little did she realize that Sikander was no ordinary man. In his time, the Maharaja had known many women, some even more alluring than this young memsahib, and it would take more than carefully calculated histrionics and a coquettish smile to seduce him.

"Madam, spare me your hysterics," he said unkindly. "Do you really intend to deny that the Major made advances towards you?"

Realizing that her indignation, however dramatic, was having little effect on the Maharaja, Mrs. Bates changed tack as effortlessly as a clipper. In an instant, the tears evaporated, and she gave Sikander a cold scowl, her features stiffening with such imperial disdain that he was tempted to break into applause.

"No," she hissed, giving up any pretense to seem delicate, "he certainly made no secret of it, so why should I? It is true that Major Russell was besotted with me."

"And it was entirely unrequited, this affection?"

"Oh, I assure you," she said icily, "I had no interest in Major Russell whatsoever. It was he who was obsessed with me. I did nothing to encourage him, but still, the man pestered me relentlessly." She shuddered. "It was dreadful. He would send me gifts, and make it a point to waylay me when I visited the bazaar and pretend it was accidental. Why, the man even turned up at our home, if you can believe it."

"He visited you, at your residence?"

"Oh yes, once or twice a month in the beginning, but then every week, as regular as clockwork. At first, he would make up the most peculiar excuses, that he was looking in to see that we were settled or that he had come by to drop off some venison he had bagged, but then, a little over a month ago, he dropped all pretense."

"Why didn't your husband tell him off?"

"Oh, he was always careful to show up while Johnny was out on maneuvers, and frankly, I was afraid to tell him what was happening. I don't like him to worry about me, you see. He has enough on his mind without thinking of some randy old bugger stamping after me."

With that explanation, she leaned forward, coming so close to Sikander that he could smell the musk of her skin. "Do you have a cigarette?" she asked huskily.

Sikander reached into one pocket of his achkan, and extracted a slim-chased silver case, filled with his hand-rolled Sobranie Black Russians. He offered it to Mrs. Bates, and she took one of the cigarettes, licking her lips, waiting until he lit it before inhaling a cloud of dusky smoke with a groan that was almost sexual.

"Gosh, it's been a lifetime since I had one of these." She laughed, a throaty murmur that made his hair stand on end. "Johnny doesn't even know I smoke."

Giving him a friendly wink, she picked at a stray sliver of tobacco from the tip of her tongue, a marvelously sensuous gesture that sent an involuntary shiver down Sikander's spine. A moment ago, she had been the naïve innocent, but now she was a Lorelei, with veiled eyes that hinted at a wellspring of hidden sensuality. Truly, Mrs. Bates was quite a handful, and he found himself wondering which she had been with the Major, the ingénue or the seductress.

"Tell me, Madame, why did you not simply refuse to see the Major? You could have turned him away when he came to call upon you."

"How could I?" she replied without missing a blink. "He was Johnny's commanding officer. The last thing I wanted to do was offend him." She let out an unkind snigger. "What a foolish old goat he was! As if I would ever want someone as old and wrinkled as him! For God's sake, the man was almost forty, if a day."

The sheer contempt with which she enunciated the word forty made Sikander stifle a groan. He was nearing forty himself; the Major had been even older, but to someone as young as Mrs. Bates, it was all one and the same. Suddenly, he found himself disliking her intensely, not just because he envied her youth, but for her insouciance, which made him feel overwhelmingly decrepit.

"Is that normal, to have men chasing after you like dogs in heat?"

"Of course," she said, as nonchalantly as if she were discussing the weather, "I am quite used to it. Men have always lost their minds around me, ever since I was a little thing." She tossed her hair and gave him a cool look. "Mostly, I ignore it. They mean no harm, and just want to buy me presents, so I put up with it and never let it get too far. But the Major…" She grimaced, as if she had just swallowed something bitter. "The truth is I didn't realize what kind of man he was. He was always very polite until this past week, when his attentions ceased to be merely cordial."

Sikander sat up, sensing they had arrived at something important. "What happened, Madame? Did he make a pass at you?"

Mrs. Bates winced, taken aback by his bluntness. "Let us just say that he became somewhat amorous, but I was able to fend him off before anything too dreadful ensued."

"Why did you not make a complaint?"

She let out a bitter little laugh, and offered Sikander a look that only a woman who has been put upon by unkind men innumerable times can master. "And to whom would I complain? The Major was the senior-most office in Rajpore, wasn't he? Besides, I couldn't take the risk. He had my husband's career in his hands, and I certainly did not wish to jeopardize Johnny's prospects." She shuddered, and brought the cigarette back up to her lips, puffing at it with a restlessness that bordered on desperation.

"You could always have left Rajpore, Madame."

"Oh, I dearly wanted to," she said with an expansive sigh. "Truthfully, I never wanted to come here in the first place. I was hoping for Simla, but Johnny wanted to come up to the Punjab. He was hoping for frontier duty, but instead, he was bogged down here, little more than a glorified Quartermaster. We asked for a transfer many times, but the Major always turned down his requests, to keep me here, I suspect, firmly under his thumb."

"Did you ever make it clear to him that his attentions were entirely unwelcome?"

"Yes, I did, more than once," she said insistently. "Just last week, in fact, he turned up, quite inebriated, swearing his undying love, and then the silly bugger tried to kiss me. I was horrified, naturally, and told him in no uncertain terms that he had to stop bothering me. I told him he was being ridiculous, that I was happily married, and had no desire to engage in a dalliance with anyone else, and that if he continued to harass me, I would tell my husband about his behavior."

"And how did the Major react to this ultimatum?"

Mrs. Bates' pretty face suffused with consternation. "He laughed at me. He called me a silly little girl, and warned me that he always had his way. And then, he threatened Johnny."

"What sort of threat?"

"He said that if I didn't come away with him, he would make sure that my husband was posted to the border." She shuddered even more violently. "Just the thought of my poor Johnny, out there with all those bloodthirsty ruffians trying to cut him to pieces, it was too much for me to bear."

Once again, Mrs. Bates let Sikander have a full broadside. Her urgency was marvelously skillful, those fiery curls wafting in a well-timed breeze, her cheeks reddening with emotion, those startling eyes brimming with tears. If he hadn't already recognized her for what she truly was, Sikander would undoubtedly have been seduced, but thankfully, he was now quite immune to her charms, ample though they were.

"Did you warn your husband about the Major's ultimatum?"

"Good heavens, no!" She looked as if she were horrified by the very idea.

"Why not?"

"I told you, I just couldn't risk it," Mrs. Bates said with a visible shiver. "Johnny is very possessive, and I didn't want him to run off and confront the Major and destroy his own career, not because of me."

"Is your husband prone to violence? Would you say he is capable of murdering a man, say, in a jealous rage?"

She shook her head, and an amused little chuckle escaped her lips. "You obviously haven't met my Johnny. He couldn't hurt a fly. He's just impulsive, that's all, and hot-headed, but he has a good soul."

"You seem to love him very much," Sikander observed.

"I do, with all my heart," Mrs. Bates replied shyly.

That might be the first truly genuine thing she has said, he thought wryly. Or was it just another lie? From what he had seen of the young memsahib so far, he found it difficult to imagine her loving anyone except herself. Beneath her comely exterior, she was a grasper, an opportunist, as relentless as Barbara Villiers herself. Did she indeed care for her husband as deeply as she professed, or had he been a convenient foil she had fixed upon like a limpet, the means to an end? Had she tethered her future to his because she believed in him, or because she was merely using him to forward her own ambitions, until she could find a more convenient man to entangle with her wiles? Sikander found he could not tell. His brain insisted she was a cold, heartless creature, but in his heart, he could not help but feel she was young and naïve enough to believe in something as hopelessly jejune as love.

"Do you love him enough to lie for him, Madame, perhaps enough to cover up a murder?"

"You're being ridiculous."

Sikander sat back, pursing his lips. "Do you think me a foolish man, Mrs. Bates, or a particularly gullible one?"

This question left the young memsahib quite befuddled. "No, of course not."

"Then why do you insist on being deceptive with me?"

Mrs. Bates' mouth gaped open. "I am not being deceptive. I have told you the unvarnished truth, I swear it."

"Is that so? Then why, pray tell, were you seen engaged in a intimate embrace with the Major at the New Year's Ball on the very night of his death?"

This question was what finally managed to make a chink in the armor of her hitherto imperturbable demeanor. Her pretty face turned a sallow shade of puce, the mask slipping momentarily to reveal a flicker of uncertainty.

"I fear I may not have been completely honest with you," she said, offering Sikander a desperate smile. "You see, it was my husband who first came up with the notion of a border posting and approached the Major, requesting a transfer. Johnny was very eager to see action. He comes from a long line of soldiers, and sitting here in the Cantonment, twiddling his thumbs, it just doesn't agree with him." She let out a forlorn sigh. "He has his head full of these dreams of adventure, but I didn't want to see him hurt. That is why I approached the Major and asked him to refuse his request."

"Is that so?"

"Yes, we came to an agreement of sorts. Each time Johnny would pester the Major for a transfer, the Resident agreed to refuse, and in exchange, I would let him play his little games."

"You mean to say you kept stringing him along," Sikander observed dryly.

Mrs. Bates shot him a withering look. "Don't look at me like I am a whore! I was trying to keep my husband safe. And I was managing just fine, until the Major decided to betray me."

Sikander tensed, sensing that she was at last coming to the truth. "How? How did he betray you?"

"A few weeks ago, he agreed to let Johnny have a transfer."

"I take it you were not pleased that the Major had contravened your arrangement."

"Of course not," Mrs. Bates snapped. "I was, quite frankly, stunned. Johnny came home and told me to start packing up. He said the Major had agreed to send him on to Gandamak, and that too after all the times I let him…" Her voice choked with outrage, dwindling to nothing. A shadow played across her features, an intaglio of emotion so intense it dismayed Sikander.

Was it guilt, or rage? He found, to his chagrin, that this once he could not quite tell.

"And that is why you sought him out at the ball, to try and dissuade him from transferring your husband?"

"Yes! I hoped to plead my case, and throw myself on his mercy, but before I could say a word, Major Russell made me a proposition. He told me unequivocally that the only thing that would keep Johnny in Rajpore was if I…if I let him have his way with me." Mrs. Bates shuddered. "And then the brute tried to force himself upon me."

"And you resisted?"

"Of course I did!"

"Let me see if I can deduce what happened next." Mrs. Bates was looking very worried by now, and had started to chew restlessly on one dainty nail. "Your husband chanced upon you as you were locked in this tussle with Major Russell, and that, I am guessing, was the cause of their altercation, wasn't it?"

She nodded. "Yes, it wasn't his fault, though. What man wouldn't stand up for his wife?" Once again, those marvelous eyes settled on Sikander, tragic this time, brimming with earnestness. "I had nothing to do with his death, I swear it, and neither did my Johnny."

"Very well, Madame," Sikander said, making a great show of empathy, although he didn't accept a word coming out of her mouth. "I believe you. However, there is still one small doubt in my mind."

"And what is that?" she asked, rather too hastily.

"If you were merely a victim as you insist so vehemently, then why did you go to his house the very night before he was murdered?"

"I did no such thing," she squeaked. This time the mask dissolved entirely, that carefully maintained demeanor of sophistication, and her eyes glazed with unmitigated panic.

"I have a witness, Madame, who saw you."

"That can't be. It was much too dark." Even as those words escaped her lips, she realized her error, and clapped one horrified hand to her mouth, but it was too late. Sikander restrained the sense of triumph that flooded through him. He had her now. He could see it on her face, the hesitant patina of guilt, brittle, fragile, but to someone of his intellect, as clear as day. *One more push*, he thought, *that was all it would take to break her, to get her to confess everything.*

Sadly, before he could press home the advantage, a shrill voice rescued Mrs. Bates from the abyss at whose edge she had been teetering so precariously.

"Get away from her, you bloody darkie."

Sikander turned to see who it was that had the gall to engage him so rudely. He was greeted by the sight of a gangly young man striding towards the gazebo. The Maharaja gazed at him in amused amazement, unable to decide whether to laugh or be taken aback, for he cut a truly peculiar figure. The first word that sprang to mind was a parrot, for this youth had that same strutting manner. The next adjective that he thought of was a word he had never quite had a chance to use until that instant. A popinjay. Lieutenant Bates, for this was undoubtedly Mrs. Bates' much maligned husband, was the very epitome of what Sikander imagined a popinjay must resemble.

While the Maharaja was nothing if not *au courant* with the latest fashions, even his splendor paled before the lieutenant, who was, by all accounts, a true dandy. Sikander had expected him to be dressed as a Trojan with a breastplate and greaves and perhaps the inevitable plumed helm, but the young man had decided, it seemed, to come as a neo-classical Hector, for he was done up in a resplendent uniform, not unlike a cuirassier from Napoleon's Old Guard, complete with a fur pelisse and a hairy shako shaped like a hoopoe's nest perched on his angular head.

On a handsome man, the effect might have been striking, but sadly, Lieutenant Bates was extremely unattractive, as tall and gaunt as a stork. In fact, everything about him was bird-like—the way he walked in short bounding hops, the way his neck bobbed from side to side gave the immediate impression of a giant emu, trying eagerly to take to the sky but unable to get off the ground.

He was a young man, younger than Sikander had expected, not more than twenty or twenty-one, for he still had a smattering of adolescent acne on his cheeks. This general air of inexperience was only added to by his affectation of a patchy little mustache that drooped deplorably at its tips, and made him seen somehow louche, almost Continental. If it had been his intention to cut a military swash, Sikander thought, the fellow had failed miserably, for all the uniform, albeit well tailored, managed to do was make him look comical, a parody of a soldier with an over-large sword at his waist that clanked against his knees with every footstep he took, threatening to entangle itself in his legs and trip him over.

From the determined scowl pasted on his face and the stern set of his shoulders, the Maharaja could tell that here was a fellow bent upon violence. Ordinarily Sikander would have spared no time putting someone like him squarely in his place, but to his surprise, this once, a pang of sympathy for the man stirred in his gut. He realized he had to shoulder at least some of the blame for the Lieutenant's ire. He could only imagine how it looked to him, to find his beautiful wife hidden away in a secluded nook in the company of another man, and an Indian to boot.

As a result, he decided to adopt a conciliatory stance rather than a confrontational one, in spite of the Lieutenant's unforgivable crudity.

"I mean no harm. I was simply talking with your lovely wife, my dear fellow."

Sadly, ignoring this attempt at conciliation, the man refused to be mollified. "Shut your bloody mouth, you insolent wog." He exclaimed, and shook one fist at Sikander.

Rather reluctantly, Mrs. Bates sprang to the Maharaja's defense. "Don't be rude, Johnny," she objected weakly. "We were just talking."

All this explanation served to do was make the Lieutenant even more livid. "Shut your mouth, you filthy strumpet," he growled, so vehement that the memsahib recoiled, paling with barely disguised terror. "First you go sniffing around that old fool of a Major like a bitch in heat, but I turned a blind eye, because at least he was one of us. But now you are cozying up to this dirty nigger, and that too in plain sight of half the damned town. How could you do that to me?" He shot her a murderous glare. "I'll see to you shortly, by God, I will."

This was just too much for the Maharaja to tolerate. While Sikander had been willing to give the young man the benefit of the doubt and dismiss him as one of that lamentable breed with too much beef in his diet, to hear him lambasting his wife with such viciousness set his hot Sikh blood aflame.

Nevertheless, in spite of his exasperation, he made one last, valiant attempt to reason with the boy. "Calm yourself, Mr. Bates. Let us…"

Unfortunately, before he could finish his sentence, the Lieutenant pulled a glove from his belt, and with immense theatricality, flung it down at the Maharaja's feet. Sikander could barely believe his eyes. Could the boy mean to call him out to a duel? No, he had to be joking, or else half-mad. It was laughable, to be issued a challenge so brazenly in this day and age. To the best of Sikander's knowledge, the last known British duel had been fought some five decades previously, in 1852, between two Frenchmen, quite ironically. Since then, it was ludicrous to think of settling arguments by single combat, but this young brat, it seemed, was in a mind to reenact the old practice.

"Have you taken leave of your wits?" Sikander said incredulously, unsure whether to be horrified or amused.

"Silence!" the Lieutenant sneered. "You have slighted my honor, and I will not rest until I have had reparation. Face me, you brown bastard, or admit you are a cowardly cur."

He was serious. The silly bugger really expected Sikander to actually fight him. The Maharaja let out an enormous chuckle. He had thought the boy a fool, but what a monumental fool he could never had imagined, not in a dream. Not only did the Lieutenant have the temerity to talk to a Maharaja like he was a mere jemadar, but he had failed to take the measure of the man he was challenging so openly to a duel to the death. Little did he realize that Sikander could kill him in the blink of an eye, with or without weapons. The only thing holding him back was that killing someone as inexperienced as this callow boy would have been little better than murder, and the Maharaja found he had no appetite for murder that afternoon. He was too tired, for one thing, and much too sober.

"Oh, grow up! I am not going to fight you." Shaking his head, he tried to brush past the Lieutenant, but Bates blocked his passage.

"Have you no honor, or is it that you are craven?"

Such barefaced insolence, it was very nearly the final straw. Sikander struggled to contain his shock. He had thought the man reckless, even foolhardy, but was he really daft enough to imagine he could get away with publicly assaulting an Indian of Sikander's rank? Was there no end to his stupidity?

"Do you know who you are talking to?" he said coldly, unable to believe the gall of the man.

"I know bloody well," the boy mocked, "a jumped-up bloody chuprassie who needs to be taught his place." The Lieutenant held up one clenched fist, shaking it at the Maharaja. "And I am just the man to teach that lesson."

"Oh, Johnny," his wife wailed, "that's quite enough." She tried to interpose herself between the two men, giving Sikander a look of desperate entreaty. "Stop this madness, I beg you."

"Just you wait, you wanton slut. You are next, once I have put this kaffir in his place." With that imprecation, the boy struck a fighting stance, raising both fists in front of him in a rather limp pugilistic guard.

"Come on then," he growled, hopping back and forth with such agility that it would have made the Marquis of Queensbury blush. "I will have you know, I was the class champion at Sandhurst, I was."

This time around, Sikander just couldn't quite hold back his amusement. It came pouring out of him, a vast torrent of laughter. "Oh, give it up, you foolish twit, before you hurt yourself."

The Lieutenant ignored this sage advice and waded in, flailing his fists so wildly that he nearly knocked out his own wife. First, a roundhouse, then a clumsy swipe at Sikander's chin, then an even more desperate hook, all of which the Maharaja evaded effortlessly, swaying away from the boy as sinuously as a reed confronted by a windstorm. He tried not to scoff. In spite of his claims of championship prowess, the boy was as unpracticed and slow as a novice.

Sikander's eyes narrowed as the boy's assaults grew more and more frenetic. It took a lot for him to resist the urge to hit back, to put Bates flat on his back, but the last thing he wanted was to cause this ridiculous situation to escalate. Instead, he satisfied himself with pirouetting away from every one of Bates' increasingly desperate assaults, until at last, the boy could swing his arms no more, gasping and huffing for breath.

"Are you quite done?" Sikander turned to the memsahib, who was watching him warily, unsure whether to be afraid of him or impressed by his agility, and made a deep bow. It had been his intent to saunter away, but before he could take more than a couple of steps, the Lieutenant summoned up a last gasp of energy and made one final sally.

This time, his rage bordered on incoherency. It was like he had lost all sense or reason. Sikander was stunned by such naked aggression. The first two times the boy had attacked him, he had suppressed the urge to retaliate. But this time, faced with Bates bearing down on him, screaming like a bashi-bazouk, his warrior instincts kicked in like clockwork.

Time seemed to slow down. Before Sikander knew it, his hand had shot out, the heel of his palm connecting solidly with the Englishman's face. With a brittle crack, the lieutenant's nose broke. Immediately, he let out a howl and fell to his knees, his hands scrabbling to his face to try and stifle the gouts of blood erupting from his damaged nostrils.

As Bates began to sob like a child, to Sikander's chagrin, it dawned on him that their fracas had managed to attract an audience. As if by magic, in that unique way that can only be seen in India, a crowd of onlookers had gathered around the gazebo, a sea of white faces, paramount amongst them Mrs. Fitzgerald, who made no move to intervene, but was instead watching the whole sordid tamasha unfold with a look of patent delight writ on her face.

Sikander bit back a curse. To his dismay, it occurred to him that somehow, he had managed become the villain of the piece. It was the boy who had been the instigator, who had attacked him first, but still, it was obvious from the panoply of scowls gazing up at him that the whites perceived him as the one to blame. Rage flowered inside him, then embarrassment. How could he have permitted things to get so far out of hand? Why had he allowed himself to lose his equilibrium in such a public fashion?

Out of the corner of his eye, he saw that Charan Singh was waving at him, trying to clear a path through the multitude. Squaring his shoulders, Sikander marched down to meet his manservant, ignoring the glares directed towards him as he pushed his way through the crowd.

Behind him, the Lieutenant had managed to regain his feet, tottering upright with his wife's assistance. "Go on, then," he shouted after Sikander, "run away, you coward."

It took all of Sikander's strength to ignore the Lieutenant's jibes. His cheeks burning with fury, he willed himself to keep walking. It would be so easy to turn and finish what Bates had started, for once and for all. From what he had just witnessed of the boy's prowess, he was no match for Sikander. Whether pistol or blade, the outcome would be inevitable. Or better still, why did he even need to sully his own hands? All he had to do was whisper a word in the right ear, and the man's career would come to a premature end. It would be so very easy.

Sikander shuddered. No other prince would have ever endured such obstreperous rudeness without retaliation. No, if it had been Patiala or Kapurthala the Lieutenant had crossed, Bates would be dead by now, cut down like a dog. But Sikander liked to think of himself as a more evolved specimen. While it infuriated him to have to endure such public humiliation, he reminded himself it was for a greater cause. Once he had unraveled the Major's murder, then he could take his revenge on the cocky young fool at his leisure.

By his side, Charan Singh let out a strangled groan, mortified that anyone could dare to take such liberties with his master. "You have only to say one word, Huzoor," he whispered murderously, more than willing to put the errant Lieutenant in his place, but Sikander shook his head.

"Leave it be, old man." Grimacing, he clenched his teeth hard enough to make his jaw ache. "Just go and fetch the car, will you? Frankly, I think I have had quite enough of British hospitality for one day.

Chapter Twenty-two

Charan Singh, long accustomed to his master's moods, was wise enough to hold his tongue until the Maharaja was settled comfortably in the passenger seat of the Rolls.

"Where to, Huzoor? Back to the killa?" He spoke warily, choosing his words carefully.

Sikander was tempted to agree. Given the turbulence of his displeasure, the notion of returning to the palace and seeking refuge in the company of a bottle of Krug sounded like a first-rate plan. But it occurred to him how little time there remained before Simla's investigator was due to arrive, so he decided the best move would be to finally track down the next person on his list of suspects, who happened to the Munshi.

"No," he commanded gruffly. "Take me to the City Palace."

As the vehicle lurched into motion, Sikander stripped off his pugree and loosened the neck of his achkan so that he could breathe more freely. Even though it was approaching eventide, the humidity showed no sign of abating. On the contrary, the sun insisted on shining down even more mercilessly, refracting off the whitewashed walls of the English bungalows as they flickered by, a haze so blinding that it caused his eyes to water.

Sinking back into the rich upholstery with a sigh, the Maharaja struggled to make sense of the disparate jumble of thoughts resounding through his skull. What a complicated muddle it was all shaping up to be! What happened to the simple murders, Sikander wondered, where the killer was as obvious as daylight to even the most bumbling of sleuths? But not this case! With each passing moment, with each new twist, it became more and more convoluted. An entirely uncharacteristic moment of self-doubt flickered through him. Could this challenge be beyond his capabilities? There were just too many questions and not enough answers, and his instincts told him there would be no quick endings in sight, that perhaps the answer to the riddle of who had poisoned the Resident might just be one that managed to defeat even his formidable powers of deduction.

It took all of Sikander's strength to force these doubts from his mind as the Rolls-Royce drew up outside the City Palace. As always, the sight of the British headquarters managed to make him wince. While he did not consider himself much of an aesthete when it came to architecture, the City Palace was undoubtedly one of the most hideous buildings he had ever had the misfortune to set eyes upon. Perhaps his opinion was jaundiced given his travels in Europe, but the place seemed even more egregious than he remembered, a hideous brick pile that combined the worst elements of Baroque, Rococo, and High Victorian. His mother had told him the story about its origins once, how his father had hired an Englishman called John Butler to design the building, but the man had refused to travel out to India to supervise its construction, choosing to dispatch the plans by mail instead, only to have them misread by the local masons. As a result, the building had been built front to back, which in retrospect was a bit of a favor to good taste, Sikander thought, considering that the exterior was so dreadful it could move a poet to tears. It was obvious that the aforementioned Mr. Butler had been a great fan of William Butterfield's School of Muscular Gothic, because he had chosen to design the entrance as a swirling labyrinth of plump pillars and ogee arches, between which were crowded enough grotesques to give any passing pigeons nightmares.

Inside, the building was stuffy and claustrophobic. There were portraits everywhere, as was expected, a massive one of the Queen looking like a jowled carthorse just opposite the entrance, and on either side of her, a row of erstwhile Residents, all of whom seemed to share the same equine superciliousness. Overhead hung a massive wrought-iron chandelier, and when he angled his neck backwards to look up, he saw that a flock of adventurous birds had made their nests in the high eaves. One squawked at him disdainfully and let loose a derisory stream that barely missed his head.

Ordinarily, the Residency was as busy as a beehive, teeming with innumerable chuprassies and vakeels and petitioners, not to mention dozens of guards, almost all of whom would have reacted with suspicion had the Maharaja of Rajpore turned up unannounced. But Sikander had timed his visit carefully. He had taken a measured guess that the large majority of British staff would be at Mrs. Fitzgerald's brouhaha, thus leaving the path clear for him to pursue his investigations.

To his relief, his calculations seemed to be spot-on. Exactly as he had hoped, the Residency was deserted, and Sikander walked right in, Charan Singh by his side, without being challenged once. There were only two guards on duty in the atrium, thankfully both native Havildars, and they were busy at a game of dice, squatting on their haunches directly opposite the main entrance, chattering and arguing, so caught up in their gambling that they did not even notice they had company until Sikander cleared his throat rather pointedly.

Immediately, they jumped to their feet, trying not to look utterly surprised. Their appearance and demeanor only served to reinforce his already low opinion of Jardine. The Havildars' uniforms were slovenly and unkempt, and their rifles well out of reach, propped up listlessly against a pillar. To his delight, Sikander realized that he knew one of the men. It was none other than Jha, the rat-faced constable who had assisted him at the Major's bungalow just the day before.

Sikander offered him a resplendent smile. "Well, Havildar Jha, we meet again. How are you, my good man?"

The Havildar's mouth fell open, taken aback at the unexpected warmth of this greeting, and it took him a minute to gather himself well enough to offer the Maharaja a delayed salute, although the best he could manage was a grunt and a sort of half wave, as if he was trying to swat an imaginary fly.

"How may we be of service, Huzoor?" Jha asked unctuously.

"I am here to speak with the Munshi. Where may I find him?"

Thankfully, rather than making a fuss, Jha had the good sense not to argue. "He is in the Major Sahib's office." He gave the Maharaja a bow. "It is the last door…"

"I know where it is," Sikander said. Pulling a fistful of coins from one of his pockets, he handed them to Jha absent-mindedly. The Havildar let out a gasp, his eyes goggling at such largesse. Even as he began to genuflect with gratitude, the Maharaja forged past the man. Charan Singh made to follow, but Sikander delayed him with a curt nod. "You wait here. Make sure that I am not disturbed, in case our friend Mr. Jardine shows up."

Leaving the big Sikh to watch dolefully as Jha and his colleague resumed their wagering, Sikander made a beeline for the Major's office, located at the far corner of the City Palace. It comprised a suite of three rooms, first an anteroom crowded with moldering filing cabinets, then a rather chintzy waiting room that smelt of mildew and tea leaves and was packed with low wooden benches, and beyond that, the Major's private sanctum, hidden behind a teak door so thick it seemed to have been wrought from an entire tree.

Sikander had been hoping to catch the Munshi by surprise, apprehend him without warning at his desk, but when he entered the office, he found he was quite alone. He let out a curse, lamenting his luck. *What a complete waste of time, he thought crossly, to have come all this way only to find that the Munshi had flown the coop!* Frustrated, he spent a restless minute poking about aimlessly through the papers on the Munshi's desk, but found nothing useful, little more than a heap of requisitions.

Just as he was about to leave, much to his surprise, a strident cacophony assailed his ears, making him wince. At first, he took it to be the sound of a stray cat in heat, screeching its heart out as it searched for a mate, but after a moment, he realized it was a man's voice, belting out a shrill and tuneless refrain. Curiously enough, Sikander thought he could recognize the song, even though it was being mangled quite thoroughly. It seemed to be the Major general's song from Gilbert and Sullivan's *Pirates of Penzance* of all things, and what the singer lacked in rhythm, he certainly seemed to be making up for in tenor.

It dawned on the Maharaja that this caterwauling was emanating from inside the Major's private office, which he had assumed was locked. Wondering who it was that could be responsible for this awful racket, he tried the door, and when it yielded to his grip, he eased it open gingerly, careful not to alert whoever might be inside and send him scarpering. To his disbelief, the source of this unearthly din was none other than the Munshi. There he was, seated in a leather wing-back chair, his dhoti wracked up to reveal his bony knees, his bare feet planted squarely atop the Major's Ceylonese cherrywood writing table.

From the looks of it, he had been in the midst of enjoying one of the Major's choice cheroots, puffing away contentedly amidst a cloud of pungent smoke while gulping down a decanter of what looked to be a rather gritty port.

"What have we here?" Sikander exclaimed, unsure whether to be amused or appalled by such an unexpected sight. "Was there a celebration to which I was not invited?"

His voice took the Munshi utterly by surprise. The old man let out a yelp of dismay. Like a jack-in-the-box, up he leaped, astonishingly spry for a fellow of his advanced years. Shooting a panicked look at the Maharaja, he divested himself of the cigar with the utmost haste, tossing it into the wastepaper basket that flanked the table. Sadly, this served only to ignite a small fire, which he then proceeded to try and stamp out, dancing from one bare foot to the other as haplessly as a buffoon in a Punchinello show.

Before the scene could devolve completely into a nautanki, Sikander crossed over to snatch up a jug of water from a nearby sideboard, and poured it over the conflagration before it could flare out of control.

The Munshi remained motionless, frozen stiff, as if he had come face to face with Medusa herself. Abruptly, realizing perhaps that no explanation could justify being caught taking such loathsome liberties, he bolted. Like a rat scurrying for its hole, he tried to edge towards the door, but Sikander had no intention of letting him get away so easily.

Before he could make good his escape, the Maharaja planted himself squarely in his path. "Not so fast, Munshi!"

The old man recoiled, backing away so violently that he nearly toppled off his feet. "Forgive me," he stammered. "I am deeply sorry for my behavior, Sahib. I am a fool."

Sikander ignored this apology. "You are a very talented liar, Munshi. You had me good and fooled, and I am a very difficult man to dupe."

"I have never lied, Huzoor," the Munshi squealed haplessly. "I am an honest man, I swear it."

"It's no use," Sikander said. "I know all about your land manipulations. Stealing from war widows; you should be ashamed."

This declaration made the Munshi's eyes widen with shock. Realizing that he was cornered, he made a most unexpected move. From somewhere deep within the voluminous folds of his dhoti, a gun appeared. It was tiny, a pocket pistol barely larger than his hand, not unlike the weapon used by Booth to assassinate Lincoln. Sikander could not tell the make, but it looked to be a single shooter, what the Americans called a derringer and the Brazilians a *garrucha*.

A lesser man would most likely have wet himself, confronted by the barrel of a gun pointed directly at his face, but Sikander did not even flinch. If anything, the Munshi seemed more terrified than he did. The old man's hand shook horribly, wavering as he tried to keep his aim steady. "Stay back," he screeched as shrilly as a woman. "I am leaving, and if you try to stop me, I will shoot."

Even as he made this threat, the Maharaja reacted automatically. With one nimble hand, he swept up the nearest thing he could reach, a heavy blown-glass paperweight shaped like a very buxom mermaid astride a prancing seahorse, which he snatched from atop the Major's table. As a boy, he had been quite a David with a slingshot, especially when it came to knocking down partridges. Thankfully his aim, it seemed, had not deserted him. Flicking his wrist, Sikander flung the paperweight at the Munshi. It connected exactly where he had intended, hammering into the man's shoulder with a meaty thud,

The glass cracked, splintering into shards as sharp as shrapnel. The Munshi let out a wail. The derringer faltered just for an instant. It was the briefest of moments, but more than time enough for the Maharaja to sweep forward in a blur of carefully composed motion. Even then, he was almost too slow. The Munshi must have involuntarily pulled the trigger, because the gun went off with a dull crack and a puff of acrid smoke, followed by a sharper thunk as the bullet slapped into the wood paneling behind Sikander's back, missing him by just a few inches.

Before the man could squeeze off another shot, Sikander's fingers closed over the gun and he twisted with all his strength. The outcome was inevitable. The old man could not have weighed more than fifty kilos on a wet day, and while Sikander was thin and wiry, his frame was corded with lean muscle. Added to that, his hands were as calloused as teak, hardened by daily training. The Munshi however was as soft as pudding, weakened by far too long spent sitting behind a desk and shuffling papers, and when Sikander jerked his hand downwards, the old man's wrist snapped, cracking like a brittle twig.

The Munshi let out a shrill squeal and let go of the gun, subsiding nervelessly to the ground, cradling his injured arm to his chest. Sikander held on to the weapon, snapping open the breech to make sure its chamber was clear, before tucking it into one of his pockets. Absently, he realized the shot the Munshi had gotten off had been even closer than he had realized. It must have creased his shoulder, leaving a ragged rent in the padding of his tunic that made him scowl.

A perfectly good outfit ruined, he thought sourly, feeling the onset of a dreadful exhaustion as the adrenalin that had been coursing through his veins began to ebb. At his feet, the Munshi was sobbing, mewling with agony, trying to move his hand but unable to do much more than flop around, like a bird with a broken wing.

Sikander stared down at him, his face a dispassionate mask. "Have you had enough?"

The man bared his teeth. Instead of replying, he hawked a gobbet of phlegm and spat violently at the Maharaja's boots, a futile, almost clichéd display of resistance that made Sikander want to roll his eyes.

"Very well," he said with a resigned smile, "if that is how you want to play the game, my friend…"

Without a hint of warning, he brought the same boot that had so recently been spat upon firmly down on the Munshi's broken forearm, pressing down with all his weight, grinding the shattered radius and ulna against each other. The old man screamed, a guttural cry of pure agony. Sikander did not even blink, remaining as unemotional as a statue. While he did not relish torture, he was not squeamish about it, pragmatic enough to understand its value as a interrogatory tool.

He knew that pain was the only language that someone like Munshi Ram would ever respect. Sadly, before he could test this theory further, at that precise moment, the door burst open, and Charan Singh came crashing in, followed by the bumbling pehradars from downstairs. Bewildered, they came to a stop amidst the room, taking in the sight of the Munshi cowering on the floor with something akin to disbelief.

"Are you hurt, Sahib?" Charan Singh inquired breathlessly.

"I'm fine."

"See, this is exactly why I cannot leave you alone for even a minute!"

Sikander silenced the old Sikh with a scowl. "Pick him up," he commanded, pointing at the sniveling Munshi.

The guards had the good sense to obey without question. Ignoring the old man's complaints, they hauled him roughly to his feet and dragged him across the room to deposit him unceremoniously on the nearest chair. The Munshi tried his best to wriggle free, but the Havildars each clamped a hand down on his shoulders, keeping him pinned firmly in place.

"Help me!" he pleaded. "The Maharaja Sahib has gone mad."

This desperate ploy was so pathetic that Sikander did not even deem it worthy of a cutting retort. Instead, he studied his fingers, wrinkling his nose in consternation when he realized, much to his disgust, that the old man's histrionics had caused him to chip a nail.

"You know, Munshi, most of my friends would have had you hanged by now. After all, you did try to shoot me!" His voice remained benign, as if he were discussing the weather, not holding the man's very life in his hands. "But I am nothing if not fair, and therefore, I have decided I will let you choose your own fate."

He smiled, a grin so entirely devoid of mirth that it made not only the Munshi shudder, but also the two Havildars flanking him shiver as well.

"The way I see it, you have two choices. Either you can decide to cooperate with me. Or, if you should choose to remain recalcitrant, I shall have to hand you over to my man here."

He nodded at Charan Singh, whose face twisted into a brutish grin. Unbeknownst to the Munshi, this was a well-practised routine. Sikander played the carrot and the old Sikh the stick, and they had rehearsed it so many times they had it down to an art form.

The big Sikh made a great show of loosening his shoulders and cracking his knuckles, as if limbering up for a particularly strenuous bit of exercise. "I am feeling my age today, Sahib," he said, giving the Munshi a withering frown. "Let us just give him to the Afghans! That should be entertaining, to say the least."

"What a capital idea!" Sikander exclaimed. "Well, Munshi, how does that sound to you? I hear the border tribes stake murderers out on a hill and cut open their stomachs, and leave them there for the crows and vultures to feed on. God only knows what they would do to a flatulent fool like you, and that too a Hindoo?"

The old man's face paled as he finally began to comprehend exactly how dire his plight was. "No, Sahib, please! Have mercy! Please, I beg of you, I have children, grandchildren!"

Sikander moved to loom over the old man, who shied away, holding up his injured arm to fend him off, as if he were terrified that the Maharaja would strike him again.

"Then stop lying to me, you worm, before I decide to take out my wrath on them!"

That was the final push the Munshi needed. The last vestiges of resistance leached out of him. His shoulders slumped, and he subsided forward, a broken man. "I admit it. I am guilty of misappropriating the land, but I am not the one to blame. It was the Major. It was all his idea. It was his scheme. I was only a pawn. Everything I did was at the Major's behest, I swear it by all that is holy!"

The old man began to blubber, breaking down. "I am not greedy by nature, Sahib, but you cannot fault me for wanting more than what I have? Why should I not make a profit, when everyone else is? Surely you cannot blame a man for taking what is offered freely, can you?"

He looked up at Sikander, but if he was hoping for sympathy, his hopes were cruelly dashed, for all he received was a frown so fierce it made him shudder.

"You think I am corrupt? Compared to the Major, I was a rank amateur."

He sucked in his breath through his teeth. "So what if I stole a little, if I embezzled a few annas here and there, if I altered the books? I thought I was being clever, that I was covering my tracks, but I did not realize what a shaitan the Major was. He was on to me from the very beginning, watching, waiting to make his move."

The old clerk groaned, a bitter exhalation of breath. "I made the mistake of becoming involved with a syndicate, and my gambling debts, they kept mounting until I had dug myself in too deep. They would have killed me, Sahib. You don't know what villains these Balochis are, Sahib! They are animals, with no hearts!"

"That was when the Major coerced you into the land swindle?"

The old man nodded mournfully. "Yes! What choice did I have left? He promised me that he would pay off my debts and keep the scandal secret if I helped him with his plan. He called it his retirement scheme. The Major Sahib had grand dreams. He was accumulating a nest egg so that he could return to England. He was going to buy a Lordship and a country manor, and live like a nabob, and he told me he would take me with him, to be his faithful retainer."

His sobs grew even more plaintive.

"At first it was just the land misappropriations, but then, I became his creature, body and soul. He made me into his procurer, Huzoor, me, a Kayastha brahman, reduced to being a pimp." He shook his head sadly. "A better man would have spat in his face, but I am weak, Sahib. He paid me well, and I took his money readily, which makes me just as evil as him."

A moan escaped his lips. "Oh, the things he did to those poor girls! How he debased them! And then when he was done, he would expect me to dispose of them, as if they were dirty laundry, to be used and throw away."

"And that is why you poisoned him, isn't it, to be free of him?"

"Oh no! Never! I admit, there were times I thought about being rid of him, when I prayed that he would be struck down, but I did not kill him. Like I said, Sahib, I am a weak man. Ask yourself this question. Why would I destroy the very creature who gave me my status, who was responsible for my wealth? Without the Major, I am nothing. While he was alive, I was a man of consequence, a personage of power and influence. Why would I jeopardize that? You must think me a fool!"

He stared at Sikander, as if to challenge him to refute the logic of this assertion. The Maharaja spared a long moment to consider his explanation very carefully. On the face of it, it made ample sense. Why would he kill the Major indeed? The man had been his meal ticket, his passport to a better life, and by the Munshi's own admission, he had been a willing accessory, which pretty much negated Sikander's earlier theory that he was being

266 Arjun Raj Gaind

blackmailed by the Major. In addition, his demeanor and his bearing, which were defiant rather than evasive, told Sikander he was not lying. That made it even more difficult for him to accept the Munshi's guilt. The man was a fool and a charlatan, but he was no killer, not unless every one of Sikander's instincts had been thoroughly fooled.

The Maharaja clenched his teeth, frustrated. He was so sure he had been on the brink of solving the case, especially when the Munshi tried to shoot him, but now, it was like he had been pushed back to square one.

"Huzoor," Charan Singh interjected, "don't tell me you believe this hogwash?"

"I don't know what to believe." Sikander exhaled solemnly, a perplexed sigh. "This is what I want you to do. Take him back to the killa, and throw him in the cell next to the Gurkha. Make sure you keep them apart, and for God's sake, do not let Gurung Bahadur find out he was the Major's procurer. The last thing I need is one of my two best suspects killing the other in a fit of bloody rage."

"I shall depute one of my sons to do as you command."

"No, do it yourself. I don't trust anyone else."

"Are you certain that is a good idea, Sahib? Every time I leave you alone, you manage to get yourself into some trouble or the other."

"Stop acting like my mother, you ox, and for once, just do as you're told."

Charan Singh looked resigned. "At least tell me where you are going, Sahib, in case you need help later?"

The answer to that question was a fairly obvious one. If the Munshi's story was to be believed and he was indeed innocent, that left the Maharaja with only one more suspect to pursue.

"I think it is time that I paid a visit to Captain Fletcher," Sikander said, pursing his lips, "and found out exactly why he has been avoiding me."

Chapter Twenty-three

Captain Augustus Fletcher had always believed himself to be an intrepid man.

It wasn't that he was particularly brave. Rather, he was blessed to have been born with a complete lack of imagination, a trait that when coupled with a brutal, amoral nature, made for an exceptional cavalryman.

Sadly, as the era of the horse soldier drew to a close and the age of artillery began, Fletcher had found that he and his kind were becoming obsolete. That was his greatest lament, that the art of mounted warfare, which he had spent his whole life mastering, had changed beyond his comprehension. There was no more nobility in it, no honor and no fanfare, no more reckless charges to the breach. No, war had become a game, played by armchair generals who had never stared death in the eye, never known how it felt to ride into the valley of death. And the worst part was that there was no place for old warriors like Fletcher in this new world. He had become what he most despised, a relic, like a lame horse, good only to be put down for once and for all.

This feeling of uselessness had only intensified as he aged, beginning as an ache in his gouty legs and then gradually spreading through his squat body, a dissatisfaction that never quite seemed to leave him. Where had it all gone wrong? Where had his career, once so filled with promise, taken a turn downhill? Now nearing fifty and still a mere Captain, Fletcher had become convinced that he had been treated unfairly, that for far too long the advancement he deserved had been awarded to those he judged to be of lesser ability. As a result, the reckless bravado that had so marked his character in his youth had soured, turned to a bitter rancor, a hostility to which he had become addicted, as surely as some men become addicted to opium or strong spirits.

The only time this resentment receded, other than when he was on horseback, was when he was running. Unlike most of the English officer class, who preferred to spend their spare time guzzling vast amounts of arrack at the club, Fletcher was a keen middle-distance runner. There was nothing he found quite as calming as a brisk five-miler, losing himself in the monotony of his stride, his heart pumping, the ever-present ache in his knees and ankles fading until all his problems seemed inconsequential, until all that mattered was the dull thump of the road beneath his heels and the sweet gasp of each tortuous breath in his lungs.

On this particular day, he had found he needed that respite even more than usual. It was the fault of that damn Maharaja, curse his bones. The jumped-up kaffir had been stalking him, like a hunter chasing down a buck, and twice, Fletcher had only been able to avoid him by the narrowest of margins, first ducking him at the club the day before, and then just about managing to escape from Mrs. Fitzgerald's charming gala before the man had been able to corner him with his tiresome questions.

Upon returning from the Ross Common, his mood had been gray, to say the least, and Fletcher had changed quickly into shorts and singlet and canvas shoes before setting out at a lively pace, taking his favorite route, a twisting, steep mountain trail that led to the Cantonment and back again. It had taken him the better part of two hours to cover the distance, which was just over seven miles, and by the time Fletcher returned to his quarters, it was nearing dusk. To his surprise, as he strode up his driveway, he noticed that the front door of the house was wide open. On the verandah, the night lanterns had not been lit, and the interior of the bungalow was swathed in shadows, so dark that he had could scarcely discern any palpable shapes amidst the murk.

"Boy," he shouted, calling for his servant, eager to give him a piece of his mind, "Where have you gotten to, you donkey?" Like every bloody Indian, the boy was worse than useless. The silly bugger was probably fast asleep, wrapped up in his blankets somewhere! *Blast the lazy scoundrel! You just couldn't trust these natives to do their jobs,* Fletcher thought angrily, *no more than you could expect them to remember their place!*

Once more he called for the boy, but yet again, he did not present himself, not even when a dangerous edge crept into the Captain's voice, that rancorous promise of violence to come. Fletcher let out another, more voluble curse, and pottered through the living room in the direction of the kitchen, stubbing his toe twice on pieces of furniture before he managed to find a storm lantern, which he lit before remembering he had forgotten to close the front door.

"Just you wait," he bellowed, "when I get my hands on you, boy, I will have your hide off, I swear it."

"You had better change out of those sweaty clothes, Captain, before you catch your death of cold," a voice said, interrupting his tirade. Fletcher let out a mighty squeal, and the lantern went clattering to the floor. His heart racing, one of his hands reached instinctively for his service revolver before he realized he was out of uniform and thus unarmed. Scowling, he struggled to see who it was that had spoken, but all he could make out was a dull shape standing in the living room, as shadowy as a wraith. As if on cue, a matchstick flared, casting a dim penumbra of radiance. In this half light, Fletcher recognized the Maharaja of Rajpore's gaunt, sardonic face watching him, his lips curving into a smirk as he lit a cigarette.

"What the devil?" Fletcher screeched, barely able to believe his eyes. "You? What in blazes are you doing here?"

"Good evening, Captain." Sikander exhaled a cloud of fragrant smoke. Nonchalantly, he crossed over to sink down into the Captain's favorite armchair, looking perfectly relaxed, dressed in a high-necked tunic of rich woven brocade so resplendent it made Fletcher feel like a beggar.

"Get out!" Fletcher snarled, taking one furious step forward. "Get out of my house, you…you…"

"Come now, Captain," Sikander interrupted him. "Calm down before you give yourself a conniption. Why don't you sit down so that we can enjoy a civilized cup of tea together?"

Fletcher's mouth fell open, barely able to swallow such barefaced cheek. It had been years since anyone had dared to order him around, not since he had taken command of the Rajpore Cavalry. True to his innately belligerent nature, he was tempted to rebel, to tell the Maharaja to bugger off. There was no reason he had to allow the man to question him like a common criminal. As far as Fletcher was concerned, royalty or not, he was just a jumped-up nigger, and he despised everything about the man—his manner, so unconcerned it bordered upon languorous, and his posture, the way he sat atop the chair like it was a throne, as if he owned everything and everyone around him.

To his dismay, inexplicably, his tongue refused to obey him. It was nothing short of uncanny, as if the man had cast a spell on him. Fletcher had heard the usual gossip, that the Maharaja possessed some sort of mystical ability that made it impossible for anyone to lie to him, but he had brushed such rumors away as nothing more than native superstition. But now that Sikander was sitting right there in front of him, watching him with those frigid eyes, Fletcher felt his resolve seeping away. In person, there was indeed something magnetic about the man, a deeply disconcerting, almost hypnotic quality that caused even him, a hardened soldier with a lifetime spent on the front lines, to falter. Some primal, vestigial instinct for self-preservation deep within the Captain's subconscious, that very essence of compliance that awakens when a predator comes face-to-face with a larger, more powerful beast, reacted automatically to the air of cold command in Sikander's voice, compelling Fletcher to retreat meekly to a nearby chair without a word of complaint.

"That's much better," the Maharaja crooned. "Now do tell, why have you been avoiding me?"

"I most certainly have not!" Fletcher replied, rather too shrilly to be believable.

"I tried to approach you at the club just yesterday, and then at Mrs. Fitzgerald's garden party earlier this afternoon, but on both occasions, you took the first opportunity you had to run away from me. You do realize how suspicious that makes you look, don't you, Mr. Fletcher?"

"It's Captain Fletcher," the Englishman replied pointedly, "and my duties keep me very busy, far too busy to waste time gabbling with the likes of you. Besides, why are you even interested in Russell's death? It is public knowledge that you didn't particularly care for the Resident."

Sikander's reply to this question was a dazzlingly impish grin. "I am bored, my dear fellow. Frankly, this is the most fun I have had in months."

Fletcher refused to be disarmed by the man, in spite of his charming manner. Instead, his sneer deepened, until his face looked as craggy as a cliff.

"You sicken me," he hissed. "A man has died, a good man, and you are acting like it is all just a merry lark."

Sikander did not seem terribly put out by such patent hostility. Leaning forward, he peered at Fletcher, examining him so closely that the Captain was quite unnerved. With most men, you could at least guess what they were thinking. You could sense some emotion, gain some insight into their character from their expression and demeanor, but with the Maharaja, he had a way of looking straight through you, as if you were transparent. And his eyes, those awful eyes, as icy and inscrutable as a fjord, they remained utterly expressionless. There was nothing there, no anger, no hatred, no calculation, just a coldness so glacial that it made Fletcher feel like he was caught in a blizzard.

"I do not expect you to understand my motives, Mr. Fletcher, or to even be civil, but I assure you, you will cooperate with me."

"And if I do not?"

Sikander's smile widened, until his lean face seemed as

cadaverous as a skull. "I make a bad enemy, Mr. Fletcher. I would advise you to test my patience at your own peril."

"Damn you," the Captain bunched his fists so hard his knuckles cracked. "Is that a threat?"

To his surprise, the Maharaja chuckled, and shook his head indulgently, as if he were speaking with a child. "Not at all! I don't make threats, my dear fellow. That was a warning. Either tell me what I want to know, or I promise you, I will do everything in my power to ruin you." The Maharaja sat back, staring at Fletcher as if he were little more than an insect. "It shouldn't be too difficult, really. A whisper in the right ear, a small bribe, maybe a favor or two called in from some people I know in Simla, and you will be drummed out of your precious regiment without further ado. A penniless old man, no rank, no pension, the laughing stock of the Officer's Mess. Is that what you want, Captain?"

Even as he made this bare-faced threat, Sikander's voice remained perfectly matter-of-fact, as though he were speaking about something entirely mundane, the weather, perhaps, or the cricket scores. A chill ran down Captain Fletcher's spine. The Maharaja seemed so utterly insouciant that for the first time, he felt an inkling of genuine trepidation, an emotion he had not experienced for decades, not since he had been a raw ensign, praying on his knees before his first skirmish.

Could the man really be quite that ruthless? Yes, he realized, as he glared at Sikander, the black bastard meant every single word. Fletcher tried not to shudder, knowing that he had lost the battle even before the first salvo had been fired. Whatever defiance still kindled within him fizzled like a damp lucifer. His broad shoulders sagged. Abruptly, he seemed to age a decade, looking for the first time an old man, gray and exhausted.

"Very well." He raised his hands to indicate capitulation, "Ask your blasted questions!"

Sikander tried not to gloat. He had indeed read the man correctly. Not only was he a soldier to the core, accustomed to obeying orders instinctively, but his limited imagination meant that when faced with a challenge, rather than trying to find the clever way out, Fletcher would always choose to keep his head down, and seek cover, so to speak.

"I thought we could begin with a bit of background. Tell me, Captain, how long is it now that you have served in Rajpore?"

This question, though harmless enough on the face of it, was one he had chosen very deliberately, with the specific intent of softening up the Captain. If there was one truth Sikander was more than certain of, it was that no man past the age of forty could resist talking about himself, and he doubted that Fletcher, albeit a taciturn sort, would forsake the opportunity to wax eloquent about his career.

"It has been eleven years now, and six of those have been as Commandant of Cavalry. I was seconded here in '97, as a Lieutenant, and gazetted Captain in '02, during the Ghazi campaign. A paltan of some two hundred Pathans had crossed at the Ramala Pass and were raising unholy hell amidst the border villages, but my men sent those bloody savages scarpering back to where they came from, and they haven't dared to show their hairy faces since." His face glowed with pride, so suffused with self-satisfaction that it made Sikander want to pity him, the poor bastard, reveling in glories long past.

"I take it, then, that you are happy here?"

"It's a decent enough posting, I suppose." Fletcher replied, non-committal. "A bit too tame for the likes of me nowadays, but the old Resident, now there was a proper gentleman. He took me under his wing, you see, and told me that when he retired, he would recommend me for his post, but the best laid plans..." He shrugged. "The job went to Major Russell instead, and that was that."

His resentment was only too obvious, but was this bitterness directed towards the authorities in Simla, or at the man who had trumped his promotion? The former could be dismissed as the fault of a choleric temperament, but the latter, given enough time, could have deepened into genuine hatred, and there, Sikander thought, lay a possible motive, certainly palpable enough to be explored in more depth. "Tell me, what did you think of Major Russell?"

"What do you mean?"

The Maharaja gave the Captain a level look, pursing his lips impatiently. "Please, don't be facetious. You worked with Russell, every single day. Surely you have an opinion as to what sort of man he was?"

Fletcher hesitated, an overly long pause before continuing blandly, as though to suggest he was selecting his words with great caution. "He was an effective administrator with a fine track record."

Sikander interrupted him with a brusque slash of one hand.

"Stop wasting my time," he growled. "I don't want you to eulogize the man. I want to know what you thought of him, one soldier to another."

"Don't you call him a soldier," Fletcher snarled, even before he had realized it. He bit his lip, as if he knew he had said too much. The pause stretched out as he considered whether it would be in his best interest to backtrack, before he decided to continue, made brash by impulsive disregard. "The Major may have had the clusters on his shoulders, but he was no soldier, not a pukka one."

Such an outburst was exactly what Sikander had been hoping for. So Lowry had not been exaggerating after all. There had indeed been bad blood between the Major and the Captain. Sikander frowned, watching the man contemplatively. Once again, Fletcher's body language was broadcasting much more than his lips had revealed. His reluctance to speak of the past, the vehemence in his tone, which had been rather petulant up to that point, the way his shoulders were squared and his jaw stiff and clenched, it was a classic defensive posture, an observation that made the Maharaja's instincts flare with suspicion. The Captain was definitely hiding something, but what?

"For a man who has just lost a friend, you don't seem very aggrieved."

"Why should I be? Will Russell was no friend of mine."

"That is not what I have heard. I was told you were very close, at least until recently."

"I thought so too, but I realize now that I was mistaken. Certainly, I spent a good amount of time with him, and on occasion, I was called upon to be his confidante, but in retrospect, I have to confess that I barely knew the man." He sighed, growing uncharacteristically pensive. "I doubt anyone knew the real Will Russell. He had always been like that, even as a young man, as aloof as a Jesuit."

"You knew him before his arrival in Rajpore then?"

"In a manner of speaking, yes." The Captain hesitated again. "I was his batman for three seasons many years ago before I was promoted out of the ranks."

"You were a ranker?" Sikander echoed, unable to withhold his astonishment.

Fletcher's florid face darkened with barely repressed shame. "Aye, I started in the ranks, and spent almost a decade wearing a sergeant's stripes." Try as he might to sound nonchalant, he couldn't prevent an edge of rancor from creeping into his voice. "I won my commission the hard way, on the battlefield during the Afghan Campaign."

This was it, Sikander thought, *the secret the Captain had been hiding, the crux of why he was so loath to speak of the past.* He had begun his career as a humble rank-and-file soldier. That certainly explained much of his bucolic choler. While the old practice of buying rank had died out with the Victorian Age, it was common knowledge that in the rarefied atmosphere of the Officer's Clubs and the Cantonments, rankers who jumped up the ladder were never welcome, unable to leave behind the taint of being common soldiers, especially with the memsahibs, who inevitably were even more snobbish than most maharanis. *No wonder he is so embittered,* Sikander thought. What man wouldn't be sour, having worked twice as hard as any other soldier, only to end up on the wrong side of forty and still just a lowly Captain, posted to a small kingdom where there were lamentably few promotions to be had?

That also explained why he had resented the Major so thoroughly. It must have been difficult, even galling for him to have to take orders from a man he thought of as an armchair soldier, a fact that was doubly aggravated by their prior history together. No doubt the Major had treated him as an upstart, an inferior pulled up from the ranks. But was that enough of a reason for a man to turn to poison? No, it seemed a bit too shaky. There had to be more to the story.

"You know, Captain, I heard a very interesting rumor just yesterday, that you had a very public spat with the Major not two weeks ago."

Fletcher's eyes dilated, just a hint, and his lips gave the slightest of twitches, but for someone of Sikander's caliber, that was more than enough to affirm that he was indeed sniffing up the right path.

"It was nothing, a minor disagreement, that's all."

"Is that so? Lowry insisted the two of you almost came to blows."

The Captain let out a violent snort, not unlike a cornered boar.

"I should have known he would be spreading scurrilous rumors, that bloody molly." He fixed Sikander with one jaundiced eye. "He's a backdoor man, you know, and he was halfway in love with the Major, I tell you. Used to follow him around like a bitch in heat, sniffing at his hindquarters." He cleared his throat, a guttural catarrh of pure disgust. "If you want a suspect, look no further than our exalted Magistrate!"

"I am well aware of Mr. Lowry's proclivities. However, that does not change the fact that you had an argument with Major Russell, in public, and that you threatened to do him grave bodily harm."

Fletcher's face tightened, as if he had swallowed a fish-bone and it was caught in his throat. "That's a damned lie!"

Sikander arched one sardonic eyebrow. "I believe your exact words were, 'I'll get you, you lying bastard, if it's the last thing I do.'"

Fletcher leaped to his feet, looming over Sikander, the bulk of him dwarfing the Maharaja. His face gleamed as red as an overripe tomato, his eyes screaming bloody murder.

"I am not scared of you, blast you," he hissed, pointedly showing no trace of deference. "I have faced down charging Afridis with naught but a cavalry saber and spat in death's own eye. Nothing you can say or do will intimidate me."

"You mistake my intentions," Sikander said smoothly, not at all perturbed. "I am not trying to intimidate you. I am trying to help you." He offered Fletcher a benign smile. "Let me make you an offer. If you stop beating about the bush and speak honestly with me, in exchange I shall endeavor to utilize my not inconsiderable influence in Simla to see you upped to Major, perhaps even appointed as our next Resident. What do you say?"

It was a reckless spur of the moment gamble. Judging by how a conflicting gamut of bewilderment and wariness played across the Captain's features, Sikander worried he would decline. For a long and breathless moment, he was sure he had overplayed his hand, but then, to his relief, the stratagem worked. Fletcher gave the Maharaja a brisk nod, inspiring Sikander to draw a relieved breath. He had guessed the Captain's price correctly.

"You're right," Fletcher whispered, "I hated Major Russell, as much as one man can despise another."

"Then why, might I ask, did you insist on toadying up to him?"

"You wouldn't understand," Fletcher said. "You've had it all handed to you, and never had to struggle. But those less fortunate are often compelled to make choices that are distasteful." He sighed. "Even though I loathed him, I still needed his patronage for advancement."

"So the rumors are indeed true? He was going to help you get a promotion, but instead, he let you down?"

"Yes." Fletcher almost groaned. "He made me a solemn promise, but it was a lie, a bloody, barefaced lie."

"Why do you think he scuppered your chances?"

The Captain replied with a bitter chuckle. "It's bloody obvious, isn't it? Other than the fact that he was a vicious, self-righteous shite, Major High-and-Mighty Russell was a bigot. I am doubly damned, you see. Not only am I not what the Russells of the world consider a gentleman, it so happens that I was born here, in India."

His voice hardened. "When I confronted him and asked why he had let me down, he told me to be content that I had made the rank of Captain. 'That is far enough for the likes of you to rise,' he said, 'quite as far from the gutter as you deserve to get.' The bastard! I fought my way to these epaulets, but he belittled me, as if I were a damned martinet."

Fletcher's face twisted into a scowl. "The truth of it, I think, is that he could not bear the thought of anyone having the same rank as him, not in Rajpore. He wanted to be the top dog in the kennel, and there was no way he would tolerate any rivals, especially not a lowborn ranker."

"That sounds a fine motive for a man to do murder."

It was a feint, a subtle probe of the man's defenses which Fletcher brushed aside adroitly. "That's a damn fool thing to say. I can think of half a dozen people who had a better motive to see the Major dead." He gave Sikander a level stare. "Take that duffer Bates, for instance. Why, he had quite a spat with the Resident just the night before last, at the New Year's Ball. They were going at it like a pair of junglee ferrets, and it would have ended in blood if I hadn't intervened."

"Ah, yes, about the ball. I believe you escorted the Major home."

"Indeed, I did."

"And when you left him at his bungalow, was that the last time you spoke to him?

"Yes."

Sikander tried not to cackle with triumph. *I have you now*, he thought. *You have just painted yourself into a corner, you lummox.*

"You're lying, Captain. I have it on good authority that you went back to the Residency later that very night. I had a most enlightening chat with Miss Jane, you see, the Major's housekeeper, and she had some rather intriguing things to say about you."

At the mention of Jane's name, Fletcher's already ruddy cheeks reddened even more, darkening to an uneasy scarlet.

"I heard that she had been stricken as well." He looked at Sikander inquiringly, and for the first time, his adamant shell seemed to soften, revealing genuine emotion beneath. "Might I ask, is she well?"

This reaction seemed out of character for a man so gruff, surprising Sikander. He cares for her, he realized, and a very great deal, judging by the moonstruck look on his face!

"Yes, she is recovering quite admirably."

Fletcher let out a sigh of abject relief. "Thank the stars! I feared for the worst."

"A fine woman, that Jane," Sikander observed, "and unless I am mistaken, Captain, she seems to have caught your eye."

Fletcher shifted in his seat guiltily, squirming like a schoolboy caught cheating in class. "A man could imagine settling down with a woman like her. Sadly, I fear I am not good enough for Miss Jane."

There was such earnest sorrow in his voice, such boyish regret, that Sikander could not help but feel a twinge of sympathy. True, Fletcher was dour as only a Presbyterian could be, and blunt to the point of being offensive, but it was patent even to an imbecile that the Captain had some small shred of romance in his soul. Unfortunately, he was quite correct in his assumption that there was no way any woman, not just Jane, would wish to take up with a man like him, someone as deeply rigid in his habits and as brusque in his manners. *Why,* Sikander thought with a sniff, *he probably treats his horses better than he treats people.*

"Is that why you went back, to see Miss Jane?"

The Captain nodded. "I wanted to apologize to her for behaving so boorishly. I did not want to leave her with a low opinion of me."

Sikander bit his lip, trying to use his finely tuned senses to determine if the man was lying to him once again, but everything about Fletcher—the earnestness in his tone, the poignancy writ on his face—led him to believe that he was telling the truth.

"Jane mentioned you had an argument with the Major? "

"I was trying to tell her how I felt, when he came upon us, and began to harangue me. He was most abusive, and told me to stay away from her." He sniffed, an audible snort of disbelief. "It was like he thought that she belonged to him, that she was his property."

Fletcher grimaced, choking back his revulsion. "And the worst part was that I had to just stand there and take it. What choice did I have? I knew I had to work with him. This is most likely my last posting, and I can't risk endangering my pension, and so I made my peace and left." He clenched his jaw so hard Sikander could hear his teeth grinding. "The bastard laughed at me, and tried to act magnanimous. He said he forgave me, that I was a fool for having aspirations that exceeded my station."

"That must have got your blood boiling," Sikander said. "Is that why you killed him?"

"For the last time, Mr. Singh, I had naught to do with his death."

"And for the last time, Captain, I simply do not believe you." Sikander decided to drop all pretense at being convivial. "This is what I think really happened. I think the Major made you a promise which he reneged upon, and then, to add fuel to the fire, he put an end to your attempt to seduce Jane. And in a fit of fury, I suspect, you poisoned him."

Sikander had expected shock, followed by a requiem performance of his earlier outrage, but Fletcher took this accusation in his stride with considerable aplomb. "You have quite an imagination, Mr. Singh. Sadly, you haven't a shred of proof to match it."

On the contrary, Sikander thought, *I have a whole bottle of proof, you presumptuous wart.* He gave the Captain a piercing glare. "Tell me, are you a drinking man?"

"I beg your pardon?"

"It is a straightforward enough question. Do you partake, Captain, of harsh spirits?"

"I most certainly do not!"

"Really? Your complexion suggests otherwise."

Fletcher bristled, lowering his brows and glowering at Sikander, his eyes filled with loathing. "When I was a younger man,

I was a bit of a hellion who enjoyed a tot of gin from time to time, but I gave it up some years ago. My dyspepsia forbids it."

"So you are not an aficionado of sherry, then? A devotee of Oloroso, perhaps, from Andalusia?"

"What is God's name are you chattering on about?"

"Perhaps I should be clearer," Sikander pressed on. "I happened to recover a bottle of wine from the scene of the crime, a very fine sherry to be precise, and upon examining its contents, I found it had been contaminated with rather a large amount of strychnine."

"I don't see what that has to do with me."

"Oh, but it does, doesn't it? As it happens, I acquired another very interesting tidbit of information from our esteemed Magistrate. When I questioned him, he told me that you provided him with that very bottle, and asked that he deliver it to the Resident as a gift."

I have you now, Sikander thought jubilantly. This was it, what duelists called the *coup de grace*, the death stroke.

To Sikander's dismay, Fletcher seemed not to miss a blink. "I think, Mr. Singh, that you have rather an overactive imagination." Offering Sikander a level look, he sidestepped the Maharaja's accusations as neatly as a fox dodging a courser. "Did I resent Russell? The answer is yes. I had good reason to. But did I kill him? I should think not. I admit it freely, the wine belonged to me. It was a gift from a friend in Cadiz, but as I said earlier, I am not a drinking man, and frankly, I wouldn't know Oloroso from arrack. Lowry however is somewhat of a connoisseur, which is why I passed it on to him. As for how the strychnine got into the bottle in question, I suggest you take it up with him."

His dour mouth curved into a grin. "Frankly, that is all I have to say on the matter."

This brusque dismissal did not sit at all well with the Maharaja. He could not help but fume, wracking his brain, trying to think of something else he could try, some new ploy, but Fletcher had managed to outmaneuver him quite thoroughly.

"Let me leave you with another warning, Mr. Fletcher," he said, keeping his voice absolutely deadpan. "I intend to find the man who killed the Major, and I will not rest until I uncover the truth. And if there is one thing you should know about me, it is that I always get my man."

With this pronouncement, he rose to his feet, summoning up as much regal grace as he could manage as the Captain's eyes followed him every inch of the way toward the front door.

Just as he was about to depart, Fletcher called after him, "Mr. Singh!"

"Yes, Captain?" Sikander turned to face the man.

"Do try and be careful where you stick that nose of yours, or who knows, you may just end up like the Major!"

His voice was so cool, so self-assured that it made the Maharaja's hackles rise. "Is that a threat?" He snarled, clenching his fists. "Are you so foolish to try and threaten *me*?"

"Oh no..." Fletcher sat back with a contented sigh "... not at all, Your Majesty! To use your own words, 'consider it a warning.'"

Chapter Twenty-four

Another dismal dusk, another dejected return to the killa.

Somewhere in the distance, a storm was gathering. The ozone tang of electricity hung in the air, accompanied by the humid groan of incipient rain. The sourness of the weather reflected Sikander's temperament perfectly. This was the phase of an investigation he hated most, once the initial thrill of the chase had worn off and the clues started to pile up, all the myriad why's and how's, but no definite conclusions managed to present themselves, no patterns, no moments of eureka when he saw how everything touched everything else.

All he really wanted was to gulp down a bottle of Bollinger and then go straight to bed, but even as he crept into the Raj Vilas, Charan Singh was waiting to waylay him yet again.

"You have a visitor," the big Sikh announced.

"Who is it?" Sikander inquired wearily. "Not that oaf Jardine, I hope."

"No, it is the journalist, Miller." He pronounced the word journalist with haughty disdain, as if it somehow tasted foul on his tongue. "He arrived about an hour ago, insisting that he needed to see you immediately."

Sikander groaned. He was much too tired to endure another bout of Miller's high strung gossiping.

"Send him away. Tell him to come back tomorrow."

"I tried, Sahib, but he would not budge. He told me to tell you that it was a matter of life and death" The big Sikh frowned, as if to suggest he did not have a very high opinion of Miller. "He is a very strange man, is he not?"

The Maharaja restrained a sigh. Typical Miller! Always so dramatic it could cause an actor heartburn. With him, everything was always a matter of life and death. There was never any middle ground. Most likely, he had turned up some abstruse, entirely insignificant piece of trivia, and that had been enough to send him into a tizzy, convinced that he had uncovered the key piece of evidence to unraveling the entire case. Briefly, he debated dismissing the man outright. But then, when he spared a moment to consider it, Sikander decided that whatever could have compelled Miller to abandon his beloved press and come all the way out to the Sona Killa was worth at least ten minutes of his time.

"Very well, I will see him. Where is he?"

"I put him in the Alhambra Room, Sahib. And I should warn you, he has already polished off a bottle and a half of your best wine."

The Alhambra Room was located at the distant corner of the north wing, not far from the topiary gardens. It was a medium-sized salon, decorated in the Moorish style with bright Alizäres tiles from Granada and Andalusian tapestries from Cordoba. When Sikander arrived, he found that Miller had already made himself very comfortable. A roaring fire was blazing away in the fireplace, filling the room with a welcome warmth. He saw that the presswallah had ensconced himself deep into an overstuffed settee, noticing with some irritation that the man had removed his boots and was now wiggling his toes in a pair of Sikander's handmade Italian slippers while enjoying a snifter of what the Maharaja assumed was his prize Rioja, as he intently perused a thick leather volume.

"I see you have managed to make yourself at home," Sikander said dryly.

Miller gave Sikander a contented smile, his face burnished bright red from the combination of warmth and alcohol. "I must confess, Your Majesty, there are times when I quite envy you. Is this really a first edition of Cervantes?"

Sikander's answer was a scowl. Crossing the room to a Cadiz armchair, he sat down rather stiffly, trying not to lose his reserve in the face of Miller's presumptuousness. "I am not in the mood for idle chatter, Mr. Miller. I take it that you have not come all this way to talk about books."

"No, of course not. As it happens, Your Majesty, I have been able to uncover some very interesting information about our dear departed Major, and I felt you should know about it post-haste."

His expression grew as self-satisfied as a cat that has just had its fill of cream. "At the risk of being boastful, let me say this much, it is as juicy a piece of gossip as you have ever heard."

"Why don't you let me be the judge of that?" Sikander sat back, tenting his fingers in front of his lips. "Go on then. Let us hear what you have dug up."

"Well," Miller said, "as it turns out, the Major had made it a habit of lying about his origins. He was not a gentleman at all, it seems." His voice thickened with excitement. "The story he most often liked to tell people was that his father was a soldier who died during the Crimean War, but from what I have been able to uncover, that was not the case. The truth is that his father was never a soldier. On the contrary, in actuality, he was a second footsman in the employ of a certain Sir William Russell."

"William Russell?" Sikander arched one eyebrow questioningly. "Do you mean to say...?"

"Yes, I believe the Major took the *nom de guérre* when he came out to India. His real name, as it turns out, was William Crawford." Miller shrugged. "I imagine he must have come of age below stairs in the real Mr. Russell's manor, envying all the wealth around him, and likely as not, dreamed of being as affluent some day, as prosperous, and thus decided to reinvent himself when he had the chance."

So the Major had not been quite as pukka as he liked to pretend, Sikander thought. He was surprised, but not quite as much as he ought to have been. Now that he knew the truth about the commonness of the Resident's origins, he had to admit, in hindsight, the signs had all been plain to see. His accent, his atrocious manners, even his peculiar patterns of speech—Sikander had noticed these incongruities often enough, but dismissed them as eccentricities acquired from a life of soldiering, camp habits that had become ingrained over time. Now however, they stood exposed for what they were, the careful play-acting of a servant's son playing at being one of his betters.

"Once I found out about the Resident's deception, I did some digging around about this other William Russell," Miller continued. "By all accounts, he was a country squire, a cloth baron who had made quite a fortune in the Levant and set himself up handsomely with a large estate near Ashford, very near the town of Maidstone. His wife died of diphtheria, leaving him with one child, a daughter he named Minerva of all things, heaven help her, who was his pride and joy."

Miller shook his head sadly. "Poor child, it seems that she became quite besotted with our Major, or rather with young Will Crawford, as he was called back then. I cannot tell for certain, but I imagine he seduced her, probably seeing her as a means for him to escape his humble origins. Of course, there was a bit of a scandal, since she was well above his class. Her father undoubtedly must have thrown a fit, but you know the old saying, 'That which love has ordained, what wisdom can tear asunder,' which was probably why he consented to permit them to become engaged. In fact, it was Sir William who sponsored our dear Resident's way though Cambridge, with the understanding that he would come to work for him as a partner upon graduation. However, that is not quite how things turned out."

Sikander nodded, as understanding dawned. "He repudiated her, didn't he…?"

A sneer twisted across Miller's face. "Yes, indeed, he did. Sir William gambled heavily on an investment with Overend, Gurney, and Company, and when the bank collapsed, he was left penniless. The man was so distraught he took his own life, leaving his daughter with no dowry and no inheritance to speak of."

"And the Major decided to jilt her because she had no money?"

Miller nodded curtly. "It was terribly ugly. The poor girl, she wrote him letter after letter, but he ignored them all. She even made a complaint to the local constable. That was when the Masters at Cambridge found out, and they took a very serious view of the Resident's conduct. As far as they were concerned, his behavior constituted a breach of promise, and was thus exceedingly dishonorable, not to say that a young lady's good name had been irrevocably ruined."

"So that is why he was sent down!" Sikander exclaimed. It was a story as old as time, and it certainly explained why Major Russell—no, Will Crawford—had fled to India. Where else could he have gone to start again, with no prospects and a reputation that was in tatters, other than the colonies? In England, he would have been a pariah, but here in India, he could remake himself, change his name, and leave his chequered past far behind.

"Do you have any inkling what happened to the girl?"

"Well, that is where the story gets interesting." The press-wallah revealed more teeth than a shark. "From what I have been able to learn, it seems young Miss Minerva Russell was rather a headstrong sort. After being jilted, rather than giving up and turning into another Miss Havisham, she was so besotted with our Resident that she followed him out to India."

"She did not?" Sikander said, aghast. Even though he was a liberal man, this revelation left him utterly shocked. It was quite unheard of, even in these modern times, that a white woman should follow a man out to the colonies, unescorted by a chaperone, but back then, thirty or so years earlier, it must have caused quite a healthy scandal for the youthful Resident.

"Yes, it's hard to believe, but it seems some months after his hasty decampment, the young woman booked herself passage on one of the fishing fleet ships out to Madras. Her arrival caused quite a sensation, I believe, especially when she confronted his commanding officer."

"Did she expose him?"

"No, on the contrary, she claimed to be his fiancée, an assertion which caused the Major, who was then a mere Ensign, quite some trouble, considering that he did not have enough seniority to enter into wedlock."

"I am guessing he didn't welcome her with open arms."

"Quite the opposite," Miller said with a salacious chuckle. "By all accounts, they entered into a rather scandalous relationship. My source, who happened to be posted in Madras at the time, insisted it was the talk of the fort for a few months, a young man and woman living in open sin, until finally Mr. Russell's commanding officer, who was a staunch Presbyterian, decided that he would rescue the young man from this immoral predicament, and sent him on to another posting, this one a front-line regiment, I believe, which did not tolerate married officers."

"And he just left her behind?"

"Oh, yes!" Miller clucked his tongue like an old woman. "Poor child! To be deserted not once, but twice, that heartless bastard!"

Poor child, indeed! Sikander pursed his lips. But then, it fit in perfectly with the Major's pattern, didn't it, as a brute, a user and abuser of women?

"What happened to the poor woman?" he asked. "Did she stay on in Madras?"

Miller shook his head solemnly. "As it happens, she had a cousin who cared enough to follow her out to India, and I believe she returned to England with him. My source told me she died soon after."

Another dead end, Sikander thought, trying not to groan with dissatisfaction. What he needed was evidence, not sad stories from the distant past. Why was Miller wasting his time with this rubbish?

"It's an entertaining story, Mr. Miller. Perhaps you should turn it into a music hall romance. A tale of heartbreak set in darkest India, with seven songs and a gay dance. However, I fail to see how any of this helps my investigations!"

Rather than being dismayed by this rebuke, the presswallah's face showed an obdurate satisfaction. "That isn't the whole story," he said. "I have been saving the best for last. The Major did not just break young Miss Minerva Russell's heart. If my source is to be believed, he managed to impregnate her womb as well."

If he had been a canine, at that moment, Sikander's ears would, quite literally, have twitched. This was a development he simply could not have predicted, not with all his skills, a twist worthy of Dickens!

"There was a child? Are you certain of this, Mr. Miller?"

"Absolutely! My source is very reliable. He has letters he can produce, if needed."

"Were you able to find out anything about the child?" Sikander almost squealed, quivering with barely contained excitement. "Was it a boy or girl?"

"It was a girl, your Highness. The Major, if my source is to be believed, had an illegitimate daughter."

Even as Miller spoke, something seemed to click in Sikander's mind, the final missing piece of the puzzle falling into place. *Of course*, he thought with mounting excitement, *that was the key to solving the whole damned case*. Suddenly, he could see the answer, visualize exactly how all the clues came together to reveal a pattern, a solution so obvious, so gloriously simple that he chastised himself for failing to discern it earlier.

Hurriedly, he sprang to his feet, reaching for the hand-bell lying on a nearby table, and began to ring it, as raucously as a town crier. "Charan Singh!" he shouted. "Get in here, you fat-headed turnip!"

Turning to Miller, he waved him to his feet. "You have done well, my dear fellow, very well indeed! I shall have twice your usual fee deposited in your account. No, let us make it thrice, shall we?"

Even though he had known the Maharaja a good long while, this abrupt volte-face left Miller understandably confused. However, the presswallah was nothing if not pragmatic, and had the good sense to keep his bewilderment to himself, considering he had just made rather a handsome profit from what seemed little more than idle gossip.

"Why, that's very generous of you, Your Highness. Might I ask, was the information helpful?"

"Oh, yes," Sikander chuckled. "Let's just say that you have just helped me solve the Major's murder."

Miller's face sagged with disbelief. "I'm afraid I just don't understand."

"Don't you worry, Mr. Miller. Everything will be clear as crystal very soon." He gave the journalist a vast grin. "Why don't you stay for dinner? Wait right here. Enjoy another bottle of wine and I shall have my man come and fetch you a little later, when everything is in place."

"As you wish," Miller replied, almost dizzily.

"Good, then it is settled."

Bidding Miller a good evening, Sikander dashed out of the Alhambra Room, just as Charan Singh finally decided to make an appearance, shambling up with a scowl.

"Why is it, Sahib," he said, "that whenever I am about to fall asleep, you seem to find some sort of emergency that requires my immediate attention...?"

The Maharaja ignored this attempt at insolence and gave his manservant a triumphant smile.

"I have a job for you," he crowed, trying not to break into a merry jig.

Charan Singh started to object, to retort that it was much too late to go gallivanting about on some ludicrous whim, but then, when he saw the exultant glint in his master's eyes, he gave a low whistle. He had known Sikander long enough to recognize that particular expression, a glee that could only presuppose one thing.

Hurriedly, Sikander entailed exactly what he wanted the Sikh to do. Charan Singh's eyes grew wider and wider as each detail was explained, and then, when the Maharaja was done, he let out a vast guffaw.

"This is going to make the English very angry," he said. "Your friend Jardine in particular will throw a fit!"

Sikander grinned, absurdly amused by the thought of Jardine's fat face turning as red as a beetroot. "How long will it take you to get everything organized?"

"A few hours at least, Sahib," Charan Singh replied. "This is going to take a lot of manpower!"

"Very well! Get to it then!"

Charan Singh nodded, but did not depart immediately. "There is just one thing I must say, Huzoor." From his expression, it was clear he still harbored grave doubts. "Forgive me, but it is my duty to ask. Are you sure of this? Could you possibly be mistaken?"

"No," Sikander responded jubilantly, "I am quite certain, my large friend. At last, I know exactly what happened to Major Russell."

Chapter Twenty-five

Leaving Charan Singh to carry out the tasks set for him, Sikander returned to his chambers for a well-deserved break.

Changing into an embroidered Damascus silk banyan coat, he retired to his bed, looking forward to taking a brief nap in preparation of the excitements to come. Unfortunately, the solace of sleep continued to elude him. He was much too keyed up, too anxious to find even a moment's rest.

After tossing and turning for what seemed like hours, drifting in and out of sleep, finally Sikander gave up. Rising lethargically, he returned to the music room with a bottle of Gosset Blanc de Noirs, and once more, sought the comfort of his piano. Beneath his restless, fidgeting fingers, the ivory felt alive, immeasurably reassuring. Over the next two hours, Sikander slowly worked his way through Ravel's *Gaspard de la Nuit*. It was a particularly complex suite, absorbing much of his concentration and thus distracting him from the fatigue that had been clawing at him all day. The first movement, the "Ondine," with its cascading chords, took him a long time to get right, but it was time well spent. As always, it relaxed him, a calm that coalesced slowly across his body. The second movement, "Le Gibet," took that calm and sharpened it to a razor's edge, leaving behind a focused clarity that came close to euphoria.

Just when he was about to try and tackle the third movement, "Scarbo," which had always exceeded his abilities, Charan Singh made his return.

"Everything is ready, Your Highness," he announced, "exactly as you wished."

"Well done! Tell me, what time is it?"

"Just past midnight, Huzoor. Your guests await your presence in the Crystal Ballroom. I have taken the liberty of serving some light refreshments, and arranged to keep them entertained until you were ready to see them."

"Excellent!" Sikander exclaimed. Springing up, he returned to his room to change into something more suitable. For this evening's denouement, he had settled upon a rather severely cut bandhgala with a very stiff collar and only the subtlest of jade embroidery around the cuffs. It made him look as dour as an undertaker, but he found it suited both his mood, and the timbre of the entertainment due to follow.

Fleetingly, Sikander cast a jaundiced eye at himself in the mirror. He looked even older than before, dreadfully tired, almost emaciated after two days without proper sleep and only sporadic meals. But still, he fancied, there was a twinkle in his eye, a gleam that intensified as he realized that this adventure, in spite of all its twists and turns, was almost at an end.

The Crystal Ballroom was the smallest of the six banquet halls in the palace, but by far, the most opulent. It had been designed by his mother, whose desire had been to try and recreate the splendor of the Imperial Ballroom at one of her favorite buildings, the Dolmabahçe Palace in Istanbul. The floor was tiled with interlocking squares of Egyptian alabaster and porphyry imported from Pergamon, the walls were mahogany, lined with gilded mirrors that reached from floor to ceiling, inset with massive baroque windows that opened onto balconies overlooking the Imperial gardens. But the pièce de résistance was the roof, a *trompe de l'oeil* dome studded with exactly nine hundred and ninety-nine gleaming pieces of peerless Baccarat crystal, each buffed to a mirror sheen, so that it seemed to all those who looked up that they were staring down at themselves, down and up, up and down, seemingly twisting onwards towards infinity.

Upon entering the room, Sikander saw that Charan Singh, as always, had taken his instructions rather too literally. He had indeed made all the necessary preparations to keep the Maharaja's guests entertained, exactly as ordered, because a banquet, it seemed, was currently in full swing. At the center of the room, a long table had been laid out, set with a dozen sterling silver place settings, and a steady stream of bearers came and went back and forth from the kitchen, delivering an impressive assortment of delicacies his harassed staff must have worked overtime to have ready at such short notice. Why, Sikander noticed with a grin, there was even a string quartet at hand, doing a fairly admirable job of playing what seemed like Liszt, but only slightly off-key.

His guests, sadly, did not seem to be having a particularly good time, with the exception of Miller, who raised a glass to Sikander and gave him a cheeky wink. Opposite him, Helene, who looked absolutely delightful draped in a sleek turquoise dress that left her shoulders bare, gazed up at him with pursed lips, as if to indicate how utterly bored she was. Next to her, an unfamiliar face greeted the Maharaja, a stranger who was watching him with a blandly neutral expression that could have been anything from curiosity to disapproval. He was an older man, dressed in a dusty black safari jacket, rigid with the unbending posture of an ex-army man. His head was entirely bald, as if he shaved it daily, and he had a hawkish nose large enough to rival the Maharaja's own, giving him a touch of the Inquisition.

This must be the famous Simpson, Sikander guessed, the hatchet man from Simla mentioned by Ismail Chacha. Frankly, he was not what the Maharaja had expected. He had imagined a bureaucrat, a lick-spittle accustomed to manning a desk, but there was nothing soft about this man. On the contrary, everything about him conveyed inflexibility, a severity of character that Sikander mistrusted at first sight.

Helene confirmed his suspicions just a moment later.

"This is Captain Simpson," she said. "He arrived from Simla this very afternoon, and when your unexpected invitation came, I thought it best to bring him along."

Rather than offering a barrage of pleasantries, the man chose to wait, leaving it to Sikander to make the first move. Obviously, it was to be a playground staring-match. The man was testing his mettle, and Sikander was not about to back down.

Raising one brow, he held Simpson's gaze, not passive but not aggressive either, two lions circling each other upon the veldt. This battle of wills went on and on, neither man willing to capitulate, until Helene let out a sigh of rampant disapproval, as if to convey how annoyed she was by their childish posturing.

"I have heard a great deal about you, Your Majesty," Simpson said finally, breaking the deadlock after offering Helene an apologetic nod. His deep, disconcerting bass gave nothing away, not a hint of what he was truly thinking.

"God," Sikander replied with a shudder, "don't believe a word! All lies, I swear it, slander spread by my enemies. Really, I am a very boring individual."

The man responded with just the slightest tremor of his lips.

"Oh, I doubt that, sir. I have a feeling everything they say about you in Simla is entirely accurate."

It was not a threat, but still...Sikander found himself more than a little worried. It looked like Ismail Chacha had been right on the money about Mr. Simpson. From the looks of him, he was going to be a formidable opponent, not at all the biddable pushover he had been hoping for.

Offering the man from Simla one last wary nod, Sikander turned to greet his other guests. To the left, the Indians waited: Munshi Ram Dev, who cradled his broken limb shamefacedly, now encased in a plaster, and by his side, the Gurkha, Gurung, who held his gaze proudly as Sikander approached. Both men were flanked by uniformed guards, and their presence managed to draw quite a few inquiring looks from everyone else, not just for their woebegone appearance, but also because they were shackled to each other.

To the right were the English. Nearest was Jane, wan-faced, dressed in a black dress that hung loosely on her slender shoulders. Sikander guessed it was a gift from Helene, who was somewhat more generously proportioned than the young Englishwoman. He gave her a brief smile, which melted away as soon as he spied Lieutenant Bates seated next to her, in uniform now, bristling with hostility but possessed, this once, with enough sense to hold his tongue. By his side, his comely wife avoided Sikander's scrutiny, keeping her eyes firmly downcast. This trepidation was mirrored on the face of Magistrate Lowry, who was seated a few metres away, watching the Maharaja warily. Next to him, Captain Fletcher was fuming visibly, his face so red that he looked about ready to combust. And last of all, Sikander's gaze intersected with that of Superintendent Jardine, who sprang immediately to his feet.

"Well, what is this dire emergency for which you have had us all dragged here, Mr. Singh?"

"Yes," Lowry chimed in, "your man insisted that there was an important message from Simla and that we should come to the Palace immediately."

Even as he said that, Fletcher cut the Magistrate off, giving Sikander a scornful scowl. "What is all the fuss about then? Go on, enlighten us."

Sikander's response to this barrage of questions was a disarming shrug. "I fear that my man has not been entirely honest with you. The truth is that there really is no emergency. It was just a pretext to gather you all here."

This confession elicited a storm of angry outbursts.

Jardine, looking confused, like a child confronted by a mathematical equation he cannot decipher: "I demand an explanation immediately."

Lowry, jowls wobbling with affront: "This is an outrage. Preposterous!"

Fletcher, frothing at the mouth like a rabid bulldog: "How dare you? Who do you think you are?"

Bates, his Adam's apple bobbing up and down with indignation: "You have gone too bloody far this time."

Their voices jarred and clashed, rising to a deafening din, until at last, it was Simpson of all people, who silenced them.

"Enough!" he exclaimed, jumping to his feet, his command-ing bass muting this spate of objections. "Calm down, all of you!"

He gave Sikander a nod, as if to inform him he had his sup-port, if only for the time being. "I am sure the Maharaja has a good reason for this deception," he said, inviting Sikander to explain himself.

"Oh, yes!" the Maharaja replied, crossing to the head of the table and sinking into the chair that Charan Singh held back for him. "The reason I have asked you all here is to inform you that I have finally managed to solve the Major's murder."

This declaration was greeted by a stunned silence.

The bearers chose that moment to begin the dinner service, which was to be *à la russe,* it seemed, and swept forward to place silver salvers in front of each guest. With a flourish, off came the covering cloches to reveal the opening course, a platter of Oysters Katharine, the very sight of which made Sikander want to be sick. Where in God's name had the chef managed to find oysters in January, and that too in the middle of the Himalayas? He shook his head and waved the plate away, turning his atten-tion instead to the paired wine, an airy Chablis which, unlike the oysters, was perfect for the weather.

Taking a sip, Sikander sat back, enjoying being the cynosure of attention. He gave Helene a contented smile, in response to which she rolled her eyes, knowing only too well how much he enjoyed theatricality. *And why not?* Sikander thought indulgently. This was his favorite part of any mystery, the summation, the denouement, the consummation. Why, in some ways, it was even more satisfying than sex.

"Well?" It was Jardine who finally spoke up, as bullish as ever, "Spit it out. Who is the murderer then?"

"Patience, Mr. Jardine! I shall get to that in just a moment. First, let me begin by saying that this has been one of the most confusing cases I have ever encountered, a conundrum that very nearly managed to stump even my not inconsiderable powers of analysis." He shrugged. "Much to my dismay, I found myself confronted by a dilemma most detectives never have to face.

After my initial investigations, it became clear to me that I had altogether too many suspects."

Sikander helped himself to another swallow of Chablis.

"There is a Latin maxim I like to consider when I judge a person's guilt—*Cui bono*—'Who stands to profit?' Sadly, the answer to that question was even more perplexing. Every single one of you stood to gain from the Major's death. All of you had a motive, each better than the last."

He made a great show of pausing, and the bearers rushed forward to offer up the second course, a creamy soup *à la Reine*, Queen Victoria's favorite. Sikander took one hesitant taste and wrinkled his nose. It was really quite dreadful, with far too much pepper and saffron for his liking, but the wine accompanying it was a decent Oloroso, he noted with an ironic grin, that he was only too pleased to sample.

"Faced with such a surfeit of suspects, I turned to the one thing that does not lie. The evidence, which in this case was the sample I had collected from the scene of the crime. Upon examining these fragments in my laboratory, I found that my initial suspicions had indeed been correct. The Major had been poisoned by rather a large dose of strychnine, which had been added to a bottle of Oloroso."

"What on earth is Oh-loh-roh-so?" Jardine interjected.

"Oh, forgive me! I forgot what a dreadful barbarian you were, Mr. Jardine." He held up his glass, its contents sparkling a molten cerise. "An Oloroso is a very fine sherry from Spain. It is exceedingly expensive and not often exported since it does not travel well, which makes it rather rare to find in India. In his youth, it seems, the Major had a marked weakness for spirits and had been known to partake of them to excess, a habit he curtailed some years ago and the very reason for his teetotaling. As it happens, his favorite spirit of choice was none other than sherry, particularly Manzanilla and Oloroso, the taste of which he acquired while serving in Travancore. How convenient then that I should find a bottle of exactly such a vintage at the scene of the crime! A lesser man might have written it off as a mere coincidence, but I do not believe in fortuity, and it occurred to me that perhaps this was the very substance that killed the Major. As it turns out, my tests revealed it was indeed contaminated by strychnine, which makes it our murder weapon beyond a doubt."

He gave the Superintendent a despairing shrug.

"Before you ask, Mr. Jardine, there is no way I can corroborate that. My samples, you see, were depleted by my tests, and who knows where the bottle is now? Not to mention the fact that I cannot even verify if the Major actually even imbibed any of the poisoned wine, not without an autopsy to ascertain the contents of his stomach and bowels. Sadly, that is the one thing we cannot do, since contrary to my instructions, the Magistrate over there," he pointed at Lowry, "has already ordered the Major's remains to be cremated.

"As a result, I found myself quite stumped, an entirely new situation for me. For the first time in my life, I was at a loss, and no doubt that is how things would have remained if an utterly innocuous comment made by Mr. Miller had not caused everything to fall conveniently into place."

Stretching the tension of the moment, he looked about him, milking it for all it was worth, until Helene finally broke in impatiently. "Enough prevarication, Sikander! Are you going to let us die of suspense, or are you going to reveal what you have uncovered?"

"Of course, *chérie*," Sikander chuckled. "Forgive my dilly-dallying, but be patient just a while longer while I endeavor to explain my logic.

"I have always theorized that to be considered guilty, a suspect must be found culpable on two counts. First, motive. Why wish the Major dead? And second, opportunity. When and how was the dastardly scheme put into effect? A good detective must always strive to establish both of these things."

"Let us consider the question of motive. As I said, all of you had reasonable reasons to despise Major Russell."

He pointed towards the Gurkha, who remained impassive, fixing Sikander with a stony, unyielding glare.

"Take Gurung Bahadur for instance, the Major's faithful syce. Do not be misled by his scarred countenance or his surly demeanor. This is no ordinary man. He is a war hero, a veritable Horatius, decorated not once but several times for conspicuous gallantry. What then could bring such a man to resort to murder? What could possibly cause him to give up his honor and take another man's life?

"The answer, my friends, is revenge." He paused, raising one hand to his chest. "What is that Shakespeare said in *Hamlet*… 'O, from this time forth, My thoughts be bloody, or be nothing worth!'" Sikander smiled. "If anyone had a valid reason to want Major Russell dead, it was this man. Not five months ago, the Major had beaten a young woman, a whore at Mrs. Ponsonby's establishment, most grievously. While she survived this assault, the unfortunate young woman was so horribly scarred by the experience that rather than live as a cripple, she chose to end her life."

A collective gasp greeted this declaration, a resounding symphony of shock and dismay and disbelief.

"Yes," Sikander nodded, "that is exactly how I felt when this dreadful story was brought to my attention. At first, I confess, I thought it a lie. I mean, the thought of our prudish Resident visiting houses of ill repute, it challenged the very limits of credulity. Could Major Russell really have been so perverse? Could he actually be so cruel, so savage as to beat a girl near to death?

"It saddens me to say it is all true, my friends. Every single word of it. As my investigation progressed, I discovered a great deal about the Major's private life, each new revelation more horrifying and shocking than the next. Not only was he a habitual whore monger, but he had more brutal proclivities, passions that were so sickening that I am loath to speak of them in polite society. Let it suffice to say that he enjoyed inflicting pain upon those weaker than himself and it was in such wanton cruelty he found pleasure, especially when it came to his interactions with women.

"It was this very perversity that drove him to ravage that hapless young girl. However, what he did not know, what even

I did not realize at first, was that she was none other than this Gurkha's younger sister.

"You can imagine that when Gurung Bahadur found out what had befallen his sibling, he was enraged. His blood burned for revenge, and if there is one thing I have learned, it is best never to rouse a Gurkha's fury, for there is nothing that will stop him once he is on the warpath, not until his wrath has been slaked by blood."

He paused, glancing at the Gurkha almost admiringly. "So, motive he had aplenty, as well as ready access to the Major's bungalow, which meant he could have easily found the opportunity to poison him. However, that was where I found myself on shaky ground. After all, what Gurkha would resort to poison? Not only is an unlikely choice for a soldier, but for a warrior raised in a society that values courage above all else, it would be so shameful as to be unimaginable. No, if the Major had been stabbed or decapitated, then perhaps this could be our man, but strychnine? That was exactly what I found difficult to accept, the thought of him taking such an insidious path, and that is what led me to dismiss him as a suspect, in spite of the mountain of circumstantial evidence arrayed against him."

As he made this declaration, the soup was whisked away and replaced by the fish course, which seemed to be baked Dover Sole. Sikander winced. It certainly looked boot-like enough, as tough as leather. To his relief, it had been paired with a delightful Muscatelle, which vanished down his parched throat with an exquisite smoothness.

Turning his attention toward the Munshi, Sikander's upper lip curled into a sneer. The man quailed, refusing to meet the Maharaja's eyes, staring fixedly down at his hands as he wrung them with a mournful expression. His sparse pate glistened with sweat, betraying his nervousness.

"So, if not the syce, who could the killer be? My next suspect was the esteemed Munshi Ram Dev, who had the dubious privilege of being the Major's vakeel." Sikander clucked his tongue with disapproval. "When it was suggested that I investigate him, I balked at the possibility. It just did not seem likely to me that he could be a killer. I mean, just look at him. On the face of it, have you seem a more harmless-looking creature? But I warn you, do not be fooled by this innocuous exterior. Here is an even better example of how appearances can be deceiving. This man is a snake in the grass, a liar and a cheat, a swindler, and a badmash."

With each successive word, the Munshi squirmed, growing ever more uneasy as the Maharaja flayed into him with no remorse.

"As I delved deeper into the Munshi's activities, I uncovered that he had quite a profitable racket going, unbeknownst to us all. For some years now, he had been preying upon war widows, delaying their grants of land so that he could acquire the allotments for a pittance, the reprehensible scoundrel! I suppose I could blame the fact that he is a Marwari and being of such ilk, he could not resist the chance to make a quick profit. But then I found myself wondering, how could such flagrant skullduggery go on under the Major's watchful eye? Could he truly have been so blind? It did not take long for me to realize it, but the answer was quite obvious. It was Major Russell who was the mastermind behind the whole scheme, and the Munshi was his willing pawn."

Sikander frowned. "And there we have a motive! The Major as good as owned him, and no man, even a corrupt one, can tolerate being owned. No doubt as the Major's requests became more and more egregious, the Munshi slowly began to realize that the only way he would ever be liberated from Major Russell's clutches was if he got rid of the man, for once and for all.

"True, he had easy access to the Major's household, even more so than the syce, which gave him ample opportunity. But that was the point where once again, doubt raised its unruly head. Time and again, as I reviewed the Munshi as a suspect, I found myself facing one persistent uncertainty. Why would he bite the very hand that fed him? I mean, he was turning a handsome profit working for Major Russell, both from the baksheesh he collected legitimately, as well as from his more nefarious activities. In addition, his reputation, his very standing in the Indian community was built on the foundation that he was the Major's most trusted employee. Why would he endanger that? Why would he risk his position and his job?"

Sikander threw up his hands, as if in surrender. "As a result, you see, I came to the conclusion that the Munshi just did not fit the bill. He is a liar and a cheat and a charlatan, certainly, but not a murderer."

Spreading his hands, as if to indicate his confusion, Sikander shifted in his seat, and the bearers took that interlude as the perfect moment to have the third course cleared. In came the entree, a game cock served on a bed of rice pilaf. It looked to be very palatable, the meat cooked to golden crispness and radiating a mouthwatering aroma of honey, but Sikander barely gave it a second glance, more interested in the rather sour Malbec Claret served alongside.

"So, you can only imagine my perplexity," he continued. "Here we have two perfectly viable motives, but neither man quite seemed to fit the role of the Major's murderer. Thankfully, I had a wealth of other suspects, all with equally strong reasons to wish the Major dead.

"The most obvious of them of course was young Lieutenant Bates." At the mention of his name, the Lieutenant glowered at Sikander defiantly. "After all, was this not the very man who had a public spat with Major Russell, not twelve hours before the Resident turned up dead? Did they not almost come to fisticuffs, in front of more than a hundred witnesses?"

By now, Sikander was quite tired of sitting down, so he sprang energetically to his feet, and crossed to stand behind Mrs. Bates and her husband, looming over them ominously.

"I must admit, when I first encountered the Lieutenant, I was almost certain that he had a hand in the Major's demise. He has all the qualities one looks for in a murderer—a choleric temperament coupled with an innate arrogance and an unrealistically high opinion of himself. He is possessive to the fault of mania, and prone to violent outbursts, considering he actually went so far as to assault me just for speaking with his wife."

With each subsequent word, the Lieutenant flinched, his face growing redder and redder, his clenched fists and bellicose demeanor conveying that he was on the brink of one of those very outbursts that Sikander had just mentioned. The only thing that kept him in his seat was the threat of Charan Singh, standing just a few feet away, and of course, his wife's slim hand on one arm, restraining him as surely as any manacle.

"It did not take much of a stretch of the imagination to find a motive that would render him culpable. First, it seemed Major Russell had repeatedly been blocking his many entreaties to be transferred to a more active posting. But that was not all. There was also the small matter of the fact that the Major had been trying desperately for some months to cuckold him, a state of affairs that had undoubtedly caused him no small amount of consternation. After all, what man would stand by and hold his peace while another pursued his wife?"

Mr. Simpson chose that moment to clear his throat rather pointedly, as if to suggest that his patience was fraying and that the Maharaja should try and get to the point.

"So as we see, Lieutenant Bates had ample justification to want the Major out of his way. However, there were three reasons why I found myself doubting his guilt. The first of course was his temperament. As I mentioned, he is hot-headed and reckless, and a young man such as him would never resort to poison. No, I can see him engaging the Major in single combat, sabres at dawn and the like, but frankly, I doubt he even knows what strychnine is.

"Second, of course, there was the matter of opportunity. Unlike the Gurkha and the Munshi, he had no access to the Major's bungalow. How then could he get to the Oloroso to add a dose of poison to it? Not to mention the fact that it would be very difficult for him to get his hands on a vintage quite so expensive on a lowly Lieutenant's stipend.

"But by far, the most compelling reason to consider him innocent is the fact that he is an exceedingly stupid fellow. There is no way I could credit him with devising such a devious and elaborate scheme. To come up with a plan so subtle takes both intelligence and patience, and our Lieutenant, I am sorry to say, lacks both of those qualities, which is precisely why I dismissed him as a suspect, in spite of the considerable evidence suggesting the contrary.

"No," the Maharaja said, turning toward the Lieutenant's wife, "there is a better suspect seated right next to him."

Unlike her husband, Mrs. Bates looked exceedingly nervous, as pale as a sheet, on the brink of falling into a faint. Nonetheless, she was even more beautiful, like some elfish dryad taken flesh, so captivating that in front of her, even Helene seemed washed out, as drab as a drudge.

"Ah, the beauteous Mrs. Bates! As I mentioned, in the course of my investigations, I managed to establish a repeating pattern of deviancy in regards to the Major's sexual leanings, an unnatural psychology. It was clear to me that the Major enjoyed preying on women. He sought them out and strove to dominate them, for it was in this very dominance that he found sexual satisfaction. It was not dissimilar to what he did to the syce's unfortunate sister, only in this case he could not beat the women he sought out, not without publicly ruining his reputation. As a result, he liked to slowly force himself upon them, to feel a sense of power not unlike what Sader-Masoch has called the inextricable coupling of desire with violence.

"At first glance, Mrs. Bates struck me as a victim, the hapless target for Major Russell's sadistic desires. And what man would not desire her? One only has to look at her to see what a comely creature she is, in the bloom of youth, unspoiled by the hardships of life, with an air of innocence that is quite irresistible."

He was about to waffle on, heaping more flattery upon the young memsahib, but he happened to notice that Helene's Gallic blood was close to the boiling point, judging by the dangerous look she was giving him. With a gulp, Sikander cut himself short.

While he was a brave man, even he was not foolhardy enough to arouse a Frenchwoman's fury.

"Are you familiar with the story of Uriah the Hittite, Mr. Jardine? It is from your Christian Old Testament. Legend has it that when he was an old man, King David, the same David who defeated Goliath and became King of Israel, saw a woman named Bathsheba bathing and became besotted with her. It turned out that she was the wife of one of his officers, a man named Uriah. Now, you would think that would have elicited some loyalty from David, but he was so overcome with lust he forced himself upon Bathsheba. As a result, she became pregnant with his child, and to avoid a scandal, David decided to rid himself of Uriah. He gave Uriah a letter to take to Joab, his commander, in which he gave an order to have Uriah posted to the forefront of a battle, where he was killed, thus leaving David free to take Bathsheba as his wife.

"In your case, Madame, you had the misfortune to be Major Russell's Bathsheba. When I first met with you, you were only too happy to pour out your heart to me. What a tale of woe you related, poignant enough to make even the most hard-hearted of men turn to putty! I confess, I was mortified when I heard of the indignities that the Major had heaped upon you, even inspired to the brink of fury.

"To tell the truth, Madame, like most men, I too was blinded by your tender charms, so beguiled that I found it difficult to conceive of you as a killer. You, a fragile woman, as delicate as a winter rose, how could you find it in yourself to kill a man? But then, the more I considered it, the more something kept nagging at me, an instinct that there was more to you than met the eye."

Mrs. Bates squirmed as Sikander's pale gaze fixed on her. Her eyes darted around the table, searching desperately for a savior, for any avenue of escape.

"That realization gave me pause, and I found myself contemplating an entirely different possibility. What if you were not Bathsheba at all, but Jezebel? What if you grew tired of being a victim, a plaything to be manipulated by men? What if you realized you could turn the tables, that you could use the Major's lechery to your advantage by applying your feminine wiles?"

He smiled triumphantly. "This suspicion was cemented when I heard from a source that you were engaged in rather a passionate clinch with the Major at the New Year's Ball. Not an embrace where he had forced himself upon you, but a consensual rendezvous where it seems you were the one who had approached him."

The Lieutenant had been listening to Sikander's diatribe with mounting dismay. With each subsequent word, he looked more and more shocked, a complex interplay of emotions crossing his features, first dismay and then consternation and lastly rage as soon as his slow-witted brain began to realize that the Maharaja was speaking the truth. A groan of pure sorrow escaped his lips, his ugly features distorted by pain, and he sprang to his feet.

Mrs. Bates responded with a whimper. "Please, Johnny, you have to believe me. He is lying." She gave Sikander a bitter, panicked look. "This is utter nonsense." Desperately, she reached out to console her husband, but he brushed off her hand roughly and strode away. Charan Singh moved forward, ready to head him off, but Sikander waved the big Sikh back, indicating he should stand down and not impede the Lieutenant's departure.

"Of course you will deny it, Madame. I would expect nothing less from a liar as accomplished as yourself."

"Leave the girl alone," Jardine interjected sullenly. "Can't you see she doesn't know a thing?"

Sikander gave him a withering frown. "Your gallantry is misplaced, Mr. Jardine. You may not realize it, but Mrs. Bates is not quite the wilting willow she likes to pretend to be. Oh no, she is a very clever woman, more than capable of murder."

"Preposterous!" Mrs. Bates exclaimed, with a hollow, unconvincing laugh. "You haven't a shred of proof."

"On the contrary, Madame, I have sworn testimony that places you at the scene of the crime, not two nights before Major Russell was poisoned. His servant, Ghanshyam, insists he saw a cloaked woman lurking about behind the Resident's bungalow, whom he mistook for some sort of phantasm. But that unearthly apparition, I suspect, was none other than you, wasn't it?"

He paused, gathering his breath and offering the young woman a triumphant smile. "Do you deny it, Madame?"

To his surprise, she did not. He had expected at least some modicum of resistance, a deluge of crocodile tears from those dramatic eyes followed by a heartfelt denial intended to evoke sympathy in the hearts of all the men around her, as was her pattern, but instead, the young memsahib gave him a defiant look, as proud as a Valkyrie.

For a moment, Sikander found himself thinking her quite magnificent. In another time, another place, he could even imagine pursuing her, and he saw at last what it was that drew men to her, like moths to a flame.

"He was an evil man," she hissed. "He deserved to die."

Every single neck at the table swiveled to watch her, disbelieving that such a slender chit of a girl could contain so much anger, but Mrs. Bates remained gloriously unrepentant, not at all discomposed to be the cynosure of so many accusing eyes.

"Don't you understand what kind of a man he was? He was a monster, with no honor, with no heart!" Her voice cracked. "I did not kill him. No, I went to the bungalow to try and reason with him, to try and beg him to leave me and my husband alone. You see, he had threatened me several times, told me that if I did not give in to his advances, he would have Johnny transferred to the frontier. I did not believe he would do it, but a few days ago, he showed me the transfer papers, signed and stamped. That is why I went to him, to offer my virtue to him if he would only destroy the orders, but when I got there, I found I could not do it. I lost my nerve."

She collapsed back into her seat, as if the strain of making this declaration had been too much for her. Utterly exhausted, a broken doll, she stared up at Sikander, her eyes brimming with moisture, looking so hapless that to his surprise, he felt a glimmer of pity for her.

"Calm down, Madame," Sikander said. "I know that you are not guilty. Just like your husband, I have been unable to establish a link between you and the poisoned wine. In addition, I do not believe that you have it in you to be a murderess. You are a temptress and a manipulator par excellence, but I believe that you lack the cold-bloodedness to take a man's life. Sadly, I cannot punish you for wanting the Major dead, but then, I imagine it is punishment enough being married to your witless excuse of a husband.

"So, it was not the Lieutenant, nor his comely wife. Who then is left for us to accuse?"

With that question, Sikander returned to his seat. He waited until the next course had been laid out—a roast saddle of mutton *à la Bretonne*, stuffed with truffles. It was accompanied surprisingly by a very dry Hungarian Tokay that he was delighted to see. Taking a large swallow, he turned his attention toward Lowry, who was trying to keep a low profile, slumped over, seemingly half asleep.

"The answer to that question must come from another gentleman who almost had me well and truly fooled. Isn't that so, Mr. Lowry?"

The Magistrate, who had been very careful to remain silent so far, hoping perhaps that he would be forgotten, straightened up at the mention of his name, offering Sikander a stolid grimace.

"I had nothing to do with any of this," he said weakly.

"Yes, Mr. Lowry, you have said so many times, so often that you almost had me convinced." Sikander gave the man a glare so frigid the Magistrate shivered. "At first, I was tempted to believe you. Frankly, if there was one man I would find difficult to imagine as a murderer, it would be you. I mean, just look at you. You are about as spineless as an invertebrate. And then there was the fact that unlike the Captain, you were so very eager to be cooperative. In fact, it was you who pointed me at Mr. Fletcher, and told me of his argument with Major Russell, not to mention his confrontation with Lieutenant Bates. But I was wrong about you, wasn't I?"

He turned to the rest of his guests. "He may seem to be as wobbly as a jellyfish, but I warn you, do not be misled by the cover of this book. Our Mr. Lowry is not nearly as ineffectual as he likes to act. He is an experienced dissembler, a pretender par excellence. Trust me, if there is any man in Rajpore who knows how to keep a secret, it is he."

Sikander hesitated, debating whether to reveal what he knew about Lowry's deviant sexual preferences. Inexplicably, something held him back. It was true that being a sodomite was not uncommon amongst the British upper classes. Why, at school, he had heard horror stories about Eton boys rogering each other as eagerly as rabbits, but still, in the rarefied atmosphere of Colonial India, being exposed as a homosexual was as bad as being branded with the mark of Cain. And while he really did not care one way or another about what people did in the privacy of their bedrooms, he was sensitive enough to understand that he held not just the man's career in his hands, but also his reputation. One word and Lowry would be ruined, not just in India, but most likely in England as well, because news this salacious had a way of traveling faster than even light.

As if to remind him of that fact, the man shot him a desperate look, his eyes beseeching him not to expose his secret. Sikander felt a frisson of pity run through him. It would be so easy to destroy him, and true, while he certainly was an unlikeable creature, the Maharaja could not deny that in this case perhaps, the punishment exceeded the crime.

"The Major had a hold on you, and he used you terribly, didn't he? He had you posted here to Rajpore only so that you could be his pawn, and you let him use you, Mr. Lowry, because you were afraid of him. You let him exploit an old friendship and your own fears, and he treated you like dirt." The Magistrate groaned, as if Sikander had physically wounded him. "But no man, even one as weak-willed as you, can live in perpetual fear. Sooner or later, a time comes when he must break, when even a mouse bites back."

"I swear," Lowry pleaded, "I did not kill him."

"Then why did you order the body to be disposed of?"

"It was his wish, I explained that."

"Was it," Sikander hissed, "or was it a convenient way to get rid of evidence? I confess, you surprised me by cremating the Major's remains with such alacrity. You almost managed to shut my investigation down, because once his corpse was gone, I had no samples to rely on other than the few I collected, and without an autopsy, I had no way to corroborate any of my theories.

"Added to that, there is the fact that you were the one who had brought the Oloroso to the Major. Of course, you explained that cleverly by deflecting attention to Captain Fletcher, saying that he was the one who asked you to deliver it on his behalf, but the fact remains that you were the last person to handle the wine. That could have made it possible for you to add the strychnine to it, not to mention that you were one of the few people who were aware of the Major's fondness for such exotic vintages."

Before he could continue, abruptly, the Magistrate sprang up, showing an admirable urgency for such a plump man.

"I must object. I take severe umbrage at such treatment." He turned to Mr. Gibson. "Sir, you are from Simla. Stop this madness immediately, I insist."

Sadly, this appeal fell on deaf ears. Mr. Simpson remained as granite-faced as a statue, and refused to make a single move to assist the Magistrate. Instead, he gave the Maharaja a curt nod, as if to urge him to proceed with his analysis.

"Where was I? Ah, yes! Certainly there was a great deal of evidence pointing towards you, Mr. Lowry. Unfortunately, in the end though, I was compelled to dismiss you as a suspect as well. The reason, quite simply, was a lack of motive. Though you had ample opportunity to poison the Major, why? Why would you wish to kill a man with whom you had a cordial relationship?" He raised one eyebrow, choosing to hold his tongue about the full truth, that Lowry had loved the Major, much to the Magistrate's unmitigated relief. "No, you had no real reason to want the Major dead, which is not something that we can say quite so readily for our next suspect, Captain Fletcher."

On cue, out trundled the dessert course, a mountainous Nesselrode Pudding in the shape of a leaping dolphin. It was paired with a fine Douro, but Sikander decided to skip it. He had already drunk far too much, and could feel the familiar onset of ennui looming, reminding him that he should try and get through the rest of his dissertation before he passed out in his chair.

"Ah, the good Captain!" He frowned at Fletcher, who was sitting ramrod straight, glowering back with an expression of supreme distaste on his face, as if to suggest he had nothing but contempt to offer Sikander. "Here we have a career soldier, a man of doughty morals and staunch principles, a veritable Roberts of Kandahar. What then could possibly drive such a person to resort to something as insidious as murder? You have to only look at him, at his unyielding posture, at his choleric complexion, to realize what his weakness is. Beneath his stiff, stout exterior, he is a deeply angry, jealous man, frustrated by a lack of advancement, made bitter from being passed over time and again, from watching men younger than him, men he judged to be less worthy, being promoted to the rank he believed he deserved. Ego, pride, hubris; call it what you may, but that, I believe, is where we must begin to examine what motive he might have had to try and kill the Major.

"At first, when I thought of him as a suspect, it did not seem to add up, I admit it. After all, wasn't it well known that Major Russell and the Captain were good friends, yes, often spotted at the club together, enjoying a game of chess, or a rubber of bridge? What then could have caused such an irrevocable rift between them, a public spat that culminated with our Captain here issuing a most forbidding promise, that he would find a way to get even with the Major, no matter what it took?

"The reason, I realized, was really quite simple. The Major and the Captain were not friends at all. Major Russell was not capable of friendship. No, to him, Fletcher was just another pawn to be used, to be manipulated, as was his habit. However, poor Captain Fletcher only realized this fact much too late."

He looked at the Captain pityingly.

"There is an old saying, isn't there, that a scorpion cannot change his nature? You asked the Major for assistance in persuading Simla to grant you the promotion for which you were so eager. You actually thought he would help you, but it never even occurred to you that there was no way he would let you match him in rank."

"God," Fletcher hissed, his voice bitter with rancor, "but you love the sound of your own voice, don't you?"

Jardine let out a snigger, which strangled in his throat when Sikander shot a look of withering contempt in his direction.

"You are lucky, Captain," he said coldly, "that I am a civilized man. Were it another prince in my place, and you would most likely find yourself with your tongue cut out for such blatant insolence."

"You dare to threaten me, an English officer, in public?" Fletcher roared. "Do you see? Do you all see the nerve of this popinjay?"

"Behave yourself, Mr. Fletcher. You are my guest. Please do not compel me do something I will regret later."

His tone was conversational, almost distant, but that only made the threat all that more chilling. Fletcher started to open his mouth, no doubt to argue, to call the Maharaja's bluff, but Mr. Simpson chose that moment to cluck his tongue rather ostentatiously, as if to warn the man to mind his manners.

Abashed, the Captain hesitated. His brow bristled with fury, but he showed enough good sense to bite down firmly on his lower lip.

"That's much better. Now where was I? Ah yes, so much for motive. As you can see, our dear Captain most assuredly had a legitimate reason to want Major Russell dead. And then of course there was the small matter of the wine, which I was able to establish originated with you, thus giving you plenty of opportunities to taint it with strychnine."

"I already explained that...."

Sikander silenced him with a wave of one hand. "Control yourself, Captain! I just said that you looked guilty, but that does not mean I believe it. Much as I would love to put the blame squarely on your shoulders, the reason I was forced to doubt you was the very same reason why I discounted Gurung Bahadur. Quite simply, it was a matter of temperament. Just like the Gurkha, you are a martial man, a man of action, and as such, I do not believe it is in your nature to choose such a pernicious path as poison. I am sad to report I do not believe you are our killer."

Sikander shook his head, feigning disappointment as the final course was trundled out, a wooden cart laden with a crystal platter of very smelly Stilton and a salver of wilted lettuce and saltine crackers, accompanied by several snifters of fine cognac.

"I seem to have run out of suspects," he said, looking at each person at the table in turn, until finally his eyes came to settle on Jane. "Or have I?"

"There was another person in Rajpore who had equal, if not more reason than all of you, to despise Major Russell. Another victim who had been hurt even more gravely by his proclivity for preying on women.

"You, Jane, if anyone can testify to the Major's cruelty, it is you. Dear, fragile Jane! I never suspected you, not for a heart-beat. I mean, why would I? You came so very close to losing your own life that it made no sense to think of you as anything but a victim. And then there was the fact that of all the people in this room, you seemed the most stricken by his passing. That led me to wonder if you were involved with him in some way, but I was mistaken, wasn't I?

"I misinterpreted your sorrow as grief, when the truth could not have been more contrary. It was not sorrow, but rather guilt. You did not love the Major. You despised him, and with good reason."

He frowned. "You were his daughter, were you not?"

The Englishwoman responded to this accusation with a gasp that was more resignation than bemusement.

"You have me, sir." She looked at Sikander sadly. "Yes, he was indeed my father."

This affirmation was followed by a crescendo of further gasps, loudest amongst them Jardine.

"I surmised as much," Sikander said. "It took me longer than usual to see it, but then, when Miller from the *Gazette* recounted a story that the Major supposedly jilted a woman when he came out to India, leaving her with child, I managed to put two and two together. That woman was your mother, I presume?"

Jane nodded, just the faintest bob of her head, as if she were too tired to hide the truth any longer.

"She was always talking about him, about how wonderful he had been, how brave and how heroic. She never stopped loving him, never believed he had deserted her, till the day she died. She was convinced he would send for her, even as she took her last breath."

Jane's shoulders slumped. "Truthfully, I never thought I would meet him. I didn't even know he was here when I came out to India, and once I entered the convent, I put him from my mind. But then," she groaned, "fate intervened. The sisters came here to Rajpore, and I with them, and there he was. It was like God himself wanted our paths to cross. I know it was. That was why I turned my back on the Church, and decided to stay here."

"But why become his housekeeper? Why didn't you tell him who you were outright?"

She shook her head. "I wasn't sure what I wanted to do. I was scared, terrified that he would rebuff me. And I was worried that I could have been mistaken, that maybe he was not my father, after all. But most of all, I wanted to wait, to get to know him before I decided to reveal my identity, to find out why he did what he had done to my mother. It was a mistake, of course. I should never have stayed."

Sikander gave her a sympathetic look. He could understand the rest—the more time she had spent with the Major, the more she had come to dislike him. It must have been excruciating, to find out that your father was a cruel, avaricious man, not to mention a sadist and a deviant. Frankly, it was a wonder she had not killed him earlier.

"What really happened that night?"

Jane bit her lip. "He was very angry when he came back from the ball, more infuriated than I had ever seen him, not to mention terribly drunk." Her voice wavered, thick with emotion. "I tried to calm him down, but then… he forced himself on me."

The words choked in her throat. Mrs. Bates groaned, holding up one hand to her mouth in dismay, realizing perhaps how close she had come to the same fate. Jardine, Lowry, and Captain Fletcher all averted their eyes in shame, and Gurung Bahadur's grim features contorted with fury, remembering what the Major had done to his sister. As for Simpson, his face showed the first real glimmer of emotion Sikander had seen from the man, a grimace of disgust as he ground his teeth together with barely repressed outrage.

Helene rose from her chair gracefully and came to stand behind Jane, resting one gentle hand on her shoulder. It was a humble gesture but it seemed to give the Englishwoman the strength to carry on with her story.

"When he was done with me, he offered me money, like I was a common whore." A boneless shudder wracked through her slender body. "That was when I…I broke down, and it all came pouring out. I told him everything, all about my mother, and who I really was."

The Maharaja shook his head. His heart went out to Jane. The poor, broken thing! How could she ever recover from this? The Major had not just stolen her innocence, he had ruined her for life. How could she ever forget what had been done to her, and that too by her own father? Part of him wished the Major was still alive, so he could have the man arrested and put on trial for his crimes. Another more, savage part wished he could have killed the man himself, cut him to pieces, and made him suffer as he had enjoyed making others. Wincing, he struggled to find something to say to Jane, any words of comfort, but nothing came to mind. It was too late for that now. The time for words was long past. "And what did the Major say when you made this revelation?" he asked softly.

Jane moaned, as if he had slapped her. "He…he laughed at me," she murmured, her voice so low it was almost inaudible. "He called me a liar and a whore and told me that I was dismissed from his service. He told me that I was to leave Rajpore by the time he woke the next morning, or he would have me arrested and locked up for being a thief."

"So, you poisoned him?"

"Yes!" She said matter-of-factly, as if she were talking about what was being served for supper. "It seemed only fair. My mother took a massive dose of poison when she killed herself. That was what he deserved, exactly the same fate."

Her voice hardened, and so did her face, growing bleak. "I had already come to the decision to take my own life. The shame of what he had done to me was too much to endure, and I could not bear the thought of going on." Her voice remained level, even as she made this macabre confession, her expression as blank as a statue. "I went to the kitchen and found the bottle of wine that Mr. Lowry had brought for the Major. I uncorked it and poured myself a glass. I knew there was an old vial of rat poison in the store room, and I rummaged about until I uncovered it."

Of course, Sikander thought, *that was where the strychnine had come from.* It was a common enough ingredient in most brands of rodenticide, and in a large enough dose, it could certainly be fatal to humans.

"I returned to the kitchen and added a generous dose to my glass, and was just about to drink it when the Major rang for me. I don't know why, perhaps it was sheer habit, but I went back upstairs to see what he wanted. Maybe some part of me hoped that he would recant his earlier words, that he would accept the truth and embrace me, but instead, he threatened me." Her words caught in her throat, choking to a mumble. "He said it was my fault, that I was nothing more than a pitiable spinster who had seduced him, who had led him astray. And then, he tried to buy me off, by offering me a very substantial sum if I would leave India and swear never to speak of what had occurred."

She ground her teeth together, so audibly that it was unnerving. "The gall of the man! He showed not a hint of remorse, neither for what he had done to my mother, nor for what he had done to me. I knew then I could not kill myself until I had first killed him."

"What happened next?"

"I accepted his offer and suggested we share a drink to seal the bargain. Then I returned to the kitchen, and emptied the remainder of the poison into the bottle of sherry. I took it up to him, along with my own glass. We drank together, and the Major raised a toast to me, calling me a very sensible woman. I left him up there and came back down to the parlor. It did not take very long for the poison to take effect. I sat there and listened as he began to scream, as he raved, begging for my help, but I didn't lift a finger."

Her voice was composed, almost relieved, as if this confession had liberated her. "What I cannot understand is why the poison did not work on me. I should be dead as well, shouldn't I?"

Sikander leaned forward and offered Jane a mournful smile. "I think I can explain that. The rat poison, was it pellets, or a powder?"

"It was a white, grainy powder."

"And how many spoonfuls did you add to your glass?"

"Two, I think, or three, I cannot quite remember."

"Was it teaspoons, or tablespoons?"

"Teaspoons, the same we use for sugar."

"There you have it," Sikander exclaimed, snapping his fingers. "Obviously the dose you took was much too mild to kill you, not immediately at least. No, while three teaspoons may be enough to kill a rat, all it did to a woman your size and weight was cause you to fall into a stupor, and luckily, as providence would have it, I arrived just in the nick of time to rescue you."

"Why? Why did you have to save me?" Jane groaned. "Why didn't you just let me die?"

With that exclamation, her composure finally cracked. She leaned forward, hiding her face in her hands as she began to weep soundlessly, entirely overcome by despair.

Both the Munshi and the Gurkha quailed, profoundly uncomfortable at witnessing such intimate candor, particularly from a memsahib. This embarrassment was reflected upon the faces of Jardine and Mr. Simpson as well, who seemed unsure of how to react to such a horrible tale. As for Mrs. Bates, she looked about ready to burst into tears herself. Lowry had the grace to look ashamed, appalled that he had never realized the depths of his beloved Major's depravity, and next to him, the Captain's face blanched pale with regret, wishing perhaps that he had been able to rescue Jane, for whom Sikander knew he cared deeply, from such a dreadful fate. His lips opened and closed soundlessly, as the bluff soldier struggled to find something to say to her, before finally giving up and averting his gaze, unable to hide his obvious despair.

Like a patient wracked by a seizure, the Englishwoman continued to tremble, her thin frame wracked by silent paroxysms of pain. Helene tried to comfort her, but to no avail. That was when Sikander decided to take matters into his own hands. Silently, he rose and crossed over to the young Englishwoman. Helene gave him a questioning look, before reluctantly stepping aside to give him enough space so that he could sink down on one knee next to her.

"I am sorry, Jane. What happened to you, to some extent it is my fault. I should have recognized what the Major was. I could have saved you, but I failed."

Gently, as carefully as if she were made of glass, he reached out and turned her face towards him, until he was staring straight into her enormous, anguished eyes.

"If there is one thing I am certain of in this case, it is that you deserve a better hand than what life has dealt you." He gave her a comforting smile. "Do you remember the promise I made to you? That I would take care of you?"

In spite of his disdain for physical intimacy, he took out his handkerchief and reached out, wiping her face clean with one corner, an almost paternal gesture.

"I want you to go with my man here. He will take you back to your room, where you will pack a bag. He will then see you to one of my automobiles which shall take you to the Railway Station. You are booked on the two o'clock mail train to Calcutta, where I have taken the liberty of getting you a first-class cabin on the P&O steamer, *Hibernia*, which is bound for Australia by way of Singapore."

He nodded toward Charan Singh who grinned and stepped forward to offer Jane a silver salver upon which lay a bulging manila envelope.

"You shall find all the necessary travel documents in there, along with five hundred pounds in cash, as well as a letter to my banker in Singapore. He will provide you with a draft for a further thousand pounds, which you can encash when you arrive in Sydney."

Jane did not take the envelope at first. She gazed up at Sikander, utterly stunned, her eyes filled with turmoil.

"Why are you doing this?" she asked as surprise faded to suspicion. "Why are you trying to help me?"

"I made a promise to take care of you, Jane, and Sikander Singh always keeps his word." He nodded at her, to urge her to trust him. She hesitated, swiveling her head to look up at Helene, who offered a kindly smile, as if to reassure her that the Maharaja meant her no harm.

It was this little gesture that seemed to do the trick, and Jane reached out for the envelope, holding it warily, as if she suspected it were booby-trapped.

"Thank…Thank you."

"I want you to make a new start," Sikander said. "Forget the Major. Forget India. Leave it all behind you, and start over. Buy a small house and settle down. Can you do that much for me?"

"I…" Her eyes welled with emotion once more, not misgiving this time, but rather gratitude. "I will try."

Jardine, who had been watching this scene unfold with a bewildered look on his face, as if he could not quite comprehend what was going on, finally chose that moment to speak up.

"Hie there! What do you think you're doing? She's a murderer. She killed the Major."

Sikander turned to the Superintendent, and Helene came to stand behind him. She patted his shoulder, looking absurdly proud of him, and he took one of her hands in his own, bringing it briefly to his lips to kiss her palm, enjoying the delicate ivory smell of her skin.

"Is she, Mr. Jardine? Are you sure of that? I mean, just yesterday, you were convinced the Major committed suicide."

"But you just said…"

"Ah yes, my theory! Certainly it is an interesting take on the whole affair, but unfortunately, there is one major flaw in my reasoning." He grinned, baring his teeth like a jackal. "As I said earlier, Superintendent, I haven't a shred of evidence. Thanks to Mr. Lowry, the Major's corpse has been cremated, and the incriminating bottle disposed of." He held up his hands, as if to signify his helplessness. "As a result, we have no substantial proof, and all we are left with are my conjectures, which frankly don't amount to much. After all, I am a well-known eccentric and a native to boot! I can't imagine my testimony would hold up in any court of law."

"This…this is preposterous. She must be arrested immediately." Jardine's voice was as shrill as a child throwing a tantrum. "She can't just walk out of here."

He gazed imploringly at Simpson, who in turn gave Sikander a stiff glare. The Maharaja glowered straight back at the man from Simla, challenging him to question his conclusions, daring him to reject them. For a long time, Simpson did not speak, frowning ever so slightly, his fingers drumming against the tabletop, a staccato tympani that betrayed his ambivalence. You did not have to be a detective to see that he was struggling to make up his mind. It had to be difficult for him, for any Englishman really, to decide to trust an Indian, especially someone with Sikander's picaresque reputation. That certainly explained why he looked disturbed, his stiff face distorted by an expression of uncertainty.

"Mr. Jardine is correct," he started to say. "This is highly irregular..."

"You're absolutely correct, Mr. Simpson," Sikander cut him off. "This has been a most irregular case. Let us not drag it out any further than we need to, shall we?" He gave the man from Simla a very theatrical shrug. "Why not let this tamasha end here, in this very room? I am certain you can count on the confidentiality of the people we have gathered here today. After all, don't each of them have a vested interest in holding their tongues, considering that if the truth were to get out, it would ruin them all? Not to mention the fact that it would cause Simla to irrevocably lose face.

"That is the last thing I desire, Mr. Simpson, to cause the British Government any further embarrassment. I mean, isn't it bad enough that a senior officer was killed? We certainly don't need the newspapers asking questions about his background, do we, poking about trying to ascertain how a deviant with such a spotty record was even allowed to rise to such a position? God forbid, all sort of shameful stories might come out!"

Sikander offered Simpson an angelic grin. Judging by the grimace he received in return, he was sure that he had pushed the man too far. *Damn it*, he thought, *why couldn't I just have reined it in a little? Why did I have to try and turn the screw just that extra little bit?*

To his relief, less than a heartbeat later, the man's craggy features broke into a grudging smile.

"Oh, well done!" he said. "Well played, Your Highness! A daring gambit, but you are indeed correct. The last thing Simla needs is any more embarrassment."

He rose to his feet with a military precision, and offered Jane a careful bow.

"As far as the Government is concerned, this is quite obviously a case of death by misadventure. I can only hope, Madame, that you find good fortune in Australia."

"Thank you, both of you. I do not know what to say." Jane staggered to her feet, clutching Sikander's envelope as if it were a life-raft, rendered more than a little unsteady by all that had just happened.

Unexpectedly, Fletcher rose in symphony with her. "If you will excuse me," he said, with abashed respectfulness, "I have a few things I should like to say to Miss Jane."

"I suspected you might," Sikander said, and gave Charan Singh a nod. The big Sikh offered Captain Fletcher an envelope as well, a twin to the one he had handed to Jane just a few moments previously. "I thought Miss Jane would need an escort to keep her safe on her journey, so I took the liberty of booking the adjoining cabin for you."

Confusion flickered across the Captain's gruff countenance, temptation warring against trepidation.

"Why would you do something like this, after how appallingly I have behaved?"

"I am not doing it for you, Captain. I am doing it for Jane. She needs a good man, and in spite of your utter lack of manners, I suspect you are one."

The man's face softened. "I was wrong about you, Mr. Singh," he said, his voice thick, unused to emotion.

"Good luck. I trust you will take good care of her."

With a brisk nod, Fletcher took the envelope from Charan Singh. Smiling tentatively, he moved towards Jane, a strangely vulnerable expression on his dour face as he offered her his arm, as if for support. Jane studied him contemplatively, and after a moment's hesitation, placed her hand in his, letting him steer her toward the door, and beyond it, to freedom.

Barely had they taken two steps when Jardine sprang to his feet.

"You cannot be serious," he growled, trying to scuttle around the table so that he could cut Jane off. "You cannot really mean to just let that little bint walk out of here? She's a killer, damn your eyes."

"That's quite enough out of you," Sikander snapped, dropping all pretense at being convivial. "I have taken all that I can endure of your incessant whining, Mr. Jardine." He gave the

Superintendent a sour frown. "Might I remind you that you are at least partially culpable for this mess? Not only did you fail to comprehend Major Russell's character, and turned a blind eye to his cruel mistreatment of Gurung Bahadur's innocent sister, but then you compounded that oversight by trying to cripple my investigation at every turn. I cannot tell whether it is because you are a bungler by nature, or if you were secretly on the Major's payroll, but I assure you, I intend to have a word with the new Resident once he arrives about whether you should be permitted to continue as *my* Superintendent."

"How dare you? If anyone deserves to be censured, it is you, for letting a murderer walk free...."

Jardine's visage reddened till he looked ready to explode, but before he could grow any more combative, Mr. Simpson intervened.

"You may leave us, Mr. Jardine."

His voice was perfectly calm, but it had an edge to it, an unequivocality so commanding it left the Superintendent entirely at a loss for words.

"But ...but..."

Simpson did not say another word. Instead, he merely raised one forefinger, as if he was scolding a recalcitrant child. For a moment, judging by the sheer aggressiveness of the glare Jardine directed towards him, Sikander thought he was about to assault the man. But whatever he saw reflected on Simpson's face soon put an end to the Superintendent's bellicosity, leaving him so chilled that he shivered, before turning and lumbering away.

Sikander hid a grin. It was impressive, really, and done as deftly as a matador delivering the *estocada* to a rampaging bull. Perhaps Mr. Simpson from Simla was someone he could come to like, after all.

"Would you care to tie up the loose ends, Your Majesty?" Simpson indicated Sikander's guests who were watching him in a daze, "or shall I?"

"I'll take care of it." Squaring his shoulders, he turned first to Mrs. Bates, who held his gaze with a sullen majesty. "You perplex me, Madame, I admit it. Try as I might, I cannot understand why you chose to marry the Lieutenant. Perhaps it was merely pragmatism, or perhaps you truly love him, but the only thing of which I am sure is that you deserve each other."

He let out a resigned sigh. "I could have your husband's career ended, after the way he behaved, but instead, I am going to do the worst thing I can think of. I am going to give him exactly what he wants. Once the new Resident arrives, I shall put in a request asking for him to be transferred out of Rajpore at the earliest, preferably to the frontier."

Mrs. Bates let out a groan, but before she could voice a word of objection, Sikander went on. "I doubt we shall ever meet again, but I feel it is my duty to leave you with a warning. Beauty fades, love falters, but character is timeless. I can only hope you will come to understand that someday when you are older."

This advice sadly fell upon deaf ears, it seemed, for Mrs. Bates rose to her feet with a scowl so acidic it could have melted steel.

"You are a dreadful, cruel man," she hissed, "and someday, when you receive your comeuppance, I can only hope I am there to witness it."

Even as she stormed off in a righteous huff, Sikander turned to the Gurkha. "I cannot say I approve of your behavior, Gurung Bahadur, but I understand your motives all too well. In some respect, I too must accept a measure of responsibility for the death of your sister, perhaps not explicitly, but implicitly. After all, it is my fault that the Major was able to get away with his depravity for so long. If I had been more observant, more suspicious, perhaps your sister might not have felt the need to take her own life. As a result, I feel I must make reparations to you. I cannot correct the wrong that was done to you. I cannot restore your sister to life, but what I can do is give you a second chance. I believe you to be a good man, an honorable man, and I will not let the life of a good man be destroyed by the deeds of an evil one.

"So…I have need of a gamekeeper for the Imperial Lodge at Ranibagh. If you are willing, then I would like to swear you into my service. Tell me, Gurung Bahadur, will you serve me?"

The Gurkha's grim visage distorted, overwhelmed by emotion, and he fell to his knees at the Maharaja's feet.

"I am your man," he said, his voice wavering with gratitude. "From now until death takes me, I am your loyal servant, on my honor I swear it,"

Behind Sikander, Charan Singh bobbed his head in unsaid approval, and one of the guards stepped forward to lead the Gurkha away. Meanwhile, the Maharaja offered the Magistrate a troubled frown.

"As for you, Mr. Lowry, let me be clear. I disapprove of people like you." He bit his tongue, reminding himself not to say too much. "You are a venial man, a weak man, but I am nothing if not fair. If I can give Gurung Bahadur a second chance, how can I, in good conscience, deny you the same? You were the Major's victim as much as Miss Jane, and I can only hope that now that you have been extricated from his influence, you will strive to redeem yourself. That is why I am willing to let you stay on here in Rajpore as the Magistrate, should you wish it."

"Oh, yes!" Lowry let out a sigh of abject relief. "Thank you, Your Highness. I will not let you down, I assure you."

"I should hope not. Understand this, you are on probation and I will be watching you very carefully. One misstep, and you will be on the next express out of Rajpore. Is that clear?"

Lowry gave him a nod, and rose and quickly waddled away, worried perhaps that Sikander would change his mind.

"Which leaves us with you, Munshi Ram," Sikander's tone grew stern. "You have twenty-four hours to evict yourself from the borders of my kingdom. If you are still here after that time, I shall have you arrested."

"But my family? My grandchildren?" the Munshi exclaimed piteously.

"They may accompany you, or they may remain here, that is their choice, but all your holdings are hereby confiscated. The land which you have misappropriated, it shall be returned to its rightful owners, the war widows for whom it was intended."

"Curse you," the Munshi sprang to his feet, his teeth bared in a snarl, "May you rot for all eternity!"

"I have been cursed by better men than you," Sikander replied, "and I am still here." With a snap of his fingers, he commanded Charan Singh to take him away. He then returned to his chair and collapsed into it with a satisfied groan.

That left only him, Helene, Miller, and Mr. Simpson still seated at the dinner-table. "That was quite an entertaining evening, Your Majesty," Miller tottered upright, clapping his hands together in mock applause, "Would you be so kind as to have one of your men drive me back to the English Town? I fear I have drunk rather too much!"

"Of course, Mr. Miller," Sikander gave the rotund presswallah an affectionate grin, "And thank you, of course, for your help."

"It was nothing at all." The presswallah doffed his hat, and then wandered away, weaving from side to side precariously.

"Aren't you forgetting something?" Helene said, giving Sikander a pout. "Isn't there someone else you should thank?"

Next to her, Simpson waited, a watchful expression on his face. "I am grateful to you too, Mr. Simpson, for your assistance." Sikander said rather grudgingly, as if it pained him to be civil to an Englishman.

Simpson smiled and said, "And I am glad to say that my superiors were quite wrong about you. That was well done, very well-handled indeed. It is going to be a pleasure to serve with you, Mr. Singh"

"Do you mean to say…?" The Maharaja's mouth fell open as he grasped the gist of what the man from Simla was suggesting.

"Indeed, it seems the Burra Sahibs have decided in their infinite wisdom that I am to be the next Resident of Rajpore." His grin grew even wider, gratified to have gotten one over on Sikander. "And might I suggest that as our first official act, we spare a moment to get our stories to match before I submit my report to Simla?"

"That's an excellent idea," Sikander retorted, recovering quickly to let out a booming laugh of his own, "but I am afraid that will have to wait just a bit longer. First, I intend to ask Madame Beauchamp here to dance."

Beaming, he held out one hand toward Helene. "It seems like a shame to let the occasion go to waste."

Helene let out a snort of bemusement, and daintily took his hand. On cue, Charan Singh nodded at the bandleader, and the orchestra launched energetically into a resounding *habañera*.

"Excuse me, Mr. Simpson." Sikander gave the new Resident a wink, and slipped his hand around Helene's narrow waist possessively. Sweeping her out onto the dance floor, he began to guide her through the complex moves of a *contradanza*. As always, they were good together, seeming to fit into each other perfectly. Helene was close enough to him he could sense her pulse quickening, a rouge coloring her cheeks when she surrendered to his lead. He spun her around once, twice, thrice as if she weighed nothing, and she responded by letting out a throaty chuckle.

"I thought you are supposed to apprehend the killer in the end," she said, "not help her get away."

"On the contrary, my love," Sikander responded with a shrug, "as far as I am concerned, my work here is done. I set out to solve the mystery of the Major's death, and wah, what a pukka murder it has turned out to be!"

Helene gave him a very odd look, as if she was seeing him for the first time, even though they had known each other intimately for years.

"You know, Sikander Singh," she whispered, arching her neck to smear a kiss on his cheek, "there are times when I cannot help but think that you are a very peculiar man."

Sikander laughed, and took her in his arms, bending low to dip her almost to the ground, causing Helene to squeal with delight.

Perhaps I was wrong to jump to conclusions quite so quickly, he thought, feeling rather satisfied with himself.

Maybe, just maybe, 1909 was going to be a good year after all.

To receive a free catalog of Poisoned Pen Press titles, please provide your name, address, and e-mail address in one of the following ways:

Phone: 1-800-421-3976
Facsimile: 1-480-949-1707
Email: info@poisonedpenpress.com
Website: www.poisonedpenpress.com

Poisoned Pen Press
6962 E. First Ave. Ste 103
Scottsdale, AZ 85251